One Weekend A Month

Craig Trebilcock

10-Digit ISBN 1-59113-892-2
13-Digit ISBN 978-1-59113-892-1

Printed in the United States of America.

First Printing – March 2006

Second Printing – September 2006

Booklocker.com, Inc.
2006

One Weekend A Month

Craig Trebilcock

Dedicated to the Soldiers and Marines

of Operation Iraqi Freedom,

whose mission was to spin straw into gold.

ACKNOWLEDGMENTS

This book is possible due to the contributions of several persons. First, to Kathy Rogers, whose technical feedback and editing was invaluable. Her supportive and helpful comments, such as, "Your first draft is terrible, dear," kept me focused and humble(d). Next, thanks to my illustrator, Joseph F. Derkowski, who agreed to create the maps so long as I didn't put his name on them. I didn't – thanks Joe.

Thanks to my family for not only tolerating my proclivity to disappear every five years or so to go to strange lands where people want to shoot me, but for also patiently enduring my subsequent hibernation to write about it.

Finally, thanks to the brothers I served with in "The Sand" for their comradery, service, and just a touch of insanity – Diesel Joe, Murph, the Evil Twin, Uncle Mikey, Powder Monkey, Pony Tail Bob, the Padre, and Grenade Juggler. *Semper Gumby.*

Let our advance worrying become advance thinking and planning.

  – Sir Winston Churchill

Do what is necessary. I'll back you up.

   –   American General briefing US Army civil affairs forces on their reconstruction mission on the eve of their entry into Iraq.

AUTHOR'S FOREWORD

One Weekend a Month is a thinly-fictionalized account of America's invasion of Iraq and the first year of occupation under Operation Iraqi Freedom. It depicts a year in the lives of an Army Reserve Civil Affairs unit thrust from the instant gratification culture of the West into the unyielding Oriental culture of the Middle East. All of the characters are fictional, although many of the events depicted are not.

In the wake of the Coalition battlefield victory in the spring of 2003, the media, often isolated in their Baghdad hotels, has largely misunderstood the Iraq reconstruction mission. The press, relying on body counts and cliché broadcasts of burning HMMWVs as a substitute for meaningful analysis daily fails to address whether our troops and treasure are making a positive difference. The Bush Administration, in turn, has likewise miscast the events in Iraq as primarily one of "terror" versus freedom, rather than a clash of cultural values. This has left an increasingly confused American public caught in the middle and wondering, "What is really going on over there?" This book seeks to answer that question from the perspective of the soldiers who spend every day out among the Iraqis trying to improve their lot.

The one item all of the 'experts' did get right after Baghdad fell was the belated realization that there was no plan for what was to happen once the large scale shooting stopped. The failure of the US to have such a postwar plan, or to even understand the players in the game so as to create a meaningful plan, is a miscalculation that will have ripple effects for the American people and the entire Middle East far into the Twenty First Century.

The key fallacy underlying the political decision to invade Iraq had nothing to do with the presence or absence of weapons of mass destruction. The fundamental misstep was the presumption that democracy would spring forth wherever the American liberty template was slapped down by the wise and benevolent USA. This naive belief had originally sprouted in the minds of US politicians in the 1990's, arising from successful populist uprisings within the former Warsaw Pact countries, the Soviet Union, and Kosovo. Those revolutions, sparked by their citizens' desire for greater freedom, radically shifted the international balance of power in favor of the United States entering the twenty first century. Iraq is not Eastern Europe, however, and the idea that democracy is valued and sought by all peoples, if only given a chance, does not apply in the tribal-dominated and submission-to-authority oriented culture of Iraq.

Left as the sole global superpower by the fall of the Soviet Union, America at the beginning of the twenty first century appeared to have an uncontested position from which to export its values and culture to a world it perceived as starving for its guidance. The 'experts' in their Washington, DC offices did not envision that an underdeveloped desert society, based upon complete personal submission to the will of Allah and communal submission to the plenary will of tribal sheiks, might not be ready to embrace Jeffersonian ideals such as individual liberty, personal determination, and equality among men (and women).

For Iraqis, democracy is something that is embraced only while the Americans are in the room. When those unwelcome guests depart, the struggle for power and position returns to its essential Bedouin roots, wherein he who controls the resources lives and he who does not dies. Accordingly, those who advocate that the US military should remain in Iraq until meaningful democracy is established better strap in for a long, long ride.

War changes the people and societies it touches in ways that cannot be anticipated when conflict begins. One could not have predicted in September, 1939, that the German invasion of Poland would ultimately thrust the USA and the Soviet Union into a half-century of military superpower status during the Cold War. One could not have predicted that an obscure naval skirmish in the Gulf of Tonkin in the mid-1960s and the subsequent US military response would provide the spark for a social revolution in the United States and the hollowing out of the US military in the 1970s.

The Iraq War, known as Gulf War II by those who fought in it, is now changing our society and our military as well, in some ways we cannot yet recognize. It was the first war of our modern era fought extensively by Reserve and National Guard troops. This narrow slice of our society has voluntarily carried the burden of this nation's 'War on Terrorism' for half a decade. One Weekend A Month is the story of a small group of well-intentioned Army Reservists from hometown America, caught up in that struggle, and forever changed by trying to deliver a gift that no one really wanted.

MAPS

Figure 1 – Kuwait and Southern Iraq

Craig Trebilcock

MAP 2 - BAGHDAD AND ENVIRONS

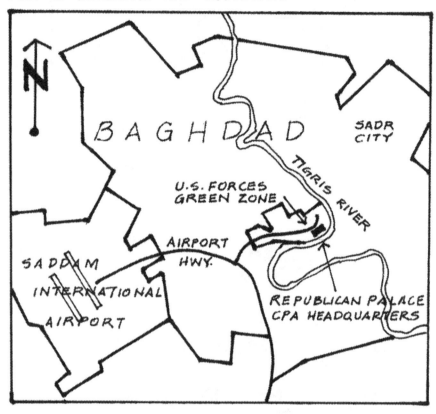

Figure 2 – Baghdad and Environs

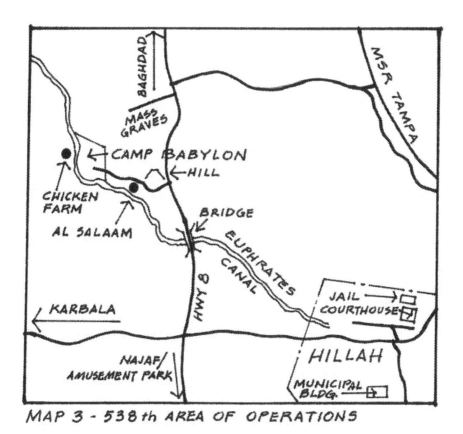

MAP 3 - 538th AREA OF OPERATIONS

Figure 3 – Camp Babylon and Hillah

TABLE OF CONTENTS

PROLOGUE

<u>Reveille</u>

Whup whup whup whup whup…

"Do you see it?"

"No."

Whup Whup Whup Whup…

"No, but I hear it."

The steady pulse of the rotors cutting through the thin desert air came closer.

WHup WHup WHup…

"It's coming from there," the private indicated, pointing to the skyline above the date palm grove alongside the canal.

"I still don't see it."

Bup, bup, bup… the deep-throated cadence of an AK-47 semi-automatic rifle spoke from the village. *Bup, bup, bup…*

They must be coming down the canal, thought the sergeant, as he glanced down at the casualty.

"Cooper, keep pressure on that wound, damnit," the sergeant ordered, as a pool of dark blood mixed with the sand beneath the soldier laying in the bottom of the irrigation ditch in which they huddled.

"Serg'nt, I'm not sure where to press," Cooper replied helplessly. "There's guts all over. I don't wanta' hurt him more."

"Press *there* and *there*," Warden emphasized, pressing Cooper's hands firmly down over a saturated field dressing centered on the man's torn abdomen. Frayed pieces of intestine protruded slightly from the corners of the small dressing. "And shut up about 'guts.' Ya' wanna' put him into shock?"

1

WHUp, WHUp, WHUp, WHUp...

They're getting close, Warden thought, quickly peeking above the rim of the three foot ditch in which they were concealed. *About damn time.* "Ridlin, pop smoke," he ordered to the soldier crouching to his right.

The casualty opened his eyes and stared blankly at the sky. "Thirsty...," he murmured weakly.

The pasty-looking private on Warden's right clenched a green cylinder in his right hand, a finger hooked through the metal ring at the top. In response to the order, he quickly stood up in the ditch as he began to pull the ring free.

"Get down, fool!" Warden bellowed, kicking Ridlin over in the ditch with a firmly placed boot to the thigh. A spray of small arms fire kicked up the dirt along the lip of the ditch where Ridlin had just stood.

"Pop it without making yourself a target, knucklehead," Warden corrected. "Ah don't wanna' hafta' write your girlfriend." Warden could feel trickles of sweat running down the side of his face and into the corner of his mouth. *Jesus,* he thought. *Just what I need is two casualties on my hands.*

Ridlin looked about in wide-eyed surprise at finding himself in the bottom of the ditch again, as several rounds snapped over his head. He still held the canister tightly in his hand.

"Toss it," Warden yelled. "Toss it onto the field, as far as ya' can – that way," Warden gestured to a flat, sandy area of scrub growth behind their position.

Ridlin scrambled back onto his knees, tore the ring free, and lobbed the canister in a high arc onto the field – this time careful not to expose himself to the enemy fire from the village.

Warden turned back to the casualty. "We're gonna' have ya' back to camp in just a minute and ya' can drink all ya' want," said Warden in a soothing voice. "Won't be long now."

"...my fault...," came the whispered reply from dry lips.

"Nobody's fault," replied Warden quietly, taking the casualty's hand in his own. It felt cold.

2

WHUP, WHUP, WHUP, WHUP – the roar of whirling rotors screamed overhead, accompanied with a hard blast of wind, as the Marine UH-60 MEDEVAC[1] helicopter broke over the top of the date palms to the east of the village, in a tight left turn.

Ridlin's canister was spewing a house-sized cloud of dark red smoke 100 feet behind their position, signaling the landing zone.

"Good Toss, Rid," said Warden, watching the UH-60 initially overshoot the smoke due to its high rate of speed. The helicopter was low enough as it passed them that Warden could see a green uniformed arm extended out the gunner's window pointing back at the smoke.

"Serg'nt, I think they're movin' round to the left," Private Jamie yelled over the chop of the rotors behind him. Jamie lay on his side in the bottom of the irrigation ditch ten feet to the left of the casualty, where he manned the 5.56mm Squad Automatic Weapon (SAW)[2]. A round-faced kid from Amarillo, Texas, he had joined the Army Reserve eighteen months earlier to get GI bill benefits for college. He wanted to be an electrical engineer – a ticket out of his small hometown, where most of his classmates ended up working as labor in the petroleum or cattle industry.

Jamie gestured to a date palm grove to the left of the village. Two men in white, ankle-length robes could be seen moving, half-crouched, behind a small cluster of outbuildings. One of the men glanced quickly in their direction and began to weave through the palm trunks to the forward left of their position, about 250 meters away. The second followed, carrying an unknown object in his right hand.

"Light 'em up," Warden barked.

---

[1] MEDical EVACuation; term commonly used to refer to movement by airborne ambulance, though technically it means any mode of medical transport.
[2] The M249 SAW is the US Army's light machine gun that can be fired using a vehicle mount, a barrel-mounted bipod, or in a soldier's unsupported arms if he is strong enough. The M249 fires the same 5.56mm ammunition as the M16A2, and can even use that rifle's magazines. The SAW has a cyclical fire rate of 750 or 1,000 rounds per minute (selectable), versus the M16A2's single-shot or three-round-burst modes.

Jamie turned back to the SAW, balancing the bipod at the end of its barrel on the edge of the ditch. Rising onto his knees, he snugged the stock into his shoulder. Leaning forward to stabilize his body against the side of the ditch, he slowly squeezed the trigger, sighting slightly ahead of the lead man. *Breathe*, he thought.

Brrring! Brrinng! the weapon chattered with a high-pitched metallic voice, as the lead man pitched forward into the dirt.

"He's runnin'," Warden yelled, watching the second white-robed target turn about and break back through the palm trunks toward the village. "Hit 'em".

Jamie swiveled the barrel and released a three second burst. A trail of dirt sprayed up at the target's heels, narrowly missing him. He dropped whatever he had been carrying – *Probably an RPG*[3], Jamie thought – and renewed his dash through the palm trunks with even greater enthusiasm.

"No, no…lead 'em, lead 'em," Warden encouraged, pointing ahead of the fleeing target as if he could guide the rounds to their intended target with his finger.

Jamie could feel his heart pounding in his chest, so hard that it hurt. Despite the tightness in his chest, he inhaled and exhaled slowly, as he had been trained, forcing his body to relax, so that his hands did not shake. Correcting his aim to a point in front of the reluctant sprinter, he placed a new spray of rounds into his path back toward the village. Dirt kicked up ten feet in front of the target, causing the now confused and terrified enemy to reverse direction yet again, cutting back toward his dead comrade.

"Light 'em up…," the casualty mimicked weakly, before a grimace of pain rendered him silent.

"Jeezez Christ, Jamie, this ain't a frickin' carnival game. Grease that Haji!" Warden roared.

Crack! The single, sharp report of a rifle sounded to their right, as the top of the target's head exploded into the air. The body pitched heavily to the

---

[3] Rocket Propelled Grenade – when referred to as an "RPG," the reference is usually to a weapon of Soviet design.

ground, its legs kicking and convulsing in the dust for several seconds more, before it lay still.

Surprised, Warden rolled onto his left side to see Ridlin still peering down the sight of his M16 rifle at the fallen man. "Well, ah'll be damned," murmured Warden. "Ridlin, we're gonna' make a soldier of you some day," he called to the pale young soldier.

Ridlin shrugged, looked over at Warden, and returned a lopsided grin.

"Serg'nt, I don't think he's doin' so good," Cooper said uncertainly, moving his hand to the casualty's throat. His blood-slicked fingers slid across the wounded man's neck, smearing the pale flesh with crimson, as he struggled to find the pulse.

A stinging blast of sand and small rocks whipped the team across their backs, as the returning medical evacuation helicopter settled onto the field behind them. Its rotor wash sandblasted everything within 200 feet, throwing up an obscuring and protective cloud of dust.

"Cover the wound!" Warden bellowed, struggling to have his voice heard over the heavy chop of the blades. "Keep dirt out of the wound," he yelled again, as Cooper laid his body over the prone casualty to shield the exposed entrails from the thick dust and flying debris.

Several rounds snapped over their heads as the gunmen in the village began to fire blindly into the dust cloud obscuring the helicopter.

"Jamie, put fire on those buildings to keep their heads down," Warden ordered. As the chatter of the SAW responded to his direction, Warden broke from the ditch through the dust cloud, toward the waiting helicopter.

The Marine side-gunner squinted through his goggles, seeking to detect any movement. He trained his 7.62 mm machine gun on a brown silhouette stumbling through the wall of dust toward the motionless and now vulnerable helicopter. Slipping his finger inside the trigger housing, he swiveled the barrel of the large weapon slightly to track the oncoming form. *Don't even blink wrong*, thought the gunner.

Warden choked as he plodded through the dust cloud toward the helo. *Feels like Ah'm tryin' to breathe inside a vacuum cleaner*, he thought. He froze momentarily as the cold realization struck him that he had left the ditch without his rifle in his haste to get help. *Too late to worry about that now*, he rebuked himself as he moved forward again. *Gotta' get help.*

The gunner saw the target hesitate momentarily, and as he did so, the familiar outline of a US helmet was silhouetted against the brown background. "Phewww," he exhaled, raising the barrel away from the approaching form.

In the open side door of the air ambulance, a Navy Corpsman - red cross prominent on his helmet - crouched and peered at the approaching soldier. As Warden lumbered up to the side of the aircraft , the corpsman yelled to be heard over the rotors. "Where's your casualty?"

"In the ditch…hundred feet…gut shot…need a litter," Warden panted back in snatches, also straining to be heard over the roar of the aircraft.

The Corpsman turned to the rear bulkhead of the aircraft and unsnapped the litter hanging there on canvas restraining straps. Shoving it out the side hatch to Warden, he dropped to the ground, ready to follow. Warden bolted for the ditch, struggling with the unwieldy stretcher under his right arm. The Corpsman followed, his emergency field medical bag banging heavily against his hip. Neither man was armed.

Warden and the Corpsman weaved back and forth to the ditch in a half-run, half crouch, trying to present as difficult a target as possible to any enemy gunman who might glimpse them through the dust cloud that still hung heavily in the air. *Brrriiinngg!* sang Jamie's SAW, and the sides of the buildings in the village puffed small clouds of dirt where the rounds hit. Warden jumped down and landed heavily next to Cooper and the wounded soldier - the ungainly litter still clutched tightly in his hands. The Corpsman dropped into the ditch behind him, falling against Warden in the crowded V-shaped bottom.

"OK, private, let me take a look," the Corpsman instructed Cooper, as he crawled around Warden and sidled up next to the casualty. Cooper continued to press on the wound, staring down without blinking. "Private, I need to look at the wound," the Corpsman repeated.

Cooper looked up dully. "Whah?" he said, looking at the corpsman with blank eyes.

"Son, I need to look at the wound," the Corpsman repeated forcefully, making eye contact with Cooper, as the young private seemed to focus in on him for the first time.

"It's OK, Cooper," Warden said to him. "He's here to help him. It's OK."

"Just move your hands away and let me peak under the bandage," the Corpsman said calmly, removing his goggles and bringing his face to within six inches of Cooper's. "I'm going to help him," he repeated slowly and deliberately, "but I need you to move your hands away first, OK? You did a good job – just let me take a look now." Cooper slowly responded, drawing shaking hands carefully back into his lap, as he sat on his heels in the dust. Drying blood and excrement on his hands stained the legs of Cooper's desert BDUs[4], but he didn't notice.

"Serg'nt, I'm getting low on rounds," Jamie yelled over his shoulder, snapping his last thirty round magazine into the SAW.

"OK, cease fire until you can see something," Warden said. "Wait,…here,… here's some of my mags," he said, tearing an ammo pouch off of his web belt and tossing it to Jamie.

The Corpsman looked up from his view under the bandage with pursed lips.

He reached up and felt the casualty's throat. He then reached down and grasped the man's wrist, feeling for any response. "I'm getting nothing," he said quietly.

"He's alive," Cooper said softly, looking at the casualty's slack face. "I was just talking to him."

"Son, he's gone," the Corpsman corrected gently. "I'm getting no vitals. Half his guts are blown out."

"He's alive," Cooper repeated slowly and firmly, his voice rising and beginning to shake. "I was just talking to him," he stated again, as if repetition would rebut what the Corpsman was telling him.

---

[4] Battle Dress Uniform – the standard camouflage field uniform worn by US force. Also know as DCUs when worn in the desert combat uniform pattern.

The Corpsman did not respond, but looked toward Warden over his shoulder and shook his head.

"He just said he was thirsty again. I heard him. You need to help him," pleaded Cooper, his voice rising slightly.

"Private, I can't do anything. I'm sorry."

"Bullshit! He's alive, damn it," interrupted Jamie rolling onto his left side to face the Corpsman, as he slapped a fresh thirty round magazine into the side of the SAW. "He's alive, OK? Cooper's right. You need to help him. Quit screwing around."

"Look, we'll send an ambulance out to collect him," the Corpsman said sympathetically, looking from Jamie back toward Warden. "We're not authorized to take bodies – only wounded. We have to save room for those we can help."

No one responded. The pulse of the waiting helicopter throbbed through the air.

"Listen, there's an MP[5] team on its way here right now to extract you," the Corpsman continued, breaking the tense silence. "They'll help you get him out. Nobody's going to leave him here. I promise." The Corpsman looked at the stony faces regarding him and felt cold sweat running down his back.

"Ya'll not going anywhere without him," Warden added flatly, retrieving his rifle from where it lay next to the casualty. "No one leaves here without him. Is that clear?"

The corpsman opened his mouth to say something – anything – to sway the three of them, but no sound came. He could see that this was not an argument he was going to win. These men were too far "in the zone" to listen to reason. Their entire universe came down to getting their comrade out alive and nothing he could say was going to stop that.

As the Corpsman saw his reflection in the flat eyes regarding him, two gray, Marine Super Cobra gunships burst over the tops of the palms with a roar, their rotor wash causing everyone to reflexively flinch lower into the ditch.

---

[5] Military Police

8

The two attack helicopters arced quickly over the team's position, as a spattering of small arms fire reached for them from the center of the village.

"That was a mistake," said the Corpsman, watching the two aircraft dive toward the deck to present a more difficult target. As if in answer to his statement, a handset on his shoulder harness crackled to life, "Evac 3, this is Evac 6," came a monotone voice over the radio. "Maintain position: we are lifting off. Zulu Charlie, out."

"Great," muttered the Corpsman. "I hate it when this happens. If you have any yellow smoke, Sergeant, I suggest you pop it now."

"Ridlin, pop a yellow smoke," ordered Warden.

"We don't have any, Serg'nt," said Ridlin. "I've got green and….green, though."

"Green means we're a target. Don't pop that," said the Corpsman quickly.

The medical helicopter lifted off in another spray of gravel and sand. It wheeled northeast as it gained altitude and quickly disappeared out of sight over the palm groves. A few random shots from within the village followed it, ignoring the large Red Cross marking on the side of the aircraft. From the north, behind the team, the sound of the Marine attack helicopters returning grew louder.

Peering over the lip of the ditch, away from the village, Warden saw that the two gun ships had come about, a half mile distant, and were now approaching them, side by side, noses down, a hundred feet off the ground. They resembled two giant birds of prey swooping down on an animal.

Oh, crap, Warden thought, recognizing the attack posture of the aircraft.

"Everybody down!" he roared, laying himself over the casualty's abdomen, as the others followed suit, pressing for the bottom of the ditch. "Get dow…," he began again, when the scream of air-to-surface rockets roaring over their heads drowned him out. The noise of the rocket motors had barely registered, when the world exploded around the team.

The debate would continue at reunions for years thereafter, as to whether the Marines had used Hellfire missiles or some other ordnance that day. To the team in the bottom of the ditch, however, the recollection they all shared was that the earth beneath them seemed to lift and pitch them skyward, as the tiny village of Al Salaam, which had existed on the banks of the Euphrates River since Nebuchadnezzar had sat on Babylon's throne, died beneath a hail of steel, explosive, and 30-caliber gunfire.

The 1st Marine Expeditionary Force situation report that day noted that a roadside bomb and sporadic small arms fire had destroyed one Army civil affairs HMMWV[6] on a routine mission. Two enemy dead were confirmed, but due to the extent of damage to the village, total enemy casualties were unknown. Civilian casualties were noted as within acceptable limits.

---

[6] High-Mobility, Multipurpose Wheeled Vehicle. Pronounced "hum-vee."

Chapter 1
The Heritage

When the 538th Civil Affairs Brigade was alerted in autumn 2002 to prepare for a possible invasion of Iraq, everyone in the unit was quite certain that a terrible mistake had been made. The 538th was a one-hundred-forty man Army Reserve headquarters unit based in Baltimore, Maryland, whose mission was to provide support to the US Army Southern Command in Miami, Florida. During the average training year this placed members of the 538th in Central America or the Caribbean, where they lived in three-star hotels, caught the local tourist sights, and coordinated civic construction projects sponsored by Uncle Sam with local foreign officials. Dig a well; build a school; shake some hands. It was all good and helped parade America's benevolence to the Western Hemisphere's underdeveloped counties, where the US might need friends someday.

The one-weekend-a-month drills for the 538th were hardly challenging and provided a nice source of extra income for unit members, who had car payments and mortgages to worry about. Drill consisted largely of generating reports, going to meetings, and attending a parade of mind-numbing briefings that the Army Reserve Command in Atlanta, Georgia, considered essential to honing its fighting force to a razor's edge – "consideration of others'" training; homosexuality in the military (another tolerance class, not a how-to course); and equal-opportunity awareness. Mix in a summer picnic and the annual Christmas party among the 24 drill days per year and any training relevant to the traditional Army mission to kill and defeat its nation's enemies in combat was almost an afterthought.

Due to the nature of its mission, 97 percent of the Army's Civil Affairs (CA) branch troops are reserve soldiers. The Army learned in WWII that having soldiers dedicated solely to the mission of interacting with civilians and civilian government officials was a valuable asset during and immediately following a war. The presence of civil affairs soldiers on the battlefield enabled the Army to reduce civilian casualties by directing them out of harm's way, and promoted civilian cooperation in areas that came under occupation of US forces. As reservists who spend most of their time away from the rigid Army social structure, civil affairs soldiers are supposed to possess the interpersonal skills necessary to build relationships and rapport with foreign civilians that full-time infantry or tank commanders might lack. A decade of peacekeeping activities in the Balkans and Haiti had confirmed the need for these citizen soldiers in order for the US to accomplish its military and political goals overseas.

As with most CA units, the 538th had a strong linguist section, concentrating in the languages of the geographic area in which the unit was intended to serve in time of war. For the 538th, the concentration was Spanish and Portuguese, to help unit members communicate with the locals they encountered in Central and South America. In view of their regional expertise and training in the Hispanic culture, it was almost inevitable that the military decision-making process would choose the 538th to be one of the first units to deploy to the Middle East for the invasion of Iraq.

Prior to their mobilization, those unit members who could tolerate the plethora of mandatory briefings – referred to by the troops as "Death by Powerpoint" – found duty in the 538th comfortable. Unit members habitually brought their civilian work in over a drill weekend to catch up from their busy civilian careers. Once every six months the troops proved their physical fitness by performing a certain number of push-ups, sit-ups, and a two mile run within Army time standards: the test was administered by the unit First Sergeant, a former boxer. Depending on his mood and the need for certain higher ranking officers to pass for promotion-eligibility reasons, the two-mile run typically averaged somewhere between one-and-a-half to one-and-three-quarter miles. Fifty-ish colonels regularly recorded physical fitness scores that would be the envy of a high school football team. Life was good.

The most strenuous military training of the year occurred due to the requirement for each civil affairs soldier to pass the annual Special Operations Command swim test. This event required each soldier to demonstrate his ability to stay afloat in deep water for two minutes while wearing his full uniform and holding a rubber rifle. This is a very useful military skill in case one is ever shot down over water while holding a rubber rifle. In preparing for war, the 538th excelled at rubber rifle aquatics.

Deep in the bowels of the Pentagon in the summer of 2002, however, the fateful course that would disrupt this martial nirvana had already been charted. When the Commandant of the Marine Corps was notified by the Secretary of Defense (SECDEF) that the Marines would spearhead a theoretical invasion of Iraq in early 2003, the Commandant requested that

Army civil affairs units be made available to secure and rebuild the theoretical civilian areas that would theoretically be occupied by his Marines. The request was immediately transmitted to the Special Operations Command at Fort Bragg, North Carolina, where Major General (MG) Oldhaus, commander of all 3,000 civil affairs troops in the Army Reserve, made the selection.

Primping before the full length mirror in the corner of his office, MG Oldhaus addressed his aide, an eager young captain from Roanoke, Virginia. "Tim, who hasn't been in the box for awhile?"

The well-groomed officer in the sharply pressed Class-B uniform responded, "Well, sir, there's the 565th CA Brigade in Seattle. They just completed simulated combat training with the 2nd Infantry Division in Korea. They're probably in the highest state of readiness. But, they were in Bosnia in 2000 – might cause some squawking from family members."

"Hell, no!" said Oldhaus, turning to view his rear reflection. "Last thing I need is a flood of whiny letters from Congressmen. Who else?"

"Well, uh, there's a brigade in Baltimore, um, let me check here – the 583rd. No, no,… it's the 538th – has never deployed. They do a lot of touchy-feely missions in the Caribbean and South America, sir."

"Fine, fine, give the five thirty-whatever to the Marines. Sounds like we won't miss them much, anyway. Say, what do you think of this belt, Tim?" asked Oldhaus, admiring the new leather general officer's belt he had picked up at the military clothing store that morning. "Does it look too tight?"

"It's terrific, sir," fawned the aide. "You'll look very impressive at the officers' wives' luncheon."

When the warning order to prepare for the invasion of Iraq finally reached the 538th, the high-ranking engineers, lawyers, medical professionals, teachers, and government bureaucrats who comprised the unit answered their nation's call: the answer was that a third of the unit's officers developed every medical malady known to man and medical science that would prevent their mobilization. Sleep disorders, joint trouble and pregnancy became rampant.

Not since a controversial conception in Galilee had so many mysterious pregnancies sprung forth. Maternity uniforms went on backorder. Knees crumpled and backs spontaneously leapt out of joint. Hearts palpitated and blood pressures ran off the charts. The snapping of tendons and the fictitious ripping of ligaments reached such a pitch that neighbors phoned the Reserve Center to complain about the noise.

Some found God, suddenly realizing after decades of military service that they could not in good conscience kill their fellow man. Company grade officers, who had snarled and strutted their martial prowess for years in combat training exercises, suddenly found themselves at peace with the universe. Conscientious objector applications flooded the S1 administrative section, as unit members fiercely demanded their right to declare pacifism.

Others, who did not want to completely surrender the eventual possibility of military retirement pay, brought forth stories of temporary family crises that would have brought Job to tears. Parents with Alzheimer's, children with learning disabilities, parents with learning disabilities, children with Alzheimer's; no angle to avoid the suddenly inconvenient military service was left unexplored. These soldiers could not possibly deploy, they claimed, without the fabric of their families and society at large crumbling into a ruined heap. When the flash flood of private physician's reports, social worker's commentaries and papal dispensations had been tallied, only 88 members of the unit's 140 were deemed healthy, emotionally secure, and pious enough to fight and die for their country.

At the 42nd Civil Affairs Command (CACOM), higher headquarters for the 538th, Brigadier General (BG) Joseph Merdier paced anxiously. "That bastard Oldhaus is setting me up," he cried in his plush office at Fort Rucker, Alabama, as he wore a path in the deep shag rug. "He sees this as his chance to embarrass me. He's intentionally picked the weakest unit I have, so he can ram it up my backside when they fail."

"Well, sir," suggested his well-appointed aide and gal-Friday, First Lieutenant (1LT) Hilton. "Why don't we send some of our better people from the 42nd down to strengthen the 538th? That would make you look good."

"Hah! Oh, Oldhaus would love that. He'd just love that," bellowed Merdier. "Then when I'm understaffed back here in the States, he can give me a flood of new requirements and taskers, and ram it up my backside when I'm unable to complete them."

"No, no, I know how to beat him at his game," he mused, a half-scowl passing over his square-jawed features. "Clear the decks and jettison the flotsam and jetsam. That's the answer," Merdier told Hilton.

Hilton, who was known as the "black widow" within the 42d CACOM, had buried two husbands in the past five years – each of whom had taken his own life under unusual circumstances. Rumor was that she was in the market again and the way she eyed Merdier made him nervous. *Like a hound dog looking in a butcher's window*, he worried to himself.

"War presents opportunity for those bold enough to seize it," he continued, pacing back and forth across his wood paneled office, wringing his hands behind his back, "And I'm grabbing this one by the throat. Send them Stoat, Rabbit, and that sneaky bastard, Burr – along with their people. They've been stealing oxygen in this headquarters for years. We'll clear out some of the dead wood and bring the 538th up to needed deployment levels. It's a win-win situation and the enemy won't be able to stop it."

"The Iraqis, sir?" asked Hilton.

"No, no – *Oldhaus*. Pay attention! Oldhaus wants to keep me out of this war, because he thinks I'm after his job. He's right, damn it, but he can't keep me from front-loading my excess baggage into the mix. That way I can keep my hands on what the 538th is up to without weakening my position back here. I want every one of those SOBs on that plane with the 538th."

"Sir," cooed Hilton pleasantly, flexing her back to fix the bun at the back of her head, "Even if we send all three colonels and their people, the 538th will still only be up to 105 personnel. We need 140."

"Damnit! Oldhaus would love to see the Marines ram it up my backside, claiming that I short-changed them. I'd like to shoot all those cold-footed bastards. I'd give anything to go and I'm stuck back here – in Alabama for Chrissakes! No awards, no battle streamer, no HMMWV with a white star on the license plate. It's not fair," Merdier choked.

15

"It'll be quiet around here, sir, with so many of the others gone," Hilton smiled, fixing Merdier with a heavy lidded stare.

"I've got it," Merdier exclaimed, continuing to pace as he ignored the suggestive banter from Hilton. "I won't let these bastards torpedo my career. Get me the commander of the 411th in Amarillo. I'll put the habeas grabbus on enough of his people to staff the 538th back up to its full manning level. We'll just call it a temporary realignment. No one will ever know the difference."

"Yes, sir," Hilton replied smoothly with a huskiness in her voice, as she smoothed her blouse.

Noticing the growing light in Hilton's eyes, Merdier turned away toward the window. "You're going, too," he declared over his shoulder. "Keep an eye on those misfits and keep me informed. Don't screw it up."

Chapter 2
The Jaguars

The 538th had one week on the ground in Kuwait in March 2003, practicing their chemical and biological warfare skills, before cruise missiles from US Navy ships in the Persian Gulf slammed into Saddam Hussein's Baghdad palace. In contrast to Gulf War I a decade earlier, which had been preceded with weeks of aerial bombardment, Operation Iraqi Freedom relied upon the element of surprise and a lightening armor thrust through central Iraq to catch Saddam's forces flat-footed and unprepared.

As the M1 Abrams tank columns sliced through Iraqi forces in the Euphrates River basin, the first civil affairs troops appeared in the small Iraqi port town of Um Qasr, which had fallen to British and US forces on the third day of the war. A civilian humanitarian emergency and a bad "CNN moment" for the Coalition was averted when a lack of clean drinking water was remedied by civil affairs troops coordinating the delivery of potable water from Kuwait, via a civilian contractor convoy. Civil affairs troops also intervened to avoid a riot when Kuwaiti truck drivers began to price-gouge their Muslim brothers by charging $5 per gallon for the free water. The importance of civil affairs had seemingly been validated again in the scheme of making war.

The 538th did not participate in the Um Qasr mission, however, as it was still in Kuwait, waiting to move north into Iraq in the wake of the Marine Corps' rapid advance. The 538th's mission was to secure order and reestablish emergency services in Iraqi towns which were now under American control. The first challenge for the 538th was to *find* the Marines, however, who were blazing across the desert at the rate of thirty to fifty miles per day. The complication was that the Marines were advancing so quickly and capturing so many Iraqi towns, that the plan as to where the 538th would begin its occupation duties kept leapfrogging forward across the desert, changing almost daily. With no reliable plan on where to begin, the 538th remained behind in Kuwait, waiting for the phone to ring.

The original plan had been for the 538th to establish its base near the major city of Basrah in the south. As the unit readied to move, however, word came back that the Marines had unexpectedly broken through the Iraqi lines at Nasiriyah, four hours to the northwest. They were therefore ordered to forget

Basrah and proceed to the captured Talil Air Base, near Nasiriyah. The evening before their move to Talil, the provincial capital of Al-Kut fell to the rapidly advancing Corps, rendering the move to Talil obsolete.

Each time that the anxious reserve troops loaded their HMMWVs to roll into Iraq, the call came back from the Marines to stand fast, as they had again broken through and were on the move. The 538th, therefore, received its first taste of war before it ever entered Iraq. Biding its time at the rear area Marine headquarters on Camp Commando, Kuwait, the 538th found itself at ground zero as the Iraqis launched multiple missile attacks against their Kuwaiti brethren in retaliation for being unable to stop the advancing Coalition juggernaut. The 538th's soldiers lived in their chemical warfare suits eighteen hours a day as they waited for the inevitable onslaught of missile-borne chemical munitions to arrive from north of the border.

"Lightening! Lightening!" came the monotone voice over the camp's loudspeakers three or four times each night, warning of incoming missiles. Saddam had used Soviet-made SCUD missiles to attack Israel during the First Gulf War, and one missile had leveled a barracks full of unlucky sleeping reservists in Saudi Arabia, as well. Taking nothing for granted this time, whenever US satellites detected a missile launch, sleepy soldiers and marines at Camp Commando were summoned from their tents to don gas masks and take cover in long, rectangular concrete bunkers covered with sand bags. The troops remained under cover until the highly accurate PATRIOT[7] defensive missiles blew the raiders from the sky, and the "all clear" was announced.

After eight days of this cat-and-mouse game, the advance guard of the Coalition ground forces in Iraq pushed the missile launchers back out of effective range. One of the amazing and under-reported stories of the Iraq war was that the advances in PATRIOT missile technology in the twelve years between the two wars with Iraq was so significant, that not one Iraqi SCUD survived its ten-minute flight to strike intended targets in Kuwait.

As the first US forces entered Baghdad and the regime of Saddam Hussein tumbled, the call finally came for the 538th to join the Marines. Their base was to be Camp Babylon, the forward Marine headquarters established on the outskirts of the Iraqi provincial capital of Babil[8] province, Al-Hillah. This

---

[7] Technically, "Phased-Array Tracking Radar Intercept-On-Target."
[8] Translated: "Babylon."

city, sixty miles south of Baghdad, was used as a country retreat for Saddam and his demented sons when they felt the need to escape the pressures of the capital.

"Hell, we missed the whole war," complained some who had hoped to pad their chances of future promotion with amazing acts of courage under enemy fire. "This is gonna' be another Bosnia – go sit in a base camp and hand out soccer balls to orphans," groused one unit veteran.

When the orders to move into Iraq were received by the 538th's S3 section[9], they directed the unit to proceed in three sections (serials) of ten vehicles apiece, by way of An Nasiriyah, an obscure provincial capital on the Euphrates River. A female Army private had been rescued from an Iraqi hospital in Nasiriyah days before, in a daring raid that was getting a lot of play in the home press. Cut off from such media hype in the desert, however, the 538th knew Nasiriyah only as an Iraqi Army stronghold, where eleven Marines whose names would not be glamorized in the press, had died securing a vital bridge over the Euphrates.

Upon the 538th's arrival at Camp Babylon, its mission would be to help secure the huge tracts of geography that the Marines had torn from Saddam's grasp on the drive to the capital. While the Marines and the US Army's Third Infantry Division had driven the Iraqi Army into extinction, they had not yet themselves moved into the power vacuum to assume active control of the many towns and cities. The 538th was coming to help fill that void and secure the victory.

To soldiers first arriving in the Middle East, the harsh climate is overwhelming. The 120 to 130 degree heat, mixed with high humidity during the summer, can wilt a man in minutes. The Kuwaitis have learned to adapt to these conditions through the wear of light clothes, light activity, and living in Paris during the summer. In contrast, US troops wear a full uniform and continue normal activity throughout the day, regardless of the heat. Most troops operate along the fine line between discomfort and dehydration only by

---

[9] The designation S3 refers to the operations section of a unit smaller than a division. The S3 section assigns all missions, directs all movement, and coordinates all unit operations on behalf of the unit commander.

the constant intake of bottled water that is stacked in palletized heaps everywhere on US camps. Troops who drink eight liters of water per day might piss out only half a liter: the rest is burned up or sweated out through the skin as the body desperately tries to cool itself.

And yet, for all of its physical discomfort, Kuwait is a land of wealth. The European-manufactured sedans Kuwaitis drive are new and the homes are modern and centrally cooled. Television satellite dishes adorn every building, pulling in the best of Western culture – reruns of Dallas and Falcon Crest. Kuwaitis wear Western fashions or the traditional Kuwaiti garb of a white shift for men or a light full-length dress for women, accented with a designer head scarf. The close relationship between Kuwait and the US, reaffirmed since American forces liberated that nation from Iraqi invasion in 1991, has further smoothed the way for an infusion of Western culture. Upscale shopping malls dot Kuwait City, and contain all of the retail store chains familiar to consumers in the United States.

Due to their vast oil-based wealth, Kuwaitis have the ability to buy whatever they wish. But this means that they must consciously work at maintaining a link to their modest Bedouin roots. This is done through the status symbol of having a traditional tent and a token flock of goats at a weekend retreat in the desert on the outskirts of Kuwait City. On weekends, families leave their posh suburban neighborhoods, drive their Mercedes out into the desert, and live in these ersatz encampments, searching for a taste of the life their grandfathers lived.

Third-country nationals, mostly indentured Filipinos, provide the manual labor in Kuwait, leaving the native population free to flee to Europe during the summer and to return to enjoy their high standard of living over the winter when temperatures dip into the sixties. To US troops living in metal-sided warehouses and stuffy tents in the Kuwaiti desert, the life of the average Kuwaiti looks pretty appealing.

In contrast is the Iraqi village of Safwan, which has the dubious distinction of being the first village on the north side of the border.

At the northern terminus of Kuwait Highway 8 sits "The Berm," a twenty-foot-high pile of dirt and sand bulldozed into place to mark the border in an otherwise featureless desert, and which extends as far as the eye can see. Immediately on the other side is Safwan, which is imprinted in the mind of every soldier or Marine who has seen it as the "sphincter of the universe." For it is in Safwan that one first encounters the grinding poverty and desperate daily struggle for survival that is the life of the average Iraqi.

The Safwan crossing point into Iraq is not just a physical crossing from one Arab nation to another – it is a time machine. It is a trip back in time thirteen hundred years. Safwan, with a population of roughly fifteen hundred people, is comprised of a loose collection of mud and brick hovels that have been forgotten by time. There is little evidence of electricity or running water, and there is no appearance of infrastructure improvements since the time Mohammed rode out of the Saudi desert. Bare-bottomed children play in the dirt as their parents try to scratch a living out of rocky patches that yield little produce. The well-to-do in the village raise skinny goats that seemingly gain their nourishment by licking the minerals out of the parched soil.

Obtaining moderately clean water and enough food for their children fully occupies the lives of the people of Safwan, who seem oblivious to world politics. The noisy arrival of the US military over the berm to their south for the second time in twelve years, therefore, did not represent either conquest or liberation to the people of Safwan; It represented opportunity.

The eight-person, two-vehicle civil affairs element known as "Team Jaguar" had been delayed entering Iraq for a day beyond the rest of the unit when its lead vehicle, Jaguar One, had fallen out of the convoy within minutes of departing Camp Commando due to a massive oil leak. After taking a day to obtain the necessary gasket to accomplish the repair, they now had to catch up with the other eight vehicles of their serial at a Marine compound named Camp Whitehorse, four hours north into Iraq.

The eight members of the team did not know what to expect when they crossed into Iraq, other than a vague disquiet that they were about to see the face of the enemy. The sole radio transmission back from the Brigade's new executive officer, Colonel (COL) Burr, had been particularly unhelpful: "Water terrible. Bring chocolate milk."

"Is that supposed to be a joke?" asked Captain (CPT) Rick Smith, the team's number two officer, as he read the message that had been forwarded through the Marine rear operations section.

"Don't know," replied Major (MAJ) Bill Trevanathan, the officer-in-charge of the team. "Hard to tell when those new guys from the 42nd are being serious or not. They know a lot about regulations and procedure, but don't seem too sharp on tactical stuff."

"Yeah, I know what you mean," replied Smith. "The first time the 'Lightening' alarm went off, I thought Lieutenant Colonel Stoat was going to crap himself. Fell out of the PortaJohn next to the TOC[10] with his pants and pistol belt tangled around his ankles. Laid there like a fish flopping on the beach, with his ass hanging out." Smith laughed heartily before recovering an air of mock seriousness. "I'd follow that man anywhere," he sniffed somberly.

The next morning at 0500 the Jaguar team huddled around their two HMMWVs as the eastern horizon began to lighten. As it was early April, the temperature was still a cool seventy degrees Fahrenheit at this early hour of the morning. A sandstorm had blown through the prior evening, covering everything with the pale yellow, talcum-like dirt of the Kuwaiti desert. The day's mission to Camp Whitehorse had been planned for an early start, as it would be 110 degrees by noon.

Trevanathan looked at each of the seven members of the team standing about their vehicles, shuffling their feet in the sand out of nervous tension. They were not sure what would be waiting for them in Iraq and he could not help with that, as information on what was happening up north did not trickle down to the level of a mere civil affairs team. They were basically driving into the unknown, with a set of map grid coordinates as their objective. Trevanathan looked steadily at each man in the growing light before he spoke.

Trevanathan's HMMWV was manned by Private (PVT) Mark Cooper, his driver; Sergeant First Class (SFC) Warden, the NCOIC[11] of the Jaguar team, and Abu bin Muhammad, their Kuwaiti translator. No one knew Warden's first name, and he didn't volunteer it. He was "Sergeant Warden" to officers and enlisted alike. Warden was a cattle rancher in the Texas panhandle and a man of few words. He had the tough, leathery skin of a man who had spent

---

[10] Tactical Operations Center – a physical groupment of those elements of a general and special staff concerned with the current tactical operations and the tactical support thereof. Usually larger and more comprehensive than a simple command post (CP).
[11] Non-Commissioned Officer in Charge.

most of his years under the unrelenting Texas sun. Bright blue eyes accented his otherwise hard features.

The second HMMWV, Jaguar Two, carried Captain Smith, another of the Amarillo, Texas, contingent, who had been a private first class in the infantry during the First Gulf War. He had left the service after the Gulf War, but rejoined as a commissioned officer after completing his civil engineering degree at Texas Tech.

The NCO team leader for Jaguar Two was Staff Sergeant (SSG) Pete Leader, a sergeant in the Baltimore City police force. Leader had grown up in Philadelphia and had never lost the accent or the ingrained street smarts when he relocated south for the job opportunity. Leader was also the most physically fit member of the unit, having played tight end and linebacker for his high school football team. He spent at least two hours per day in the gym, maintaining his imposing physique.

Sergeant (SGT) Tim Mantis, another crew member aboard Jaguar Two, had pinned on his NCO stripes at Fort Bragg as the 538th was processing through on their way to Iraq. Accordingly, he was the youngest and most inexperienced NCO in the unit. He had been purposely teamed with Leader so that he could learn how to lead troops. A political science major at University of Maryland – Baltimore Campus (UMBC), he had a lot of opinions and a mouth big enough to deliver them.

The driver of Jaguar Two was Private (PVT) Darren Ridder, who had graduated his civil affairs training course only three weeks before deployment. Due to being so green, he was the favorite target of torment for Mantis, as Ridder struggled to learn how to be a real soldier. A computer geek from Doylestown, Pennsylvania, Ridder was regarded as a hyperactive, ADD poster-child by most members of the unit. At the mobilization station at Fort Bragg, he had been dubbed with the nickname "Ritalin," due to his penchant of talking and rambling about the barracks at night when others were trying to sleep. Over time the moniker had eroded to simply "Ridlin."

"OK, listen up," Trevanathan began. "Our mission is to link up with the other eight vehicles of serial 3 outside Nasiriyah. We'll proceed up Highway 8 to the border, cross at Safwan, and follow MSR[12] JACKSON to Camp Whitehorse outside the city. We'll link up with Colonel Rabbit and the rest of the serial there."

An unsolicited groan came from somewhere in the assembled group at the mention of Rabbit's name.

"Steady," cautioned Trevanathan in a deep voice, not looking up from his briefing notes to see who the culprit was. "All Phase 3 Rules of Engagement remain in effect. My call sign is Jaguar One; Captain Smith's is Jaguar Two. The radio frequencies were pre-loaded by Sergeant Warden last night before the storm hit. We'll do a radio check, but nobody mess with the radio settings without Sergeant Warden's permission. Any questions?"

"Can we go home now?" joked Leader.

Trevanathan smiled appreciatively, as the rest of the team laughed quietly. "Sure," he replied. "We just need to make a quick detour by way of Iraq." The team laughed again. Trevanathan noticed that the banter had helped the grim looks he had seen on his team's face at breakfast ease a bit. *That's good*, he thought to himself. *I don't want them wrapped too tight.*

"Let's mount up," the officer ordered. "SP[13] in 5 minutes."

"Well Cooper, this is your big scene," chided Trevanathan gently, as the occupants of Jaguar Two drifted back to their HMMWV for one last equipment check. "Are you ready?"

"What scene, sahr?" asked SFC Warden in his slow Texas drawl, as he climbed into the right rear passenger seat of the HMMWV behind the major. The canvas doors of the vehicle had been removed and stored to increase visibility and weapons mobility: doors get in the way if you have to fire a rifle. The HMMWV now resembled a large, boxy, sand-colored dune buggy with a roof.

"Cooper and I have a running joke," said Trevanathan over his left shoulder, raising his voice to be heard over the cranking of the two HMMWV motors.

---

[12] Main Supply Route – a route designated within an area of operations upon which the bulk of traffic flows in support of military operations.

[13] Start Point – or less literally, departure time and location.

"He reminds me of the All-American kid who buys it in the opening scene of those old WWII movies. You know – the kid that everyone wants to avenge after he gets greased."

Cooper laughed appreciatively. He was used to being ribbed by the other members of the unit due to his quiet and unassuming demeanor. "Yes, sir, but I hope you won't mind if I don't fulfill my destiny today."

Trevanathan, smiled at Cooper's usual even-keeled temperament. Trevanathan, who was known as "Major T" to his team for ease of pronunciation, was one of the brigade officers who had spent the most time in the active Army – eight years. A civilian trial attorney in a small law firm in Pennsylvania, he was a reserve officer in the Army's Judge Advocate General's (JAG) Corps. As the Army frequently reminded him, however, he was a soldier first and a lawyer second – a fact that was abundantly clear this morning as he assumed responsibility for the lives of seven other men.

Six feet three inches tall and lanky in build, Trevanathan had an easy-going, quiet air about him that made people not take notice of him at first. His prematurely-graying hair helped add a bit of maturity to an otherwise boyish face. Quick-witted and with an irreverent sense of humor, only those who knew him well realized the seriousness with which he approached his duties as an Army officer.

Waiting for Jaguar Two to finish preparations, Trevanathan thought back on the decisions that had brought him to this moment. William "Bill" Trevanathan had joined the JAG Corps as a "direct commissioned" first lieutenant after graduating from the University of Michigan Law School. After enduring the corporate law mentality of his peers at Michigan for three years, Trevanathan had decided to find something meaningful and different to do with his legal career than to become a corporate tool. The Army had been something different. His wife, Ann, an economist, had reluctantly agreed to try on the role of an Army wife.

For his first tour of duty, First Lieutenant Trevanathan had been stationed in the border town of Wildflecken, West Germany. When the Iron Curtain, 17 kilometers away, had evaporated in 1989, liberating millions of Eastern Europeans, Trevanathan had his first up-close exposure to those who had lived their lives under a tyrant's yoke. Seeing the grateful and relieved faces of those who escaped from the spirit-crushing burden of communism left a deep impression upon him.

Promoted on time, Captain Trevanathan had remained in Europe for six additional years' of service in Germany, Hungary, and Bosnia-Herzegovina and was seriously considering a twenty-year Army career when his first son, Alex, was born. Looking back on his own pleasant small-town childhood, he knew he did not want to drag his family from Army post to Army post every three years for the rest of his life, and instead left active duty to settle with his family in Shrewsbury, Pennsylvania, a rural town of 3,000, where he worked for a small, general practice law firm.

After participating in the Army Reserve "weekend warrior" program for a couple of years, during which he was promoted to Major, he left that program, too, when his second son, Jeffry, had come along. With a growing family and a full-time legal practice, time had become too precious to spend shining boots and sitting in a reserve center on weekends, processing bad discharge papers for kids who smoked dope or committed other minor UCMJ[14] infractions. When the twin towers fell in New York, however, he had sensed what was coming for the country, and had rejoined the Army Reserve, this time in a deployable civil affairs unit. He felt he wanted to have the chance to make a difference for his country and his family. His wife had not been pleased, but understood when he explained that by his serving now maybe his children would not have to do the same someday.

Trevanathan shook himself out of his reverie and picked up the handset to the secure SINCGARS[15] radio mounted between the two front seats. He pressed the button on the side of the hand-set to activate the send function. "Jaguar Two, this is Jaguar One, over," he spoke into the mouthpiece.

Through a crackle of static came the Texas drawl of CPT Smith, sitting fifty feet behind him. "This is Jaguar Two, go ahead One, over."

"Jaguar Two, what's the action on Cooper's life expectancy today?" said Trevanathan into the handset with mock seriousness.

---

[14] Uniform Code of Military Justice.
[15] SINgle-Channel Ground and Airborne Radio System, a family of encryption-ready radios used by the American military, which may be operated in frequency-hopping mode.

"Aah it's a little light, Jaguar One," came the amused reply from Smith through the crackling radio speaker mounted above the windshield. "I have him hitting a mine within the first 5 miles, while Serg'nt Leader thinks it will be a sniper before we reach the highway; over."

"Roger, Jaguar Two. Jaguar One, out." Turning to his driver, Trevanathan said "There you go, Cooper; your potential is limitless." Trevanathan beamed, invoking the gallows humor that only soldiers and cops truly appreciate.

"Yes sir," replied the tall, blonde Cooper, good-naturedly, "I'll try not to disappoint the team by beating the odds."

"You have an interesting sense of humor, sir," said the team's Arabic translator, Abu, who stood nervously next to the Major, shifting his feet in the yellowish dirt, apparently not anxious to begin the trip, nor appreciating the humor in any of this. Abu was purportedly a contractor hired by the Kuwaiti Ministry of Defense (MOD) to assist the US forces in their operations in Iraq. It was assumed by every member of the team that Abu was likely also tasked with keeping the Kuwaiti MOD informed of US activity in Iraq. In short, while he would be an invaluable help with translating, he was also regarded as a benevolent Kuwaiti spy.

Abu was a particularly nervous spy, as his family had suffered greatly at the hands of the Iraqis during the 1990 invasion of Kuwait. His eighteen year old brother had been hung from the light pole outside their home for interfering with an Iraqi officer who was attempting to seize the family's Mercedes for his personal use.

"I do not find this funny at all, sir," said Abu seriously. "There is great danger ahead. We should not speak lightly of such things," he concluded with great indignation. Abu wore the same desert camouflage uniform as the rest of the team so that he would blend in at a casual glance. The only difference was that he wore no rank and carried no weapon.

"Well, Abu," cut in Warden, "There's gonna' be danger and we can either shat ourselves silly over the idea, or stay loose and make the best of it."

"I see nothing humorous about this situation," sulked Abu, turning and walking behind Jaguar One to take the remaining seat behind Cooper.

"OK, enough," said Trevanathan. Triggering the handset, he transmitted, "Jaguar Two, this is Jaguar One. Let's go to war, over."

"Roger, Jaguar One. Jaguar Two out," Smith replied.

The two HMMWVs, heavily loaded with equipment, rolled forward, beginning their slow exit from Camp Commando. Exiting the sand two-track road from the front gate, the engines strained to bring their heavy load up the long, sandy slope toward the main north/south highway that ran from Kuwait City tow Iraq. *It was down this same highway in 1990 that Saddam's Republican Guard had traveled to "liberate" their 19th province, Kuwait,* Trevanathan reflected.

The small convoy bounced up onto the highway from the makeshift side road and turned north. Within minutes, any vestige of the twenty-first century disappeared in the side mirrors of Jaguar One, replaced with mile after mile of stark desert. The two vehicles droned through the wastes, encountering only occasional military traffic heading south. Every mile looked the same – flat wasteland to the horizon, accented with occasional scrub brush. The only sign of life was a herd of several dozen wild camels that ignored the vehicles as they grazed peacefully next to the highway. *Every time I see those things I feel like I'm in a nativity set*, Trevanathan mused to himself. He could feel his blouse begin to saturate with sweat under the twenty-five pound flak jacket that enveloped his torso like a cocoon. He resisted the temptation several times to loosen it, despite the discomfort. *I need to get used to this damn thing eventually*, he thought to himself.

Despite the unchanging scenery on the other side of the windshield, progress was made. After an hour the team saw a wall of sand rising out of the desert. It was "The Berm,", the wall of sand that combat engineers had constructed in the featureless desert to mark the border between Iraq and Kuwait, years earlier. Trevanathan noticed that even though the Iraqi Army was essentially destroyed at this point, US tanks and Bradley fighting vehicles were still spaced every half kilometer or so down the length of the barrier as far as the eye could see, their barrels pointing north into Iraq. Ahead of the team, a convoy of 15 to 20 deuce-and-a-half[16] trucks was entering a cut in the berm, carrying supplies across the border.

---

[16] Two-and-one-half ton capacity cargo hauling trucks.

The two HMMWVs slowed and then stopped,, as they waited to be waved forward by the military policemen controlling border access through the checkpoint. After the truck convoy disappeared through the berm, a five-ton truck hauling a trailer came south through the narrow cut. As it lumbered past them, Trevanathan could see that a damaged Bradley sat on the trailer. The twisted metal and torn tracks on the left front of the vehicle revealed where the infantry carrier had apparently hit some type of mine. Scorch marks blackened the front and side. It passed them in silence. No one commented, but all eyes in the two HMMWVs marked its passage.

"Make sure everyone is locked and loaded," Trevanathan said to the occupants of Jaguar One. "No one fires unless there is an immediate threat on this convoy, does everyone understand? I don't want any dead civilians on my hands."

"Yes sir," came the reply from each member of Jaguar One. "Jaguar Two, no one fires unless there's an immediate threat, understand?" Trevanathan repeated over the radio.

"Roger, sir," said Smith, following his habit of calling Trevanathan, "Sir," whenever they were acting in their official capacities. Trevanathan and Smith were friends and on a first name basis when out of earshot of the enlisted. However they maintained the necessary military decorum when in the presence of subordinates or superior officers.

"Sir, what do we do if they throw things at us," asked Abu nervously, his large, liquid brown eyes seeming to bulge further out of his head for every yard they came closer to Iraqi soil. "During the first war the people of Safwan would stone passing convoys if they did not give them food."

"I suggest you duck, Abu," replied Trevanathan seriously. "We're not shooting people for throwing things unless it's going to kill us. People threw shit at us all the time in Bosnia. With these flak jackets and helmets they can't really hurt us."

The team moved slowly forward, as a young MP waved them forward from the end of the paved highway to a temporary dirt road that had been cut through the berm. "Where you headin', Sir?" inquired the corporal controlling the intersection, as he leaned in Cooper's side of the vehicle.

"Whitehorse," said Trevanathan. "Hooking up with our main element."

"Awful small convoy to be going that far, sir," said the corporal dubiously, looking at the HMMWV and its lack of armor. He observed the canvas coverings of both vehicles and the lone SAW machine gun hanging out the driver's side of Jaguar Two. "Not a lot of firepower either, Sir," noted the MP soberly.

"Tell me about it," said Trevanathan. "We're not happy about it, either: but orders are orders."

"Roger sir. Understood. You gentlemen have a good Army day," he concluded, waving his right arm across his chest to signal the vehicles forward.

"Corporal, any trouble in Safwan today?" Trevanathan hollered over the engine as Cooper began to edge forward.

"Sir, there's always trouble in Safwan," the corporal laughed, as he disappeared behind them in the cloud of dust kicked up by the tires.

"That's encouraging," Trevanathan said under his breath.

The convoy moved slowly toward the opening in the berm, and each member of the team became silent, their eyes collectively straining to see any threat ahead through the narrow exit. The height of the berm prevented the team from seeing into Iraq, except through the narrow passageway. After years of training exercises, simulations, lectures, and military schooling, each team member was finally going into harm's way in an enemy country for the first time. Glancing sideways down the length of the Kuwaiti side of the berm as they entered the cut, Trevanathan noticed the vehicle crews perched on top appeared relaxed – *a good sign*, he concluded.

What the hell am I doing here? Trevanathan thought momentarily, while he watched Iraq begin to grow at the other end of the cut. His thoughts jumped momentarily to his family in their quiet home in Pennsylvania. *If they could see me now…*, he thought. Quickly suppressing the daydream, Trevanathan chastised himself silently. *Time to cut the bullshit and get serious about the mission*, he impressed upon himself. *No more time for philosophy – this is the real deal and these guys are depending on you.*

The two vehicles passed through the berm and up onto a small portable tank bridge. Combat engineers had laid the twelve-foot -wide bridge across an

Iraqi tank ditch on the immediate far side of the berm, which had been naively intended to slow any Coalition advance. Jaguar One slowed slightly to mount the twenty-foot long, one-lane metal span. They clattered slowly over the metal roadway and then, with a sudden thump as each vehicle dropped down from the lip on the far side, they were in Iraq.

Chapter 3
The Crossing

The military supply road through Safwan skirts the western edge of the village so that convoys do not lumber through the center of the small settlement. The idea was to avoid the civilian interference that had been prevalent in this area during the first Gulf War by simply bypassing the town. The idea made no difference, however, as the poor Shiite villagers in Safwan simply hiked the extra mile out to the new bypass each morning in order to beg from the passing convoys.

A small herd of goats paid no attention to the two Jaguar team HMMWVs as the vehicles chugged up the loose sand road toward the MSR, a mile distant. The ill-fed animals had long ago become used to the passage of military vehicles through their grazing area. A skinny brown and black mongrel, with large portions of its fur burned off, trotted alongside the vehicles for fifty meters or so, on its way to points unknown. As it cantered alongside the slow moving convoy, with its head held high, Trevanathan was repulsed to see that it had a gray, sandy human hand dangling from its mouth. *Welcome to Iraq*, he thought, swallowing back the bitter liquid that rose into his mouth.

While the Jaguar team had tensed to face the enemy, what they encountered along the short, two-lane connecting road was an unexpectedly boisterous atmosphere. The road ahead, as far as the team could see, was lined with children and teenage Iraqis waving, gesturing, and yelling to each military vehicle as it rolled past. Each Iraqi rubbed his stomach, pointed into his or her open mouth, and shook their head to claim hunger in the hopes of a handout. The effectiveness of the signal was diminished somewhat by the laughter, jeering, and occasional obscene gestures of the roadside beggars.

"Are they hungry, sir?" marveled Private Cooper, as they entered the seemingly endless gauntlet of animated Iraqi youths.

"Not anymore, Cooper," replied Major Trevanathan. "Saddam cut off food shipments down to this area in order to prompt a humanitarian disaster in case we invaded. The Coalition has been pumping food and water into Safwan for over two weeks now. These kids are just bored and we're the circus coming to town."

As Jaguar One passed a group of young teenage boys, Trevanathan was surprised to hear them yelling to him in English: "Water, meester! Gif me water!" "Dollah meester! Gif me dollah!"

"Meester, buy Saddam dollah!" yelled one small barefooted boy running alongside Jaguar One, waiving a handful of blue-colored notes in his tiny fist. As with most of the boys along the route, he wore a dirty, off-blue full-length shirt and no shoes.

It quickly became apparent that each small cluster of urchins controlled a certain stretch of the roadside that comprised their "turf." They ran alongside the slow-moving convoys as the heavily laden trucks and HMMWVs chugged up the dirt track in the direction of the distant paved highway, MSR JACKSON, which ran southeast to northwest across central Iraq. The sprint would last until the youth reached the turf controlled by some other group, at which point they would peel off, yelling some parting words in Arabic toward the rear of the HMMWVs. If one of them ran too far in their pursuit of a handout, thereby encroaching upon another group's self-declared turf, he was greeted by a hail of slaps and kicks from the owners, until he retreated.

"Stay alert," said Trevanathan, his eyes rapidly darting from group to group as they passed, looking for any sign of someone who might be concealing a weapon or an explosive charge to lob into their vehicle. The Marine G2 intelligence section in Kuwait had briefed them that the Fedayeen[17] were paying a bounty of $1,000 in US currency to anyone who attacked an American convoy with an RPG or grenade. At their current 20 MPH pace down the sand track, they were prime targets. *Three years' pay to an Iraqi for one moment of bravado*, thought Trevanathan uncomfortably, his eyes quickly searching each group for any sign of hostility.

The team had modified their vehicles prior to entering Iraq for maximum fields of fire. In addition to the removal of the doors, the rear canvas flap window had been tied up so that they were not blind in that direction. Seat belts that Army regulations deemed mandatory went unused, as they restricted the passenger's ability to swivel for vision and fire when worn over bulky flak jackets. Loaded, the sand colored HMMWVs now looked like dune buggies

---

[17] The Fedayeen were irregular troops, controlled by Saddam Hussein's sons, who were responsible for harassing US convoys and other lightly-defended targets, as well as exacting revenge against any who cooperated with Coalition forces.

owned by the *Beverly Hillbillies*. Cots, equipment, boxes of prepackaged food, and crates of bottled water filled the small truck beds at the rear of each vehicle. Canvas barracks bags lashed to the loading brackets in the bed of the vehicle carried all of their excess equipment and the few modest, worldly possessions that had to maintain them for the next six months. Strapped on top of the load, under a piece of cargo netting in the back of Jaguar Two, were the four precious cases of sealed chocolate milk which had become a last minute operational necessity to their forward detachment.

"Keep an eye on that minaret," Trevanathan called over his right shoulder to Warden. The small two story tower, adjacent to an outlying mosque one hundred meters to the east, was the only structure that provided a potential elevated firing platform within sight. Each occupant of the HMMWV had responsibility for maintaining watch over an imaginary quarter circle surrounding them. This division of labor ensured that there was a set of eyes in all directions at all times.

Abu turned from his quarter of the circle and spoke, "Sir, no Muslim would ever use a mos…". Without warning Trevanathan was slammed forward by the sudden braking of Jaguar One, the top of his helmet smacking the windshield.

"What the hell?" he exclaimed, lifting his helmet from up over his eyes. His head rang from the force of the impact. But before he could recover his senses, a young Iraqi boy of about 12 years lunged into the open right side of the HMMWV, scratching Trevanathan across the nose as he tore the sunglasses from his face.

Trevanathan recoiled in surprise, his eyes watering from both the helmet impact and the unexpected snatch-and-grab. As he wiped the tears out of his smarting right eye, he saw the back of the young thief disappear through the cluster of younger Iraqi children who now surged forward like a wave to the side of the stopped HMMWV, shrieking "Meester, water, meester!" as they clutched at his arm.

Trevanathan turned quickly to face a white-faced Cooper on his left. "Cooper, what the hell are you doing?" Trevanathan roared. "Get us out of here!"

"They threw a kid in front of us, sir," Cooper replied in a high, shaky voice, tears welling up in his eyes. "Jeezus, sir, two of the bigger kids just picked up a kid in a red shirt and threw him right in front of us." Trevanathan could see Cooper's hands, trembling and white knuckled, as they tightly gripped the steering wheel.

"Water, Meester!" came the demanding cry from the Major's right, where several children were now tugging vigorously on his sleeve to get his attention. "Saddam donkey!" cried another in a high piping voice, apparently seeking to ingratiate himself with the Americans.

"Get outta' here, ya' lil' terrerists!" Warden bellowed from the back seat, kicking his boot out the door at several of the group who came nearest to him.

The rear of the HMMWV sagged unexpectedly, as a group of four teenagers swarmed onto the vehicle, jabbering excitedly in Arabic. They began to tear through the cargo netting, grabbing whatever was first at hand and tossing it to three other young toughs who stood behind the tailgate, waiting to bolt with the goods.

Trevanathan was feeling overwhelmed. They were pinned in place by a child who might be lying hurt in front of their wheels, while a swarm of teenage locusts were openly stealing their equipment. Using weapons was out of the question. He glanced quickly back over his shoulder through the rear window at the punks trying to get their hands under the cargo net, while the continued tug on his arm from the right and screams for water became more insistent "Where's the kid?" yelled Trevanathan, with a noticeable tremble in his voice, not able to see over the massive hood of the HMMWV to what lay before them. The press of bodies against the side of the HMMWV prevented dismounting.

"I don't know, sir," cried Cooper, his voice rising again. "I don't know if I hit him."

In the back seat of the vehicle, Abu had curled into a fetal position as a competing pack of teens arrived on the left side of the vehicle, pawing at him and jamming their hands into his pockets in search of anything of value. Warden had begun wielding the butt of his M16A2 rifle through the open back window of the HMMWV, painfully connecting it with the knees of the invading teenagers who were swarming over the rear of the vehicle.

"Sahr, we're gettin' stripped clean," yelled Warden forcefully, smacking the shin of another looter, who howled painfully.

Snapped out of his uncertainty by Warden's voice, Trevanathan bellowed, "Move it, Cooper - gun this damn thing!" As he yelled, Trevanathan fended off the grasping hands of a ten year old girl who manically lunged into the front passenger opening at a half eaten Army ration lying under the radio mount. "Gun this damn thing!" Trevanathan ordered again.

"Sir, I can't see the kid," Cooper sobbed, tears streaming down his face.

"I said gun it, Private! Do it now!"

The engine of Jaguar One roared as Cooper mashed the accelerator to the floor. The huge all-terrain tires dug into the sand, as the truck lurched forward and the tearing hands of the frenzied crowd ripped loose from the team. In the cargo bed, bodies flew off the HMMWV in every direction as the looters were caught by surprise by the sudden movement of their previously dormant prey. As Jaguar One broke clear of its snare, Trevanathan looked back through his side mirror, seeing an identical scenario playing out on Jaguar Two, as it too shed a skin of unwanted visitors with a leap forward.

Trevanathan grabbed the radio handset and – forgetting military discipline – blurted, "Rick, is everyone OK?"

Dead silence.

"Rick," repeated Trevanathan, "is anyone hurt?" This time an excited Texas drawl came out of the speaker. "No injuries, sir. We're battered, but OK."

"Jaguar Two, look behind you. Did we run over anyone – a kid in a red shirt?" asked Trevanathan, dreading the reply.

No answer.

"Shit," exclaimed Trevanathan, to no one in particular, as he waited for the answer.

Smith's voice sprang from the speaker mounted above the windshield. "Negative, Jaguar One," as military discipline returned to the shaken team members. "No civilian casualties. Kid in a red shirt is back there with his buddies giving us the finger."

"Phew," breathed Trevanathan to himself, closing his eyes momentarily in relief. "We didn't hit anyone Cooper," he repeated to his driver for emphasis, and watched a look of relief wash over the Private's pale face.

"Thanks, sir," said Cooper. "Sorry about back there. I just froze."

"It's OK, Cooper. You got us out of there. You did OK."

The team rode in silence, shaky as the adrenalin began to drain from their systems. *You're the one who screwed up, bud,* Trevanathan admonished himself silently. *If that hadn't been a bunch of kids we'd all be dead now. I froze and Warden knows it, I'm sure.*

The Major felt the actual weight of being in charge of whether other men lived or died for the first time in his career and it was not a pleasant feeling. *These guys all have families waiting for them at home,* he thought again. *Need to get my shit together. I'm not sending these guys home in a bag.*

"Jaguar One," crackled the speaker, Smith's voice interrupting his thoughts.

"This is Jaguar One, Go ahead Two," Trevanathan breathed heavily into the handset, as the small convoy turned westward onto MSR JACKSON.

"I regret to inform you that four cases of chocolate milk were lost in the battle of Safwan," Smith reported with mock seriousness.

"War is hell, Jaguar Two. One out," Trevanathan laughed sourly, as he dropped the handset into his lap and closed his eyes in relief.

Chapter 4
The Rabbit

The balance of the trip to Camp Whitehorse went by without event. With a complete absence of civilian vehicles on the road, it was as if the Jaguar team existed in their own universe. The terrain between Safwan and Nasiriyah was the same wasteland they had experienced in northern Kuwait. High-voltage utility towers, built for carrying power to Basrah, punctuated the barren landscape. Many of the towers were sheared in half from Coalition air strikes, leaving a tangle of steel and wire along the MSR.

Only an occasional destroyed Iraqi armored vehicle was evident this far south, as the balance of the Iraqi Army had fallen back 170 kilometers to Nasiriyah in the first days of the conflict, in order to block bridges along the Euphrates River.

The Jaguars arrived at the former Iraqi military post outside Nasiriyah shortly after noon. A white, two-meter high concrete wall, riddled with machine gun fire, surrounded the 15,000 square meter complex. The camp exhibited none of the spit and polish that Trevanathan had come to associate with the Marines, even in the austere Kuwaiti desert. In contrast to the well-manicured Marines they had left behind at Camp Commando, these troops resembled scruffy desert marauders. Ragged, salt-stained uniforms hung loosely on the lean frames of gaunt men with patchy facial hair. The camouflage blouses of many had been dispensed with in favor of the cooler, olive green shirts underneath. Brown desert boots were ripped and stained, the sole of each bearing the blood type and medical allergies of the owner, recorded in indelible marker along the side.

Several Marines reclined in doorless doorways, cleaning their weapons. Others glanced out empty windows with dull eyes as the two freshly-painted Army HMMWVs with their black Jaguar stencils on the sides chugged past. The scene had a slight refugee camp air to it. Torn clothing hung on green 550 cord[18] strung between bullet-pocked, windowless buildings. Two Marines

---

[18] Nylon cord used for parachute suspension lines, also known as "parachute cord." Usually green, the cord has a 550-pound test breaking strength, and is as obsequious as "duct" fabric tape among marines and soldiers. Military fabric tape is generally

worked by the water buffalo[19] alongside the road, washing their blouses in a 5-gallon bucket of grey water and working the excess water out by hand. One Marine sat against the white wall of a former Iraqi barracks, his head between his knees, asleep, a lit cigarette burning between his fingers.

"These boys look like they've been through the mill," commented Trevanathan quietly from the front passenger seat, as the small convoy rolled through the camp.

"Ah've seen it before, sahr," commented Warden from the back. Warden had served on active duty with the Army's 10th Mountain Division in Somalia before entering the Reserves. "Don't let appearances fool ya' none. These boys will lay a world of hurt on anyone who messes with 'em. They don't look lahk much layin' round here, but when the balloon goes up, they're all bizness."

The team parked their vehicles in a makeshift motor pool consisting of a circle of concertina wire. After checking in with the Gunnery Sergeant in charge of the billeting space, the Jaguars set up their sleeping quarters in an abandoned one-story building near the northern perimeter of the camp. The cement-block building lacked windows, doors or beds, but made up for the absence with plenty of insects. The team spent a restless night on the sandy, concrete floor, where their futile efforts at sleep were disrupted by waves of sand fleas, Euphrates River mosquitoes, the sporadic rifle fire of sentries dispatching wild dogs outside the wire, and by a pair of particularly amorous and vocal feral cats sharing a moment of quality time at the far end of the row of barracks.

Trevanathan rose the next morning feeling like he had been dragged to Whitehorse, rather than riding. Shuffling to the doorway, he looked out blearily at the moon-like landscape surrounding the camp. In every direction the vista was identical – gray and yellow dirt lying across a flat landscape, devoid of plant or animal life. A towering pillar of black smoke billowed into the sky an unknown number of miles to the northeast. Distance was difficult to determine in a landscape with few landmarks.

---

olive drab green, and commonly referred to as either "90 MPH" or "100 MPH" tape, alluding to its use in binding nicks in helicopter blades during the Vietnam war.
[19] Nickname for the 400-gallon portable water trailer used by the military, which can be towed by a HMMWV or larger vehicle.

"Mornin' sahr," said Warden, looking up from the small open fire he had built outside the door. The ever-resourceful NCO had built a makeshift camp stove of broken bricks taken from the rubble of the neighboring building. "Want some coffee?"

"Yeah," said the Major, returning inside to retrieve his metal canteen cup from his web gear. "Thanks," he said, handing the cup to Warden.

"Wonder what that is?" Trevanathan nodded absently toward the pillar of smoke.

"Gouge is the Air Force took out a brigade of Haji armor last night that tried to counterattack. Bad move on Haji's part, getting caught out in the open."

"Which way were they heading?"

"Here," Warden replied flatly. "Lucky for us they don't have any artillery left to speak of or it woulda' been an exciting night here at the ranch." Warden lifted the pot from the open flame with strong, calloused hands that did not seem to mind the heat from the metal handle. Generously filling the steel canteen cup, he handed it back to the officer.

Taking a deep pull on the harsh, oily liquid, Trevanathan felt some life returning to his aching muscles. "Gotta' do better today," he said to the horizon, thinking of the prior day's debacle in Safwan.

"No harm, no foul, sahr," replied Warden, pouring the dregs of the small camp pot into his own cup.

"We were lucky this time – but luck isn't gonna' cut it out here. What about next time?" Trevanathan mused, looking into his cup for an answer. "What's the right answer when someone chucks a kid in front of your wheels?" He took another long swallow of the hot, bitter liquid. "Am I just supposed to run 'em down like a dog and keep going?"

"Sahr, if ya' don't mind me sayin' so, this is a place where thinkin' like ya' do back home will get ya' killed. Back home in Texas, you'd roll your truck to avoid a kid in the road. But it's different here. Here, ya' just gotta' keep on goin'."

"That's awful damn harsh." replied Trevanathan. "How do you live with yourself afterwards?"

"Sahr, how's someone gonna' live with themselves if they stop their men in a kill zone and get 'em whacked in an ambush? These terrerists know our weaknesses and they're gonna' use that against us. Hurt kids, hurt women. They're all bait for suckers like us. Next tahm there's gonna' be someone waitin' with a grenade, or worse – 'stead of just stealin' food. There's no right answers over here. Only bad choices – ones that get ya' killed or ones that keep you alive - but maybe get someone else killed."

Trevanathan nodded in silent acknowledgment, but could not bring himself to verbalize agreement with the hard philosophy Warden was laying down.

"Sahr, you're gonna' do jest fine, 'cause you care what happens to your people. Ya' even care what happens to these damn Iraqi terrerists. If you don't mind me sayin' so, the trick is gonna' be for you to know that people are gonna' die over here and there's not a helluva lot ya' can do to stop it."

Trevanathan sighed wearily. "Yeah, you're right, Sergeant Warden. That's gonna' take some getting used to." He turned to enter the barracks to clean the prior day's dust and grit out of his M16 before the day's mission began. "Thanks for the coffee," he called over his shoulder.

The serial was scheduled to depart from Whitehorse to Al Hillah and Camp Babylon at 0630; the ten-vehicle convoy faced a grinding eight-hour drive across the heart of the central Iraqi desert. Few towns, no water. Nothing much but sand, heat, and scattered teams of enemy Fedayeen who had not yet accepted that the reign of Saddam Hussein was over. The convoy's objective was to link up with the rest of the 538th CA Brigade at Camp Babylon before dark. Even with night vision equipment, this was Iraqi turf, though, and the lightly armed civil affairs troops did not relish the thought of picking their way through unfamiliar, potentially mined territory in the dark.

Tomorrow they would begin their mission of reconstructing essential government services in the huge area of southern Iraq between Baghdad and Kuwait occupied by the Marines. Today they had to *find* the Marines.

The 538th would spend the next six months providing the combat-minded Marine Corps commanders with the legal, political, economic, medical, and civic engineering expertise needed to rebuild and administer a territory the size of the Eastern United States from New York to North Carolina to Ohio. They now owned that area, whose social and governmental infrastructure had collapsed as soon as Saddam's control had disappeared. As Trevanathan and his men knew, the Marines were great at breaking things, but their ability to glue them back together afterward was still to be tested.

The Jaguar team took position as the second and third vehicles in the convoy, positioned immediately behind the convoy commander, Colonel (COL) Walter Rabbit. The enlisted soldiers had already nicknamed the officer, "Ricochet Rabbit," after an old cartoon character from the Sixties, due to his remarkable inability to stay focused on any matter for more than a few seconds at a time.

"Good morning, men," Rabbit said briskly, as he walked past Jaguar One to the lead vehicle of the convoy.

"Morning, sir," came the unenthusiastic reply of the enlisted personnel leaning against Jaguar One. Saluting was not done in a combat zone, as it made the ranking officer an obvious target for snipers. In Rabbit's case the men were willing to make an exception.

Colonel Rabbit was one of the staff officers that BG Merdier had exiled to the 538th from his Alabama headquarters when he was cleaning out his dead wood. A 27-year veteran of the Army Reserve, Rabbit had not spent any time on active duty during his career, except for the two week summer camps required of all active reserve personnel. Many of those summer tours had been served at various Army "gentlemen's courses" or in the air-conditioned control cells of battlefield computer exercises.

"That's beautiful," commented SSG Leader to Warden as they loaded cases of water into the small truck bed of Jaguar Two. "We're about to cross eight hours of enemy desert with an OIC[20] who has the equivalent of one year and two weeks active duty time in his career – all in CONUS[21]. Second lieutenants have more field experience."

---

[20] Officer-in-Charge
[21] Continental United States

"He might be OK," said Warden in an unconvincing fashion. "Ya never know."

Leader snorted. "Do you remember even seeing him at Bragg when we were practicing quick reaction drills to enemy contact? He laid in the barracks reading books in his private room. I'm tellin' ya', he's one of those officers who got his rank by just hangin' 'round long enough."

"Well, there's nothin' we can do about it, so no use bitchin," said Warden in his usual stoic manner. "Just listen to the boss and Captain Smith and hope they don't screw up."

"Major Trevanathan," came the high, nasally twang of Colonel Rabbit from the front of the line of vehicles waiting alongside the main exit road from the camp. "Major Trevanathan, we have an SP of 0630 and your team is not ready to go. It is 0627 and they are not ready to depart," he admonished, his nostrils flaring, as he leaned out the front passenger door of the lead HMMWV, "Gator One."

"Sir, the NCOIC for the ammo distribution point is not available until 0630," replied Trevanathan, walking toward the Colonel. "Ridlin is over at the ammo point drawing additional ammunition belts for the SAW as soon as it opens up. We'll be out of here by 0635. Everything else is good to go."

"That's unacceptable, Major. We have an SP of 0630 and I mean to move out at 0630. I have never missed an SP in my career and this will not be the first time," Rabbit snapped, conveniently forgetting that he had never been in charge of any military movement previously in his career.

"Yessir, I understand," said Trevanathan. "But the Marines would not let us draw the additional SAW ammo last night and would not open until 0630 this morning, so we're kinda' handcuffed. We could only draw one belt at Commando. It'll be just a couple minutes more."

"It will not be a couple minutes more. Start your vehicle now. It's 0628. We are leaving."

"Sir, the SAWs are the only automatic weapons we have on these vehicles. We have no real firepower without that extra ammo."

"Don't tell me how to lead a convoy, Major," snarled Rabbit, his nasally twang climbing even higher than normal. A large blue vein on his temple throbbed noticeably. "Mount up – *now!*"

"Yessir," said Trevanathan, recognizing that further argument would be futile. Resigned, he moved back to Jaguar One, where his team had gathered to listen to Rabbit's tantrum. The air was filled with the now familiar smell of idling HMMWV exhaust.

"Listen up…," Trevanathan started, before Sergeant Mantis interrupted him. "Sir, we can't go anywhere without that SAW ammo," blurted Mantis. "We'll be hanging out for every raghead along the route to light us up," he panted, his eyes bulging out from under his kevlar helmet.

"Thank you for that newsflash, Mantis," Trevanathan snapped. "May I be in charge now?"

Mantis dropped his eyes and scowled, his cheeks flushed. "Sorry, sir."

"Sergeant Warden, we need to mount up and follow the Colonel – no choice," Trevanathan ordered quietly. "Jaguar Two, you are going to have trouble turning over your engine and fall to the rear of the convoy. Wait until Ridlin shows up with that SAW ammo and then follow us."

"Yessir," said Smith.

"Mantis you are with me. Abu, ride with Leader. Sergeant Leader, get that ammo ASAP, even if you have to steal it."

"Yessir," replied three voices at once.

"Major Trevanathan," interrupted the high pitched twang of COL Rabbit's voice from the lead vehicle as it reached an ear-splitting octave. "It is 0630. We must leave now. NOW, Major. Do you understand?" Several Marines, standing in a nearby doorway smoking, openly smirked at the histrionics of the reserve officer.

"Roger, sir," replied Trevanathan, embarrassed that they were creating such a pitiful scene in front of these battle-tested troops.

Climbing into the front right seat, Trevanathan waved SSG Leader over to the side of his vehicle. "Sergeant Leader, listen up. In fifteen minutes Jaguar One will overheat and pull off the MSR for minor repairs. That will allow you to catch up. We'll see you there. Let's go."

"Roger, sir," replied Leader to the Major as he turned and headed back to Jaguar Two.

Rabbit's HMMWV was already rolling out the gate of the compound, as Private Cooper scrambled into the driver's seat of Jaguar One. He shifted into gear and they lurched forward to catch up. As they passed underneath the arm of the makeshift traffic control barrier at the front gate, Trevanathan made eye contact with the young marine standing guard to the right of the exit point. He raised his right hand in acknowledgment of the sentry's slight head nod to their passing, and noted that the young man had the face of a twenty year old boy and the dead eyes of a combat veteran. *Wonder what that kid has seen?* Trevanathan mused to himself.

"Well, we made his SP, sir," Warden laughed wryly from the seat behind the Major.

"Yeah," yelled Trevanathan back over the noisy drone of the engine. "With no SAW ammo, no ROE[22] briefing, and he didn't even think that he was leaving Ridlin behind. I've never seen such a goat screw in my life."

They caught up to Rabbit's vehicle as it turned left onto a paved two-lane road that led back to the main supply route, MSR TAMPA. TAMPA would take them to the outskirts of the provincial capital of Al Hillah, before turning sharply north toward Baghdad. Due to their early start, the sun still hung relatively low in the east behind them, with the temperature still a relatively cool 95 degrees. The breeze caused by the movement of the HMMWV was almost pleasant.

After a short stop when Jaguar One had inexplicably overheated, the convoy made good time across the flat, barren reaches of central Iraq. Contrary to popular belief, Iraq's desert is not really comprised of sand, such as one finds at the beach. Rather, it is mile after mile of fine, powdery dirt. The dirt is so fine that the slightest wind or movement causes it to billow into the air, where it then settles into every nook, cranny, and crevice of vehicles, weapons, and personnel. Even on a perfectly clear and still day, the fine dust hangs in the

---

[22] Rules of Engagement – the military orders that define when troops may use deadly force.

air, wearing down mechanical parts and irritating the eyes with its abrasive quality.

Within an hour of their departure from Whitehorse, the sun had climbed high enough into the sky that the springtime norm of 120 degrees had been reached. Combined with the heat thrown off by the straining engines, the open passenger compartments of the convoy's vehicles approached 130 degrees Fahrenheit. No towns or hamlets were visible in the wastelands that surrounded them. The terrain was identical in every direction – flat and featureless except for the increasing number of destroyed and burned out Iraqi tanks and armored personnel carriers as they headed northwest. Most often, the clusters of dead vehicles were in the vicinity of highway bridge overpasses, which the enemy had used as defensive positions in the otherwise featureless topography.

"I can't wait until summer hits in two or three weeks," Trevanathan said to Cooper. "Then it is supposed to average 130 degrees until October. Really makes you wonder what the hell the first group of people who traveled through this area saw that made them decide to stay."

Cooper shrugged without taking his eyes off the road. Overpasses were not only a favorite defensive position of the Iraqi Army, but also of the Fedayeen, who attacked supply and troop convoys with hit and run tactics. The Fedayeen would place remotely-detonated bombs against the support pillars of a bridge, and position one man out of sight on the far side with an RPG. As the lead vehicle appeared from under the overpass into the apparently safe open road, it would be hit from behind by the RPG, causing the convoy to jam up behind it under the overpass. The IEDs[23], usually comprised of 122mm or 152mm artillery shells, were then remotely detonated, causing massive casualties among the Coalition forces, especially reservists traveling in canvas-covered vehicles.

The Coalition had developed countermeasures in response, of course, including facing weapons rearward as vehicles entered under an overpass. Should any Iraqi be unwise enough to be on the far side of the bridge embankment when the lead vehicles exited, they were taken out without

---

[23] Improvised Explosive Device – a homemade weapon used by insurgents in Iraq to attack US vehicles, often made from an artillery round linked to a detonator that is in turn triggered by a doorbell, garage door opener, timer, or even a cell phone.

waiting to determine if they had hostile intent or not. When the difference between life and death for the convoy might be the slightest triggering pressure of a thumb upon a doorbell or garage door opener – the favorite detonators for IEDs – there was no time for hesitation or second-guessing.

"Jaguar One, this is Gator One", came the squeaky voice of Colonel Rabbit through the radio handset that Trevanathan had wedged next to his ear under his helmet's chinstrap. The speaker box mounted above the windshield had quit working during the passage from Safwan, apparently a casualty of the heat and dust.

"Gator One, this is Jaguar One, over," replied Trevanathan.

"Jaguar One, is that MSR TAMPA on our left?" asked Rabbit.

Trevanathan glanced over at the six-lane divided highway that paralleled their current direction of travel, one hundred meters away. "Uh, that's right, Gator One, but the entrance ramp is not for another six klicks[24] according to the map."

"Well we can make better time on the MSR. I'm looking for a place to cross. Gator One, out."

Uh-oh, Trevanathan thought to himself. The S2[25] for the Marine infantry brigade in Nasiriyah had briefed them the night before that this entire area was heavily mined due to its importance as a direct avenue of approach to Baghdad.

Trevanathan turned to his driver. "Cooper, if Colonel Rabbit drives off of the road I want you to wait until he clears any unpaved area before following. Do you understand?"

"Yessir," said Cooper, keeping his eyes on the road.

"Then, only if he makes it through safely you need to drive exactly in his tire tracks, understand?"

---

[24] Slang for *kilometers*

[25] S2 is the designation for the intelligence section of a unit smaller than a Division. G2 is the designation for an intelligence section of a Division or a Corps-size unit, or any other unit that is commanded by a flag-grade (general) officer.

"Yessir," replied Cooper again.

"I don't want us getting turned into spare parts because Gator One is in a hurry," Trevanathan reaffirmed.

The importance of what the officer was telling him suddenly struck Cooper, who gave a wide-eyed look at the officer. Trevanathan recalled that same expression from the gas chamber training at Fort Bragg before they had flown to Kuwait. Trevanathan had been teamed with Cooper for the task of switching filters on the gas masks, while standing in a room saturated with tear gas. This was a necessary skill to master in case of chemical warfare, which the US troops expected Saddam to use in defense of his regime.

The disposable mask filters only lasted a few hours when exposed to toxic gas, which made it necessary to be able to switch them out regularly while wearing the gas mask in a contaminated area. Once the canister-shaped filter was unscrewed from the front of the mask, the wearer had to hold his breath until the new filter was screwed in or be exposed to the contaminated atmosphere. During training a mistake would result in a snoot full of irritating tear gas. In combat, such an error would result in exposure to nerve gas and a quick but painful death.

In the training chamber at Bragg, Trevanathan had quickly switched Cooper's filter out for him in a matter of a few seconds as the Private held his breath. When it was his turn to return the favor, however, Cooper became so nervous that he removed Trevanathan's old filter canister, dropped the new filter to the ground, and then fumbled it across the length of the twenty-foot chamber. By the time Cooper retrieved the errant canister and attempted to screw the filter back onto Trevanathan's mask, Cooper's hands were shaking so badly he could not complete the task. As Trevanathan had inhaled a searing lungful of the CS gas through the unprotected opening, he remembered hearing Cooper's muffled voice through the rubber skin of his mask, chanting over and over again, "I'm sorry, sir, I'm sorry sir…"

After heaving his guts outside the gas chamber to the great amusement of the other members of the brigade, Trevanathan found Cooper hiding in back of the deuce-and-a-half truck that had brought them to the gas training chamber. Cooper's face was buried in his hands. As Trevanathan climbed into the back of the truck, Cooper had looked up at Trevanathan with those same huge frightened eyes. "Cooper…," began Trevanathan slowly, still coughing, "…if we're ever in a situation like that again – and God help us if we are – you need to take it slow and easy and maintain regular breathing, OK?"

Cooper had nodded.

"If you start tightening up and hyperventilating like you did in there, you're going to be no good to anyone, understand?"

"Yes sir, I'm sorry…"

"You don't have to be sorry, Cooper. Shit happens. Just make sure the shit happens here and not on the battlefield. OK?"

Trevanathan was snapped out of his memory by Gator One, two hundred feet ahead, making a quick and unannounced left turn onto the 100 meter wide dirt strip between their road and the highway. Dirt spun up behind the vehicle's wheels, as its tires dug deep into the soft yellow surface. Rabbit appeared to be following the thin tracks of a cart or wagon that had gone across this same stretch earlier.

"Stop here, Cooper," said the Major. "I'm not ready for you to be a red shirt, yet."

Jaguar One groaned to a stop, as Trevanathan watched Gator One plow across the dirt strip toward the MSR, churning up a great cloud of dust in its wake. Trevanathan tensed to see if the vehicle went up in an orange flash of smoke and flame. Gator One successfully crossed the stretch, however, churned up a slight rise to the highway, and turned right onto the empty MSR.

"Sometimes it's better to be lucky than smart," said Trevanathan to himself. Picking up his handset he depressed the *send* button on the side and spoke into the mouthpiece, "All serial elements, follow Gator One to the MSR, Jaguar One, out." *I shouldn't have to be relaying instructions for Rabbit,* Trevanathan thought. *He's the convoy commander. He needs to let all of the vehicles know what he is doing, not just me.* Trevanathan felt a growing frustration with the senior officer, who should have been providing guidance and leadership to the green reserve troops, not playing some self-absorbed "lone ranger" role.

Trevanathan could see that Rabbit's vehicle was now accelerating up the highway without waiting for the rest of the convoy. *Typical,* thought

Trevanathan. *Hope he doesn't run into any unfriendlies before we catch up. Not much, anyway.*

"OK, Cooper, let's go." Trevanathan ordered. "Follow Gator One's tire tracks."

Cooper pulled off the hard surface of the two-lane road and nosed Jaguar One slowly down the slight slope onto the dirt strip, carefully following the tracks left behind by Gator One to prevent plowing new and potentially deadly ground.

Trevanathan turned around in his seat to see that Jaguar Two was following closely behind him. Behind Smith's HMMWV, a fourth vehicle, "Red Raider One," was completing its own turn onto the dirt strip between the two roads. Satisfied with the progress behind him, he turned back to the front, where several twisted, rusty pieces of rebar sticking up out of the sand to their right momentarily drew his attention. Trevanathan glanced away momentarily to his left and then performed a perfect cartoon-style double-take, as he snapped his attention back to the snarled rebar, next to which were three white, cake-pan-sized objects lay plainly on the surface a few feet away. The Major looked ahead at the tracks left behind by Gator One, as he fumbled for the radio handset's *send* button. A fourth white disk lay half-buried twenty yards ahead, sitting at a 45 degree angle, two feet to the left of Gator One's path.

"Mines!" Trevanathan barked into the handset, as his thumb depressed the button. "All elements halt. We're in a minefield."

The vehicles lurched to a stop as their drivers mashed on the brakes.. Three HMMWVs had followed Jaguar One onto the dirt strip between the MSR and the two-lane road: the remaining five sat idling on the road behind them, waiting their opportunity to cross.

"What do we do now?" Mantis bleated from his seat. He looked out the left side of the vehicle at the ground below him as if a mine might jump up and bite him at any moment.

"Mantis, shut your pie hole and wait for orders," barked Warden, who had already grown weary of Mantis' temporary presence in Jaguar One. Mantis shot a hurt look at Warden, but obeyed.

Trevanathan looked back over his right shoulder at Warden, who sat as calmly as if they were waiting for a traffic light to change. Warden had a round tin of chew in his hand and was extracting a generous pinch to deposit inside his lower lip.

"Gator One, this is Jaguar One, over," said Trevanathan into his handset. There was no response.

"Gator One, this is Jaguar One. We've encountered a minefield."

The unreliable speaker mounted at the top of the windshield crackled unexpectedly to life with a hiss. "Jaguar One, this is Gator One. You have fallen behind, over."

"Nice of him to notice," said Trevanathan to himself, without depressing the transmit button. Activating the handset, he said "Gator One, we have encountered a minefield, over."

"Jaguar One, we don't have time to deal with this now. Mark the grid coordinates and we'll report it when we get back. You need to catch up, over."

"Gator One, we are in the minefield. I repeat, we are sitting in the minefield, over."

Silence.

"Gator One, do you copy? We are in the minefield, over."

"Jaguar One, did you cross where I did? Over."

"Roger, Gator One, you drove through the minefield."

Silence.

"Do ya think he's figgered it out yet, sahr?" Warden asked calmly from behind, leaning out and directing an expertly-aimed stream of brown tobacco juice onto the sand.

"When you hear the sound of him loading his drawers over the radio you'll know the light bulb went on," Trevanathan replied.

Determined not to hesitate again, Trevanathan began giving orders. "OK, we need to get out of here. If some Fedayeen bastard has this minefield zeroed in and starts dropping mortars on us we're screwed. Cooper, Warden, I want you to probe ahead of the vehicle to the right of that mine up there. Rabbit must have stirred it up with his passing."

Trevanathan triggered his handset, "All elements, I want the last five vehicles to proceed along the hardball to interchange Foxtrot. Rendezvous with Gator One and wait for us there. Jaguar Two, Red Raider One, and Sierra Seven-Two maintain position until we clear a new track, over."

Acknowledgments came over the radio from each vehicle in the convoy, with the exception of Gator One. Trevanathan watched enviously as the last five vehicles in the convoy disappeared along the mine-free, paved road toward the rendezvous point.

Cooper and Warden dismounted to clear a safe path for Jaguar One and the other three HMMWVs. Warden reached into his fanny pack and produced a pair of plastic chopsticks that he had liberated from a Chinese restaurant at Fort Bragg for just this purpose. Mines are often triggered by weight upon a pressure fuse, however, more sophisticated mines may also be triggered by a shift in the magnetic field surrounding the mine, such as might occur when a vehicle or metal probe comes too close. A cheap chopstick, therefore, makes a good probing tool. Slid into the ground at a thirty degree angle to avoid depressing the detonator, the chopstick encounters resistance when it touches the side of the mine. Advancing only six inches per probe into the dirt, the work of searching for mines without a sophisticated detector is as dull as it is deadly. As the instructor at Fort Bragg had told them before they shipped out, however, there was no need to rush the process, because they had the rest of their lives to do the job properly.

"Jaguar One, this is Gator One. What is your status? Over." the speaker crackled.

Trevanathan began to respond, but hesitated.

"Jaguar One, this is Gator One. Report your situation, over."

Trevanathan waited again, staring ahead through the windshield at the two soldiers crawling on their hands and knees, methodically probing, while waiting for their worlds to end.

"Sir, aren't you going to answer him?" Mantis asked from the back seat.

"I think I'm having radio trouble, Sergeant Mantis," Trevanathan responded, as he looked at Mantis seriously. "It's a shame the radio is malfunctioning. Colonel Rabbit might think for a moment that his screw-up has gotten us killed. A few minutes of discomfort might cause him to think twice before joyriding or leaving us again, don't ya' think?"

"Boy, I hope I can fix this," Trevanathan said sarcastically as he lightly hit the side of the SINCGARS radio with his fist.

"Jaguar One, report," came Rabbit's voice again, now rising to the same strained pitch it had when the all-important departure time had been in danger.

"That's what happens when you go to the low bidder," Trevanathan said in mock concern, as he continued to lightly tap the radio.

"Jaguar Two, this is Gator One, do you read?"

Captain Smith reached for his handset to respond, but saw Trevanathan signal a slashing motion across his throat as he held his handset in his right hand. "Shoot," said Smith to his team, shaking his head. "Radio trouble again."

Ahead of Jaguar One, Warden and Cooper spent twenty minutes probing a fifty foot long safe route away from the half-buried mine to their left and then back onto the trail that Rabbit had blazed with his passage. They had encountered no other mines, and marked the new safe route with strands of brightly-colored engineer tape that they pushed into the dirt with their chopsticks.

"All right, let's take it nice and slow," said Trevanathan to Cooper as the Private settled back into the driver's seat. Trevanathan unknowingly held his breath as Cooper swung off of Rabbit's original track, away from the uncovered mine, and onto the alternative course they had just probed. *I hope they didn't miss any*, Trevanathan thought to himself.

As they inched forward, Trevanathan recalled how one colorful EOD[26] instructor at Fort Bragg had explained how it was better to be killed by a mine, rather than wounded, when riding in the front right seat of a HMMWV.

---

[26] Explosive Ordnance Disposal

This was because the force of an explosion often caused the vehicle batteries mounted beneath the front passenger seat to blow up through the canvas seat and rather forcefully enter the passenger's hindquarters. "That'll make your eyes water," the instructor had joked, with the gallows humor typical of Army combat skills instructors.

Rejoining Gator One's track at a point beyond the half-buried mine, Jaguar One passed through the remainder of the dirt strip without incident, as did the other three trail vehicles. As they bounced successfully up onto the paved highway, Trevanathan pulled his GPS[27] out of his pants' cargo pocket and marked the grid coordinates of the minefield so he could report its location when they reached Camp Babylon. EOD would eventually send a team to clear or blow the mines, unless some other fool followed their trail and detonated them first.

The Major reflected that the cart tracks they had viewed as a sign of safe passage initially may well have been the cart that carried the mines out in the first place. *That's a good lesson to remember*, thought Trevanathan. *A track doesn't always mean safe passage.*

Only after all four vehicles had made it safely to the hard surface of the MSR did Trevanathan trigger his handset. "Gator One, this is Jaguar One. Have cleared obstacle and am proceeding to rendezvous at interchange Foxtrot, over."

"Roger, Jaguar One. Gator One, out," came the clipped response.

"Sir, isn't Colonel Rabbit going to be pissed that you didn't return his call earlier?" asked Mantis as the four vehicles picked up speed on the highway.

"Mantis, ya' ever stop runnin' that gash under your nose long enough to think before ya' speak?" cut in Warden. "Ya' don't question the Major's calls, shitbird."

"I'll tell you, Mantis," said Trevanathan turning around to face him so everyone in the HMMWV could hear clearly, "I respect the rank, regardless of who wears it. But I take it seriously when one of these amateurs from the 43d starts getting careless playin' soldier, and almost gets my team killed.

---

[27] Global Positioning System

CAPOC[28] looks the other way and puts up with crappy officers at home station because they need numbers. Commanders with full rosters get promoted regardless of how badly trained or stupid their personnel are. That's how these paper colonels got where they are in the first place. But the minute it's gonna' get my men killed, I start to take it personal."

"Yes, sir," said Mantis quietly, not sure whether Trevanathan was angry at him, or Rabbit.

"Never mistake rank for leadership ability in the Reserves, Mantis," Trevanathan continued. "Maybe the next time Colonel Rabbit is about to do something stupid, he'll remember how crappy it felt not to be sure if he had just got his people killed, and some poor schmuck won't go home in a bag because of it."

"Yes, sir," mumbled Mantis, looking away. He was surprised at the ferocity of Trevanathan's response – especially about a full colonel. The officers did not usually share their opinions of each other in front of the enlisted personnel. The fact that Trevanathan had spoken his thoughts on the matter was surprising to him, and seemed to be a breach of the unwritten code that officers' business was not paraded before the NCOs. *Things are starting to change around here*, Mantis thought to himself.

Jaguar One and the other three vehicles found Gator One and the rest of the convoy waiting for them at interchange Foxtrot as planned. As they pulled back into their respective places in the convoy, Colonel Rabbit again took the lead – this time proceeding at a pace that kept the nine other vehicles within his view. No words were exchanged between Rabbit and Trevanathan.

---

[28] Civil Affairs and Psychological Operations Command – pronounced "kay-pock."

Chapter 5
The Jacket

The convoy continued its relentless westward passage. Waves of heat shimmered on the six-lane divided highway. Sweat-saturated uniforms clung uncomfortably to the team's skin beneath heavy flak jackets. Major Trevanathan had to concentrate to keep himself from nodding off. Despite the potential danger around them, the steady throbbing of the engine, the unchanging terrain and the relentless heat created a lulling sensation. Trevanathan looked back over his left shoulder and saw that Abu had already succumbed – his helmeted head leaning forward on his chest.

Looking over his right shoulder, Trevanathan saw SFC Warden was still maintaining his vigil over the unchanging scenery. Trevanathan signaled to him to wake Abu, so that they would have 360 degree visibility around the vehicle. Warden reached over and slapped the top of Abu's helmet with unrestrained enthusiasm.

Abu jumped awake, momentarily disoriented as to his surroundings. "'Less ya' wanna' make Iraq yer perm'nent home, I suggest ya' keep yer eyes open," Warden warned. "Everyone on this team depends on everyone else to stay alive – 'cluding you."

"My apologies, Sergeant. It will not happen again," stammered the Kuwaiti, embarrassed at nodding off. Warden nodded without comment and turned back to his portion of the desert.

The monotony was broken for several moments as they came upon the first evidence of a major combat engagement. Several hundred destroyed Iraqi Army vehicles lay in the median and along the sides of the highway, marking a point where they had unwisely sought to make a stand – or perhaps had been caught in the open by the Air Force. Either way, the extent of the destruction was so thorough that it was impossible to tell how the twisted heaps of metal had been destroyed. Tanks, armored cars, armored personnel carriers, trucks, cars, and buses were piled one upon the other, as if a giant hand had reached down and smashed them like toys into a pile.

Trevanathan stared at the destruction with a strange combination of sympathy for the dead Iraqis and admiration at the effectiveness of the Coalition's fighting ability. *They didn't have a chance*, he thought. One Iraqi T-72 tank sat tucked behind a small dirt berm to the right of the highway, facing south. The turret had been blown into the air and had landed upside down exactly at the point from which it had launched. *Well, these bastards have been using their army to kill Kurds, Kuwaitis, and their own women and children for a decade*, Trevanathan thought. *Payback's a bitch.*

"The best Soviet military equipment money can buy," mocked Warden from the rear seat.

"They deserved to die," spat Abu. "They are animals. They do not know how to live in a civilized way."

"Now I thought that the Koran says ya'll boys are brothers, Abu. Isn't that raght?" probed Warden, looking back at Abu. Warden had had his fill of street preachers in Somalia, who lauded Islam as a religion of peace during the day and then targeted the US and UN peacekeeping forces at night. What little empathy he had brought with him from the Texas panhandle for the Arabs had evaporated in the Mog[29],the day that his best friend in the 10th Mountain Division had been killed by a sniper, while playing a pick-up game of soccer with the local children.

"All Muslims are brothers. These Iraqis…they…are not good Muslims. It…is very complicated. I do not expect you to understand."

"I understand more than you might think, Abu," said Warden, ending the conversation by turning his back on the translator.

At occasional intervals an Iraqi child, or sometimes two, would stand next to the highway, waving at the convoy as it passed. Some waved empty plastic water bottles or pointed fingers to their open mouths to indicate they were hungry and wanted food. The team had learned in Nasiriyah, however, that there was no food shortage in Iraq. The markets and roadside stands of Iraq were overflowing with produce in every town and city they had passed through.

---

[29] Soldier slang for Mogadishu, capital of Somalia.

Trevanathan was amazed that these roadside children seemed to appear out of nowhere, standing along the highway unsupervised, with no dwelling or village within sight for at least fifteen miles across the flat, barren landscape. The teams had been briefed prior to entering Iraq to not distribute food or water along the MSR, even though it might seem the humanitarian thing to do. From prior operations in the Balkans, the Army knew that if one kid was given a bottle of water today, tomorrow there would be twenty kids begging along the same convoy route, and fifty the day after that. The result would be the creation of another Safwan and the slowing of precious supplies from Kuwait and the Iraqi port at Um Qasr. A number of Iraqi kids had already been killed due to soft-hearted soldiers throwing an MRE[30] out the window of their truck, which then drew the little beggars in front of the next convoy vehicle following behind.

Colonel Rabbit's convoy rode in the middle lane of the three lane highway. At an average convoy speed of 55 MPH, this meant that even small-engine Iraqi vehicles would occasionally overtake the convoy, requiring the team to remain alert. Civilian vehicles were still rare on the MSR, but the end of the major fighting and the growing need for trade to resume between the far-flung towns in the South was gradually changing that.

Trevanathan could see in his side mirror that a small white Toyota pickup truck was overtaking them on the right. He shifted sideways in his seat, his right foot dangling out of the open doorway, inches above the pavement, so that his M16A2 rifle could cover the small truck as it came abreast of him. Warden had the vehicle covered as it approached from behind. Several drive-by shootings had occurred in the past week, when a seemingly innocent civilian vehicle had come up quickly on a convoy and unloaded a barrage of automatic weapons fire at US troops, before cutting off onto a side road.

This truck was apparently on its way to some market, laden with livestock and people. Trevanathan marveled at how the Iraqis used small pickup trucks to carry so much. The front seat was occupied by three dark skinned men, who waved at Trevanathan as they drew alongside. Each wore a red and white checkered scarf on his head and flashed smiles of great enthusiasm.

---

[30] Meal Ready to Eat – prepackaged field rations carried by US troops; each meal is sealed in its own brown plastic bag.

As the rest of the truck passed alongside, Trevanathan saw that a cow had somehow been loaded into the tiny bed and tethered to some unseen hitch. Three sheep were jammed together in a mass behind the cow, creating the illusion that there was but one sheep with three heads sticking out of a single large wooley body. Their eyes rolled nervously at the sound of the HMMWV's deep engine roar beside them. Huddled in the near front corner of the truck bed, closest to Trevanathan, were two middle-aged women wearing traditional black burkhas. Only their faces were exposed. Their skin was leathery and deeply lined, the result of years spent unprotected beneath the harsh Iraqi sun. On the lap of the younger of the two sat a boy of about three years of age, who stared somberly at the large foreign vehicle and the strange creatures who occupied it. From the viewpoint of the toddler, the soldiers with their large goggles, armored exoskeletons and strangely shaped helmets, created an almost insect-like appearance.

Trevanathan lowered the barrel of the rifle he had trained on the door of the truck, despite all of the smiling and waving that had greeted them. He had learned to nod and smile whenever the occupants of an Iraqi vehicle extended a friendly greeting, but he never removed his hands from the weapon that kept everyone honest during a brief highway encounter. Despite knowing that it was not good security to lower his guard, he could not bring himself to keep his barrel trained on a kid. *I'll take the risk*, he thought to himself, *rather that than have that kid grow up with memories of a US soldier drawing down on him and his mother.*

The truck passed by them and slowly drew ahead of the convoy. *I'll have to ask my wife to ride in the back of the truck with the animals when I get home*, thought Trevanathan to himself, with a smile. *Yeah, that'll go over big.*

"All convoy elements, this is Gator One," twanged Rabbit's voice over the intercom. "We are approaching Fuel Point Dragoon. We'll fuel up here and take a break for latrine and chow, out."

Fuel Point Dragoon was a dusty patch of desert halfway between Nasiriyah and Baghdad that the Army had established as a refueling point. Long rows of green tanker trucks sat baking beneath the sun, filled with diesel to keep the flow of supplies and personnel for the US war effort moving. A few sleeping tents for the soldiers of the fuel detachment dotted the area, along with a makeshift mess tent that doled out bitter coffee, hot bottled water, and MREs.

The convoy parked in the shade of the tankers and dismounted, stretching their cramped legs. Staff Sergeant Leader removed his flak jacket and flung it to the ground, cursing. Trevanathan noted the uncharacteristic reaction of the normally even-tempered NCO. "What's the problem, Sergn't Leader?"

"Nuthin' sir. Sorry."

"Bullshit, what is it?"

"Well, this flak jacket is just too small, sir. When I went through CIF[31] all they had left was medium. It barely covers my chest and the small arm holes are causing a rash. The itching is driving me nuts in this heat."

"You're too bulked up for your own good, Sergn't," sneered Mantis, who envied Leader's impressive build.

"Hey, maybe I could go shop at the fat boy shop next time like you, Mantis," Leader fired back. "Do they sell Kevlar bras for your man-titties?"

Ignoring the exchange, Trevanathan removed his own 25-pound jacket and laid it on the passenger seat of Jaguar Two. He picked up Leader's jacket and slipped it on over his blouse. "Well, I can see why it doesn't fit you Sergeant Leader; it just barely fits me. You go ahead and take mine – it's a large."

"No sir, it's fine, I'll just put some powder under my arms when we reach Camp Babylon, really."

"Negative. I need you in top form on that SAW with plenty of room to maneuver. If you're all bunched up in a flak jacket that's too small you can't do your job. Medium will be fine for me, I'm skinny. Anyway, the smaller plates[32] don't weigh as much, so I'm getting the better end of the deal," Trevanathan laughed.

"I feel bad takin' your flak, sir," Leader muttered, embarrassed to have complained and even more chagrined that Trevanathan was giving up his own flak jacket.

---

[31] Central Issue Facility – the building where troops draw necessary field gear prior to a deployment.
[32] The Interceptor® body armor vests worn by US forces in Iraq have large pockets into which slip bulletproof plates – these provide protection against high-velocity projectiles such as rifle bullets and shrapnel.

"It's the best thing for the team. Besides it's an order, so you don't have a choice."

"Roger, sir. Thanks."

"Don't thank me. I expect you to use that big old flak jacket to save my ass if we get into trouble. Now go get some chow."

"Yessir," said Leader, turning and walking toward the makeshift mess tent. "C'mon Mantis," he continued, "You might blow away if you don't shove some more calories in your pie hole."

"Mantis," Trevanathan ordered, "you're with me for the next leg." He had decided in the interest of international relations to separate Abu and Warden for awhile.

"Roger, sir."

As the two NCOs walked away, Smith approached Trevanathan, munching on a hunk of pineapple upside-down cake from the MRE he had just opened. Trevanathan eyeballed the yellowish cake, which was his favorite MRE dessert. Smith caught his obvious look and broke the chunk in half, handing the larger piece over with dirty fingers. Trevanathan popped it into his mouth, and mumbled, "You're so good to me," through his mouthful of crumbs.

"I can't stand those big dog eyes you make when someone draws the pineapple cake," Smith laughed. "Say," he continued, "did you trade your flak jacket? Your other one was desert camo wasn't it?"

Trevanathan looked down at the woodland green camouflage pattern of the smaller vest. "Yeah, I thought this went better with my eyes." He finished off the sweet morsel and licked the crumbs from his likewise dirty fingers.

"Well, I hope you like the color, because it's so small on your lanky-ass frame that it looks like a training bra," Smith chortled, pleased with his own joke.

"Hey, just because you gave me some cake doesn't mean you can talk dirty to me," Trevanathan replied with mock hurt in his voice.

"Major Trevanathan!" came Rabbit's high-pitched voice from the lead vehicle. "I'll be in the mess tent. Call me when the vehicles are refueled."

"Thy master's voice," Smith mocked in a low voice.

"Yessir," said the Major, ignoring the comment and moving off to locate Warden to begin the refueling.

Chapter 6
The Passage

The miles continued to drone by as the convoy approached the end of its journey. Saddam Hussein had built the highway as a testament to the modernization of his nation, as well as a high-speed avenue of approach to his neighbors in Kuwait, Saudi Arabia and Southern Iran. Except for the endless wastelands on either side of the highway, it could have been a major highway anywhere in the USA. Such a high-quality roadway is a rarity in the Middle East, where the costs of maintenance under the harsh desert conditions are a disincentive.

Despite the smooth road, however, the passage across central Iraq was as unpleasant and draining as it had been for millennia. Major Trevanathan had wrapped a green camouflage bandana across his face to filter out some of the dust that was beginning to cause him to cough chronically.

Iraqi dirt plays havoc with uninitiated respiratory systems. Most troops develop the "Iraqi crud" within a week or two of arrival in theater. The "crud" is a combination of bronchitis and asthma-like symptoms that leaves one choking his lungs up for a week or two until his system adjusts to the perpetual irritants hanging in the air. When the springtime sandstorms stir up the atmosphere, one can actually taste and see the dirt in the air with each breath.

Trevanathan knew that they were approaching the end of the southern wasteland when he spotted the first reeds of a salt marsh alongside the highway. After hours in the lifeless terrain, even the appearance of scrub brush and stunted grass looked lush by comparison.

"Look at that, sir," Mantis called from the back seat, pointing to a group of women kneeling in the mud fifty meters off one side of the highway. Dressed from head to toe in their black burkhas, the women were extracting salt from the fetid soil using what appeared to be homemade wooden rakes to drag the surface. School-age children gathered the salt scum and pounded it into small white mounds to dry in the sun.

Colonel Rabbit slowed the convoy as it passed the women, transfixed by the sight of these heavily clothed women performing their labor under the relentless sun. Small brown children, of perhaps two or three years, squatted quietly nearby, observing their mothers and digging in the ooze with their fingers.

Several women looked up momentarily at the noise of the slow-moving convoy. Eyes from the Seventh Century ran across the modern weapons and soldiers of the most recent empire to conquer their land. Seeing no threat, they quickly returned to their task. One of the older children, of perhaps eight or nine years, looked up from his salt mound and fashioned an imaginary pistol with his fingers, pointing it at the convoy.

"They start 'em early, that's for sure," Mantis muttered.

"Just think about it," Trevanathan commented, "These people have probably been getting their salt this same way for the past three thousand years. They've been dragging their children out here and working in the sun until they keel over dead and the next generation takes over."

"Pretty damned stupid if you ask me," Mantis replied.

"Mantis, these 'stupid' people created the first city-states on the planet, wrote the first set of recorded laws, and controlled an empire that ran from the Atlantic Ocean to India for centuries. They're not stupid. What they are is very slow to change and very slow to accept change. We better remember that in dealing with them," corrected Trevanathan.

"Where's the men, sir?" Mantis continued, ignoring the mild rebuke.

"Don't know," replied the Major. "I know the women do most of the work around the home, but I don't know what the deal is with working in the fields."

The convoy passed more and more groups of women and children working the marshes as they approached Hillah. There were subtle changes to the terrain now, as the highway once again drew near to the Euphrates River. Huts made of dried reeds sat alongside brackish pools of water, bordered by black mud. Palm trees began to appear in the distance: at first just a blur on the horizon, but gradually the green fronds and the long brown trunks became distinct.

The other change in the countryside was the renewed frequency with which damaged Iraqi tanks and armored personnel carriers littered the sides of the roads. Hillah had been part of the "Ring of Death" that Saddam had established roughly 100 kilometers south of Baghdad. This was where his vaunted Republican Guard was to have made their heroic stand, and where the Americans had feared Saddam would use his chemical weapons when the noose began to tighten. Recognizing that the game was up for their leader, however, many Republican Guard units turned tail as soon as US forces had lumbered into view.

Waiting to run until the Americans were visible was a bad idea, however, for the effective range of the US M1A2 main battle tanks is in excess of three kilometers, over 1,000 meters more than the Republican Guard's fleet of Soviet-made T-72s. By the time the Iraqis had visual contact with the advancing US armored columns, it was already too late to run. Most of the destroyed Iraqi vehicles around Hillah were facing north toward Baghdad when they were destroyed – instead of south toward the advancing US forces – as their doomed crews tried to escape.

The convoy reached its exit coordinates from the MSR without incident. Everyone was too exhausted from a day in the desert heat to exhibit much enthusiasm, though. Only Trevanathan appreciated that the small convoy had successfully accomplished a crossing that had destroyed countless waves of invading armies over the past thirty centuries.

Instead of an exit ramp, a recently-constructed one-lane dirt road intersected the side of the highway. The narrow road led back into a cluster of date palm trees one hundred meters distant where another paved road began. The exit was marked only with a makeshift sign stating "Babylon," with an arrow pointing west. Gator One led the convoy off MSR TAMPA onto the shaded lane toward Camp Babylon, twenty kilometers distant.

The longest day of my life, Trevanathan thought to himself, as they drove beneath the date palm trees toward their new home.

Chapter 7
The Hospital

"Let's start at this end of the hall. There's two kids in here," the officer indicated. The pediatric ward of Saddam Hospital in Hillah more closely resembled a series of rooms in a by-the-hour motel than a treatment unit. The only hint that the soldiers had entered a hospital room was the little girl in the bed nearest the far wall with an IV stuck in her left arm. That, and the overpowering stench of sickness. Otherwise, it was just a faded yellow, plaster-walled room containing two old metal-framed beds. One sheet and a faded, pink-striped pillow without a case on each bed completed the scene. There were no medical monitors, nurse summoning buttons or even a pitcher of water. A woman in a dark brown burkha sat in a metal folding chair between the two beds with her eyes cast at the floor, seeing nothing.

As the three soldiers and their translator walked gingerly into the room, the little boy in the bed nearest the door sat up quickly and stared at them unblinking. The girl remained turned to the wall. The Iraqi woman did not even look up, apparently used to the comings and goings of the hospital staff. "Hi there, little guy, would you like a toy?" asked Major Matthew Heller, timidly. The boy continued to stare at them, unblinking. His lower lip trembled slightly.

Heller was one of the civil affairs officers from the 411th battalion in Amarillo who had been scooped up in Brigadier General Merdier's last-minute effort to replace the defecting 538th personnel. A registered nurse by trade, he, like many army personnel with any level of medical training, instantly earned the nickname "Doc" from the unit's soldiers. His job with the 538th was to develop a rapport with the local Iraqi health officials and to assess what support was needed to prevent an outbreak of cholera or other life-threatening diseases in an environment where clean water and waste treatment was almost unknown.

An easygoing and likeable officer, Doc had sandy hair and a freckled complexion. His lean, six-foot tall frame gave him the appearance of a runner. He had meshed well with the younger officers of the 538th after demonstrating he possessed an unfailing bullshit detector that he was not afraid to use. The first inkling of this skill was when he was told by local Iraqi Ministry of

Health officials that medical supplies were unavailable for the local hospital. Smelling a rat, Doc had led a convoy of supply trucks into the Ministry's own compound and seized a small warehouse full of medicine, bandages, and antibiotics that were being hoarded by the officials for sale on the black market.

Today, his mission was improving public relations at the local hospital, distributing stuffed animals to sick kids to show the compassion of the US forces. As he did not have his own security escort, Doc had cajoled Captain Smith and Jaguar Two to accompany him into Hillah with several boxes of toys obtained from the officers' spouses' association back home.

Doc reached into the cardboard box carried by Sergeant Mantis and pulled out a cute brown rabbit, with soft fur and small brown glass eyes. He held it out toward the tentative child with a smile. The boy did not move, his eyes still locked on the officer's face.

"Abu, tell him it's a gift for him," Doc told the translator. Abu rattled off something in Arabic, causing the mother to look up, noticing the entry of soldiers from a foreign country into the twelve by ten foot room for the first time.

The boy did not move. "Doc, maybe he's scared of you," suggested Smith, who also normally served with Heller in the Amarillo unit. "Why not just lay the thing on the bed and let's get moving?"

Doc put the rabbit on the foot of the bed and moved over to the little girl. "Hi honey," he began, "Do you want a toy? A nice kitty?" he added, pulling an imitation white Angora cat out of the box. The toy had bright blue glass eyes and a pink satin ribbon around its neck. The boy's mother instantly fixed her eyes upon it. As Abu translated the offer, the girl turned her face away from the wall toward them for the first time. Doc saw that she had bandages over both eyes and massive facial burns. The skin of her right cheek was purple and shriveled like a prune. The left cheek was smooth and a flawless light brown.

"What happened to her?" blurted Mantis.

"Shut up, Mantis," ordered Doc, who was accustomed to viewing serious injuries. Abu spoke gently to the girl in Arabic and she quietly replied.

"She says she was picking up scrap metal with her brother along the road near the river," said Abu. "They spotted some shiny metal object in the ditch and her brother ran to retrieve it. It exploded."

"Maybe a cluster munition," Doc said, quietly.

"Is this the brother?" said Smith, gesturing toward the boy who had picked up the rabbit, and who did not seem badly injured by comparison. Abu asked the girl. "She did not see it, sir, as she was blinded by the explosion, but her mother told her he is in paradise now."

"This place gives me the creeps," Mantis muttered petulantly.

Ignoring the NCO, Doc spoke softly, "Honey, here's something for you – Abu tell her." Doc held out the toy. The girl reached out gingerly in response to Abu's words and felt the soft long-haired coat of the toy. She lifted it gently from Doc's hands and stroked it softly, a small smile coming over her twisted face.

"Well, we made someone's day at least," said Smith as he felt a small tug at his sleeve. Looking over his right shoulder Smith saw the boy's mother standing at his elbow, gently tugging the material of his uniform. She looked up at Smith with dark, bloodshot eyes and smiled, revealing a row of uneven, brown teeth.

"Yes ma'am?" asked Smith, turning to face her. The mother held up the small brown rabbit and then pointed to the cat the girl was hugging. "Oh, you're welcome ma'am," said Smith, smiling, before turning back to Doc and the girl. The mother pulled at his sleeve again, only more insistently this time. Smith looked back again and the mother held the small rabbit out to him with both hands. She shrugged and nodded toward the girl, as unintelligible words spilled from her mouth.

"What does she want, Abu?" asked Smith, looking at the translator who stood uncomfortably in the doorway. "Nothing, she wants nothing," replied Abu, his dark complexion flushing. Smith frowned as Abu spoke quickly and sharply to the mother in Arabic, prompting her to return to her chair clutching the rabbit. She once again cast her eyes solemnly at the floor as her son stretched to reach the toy that she held beyond his reach.

"What'd you say, Abu?" asked Doc, who had now been distracted by the fuss behind him.

"I told her that you accept her thanks and she must leave you alone, as you are very busy men."

"Uh huh, well, take it easy on her, OK?" said Doc, stooping to pick up his cardboard box of stuffed animals. "She has a sick kid – and remember, we're supposed to be winning these people over, not yelling at them."

"Yes, Major," replied Abu as his skin flushed darker.

"Let's get onto the next room," said Doc, moving toward the door.

The next room on the opposite side of the hall had just one patient – a boy about eight years old – laying in a single bed just inside the door. His right leg was missing below the knee. An IV drip hung from a bent metal stand next to the bed.

"Hi son, would you like an animal friend?" asked Doc. The boy's father sat tensely next to the bed as the soldiers entered the room, but visibly relaxed when Doc pulled a stuffed panda bear from the box and held it out to the boy. The boy sat up and quickly snatched the toy out of his hand, then curled himself about it in a fetal manner.

"Thank you... bery much," said the father in heavily accented English, as he stood up from his chair. "You are bery kind." Like many Iraqis, the father was relatively short, standing approximately five foot four. He had jet black hair, a long thin face, and a bright smile below his mustache.

"You're welcome, sir," answered Doc. "How is your son doing?"

"He is very sick," said the man somberly. "He has a disease that the doctors were unable to treat before. He lost his leg to it. We hope that with you Americans here now he will be able to get the medicine when he needs it. Enshalla."

"What is his condition?" Doc asked, his professional medical demeanor exerting itself in the way he questioned the father.

"I do not know the word in English," apologized the father, "but the Arabic translates as sugar disease."

"Diabetes? Your son is diabetic?"

"I think that is one of the words the doctors used, but I am not certain."

"That should be very treatable," commented Doc. "Are they giving him insulin?"

"I do not know the medicine," answered the father, "but they are giving it to him now and he looks better. The leg turned bad during the fighting when there was no medicine."

Smith listened to the exchange and sadly thought, *So many victims. People have no idea how many innocent people get hurt by a war who aren't even near the fighting.* He felt a tug at his sleeve and turned to see that the mother from the first room had quietly slipped in. Clutching the little brown rabbit she pointed back at her son's room and rattled off a long string of unintelligible Arabic, gesturing and speaking with increased volume and emphasis.

"What does she want?" asked Smith, a bit of irritation creeping into his voice. He was finding it increasingly disconcerting to have this woman repeatedly sidling up behind him unnoticed and plucking at him like a chicken in the market.

Abu shifted uncomfortably. "I am very embarrassed sir, but she wants to know why her son received only a small brown rabbit, when the girl received a very rich looking cat. She says that the girl's family is known to be Ba'ath[33] party members, and it is unfair for her to receive such favoritism."

Smith was speechless. "You mean," he started slowly, "that she is bitching about the toy we gave her kid?" He felt his cheeks burning.

Abu did not answer. The mother raised her voice shrilly again, gesturing at the door to her son's room, and began to shake the rabbit by its neck.

"She is from a tribe that has no honor," interrupted the father of the diabetic boy, pointing an accusing finger at the woman. "They are murderers and

---

[33] The Ba'ath Party was controlled by Saddam Hussein, and was dominated by the 20% Sunni Muslim population of Iraq. Sunni Ba'ath party members enjoyed the best standard of living in Iraq under Saddam, while the 60% Shiite Muslim population, predominantly in the southern part of the country, generally lived in poverty.

liars," he continued. "My cousin was killed by a member of her tribe. I know."

Abu cut the father off with a quick stream of Arabic that clearly meant for him to shut up.

"Look, I don't have time or patience for this," said Smith. "Doc, can we give the crazy old bat a better animal so we can get moving?"

Doc rummaged through the box. "How about this Mickey Mouse?" asked Doc, holding up a version of the famous rodent dressed up as a wizard.

Smith snatched the stuffed toy and turned to Abu. "Does this meet Lady Di's requirements?" he snarled . The mother's eyes glowed with avarice. She grabbed the mouse from Smith, dropped the rabbit, and scuttled out the door without a word.

"Charming," said Smith dryly.

Trying to suppress his own disgust with the entire exchange, Doc said, "I hope your son feels better, sir."

"Salaam Alekim," the father responded, bowing slightly and touching his chest above his heart as the soldiers left the room.

As they walked down the hall, Doc spoke quietly to Smith. "That kid would have probably never lost his leg if the Iraqi Army wasn't warehousing all their drugs for military use. These people are their own worst enemy, sometimes. All the oil money in the world and they don't provide even basic health care to their people."

"Well, we're gonna' change all that, right?" Smith replied with more question in his voice than certainty.

The team continued down the long hall, handing out toys to the dozens of children on the floor. Each room presented the same empty walls and bare beds, with only an occasional vestige of medical treatment apparent, usually an IV bottle. "The main killer of kids here is diarrhea," explained Doc. "They get some bad water or bad food and there's nothing that stops their systems from quickly becoming dehydrated by the lack of fluids. The sad thing is that it's not the dehydration that kills them, most often, but the treatment. They come in here and are re-hydrated with reused IV needles due to the shortage of medical supplies. That leads to staph infections that kill them. Some over-the-counter Immodium® and a glass of clean water would do the job better."

From the far end of the hall behind them came the crash of a metal pan and the sound of breaking glass. The yelling of high-pitched voices quickly followed. The mother from the brown rabbit incident stormed down the hall toward the team, knocking aside a staff member. She was followed by six mothers from other rooms in which they had already distributed toys. Over her head, like a sign of protest, the leader carried the white cat, its bow now torn and one of its eyes missing. Shaking the cat and yelling in Arabic she pointed at Smith. The other mothers gathered about her, also yelling shrilly and shaking an orgy of Sponge Bobs, teddy bears and Tweety birds. The gifts twisted grotesquely in the shaking hands of the outraged mothers. "Abu?" asked Doc with a raised eyebrow.

"Sir, they are angry that the child of a Ba'athist receives the finest prize of all from the Americans. They have compared the items and state that this shows nothing has changed in Iraq. That there is no justice for those who have suffered under Saddam."

"You've got to be kid…" began Doc, before a Tweety bird smacked the left side of his face, causing his eye to begin to water unmercifully.

"Great: four US troops killed in stuffed animal riot," muttered Mantis under his breath as the angry group pressed forward, their voices becoming more shrill.

"Jesus Christ," cried Smith. "These people don't have a pot to piss in and they're upset over the stuffed animals we gave 'em?" His comment was drowned out as the wave of women surged forward, smacking him with their plush arsenal.

"OK, this is nuts," said Doc, holding one hand to his watering eye. "We're out of here." The team retreated down the hallway toward the stairs, followed closely by the posse of cursing, ferocious mothers, brandishing the discounted treasures.

As the team hustled down the two flights of stairs to the ground floor, stuffed animals rained down upon them through the stairwell. Looking up, Smith was relieved to see that the women were not following. This was one of those no-win situations where the enormous might of the US Army did not matter a bit. They could stand fast and look ridiculous as they were assaulted with stuffed animals or rapidly leave and look equally ridiculous.

The soldiers slowed as they reached the ground floor and exited the stairwell at a semi-dignified pace. Exiting the main lobby to where the two HMMWVs sat outside, Doc yelled, "Let's go," to his waiting driver, Sergeant Mancuso.

"So, how'd it go, sir?" asked Mancuso as he turned the ignition and slowly shifted the vehicle into drive.

Heller eyed the main door to the hospital nervously, wishing Mancuso would hurry up. "Oh, great…just great," he said wearily as they pulled away. "We're doing a helluva job winning these people over."

Chapter 8
The Palace

The new home for the Jaguars was first-rate by field living standards. Saddam had built his palace atop a manmade hill, towering two hundred meters above the surrounding countryside. From the large stone veranda surrounding the dirt-brown structure, one could see forty miles in any direction. Due to its large number of supporting outbuildings and the preexisting security walls and fences, the Marines had taken over the four-square-mile compound for their headquarters and renamed it "Camp Babylon."

Below the palace hill, an endless horizon of date palm groves lay on the far side of the Euphrates River canal that was the western boundary of Camp Babylon. To the east were a series of low rolling hills in which lay the ruined foundations of the ancient city. The eastern portion of the compound also contained the original, partially reconstructed ruins of the original palace of Babylon. Seven kilometers to the south was the center of the city of Al Hillah; beyond that, arid wasteland ran all the way to the Kuwait/Saudi border. To the north, the Euphrates canal disappeared between another set of low lying hills in the direction of Baghdad.

The location for this palace had been personally chosen by Saddam, specifically because it overlooked the ruins of Babylon – home of the greatest Babylonian king, Nebuchadnezzar. It was at this now-ruined site where Daniel had been thrown into the lion's den, according to the Bible. It was the place to which the Jews had been exiled during the Diaspora. In the throne room of the ancient ruined palace, Alexander the Great had died, returning from conquering the known world. Viewing himself in the same vein as Alexander and Nebuchadnezzar, Saddam had built his palace to look down upon their former seats of power. Despite periodic interference from the meddlesome and waffling Americans, Saddam had been convinced that he would one day be recognized as a great Arab leader.

Babylon had new landlords now, however – the US Marine Corps, and its supporting Army elements – who quickly made the palace their home. Much of its grandeur had been lost in the frenzy of looting by the Iraqi people upon anything that symbolized the former regime before the US forces arrived. Not a door or window remained in the building: all had been stolen or destroyed by the mob. Only the massive chandeliers that towered ten meters above the intricate tile floors remained untouched.

Electricity was nonexistent, not only because there were no generating plants operating, but also because the looters had torn every electrical outlet and switch right out of the walls. Ornate bathrooms that had previously featured gold leaf toilet and faucet fixtures, were empty except for human waste left on the floor by the pillagers as a sign of their disdain for their former ruler.

Essentially the palace was a big, empty shell.

The Jaguar team loved it, however. The three story edifice was made of concrete and stone in the Nazi-like architectural style that characterized most of Saddam's buildings. Walls up to a meter thick provided protection against the stray rounds or mortar fire that occasionally found its way into the camp from unfriendly neighbors. Each soldier had a small area to himself, a little larger than two cots side-by-side, in which to sleep and keep his equipment, an absolute luxury compared to the cramped tents in Kuwait. Real slit trench wooden latrines, complete with privacy doors, had been built by the Navy Seabees on the back of the hill above the motor pool.

"I think I've died and gone to heaven," said Doc, mimicking tears of joy as he gazed lovingly over the two rows of rustic, outhouse-style latrines. His memories of the open pit toilets at Camp Whitehorse were still fresh.

A mess hall was established by the Marines in an ornate, one-story building on the lower grounds which had been used by Saddam for entertaining guests. The mess hall was located roughly a hundred meters from the bottom of the palace hill, on the bank of the canal. Although the food was T-rations[34] served out of large, heated plastic bins, it was a welcome change from the prepackaged MREs they had lived on for weeks.

Another of the luxuries available was internet access. As a civil affairs unit, the 538th's ongoing mission was to coordinate between different Government

---

[34] Thermostabilized Rations, or "T-rations" are large, pre-packaged metal trays containing a variety of foodstuffs, one item per tray. Opened with a standard can opener, each tray holds enough servings for 18 soldiers under normal conditions. A meal normally consists of items from several trays, and the trays themselves are normally brought to serving temperature in a special module into which multiple trays slide.

and humanitarian organizations to help rebuild Iraq. Accordingly, their standard list of unit equipment included thirty laptop computers. At Camp Babylon, the Marines had established networks by which these computers could actually communicate with the rest of the world. To soldiers who had been out of touch with their families since the major fighting began, network access meant precious contact with home. E-mails flew, advising anxious loved ones that everything was OK.

Having finally reached a place of semi-permanence, the reservists began the "nesting" phase of their deployment. A parade of internet camping store air mattresses, single man tents and solar showers began to clog the military transports heading to the Gulf from the United States. To troops who had spent weeks sleeping in the field, wearing the same uniform and not showering, the end of the fighting also meant the ability to get clean on a regular schedule. The Jaguars cobbled together some lumber "liberated" from the Seabees into a makeshift hangman's style platform, from which they reverently hung Captain Smith's solar shower. The one advantage of Iraq's 135-degree summer day was that water placed in the insulated reservoir of the five-liter solar shower was piping hot within ten minutes.

If the first casualty of war is truth, the second is modesty. Soldiers of both genders in wartime sleep, wash, and relieve themselves in proximity to each other that would be unimaginable in the civilian world. On a convoy, the men piss on one side of the road while the women squat in the open on the other side. Everyone is too tired, filthy and stressed-out to worry about anyone "seeing" anything that would be considered private back in the real world. They simply do their business and move on. Camp Babylon returned the luxury of privacy in such matters. Although their living conditions would have brought a flood of humanitarian aid groups to their doorstep in protest if they had been "inflicted" on anyone back home, the Jaguars were grateful for their windowless, looted building.

Despite the intense sun, few soldiers have suntans. For protection from insects and the elements, full length pants and tops are almost always worn, with only one's hands being exposed. Faces are shielded by floppy-brimmed "boonie" style caps. This manner of dress leads to the "monkey paw" look, where troops with ghostly white bodies have darkly tanned hands. So, when Sergeant Mantis walked out of the living area down to the shower on the lower veranda, he was a sight to behold. Wearing only the Army running shorts and orange thong sandals he had bought at the PX before deploying, his portly white frame glared obscenely in the harsh Iraqi sun. Stepping onto the plywood shower platform, he opened the small plastic valve at the base of the five-liter bag to release the flow of hot water.

"AAAhhhhhhhh…" moaned Mantis. The stream of water poured through the small nozzle rejuvenating his almost-forgotten memories of cleanliness. "Aaaaagghhhhh," he moaned again deeply, as his monkey paws scrubbed away the accumulated grime, sweat, and stink of living in the same clothes for two weeks.

"Mantis, knock it off," Warden called down from his chair on the nearby upper veranda where he sat to watch the sunset. "You're getting me excited."

"Can't help it, Sarg'nt," replied Mantis. "This is better than sex."

"How would you know, Mantis?" jibed Leader, walking past as he returned from the evening meal. "I hear tell you and those monkey paws are the only action in this place."

"Oooh, it's good, Sarg'nt. Not even you can ruin my mood tonight."

"All those rolls and no butter," replied Leader with a sad shake of his head, as he glanced at Mantis' flabby frame before mounting the steps to the upper veranda.

"Hmmpphh," said Mantis, ignoring the barbs to focus on the short-term pleasure of feeling clean.

The chair occupied by Warden, was one of the folding "soccer mom" type, which would soon become the rage of Camp Babylon. One does not realize what a great luxury it is to have a chair to sit upon at one's convenience until there are no chairs to be had within several hundred kilometers. After 16 hours in hot combat boots, the ability to kick them off and put his feet up on the low concrete wall around the veranda was one of the simple pleasures that got Warden through the day. Within a month after the arrival of Warden's first chair, every soldier and Marine in the camp counted his rifle, his kit, and his own "soccer mom" chair among his most prized possessions.

Matters that are taken for granted in the United States are beyond imagination to the average Iraqi, and often but a faint memory to the soldiers serving there. The eight-dollar, lightweight, collapsible chairs were such a luxury to troops denied even the basic trappings of civilization that rules of etiquette sprang up that were enforced with humorless severity. Soldiers would not think of sitting on another's chair without permission. Taking someone's chair without permission was an offense that could only be appropriately settled upon the field of honor with an old fashioned ass-whipping. The affront of resting one's dirty combat boots upon the seat of another's chair would likely end the same way.

Having one's own bathroom, a bed off the floor, indoor plumbing, running water, air-conditioning – these are luxuries that most Iraqis, especially in the areas outside Baghdad, will never know. Windows in buildings outside the cities often do not contain glass and are instead open to the elements. Water is drawn from a river, canal or well and is hand-carried. In most of the country, the donkey is still the primary means of hauling loads over distance. Donkey carts fight for space on roads aggressively patrolled by taxi drivers in their orange-and-white late-model sedans.

Most Iraqis are born, live and die within ten kilometers of where their parents and grandparents made their lives. They pray in the same manner and in the same place that their ancestors have done so for centuries. They also bear the same prejudices and vendettas against neighbors whose ancestors may have slighted their own family's predecessors in some manner decades or centuries before. It is into this sloth-like pace of life that the reservists of the 538th settled in to bring fast and dynamic change to the Iraqi people.

Chapter 9
The Barracks

The enlisted and junior officers of the 538th had procured the ceremonial entrance hall and adjoining formal dining room of Saddam's palace as their barracks. The dozen colonels and two dozen light colonels of the unit had settled into "field grade" housing with the Marines on the lower level of the compound. It was an arrangement of mutual convenience, as the higher ranking officers from General Merdier's command had done little to meld with the 538th during the five weeks of training at Fort Bragg – obtaining rental cars and private rooms for themselves on post, while the rest of the unit lived in open-bay barracks and were transported in the appropriately named "cattle cars" from training site to training site.

Beneath a large crystal chandelier and an elaborate ceiling painting depicting the past glories of Babylon, the team had carved out makeshift living quarters. Cots, mosquito netting, duffel bags and piles of olive-drab equipment littered the two large rooms.

"Hey, listen to this ya'll," announced Warden from his green soccer-mom chair. He sat atop the small dais in the palace's ceremonial entrance hall, which had previously held one of Saddam's many thrones. "The President's national security advisor says in Stars and Stripes[35] that we're fighting to bring democracy to the Hajis[36]."

"Who's that?" asked Ridlin vaguely, sitting on his cot as he furiously punched buttons on his Gameboy.

"Who's who?" replied Cooper, sitting next to Ridlin, watching his progress through a gauntlet of zombies on the small screen.

---

[35] The daily newspaper produced by the Department of Defense for military personnel.

[36] "Haji" is military slang derived from the Muslim title of respect for one who has completed the Haj, or pilgrimage, to Mecca that is the obligation of all Muslims who can do so. As employed by soldiers and Marines at the time of the invasion of Iraq, it was a general reference by US troops to all Arabs, regardless of nationality.

"The security watchamacallit," Ridlin replied, not removing his eyes from his game.

"That's that buck-toothed black gal you see on TV all the time, 'splainin' why it's so important to help the terrerists," explained Warden.

"Condoleeza Rice," interjected Mantis with a superior air. "She's the President's national security advisor. One of the smartest people in Washington."

"She must be smart," said Leader, as he rummaged through his rucksack for a tin of chewing tobacco. "She ain't over here."

"Anyone else notice how the talk 'bout the WMD[37] is gone as our reason for bein' here? Or 'bout replacin' Saddam? Seems like they keep movin' the target," observed Warden, as he thumbed through the paper.

"No, no," chimed Leader mischievously. "I've got some WMD right here I found last week…oh, wait,…no,…that was pocket lint. Sorry."

"I thought the national security advisor was that Air Force guy," said Cooper, as Ridlin's videogame advanced to the next level with a series of bloops, beeps and music.

"Nah, he's the Chairman of the Joint Chiefs of Staff," corrected Mantis. "Don't you guys know anything?" Mantis, a political science major, relished the few opportunities presented when he could flaunt his knowledge of political issues in front of the team.

"How the hell can an Air Force guy give advice on a ground war in Iraq?" asked Warden, to no one in particular. "That makes a helluva lot of sense – take a guy that's never carried a rifle in combat and make him top dog."

"Hey, now; don't be bad mouthin' the Air Force, Sargn't Warden" Leader answered with a straight face and a feigned air of admiration. "It's a viable alternative to military service."

Everyone but Mantis chuckled appreciatively at the old joke. "Hey, my dad was in the Air Force," he snapped, peevishly

---

[37] Weapon(s) of Mass Destruction – chemical, nuclear or biological weapons.

"I thought your mother was in the Air Force, Mantis," said Leader, with a twinkle in his eye, "or was it the other way around?"

"Screw you, Sergeant," snapped Mantis, his cheeks flushing.

"Don't know that ahm happy with a guy givin' direction on how to fight a ground war who has spent life lookin' at the world from 30,000 feet," replied Warden, shaking his head again.

"I don't know why I talk to you guys," pouted Mantis. "All you want to talk about are NASCAR and women."

"Speaking of which, you're sportin' a pretty nice rack there yourself, Mantis," jabbed Leader. "Did you get those from your mom, too?"

Cooper blew the Gatorade he was gulping out both nostrils and began choking for breath as Mantis fumed. Ridlin edged away from Cooper on the cot to protect his Gameboy screen from the flood, his fingers continuing to fly at a frenetic pace.

"I swear: if I wasn't married, I could fall in love with that pair," chided Leader, as he spat into his chaw cup and began to field strip his SAW for cleaning. "Better not sleep on your stomach tonight Mantis. I'm feelin' randy."

Mantis was one of those guys who never seemed to ditch the baby fat, no matter how much he ran or how many weights he lifted. Standing up from his folding chair near the door-less entrance, he began, "Look sergeant...," His face darkened as he considered his next move.

"Mantis, you should know better to quit while you're behind when Leader is on a tear. Sit down." directed Warden, cutting him off with his casual authoritative air.

Mantis sulked back into his chair, glaring sullenly at Leader, who had fished his cleaning kit out of his rucksack.

Bored with tormenting Mantis, Leader began one of his occasional but trademark manic soliloquies, to his team's entertainment. As he rambled, his experienced fingers continued to strip the automatic weapon down to its base components for cleaning.

"Ah yes, Meester. We want democracy," he began in a singsong Middle East accent. "President Bush, he give me democracy. He give me new refrigerator. Yes, yes, we need democracy. Today we vote to crap upstream from village. Tomorrow we vote to crap downstream. We have big time democracy here. I want to be American. Drive big car, go to the mall. Kick shit out of third world countries. Give me water, meester. Invade Kuwait. Vacation in Poconos. Big time democracy."

Warden smiled and shook his head as he set his paper aside to watch the performance.

"Ever watch ET?" Leader asked rhetorically, the cadence of his monologue picking up as he dropped the accent. "There's a great movie. It's so sweet the way they take that poor li'l guy in. Know what I'd do if I found that ugly SOB hiding in my tool shed?

"Boom", he mimicked, quickly standing and pretending to pump an imaginary shotgun.

"Hey ET, wanna ride my bike?

"Boom, Boom," he roared again, pumping his pretend shotgun.

"Wanna phone home ET?

"Boom.

"I ain't no damn Ma bell. Boom, Boom.

"Then I'd go get Alan Alda and Jane Fonda.

"Boom. Boom.

"Hey, Barbarella. Boom.

"Hawkeye! Over here!

"Boom.

"Then that Haji lovin' bastard, Sean Penn.

"Boom."

Ridlin had stopped playing his game and was giggling on his cot, while beside him Cooper was still choking on his Gatorade. Even Mantis was grudgingly smirking, realizing that Leader's earlier verbal assault had just been part of the day's entertainment and was nothing personal.

Leader had the type of irreverent humor that came from growing up in the city – sharp and as biting as acid. No one was safe from it, especially the officers. In civilian life Leader was a beat cop in one of the rougher neighborhoods of Baltimore. There, he used his sense of humor and imposing physique to defuse many situations that might otherwise turn ugly. A guy who was as serious and professional as they came when the mission got dangerous, he had a wit that could cut a person to ribbons and also delight the team when they needed a lift. But now, having exhausted his repertoire of material for the moment, Leader settled back onto his cot and began scraping residue from the SAW's firing pin with a wire brush.

"Air Force, Ah can't believe it…" murmured Warden, picking up the paper again and turning to the sports page.

The next day the Jaguars were ordered by the operations section to escort Colonel Rabbit to a courtesy call on the mayor of Hillah. Each of the eighteen provinces of Iraq was administered by a provincial governor, who doubled as the mayor of the provincial capital. In Babil Province, the mayor was Ali bin Muhammad, a Shiite politician who had managed to survive Saddam's purges of the Shia elite following the First Gulf War.

While viewed as a Ba'ath party loyalist by the regime, Mayor Ali had immediately welcomed the arrival of the Coalition forces with open arms. He had survived under the Sunni-dominated regime of the Hussein family at the mere whim of Saddam and his two insane sons, and the mayor was relieved to see them gone. *And who knows?* the mayor mused, *the Americans might bring new opportunities for those of a proper mind-set.*

There was a level of excitement among the team that morning at beginning their first real mission to rebuild the Iraqi Government. Everything they had done for the past three months was designed to train and move them halfway around the world for this purpose. Warden, Leader, and even Mantis were all highly trained civil affairs operators in their own right. This mission would give them their first real opportunity to employ the cultural knowledge, communications skills and military training they had developed over a combined thirty-two years of Army service.

Captain Smith remained behind at Camp Babylon to coordinate a reconstruction plan with the planning staff of the I MEF[38], so the team arranged positioning of the personnel in the vehicles to put Rabbit in the back seat of Jaguar Two. From their experience of two days before, the Jaguars wanted to minimize the possibility of having to follow Rabbit's directions anywhere.

Major Trevanathan guided the way to downtown Hillah from the front passenger seat of Jaguar One. He had plotted the route on the map the evening before, while Rabbit had been watching movies in the mess hall. The route took them out the main gate of the base, down the winding two-lane asphalt road past the small village of Al Salaam, and to the four-lane divided Highway 8. Highway 8 took them across the narrow bridge over the Euphrates river canal as it made its way into Hillah.

The municipal building, a two-story white concrete building, surrounded by a five foot high concrete wall, was on a side street on the south side of town in a residential neighborhood that was upscale by Iraqi standards. An Iraqi policeman opened the black metal gate in the wall to admit the two HMMWVs into the open parking area next to the building. Trevanathan noticed uneasily that the guard was carrying an AK-47 with a folding stock across his back. *One day they're enemies, the next our allies*, he thought uneasily. *The question is, do they know that they're our allies now?*

As soon as the vehicles stopped, Rabbit – true to his nickname – jumped out of Jaguar Two without a word to the team and strode quickly toward the building.

"Sahr, should we follow the colonel?" Warden asked as he dismounted from the left rear seat. "We haven't secured this area yet – he's takin' a helluva risk." As he spoke, Rabbit turned the corner of the building and disappeared

---

[38] I MEF or IMEF is the shorthand abbreviation for the 1st Marine Expeditionary Force, the corps-size unit led by a three-star Marine general that the 538th was assigned to support. The abbreviation is "I" instead of "1" because US corps are designated with roman numerals.

from sight, leaving the rest of the team with no instructions or sense of what they were supposed to do.

"I'm not sure what he expects," replied the Major, quickly surveying the area for potential threats. "He left no instructions." Seeing nothing but quiet, well-tended homes surrounding the area, he said, "Sergeant Warden, I'll go find out the colonel's intent and be right back. Keep two men on watch. If you hear anything exciting, come a runnin'." With that, Trevanathan jogged off in the direction the colonel had gone, his battle rattle[39] bouncing along with each stride.

"That's beautiful," remarked Leader, as he joined Warden standing next to Jaguar One. "May I park your vehicle, sir?" he asked sarcastically.

Three hours later the team was still baking in the 130-degree heat, with no further word from Trevanathan or Rabbit. "Man, I'm so glad I went through the Civil Affairs NCO course so I could be the valet for Rabbit," said Leader sourly, taking a pull on a hot bottle of water. "All that time away from home, training and studying – this makes it all worthwhile," he said without humor, as beads of sweat ran down his face.

"They, too, serve who sit and do jack shit," muttered Mantis from the back seat of Jaguar Two.

"What did you do in the war, daddy?" Leader continued to himself aloud for his own entertainment. "Why I was a parking bitch, son. One of the finest parking bitches in theater," he mimicked in a deep baritone voice.

"Everybody, keep drinking water," ordered Warden, ignoring Leader's soliloquy and raising his voice so the entire team could hear. "I don't want any heat casualties."

The sun was well past its zenith when the two officers finally returned. Rabbit sipped on a coke, beaded droplets of cold water running down the side of the can. He approached the team, oblivious to the longing looks fixed on the cold drink. They had spent the afternoon shielded from the withering sun by a thin

---

[39] "Battle rattle" is a nickname for the personal field gear troops carry on their bodies, which includes body armor, helmet, and load-bearing suspenders and belt to which are attached such things as ammunition pouches, canteens, flashlights and first aid kits containing field dressings.

piece of canvas roofing, sucking hot water from plastic bottles, and cursing the two officers. Their mood was near mutinous.

As Rabbit quickly took the Major's place in Jaguar One, Trevanathan walked over to Warden, who was slumped in the driver's seat of Jaguar Two. "Good meeting, sahr?" Warden inquired with a raised eyebrow as Trevanathan walked up.

"He kept me there," replied Trevanathan, knowing that Warden was pissed off, and for good reason. "Said he didn't want to overwhelm the mayor with 'other' people," he said flatly, recognizing that his troops had been screwed. He could see the impact of the unrelenting heat in their rounded shoulders and darkened eye sockets.

Trevanathan pulled two cold cans of coke from his pant's cargo pocket and handed them to Warden. "It's all I could sneak out. Share."

"Hoo-rah, sir," replied Warden appreciatively, his expression warming toward the officer.

"Let's go," cried Rabbit impatiently in his nasally twang, as he polished off the last of his icy can of soda. "I don't want to miss dinner."

"Ah could make it look lahk an accident, sahr. Really, Ah could," Warden joked weakly to Major Trevanathan.

"Don't tempt me," replied Trevanathan, placing his helmet on his head and climbing into the passenger seat.

That night back in the palace, Leader began slowly. "NCO dumb," he said suddenly, breaking the quiet in the entrance hall where the team had collapsed onto their cots after the mission. He bit off a piece of jerky and chewed it vigorously. He and Warden had missed dinner, as they had to first check Jaguar One and Jaguar Two back into the motor pool after first dropping Rabbit at the mess hall. By the time that task was completed, the mess hall was closed, leaving only MREs or their private stashes of pogey-bait for dinner.

Leader swallowed the chunk of jerky. "NCO dumb," he repeated in his imitation Iraqi accent. "NCO no need water. He no need Coke. Coke is for officer. Kick NCO in ass. He happy."

"What about Rabbit?" encouraged a tired Cooper from his cot, sensing another Leader performance.

"Colonel Rabbit he great leader," said Leader, now changing to an overplayed American Indian accent. "He get heap big medal. Him leader of men. NCO dumb. NCO sit in sun. He no need medal. He shine Rabbit's boots. He happy."

"Pete."

"Rabbit bend NCO over log. He no gay – NCO gay. He like it on log." Leader continued, now changing to a fake, sing-song Vietnamese accent. "Buy refrigerator for sick grandma, Joe…me love you looong time…"

"Pete!" cut in Warden, catching Leader's attention, as he motioned his thumb toward the entrance where heavy wooden doors had once stood. Major Trevanathan stood in the doorway, his arms crossed over his chest, his rigid outline silhouetted against the darkening sky behind him as he peered silently into the interior.

The team sat stone quiet, bracing for the expected remonstration for their open disrespect. A quiet side comment could be forgiven, but Leader had gone far beyond that.

"Colonel Rabbit needs his boots done, Leader," said Trevanathan. "Don't forget your log." He turned and was gone.

As Trevanathan's footsteps faded, the team broke into roars of laughter and high pitched giggles of relief. Leader, slumped on his cot, felt the blood burning in his cheeks from embarrassment as a feeling of relief washed over him. "That skipper," he said in a low voice to himself, "he's alright."

Chapter 10
The Hope

During the first two months following the invasion, it appeared that the occupation might well turn out as the Bush Administration had hoped, with the locals in Southern Iraq generally welcoming the US military presence, as well as their American dollars. Although security was maintained at a high level by the Marines, the number of actual direct, organized attacks on US troops south of Baghdad was relatively low. The main security problem was common thievery and robbery of civilians by gangs of armed thugs, many of whom had deserted from the Iraqi military. Baghdad was still unstable, but the major Shiite population centers in the South were quiet. During this time, the Jaguars settled into a routine of visiting the provincial capitals throughout the South, assessing wartime and looting damage to municipal buildings, and reporting their findings to the US controlled Coalition Provisional Authority (CPA) in Baghdad. CPA was the de facto occupation Government of Iraq, charged with coordinating and funding all reconstruction activities.

"Hey sir, look at that," said Cooper, gesturing out the left side of Jaguar One as the team returned from assessing the damage looters had done to the courthouse in Najaf. Trevanathan's eyes followed the line of Cooper's gesture to a Ferris wheel that rose above the three meter, sand-colored brick wall sitting along Highway 8, south of Hillah. As they passed the entrance to the compound, Trevanathan caught a quick glimpse of other amusement park rides, and green trees, behind the wall.

"Whip around, Coop," said Trevanathan. "I want to see that."

Cooper eased the HMMWV over to the left lane of the divided four-lane road. Slowing slightly, he cranked the wheel over and the great tires of the vehicle easily climbed up over the low curb separating the two directions of traffic. Seeing no oncoming traffic, he cranked the wheel again to complete the 180-degree turn and accelerated back in the direction from which they had just come.

This time, they turned right onto the short paved driveway leading to the gateway into the park. "Amazing," said Trevanathan, as Cooper stopped before the entrance, "These people don't have adequate medical care or clean water, but they build amusement parks."

"Actually sir," Abu spoke from the seat behind the Major, "This park is not for everyone. It is…, that is,… *was* only for high level Ba'ath party members and their families. One had to reach a sufficient stature in the party before he could bring his family here. It was considered quite an honor – giving great prestige to the family of the party member."

"Cooper, Sergeant Warden, check out the entrance for IEDs, would ya'?" directed Trevanathan. As the two soldiers dismounted, rifles in hand, Trevanathan picked up the handset and depressed the SEND button: "Jaguar Two, this is Jaguar One, over."

"Go ahead, One," answered Smith's familiar drawl from the trail vehicle.

"We're gonna' check out the entrance to this place. Keep an eye behind us, over."

"Got ya' covered. Jaguar Two out."

"Abu, what is this place called?" Trevanathan asked over his left shoulder.

"Saddam Park, sir."

"Silly of me to ask," smirked the Major. He watched Warden carefully approach the opening in the wall as Cooper provided him with cover from ten meters to his left. Warden walked slowly and deliberately, his head moving from side to side as he scanned for activity. Trevanathan checked his side mirror for any movement behind him.

In the mirror, Trevanathan could see the large frame of Staff Sergeant Leader dismount from Jaguar Two, his M16A2, with its M203 grenade launcher beneath the barrel, held at the ready. *All business.* Leader did a quick 360-degree scan of the surrounding area. With a set of dark shades shielding his eyes, he posed more than a passing resemblance to the Terminator movie character popularized by Arnold Schwarzeneger, which made Trevanathan smile at the thought.

Trevanathan had copied Leader's habit of wearing dark goggles or one-way sunglasses when out on a mission. "It prevents an enemy from knowing where your attention is focused at any one time. Someone who can't tell whether you have their number or not is less likely to mess with you," Leader had told the team back at Fort Bragg during urban combat training. "When I'm out on the beat, my eyes are dartin' all over the place without anyone realizing it. A half second delay by the enemy might save your life," he had advised.

"All clear, sahr," said Warden walking back to the officer's side of the vehicle. "Looks lahk someone put up a fight here at one tahm. There's a buncha' 7.62 brass up around the gate, but no sign of IEDs. Tire tracks show that other vehicles have been through here recently."

"OK, let's go in then," said Trevanathan.

"Roger sir. Umm, 'zactly what are we doin' here, if you don't mind me askin'?"

"Why, we're having a picnic, Sergeant Warden," Trevanathan smiled, as he raised his right arm and made the circular hand motion to mount up. Warden smiled and shook his head as he walked back around to his side of the vehicle. "Major T" was always coming up with something new to keep him slightly off-balance.

"Where to sir?" asked Cooper, as Jaguar One nosed through the gate and came to a Y-shaped intersection in the gravel road.

"Let's head down to those trees near the merry-go-round," indicated Trevanathan, pointing toward a shady spot about 200 meters from the entrance. As they slowly rolled through the empty park, Trevanathan looked about at the brightly painted amusement rides – such a contrast to the monotone dust color that characterized the rest of the country. All of the rides from any cheesy carnival in the USA were there: bumper cars; kiddie motorcycle rides, a small train track that wound through the park, and a Viking longboat that swung back and forth on a pendulum. *No self-respecting Viking would be anywhere near this place*, he thought.

The park was one of the greenest places Trevanathan had seen since arriving in the region. A series of cypress, olive, and other trees he didn't recognize lined the service roads and footpaths that wound through the rides. *It must have cost a fortune to bring in enough water to keep this place green*, he thought. Ornamental and drinking fountains, both now dry, dotted the landscape. *I suppose this place looked like paradise to people who have only known the desert,* he mused. *I can see how some bureaucrat could have been enticed to remain loyal to a regime that could give his family these perks.*

"Park over there, Cooper," said Trevanathan pointing to a spot between two towering trees a dozen meters from the merry-go-round. Cooper eased the HMWWV to a stop in the cool shade, beneath their canopy.

Trevanathan dismounted and took in the surrounding landscape. *It feels almost comfortable under these trees*, he thought. *Must be no more than 110 degrees here, out of the sun*, he estimated. The other members of the team likewise dismounted and became mesmerized by the surreal landscape of greenery and carnival rides in the midst of so much destruction and want. The park covered an area of approximately ten acres, being insulated from neighboring residential properties by the wall that marked the entire perimeter. Several multi-story buildings and the minaret of a mosque were visible half a klick away, but the intervening wall provided some security from the team being observed from anything within effective sniper range. *The Iraqis can't shoot worth a damn anyway*, thought Trevanathan. While the hidden bombs they placed were of significant concern, the lack of training and discipline in firing their weapons made the marksmanship of most Iraqi insurgents a secondary concern.

"Lunch time, gentlemen," declared Trevanathan happily. "We're going AWOL from the war for a half hour, so get some chow and enjoy this nice shade."

"Cooper, break out one of those tasty MREs for me wouldja?," Leader asked the young private, who was foraging through a cardboard box in the back of Jaguar One.

"What flavor, Sergn't?"

"Give me something with pork in it so I can spit it on the ground," Leader laughed. Warden grinned at the insult to the Muslim custom against consuming or touching pork, but Abu did not look amused as he stared sullenly at the ground.

"Ridlin, you're on guard while we eat, then someone will spell you," Smith directed.

"Roger, Sir." Leader settled down with his back to one of the big trees as he tore open MRE #8: Pork Chow Mein. "Did I tell you that while I was in Nasiriyah, this Haji came up to me?" began Leader. The team paused from opening their own plastic meal packets, as they could sense a Leader story in the brewing.

"Yeah, he told me he wanted to see Rajah," continued Leader. "I couldn't understand him, so I asked him again who he wanted, and he repeated that he wanted to speak with Rajah." Leader paused for dramatic effect, as he peeled the top off one of the dark green foil packets. "So I said, 'Hey Mr. Haji, I don't know any Rajah,' but he became pissed and started yellin'. He said, 'You lie! I know Rajah is your boss and I want to speak to him.'"

Warden made eye contact with Trevanathan and rolled his eyes in good humor, sensing what was coming.

"So, I said 'why do you think Rajah is my boss, Mr Haji?' and he said "I know he's the boss because I hear all of the soldiers saying "Rajah, sir," whenever they speak to him on the radio."

The team chuckled at the bad joke, as they returned to their meal packets.

"Booo. You need some new material Sargn't," chided Mantis. "Ridlin has better material than that."

"Come smell my ear infection, Mantis," said Leader, digging a dirty finger in one ear that had been aching for a few days now.

"MMmm, that whetted my appetite," said Smith, tearing open the prized Beef with Barbecue Sauce entrée from his packet. Beef with Barbecue sauce is one of the few MREs that actually taste like the description on the cover. He sighed deeply upon taking a deep whiff of the packet's contents. "Just like Mom used to make," he said wistfully. "Of course, mom was a shitty cook," he laughed, emptying the small bottle of Tabasco sauce from the MRE into the foil envelope.

"Anyone want mah Charms?" asked Warden, holding up the roll of the square, hard candies he had received in his meal pouch.

"Marines won't eat Charms," said Trevanathan. "Superstitious. They think you'll get whacked if you eat 'em."

"I'll take 'em, Sergeant," said Ridlin, turning from his observation duties next to the front of Jaguar Two..

"Ridlin, keep your damn eyes on your guard duties, not on candy," lashed out Mantis in a harsh tone.

"Mantis, don't make me force feed you," interrupted Leader, irritated at the manner the young NCO spoke to Ridlin in front of the group. "You look like you ate a truckload of Charms by the size of your ass."

"Sure, sure, Sergn't," whined Mantis sourly. "I'll shut up and we'll get whacked because A-D-D boy there can't keep his eyes on the job." Trevanathan had learned to stay out of NCO business by now, but did not want the enlisted men exposed to this exchange.

"Cooper, go check out that utility shed over there," Trevanathan indicated, pointing to a small brick structure fifty meters from their position, next to the wall surrounding the park. *I should have cleared that before we sat down here*, Trevanathan chastised himself silently. "Take Ridlin with you."

"Roger, sir," said Cooper jumping to his feet and grabbing his rifle from where it reclined against the tire of Jaguar One. "C'mon, Rid."

"Rajah, sir", mimicked Leader, causing another round of appreciative chuckling from everyone, except Mantis, who was sullenly shoveling beef macaroni into his face.

When the two soldiers men had moved out of hearing, Trevanathan turned to his three NCOs. "Gentlemen, I don't want you airing the family laundry in front of the enlisted. You don't have to love each other, but those kids need to feel we're a team and will back each other up, OK?"

"OK, sir," said Warden.

"Got it, sir," said Leader, serious for a moment.

Mantis remained quiet, eyes cast downward at his meal.

"I need to go see a man about a horse," said Trevanathan, standing slowly and looking about the immediate area for a likely place to relieve himself. "Rick, come keep an eye out for me, wouldja'?"

"Yessir," said Smith, polishing off a chocolate covered brownie, one of the few truly tasty items in an MRE packet. "I can't think of any better way to end a fine meal than to watch you take a dump," he joked with a wry smile.

Abu had curled up under one of the nearby trees and was catching a quick nap in the shade.

When the officers had walked out of earshot, Warden turned to face Mantis on his right, who was still avoiding eye contact with anyone.

"Look, dumbshit," drawled Warden. You're wearin' tham stripes, but you don't know the first damn thang 'bout leadin' troops. Civil Affairs ain't 'xactly hard core, but you need to earn the respect of the enlisted if you want 'em to follow you." Mantis tilted his head slightly so one eye looked at Warden peevishly.

"You were raght to correct Ridlin," Warden continued, noting the red flushed streaks on Mantis' otherwise pale cheeks. "But the way ya' did it embarrassed him in front of everyone. Correct him, but do it without swearin' at him or if ya' need to swear, then take 'im off to the side and chew his ass. But don't ream him out in front of everyone. It makes you look weak and he doesn't learn anything, 'cept you're a bully. Remember, he might just save your ass someday."

"Or not," added Leader seriously.

"Fine, sergn't," said Mantis in a clipped tone. "But it undercuts my authority when Sergn't Leader is always on my ass in front of them."

"Mantis, you start actin' like an NCO and I'll start treating you like one," said Leader sharply. "Right now you're a senior specialist as far as I'm concerned. You got those stripes 'cause you have some college, not because you know how to lead men."

Their debate was cut short by the sound of Cooper yelling from beyond the HMMWVs, "Stop it! Hey! Knock it off. Knock It Off!"

Warden jumped to his feet and peered over the rear of Jaguar Two in the direction of the noise. He could see a group of kids pushing and swinging their arms, as Cooper tried to pull them away from the entrance to the utility building. Ridlin was likewise occupied on the left side of the small melee, defending himself against a flurry of flailing arms and legs.

Trevanathan, who was momentarily indisposed behind a tree in the opposite direction, heard the disturbance as well, and pulled his trousers up to head toward the source of the ruckus with Smith following. Rounding the corner of the shed, Trevanathan saw Cooper and Ridlin trying unsuccessfully to break up a melee of young Iraqi boys, who were trying to force their way inside. One smaller boy, with a determined look on his face, barred their way with a series of kicks and punches. As Trevanathan's tall frame rounded the corner, the aggressors were momentarily distracted, allowing the younger boy to lash out with his foot and catch the largest boy squarely in his unprotected crotch. "Whoof," uttered the larger boy as the air went out of him, and he dropped to his knees clutching his battered goods with both hands.

The felling of their champion and the appearance of this tall soldier caused the remaining four youths to back off momentarily, forming a wary semicircle around the front of the shed. Anger and uncertainty flashed in their eyes.

"Cooper, what's going on here?" Trevanathan demanded, as Warden and Leader arrived from the HMMWVs.

"Well, Sir, Rid and I went in to check out the shed," said Cooper. "It looks like somebody is squatting here – using it as a shelter. We found some blankets and cooking stuff. When we came out, this group here…,"he indicated with a gesture of his hand that caused one of the older boys to start slightly, "they were chasing this little guy up to the front of the shack. We tried to stop them, but they blew right by us and started trying to force their way in to the shed."

Trevanathan looked at the small boy in the door, who appeared to be about 7 years old from his size. He glared defiantly at the older boys, who appeared to range from 11 to 13 years old. Like most Iraqi kids, the small one had a full head of thick black hair and a dusky complexion. A small round face held a small, thin-lipped mouth that was tightly set. His eyes flashed and the nostrils of his small, round nose flared, as he inhaled deeply. He wore a short-sleeved blue plaid shirt and a pair of dirty, dark blue pants that looked as if he had owned them for more than one season. There were no shoes on his dirty feet.

Two features, other than size, distinguished him from the pack of glaring street rats. The first was that the boy possessed a set of shockingly-blue eyes, a rarity in Iraq. The second was an enormous orange-sized growth on the right side of his neck.

"Abu, get over here," yelled Trevanathan, as the large boy on the ground moaned piteously and raised himself onto his knees. The foot of the small boy lashed out again, catching his assailant in the ribcage, and knocking him over again. This move shook the remainder of the gang from their dormancy and they lunged for the boy again, as one group.

Trevanathan quickly stepped in front of the intended target, interrupting their charge as Cooper and Ridlin grabbed two of the attackers from behind. The third, another large youth with a bad complexion, was unable to counter his momentum and bounced off of Trevanathan's flak jacket, recoiled backwards, and fell over the fetal form of the leader.

Abu jogged up to the scene as the boy who fell to the ground let loose with an angry torrent of Arabic in the direction of Trevanathan and the smaller boy.

"Abu, find out what is going on here," ordered the Major. Abu dutifully engaged in a conversation with the group and the young boy in Arabic that involved much arm waving, finger pointing and raised voices, before Trevanathan cut the conversation short.

"Abu, we have to get going. Give me the Reader's Digest version."

Abu frowned at the unfamiliar reference. "Well, sir," he said, "the young boy says that he and his grandfather live in this shed since his father died. He says that his grandfather sent him to the market to buy bread and he was coming home when these boys began chasing him and throwing stones at him."

"What's their side of it?"

"They say that he is marked by the devil and they were driving him away from their neighborhood, so that he does not spread his evil to them. They say that their parents have told them that the mark on his neck shows he is cursed and not favored by Allah."

Trevanathan winced. The brutality of everyday life in Iraq should have ceased to amaze him by now, but it had not. "So, because the kid has a sickness they're going to stone him, is that it?" he asked, opening his eyes to wait for the inevitable answer.

"It is not uncommon with the primitive Iraqis," stated Abu with obvious disdain. "It is their tradition to weed out the weak from the tribe in order to keep it strong."

"Haji Darwinism," snorted Warden. "Wonderful."

The pock-faced boy who had collided with Trevanathan, raised himself to his feet and glared at the tall American, as if assessing his chances of reaching the smaller boy behind the mountain of armored camouflage. His three partners shifted uneasily from foot to foot, looking angry and unsure while their leader remained prone, whimpering softly into the dust. Trevanathan's sharp look quickly assured the youth that further attempts might prove unsatisfactory.

Trevanathan glanced back over his right shoulder at the small boy who stood defiantly with his hands on his hips. The boy looked up solemnly into Trevanathan's face with his clear, penetrating eyes.

"Hey bitch," the boy intoned evenly, not changing expression, his serious eyes locked onto Trevanathan's. The Major looked at the small figure in disbelief, as if the boy had just spoken to him in Martian. "Wha...?" Trevanathan guffawed, a smile breaking across his face, as the boy continued to stare seriously into his eyes.

"Bling, bling," intoned the boy again, with complete seriousness. "Hook a brother up?" he recited without changing expression

The team around Trevanathan started to snicker, as the street gang looked at the Americans with confused expressions.

"I think we can safely assume we're not the first Americans he's met," deadpanned Trevanathan.

Trevanathan looked at the four youths who continued to shift their feet and glare menacingly at the younger boy. He knew that the moment the Jaguars left, these punks would be all over the kid. *I am sick of the expectation that the strong get to dump on the weak in this country*, he thought wearily. Reaching into the Velcro pocket of his flak jacket, he retrieved a shiny, gold-colored Major's oak leaf he had stashed there. "Abu," Trevanathan stated, as he turned toward the younger boy, "Tell these others that I am putting my mark on this boy." Trevanathan knelt in front of the child, as Abu translated his statement.

"Tell them…," Trevanathan continued, as he pinned the bright insignia to the collar of the boy's dirty shirt, "that my mark is stronger than any curse they believe he may have." The boy's deep blue eyes looked down at the shiny pin that Trevanathan has fastened to his collar, a look of wonderment in his eyes. Abu continued his translation. "Tell them that this boy is under my protection and that anyone who harms him will answer to me." As Abu completed his translation Trevanathan stood, turned toward the group, and drew himself up to his full height for added emphasis, glaring with narrowed eyes at the increasingly uncomfortable vigilantes.

"Now tell them to leave and spread the word that this one is protected. If that protection is violated, I will find them." Trevanathan widened his eyes dramatically, as if overplaying a part in a grade-B movie. The group, which now included the chastened leader, standing on his shaky legs, looked at the badge gleaming on the boy's collar, looked at Trevanathan's huge frame and fierce glare, and simultaneously broke for the northern wall of the compound to escape this mad American soldier.

Chapter 11
The Chicken Lady

The team quickly fell into a routine in their new home at the palace. Each morning, the Jaguars began the day by sweeping up the accumulated bat guano from the two rooms, which blew in during the night from the veranda. Each soldier would then shake out his clothes and equipment in search of scorpions or the occasional camel spider, which would sneak in during the night, attracted by the heat of sleeping bodies.

After shaving with bottled water in the side mirrors of the Marine HMMWVs parked on the road winding up the hill to the palace, the officers would trudge down the steep path to the TOC for morning briefings and intelligence updates on overnight enemy activity in the region. The enlisted soldiers would attend physical training and then perform weapons and vehicle maintenance. On mornings when they were to oversee a reconstruction project or attend a meeting off-post, the team would depart in Jaguar One and Two as early as possible in order to beat the mid-day heat. They always returned before dusk in order to avoid the growing number of insurgents, who preferred to operate under cover of darkness against lightly defended targets, such as supply trucks and canvas-covered civil affairs HMMWVs.

When an off-post mission was not scheduled, the team would try to find a place out of the sun to conduct training, such as map reading or emergency medical care. The officers would also attempt email or radio contact with the outlying provinces to monitor the various legal, medical, or engineering reconstruction projects that the Marines were initiating to stabilize their region. Communications were haphazard and not well coordinated, however, often leaving those responsible for coordinating reconstruction in the dark as to what was occurring over the horizon. As is so often the case with an army at war, there were also huge periods of inactivity where boredom and thoughts of home played heavily on the soldiers' minds.

The highlight of the daily grind came when the sun dipped below the western horizon. At dusk, the wind would pick up, bringing some relief from the day's stagnant, heated air. Hundreds of bats, living underneath the roof of the two-story alcove immediately outside the ceremonial hall, would stream out, filling the darkening sky with their rapidly darting forms. The bats performed their wild aerial ballet in pursuit of the swarms of mosquitoes that rose from the canal, as the diminishing strength of the sun liberated the malaria-carrying insects from their hiding places along the muddy banks.

It was at this time of day that the officers would gather on the upper veranda of the palace, their row of soccer-mom chairs facing West, to breathe a sigh of relief that another day in Iraq was done. The cooling wind, which dropped to a brisk 105 degrees after sunset, blew away the frustrations and anxiety of the day. Rank was put aside and a dozen or so 538th officers would kick back for the evening show. The enlisted performed a similar ritual on a separate section of the veranda, where they would be free to bitch about the officers without being overheard. Watching the bats feast and cavort was the opening scene of the nightly entertainment.

During May of 2003, electricity had yet to be restored to many portions of Iraq. Accordingly, as soon as the sun went down, the countryside around the palace became black, *very* black. Under such conditions the sky in central Iraq was spectacular, with little light or pollution to eclipse the starry carpet draped over them. As cigars were produced from cargo pockets, the officers made a contest of counting the number of satellites passing high overhead – a feat virtually impossible in the cloudy and artificially-lit skies of home.

The main event of the evening's entertainment had evolved without plan. On one of their first nights in the camp, the low stutter of an AK-47 several hundred meters away had interrupted the conversation among the officers. *Oh, crap, welcome to the neighborhood*, thought Smith. The cheering and whistles of the Marines gathered outside the palace's back entrance made it apparent there was no danger from the gunfire, however. "Well, doesn't sound like an attack – let's see what's up," said Trevanathan, as he rose from his chair.

The low stutter of the assault rifle became louder as the officers wandered the fifty meters down to the half-circle patio outside the throne room. A group of young Marines lounged on the stone railing.

"You go, girl!" yelled one. "Get some, get some!" yelled another, while the balance of the small group of five or six whooped or made the characteristic Marine Corps barking sound.

Trevanathan looked past the group down into the darkened date palm grove on the other side of the canal. There, the flash of orange-red streaks cutting through the trees was followed by an almost immediate, low throated *Bup, Bup, Bup...* cadence from an AK-47. Several returning flashes of light appeared from the receiving end, directed back toward the original shooter.

"What's going on, Marine?" asked Trevanathan, noting that none of the young, closely shaved Marines appeared to have the slightest concern for taking cover, despite the weapons firing only a few hundred meters away.

"It's the Chicken Lady, Sir," replied one lanky marine with a slight accent in his voice.

"What's a 'Chicken Lady?'" inquired the Major, conjuring up a mental image of a sideshow freak attraction.

"There's an old Haji woman that lives in the date palm grove on the other side of the canal, sir," the Marine explained. "She has a chicken farm there that she tends to by herself. Every night when the sun goes down the villagers try to sneak into her place and steal the chickens. And every night she lights 'em up."

"That's an old woman down there, laying down all that fire?" asked Trevanathan with wonder, as another burst of gunfire below appeared to drive the attackers back.

"Not just any woman, Sir. The Chicken Lady is the toughest Haji in these parts. The locals say that even Uday and Qusay stayed clear of her place when they'd come down here to violate some of the local girls." As if to confirm his statement, another burst of reddish fire ripped through the palm trunks on the other side of the canal, followed by a sharp shriek of pain.

"We've been here six weeks, Sir, and every night's the same," the marine continued. "The chicken lady is 29-0 in driving off those looters. Ya'd think they would have decided to pick on an easier target by now. I suppose it's become a matter of pride that the men don't want to be run off by a woman."

Trevanathan watched in amazement as the gunfire decreased to a few scattered bursts heading back in the direction of the village. Then, with one final burst from the Chicken Lady, the show was over. As one, the young marines rose to their feet and applauded heartily in the direction of the now-dark trees.

A Marine sentry called down to the patio from his post on the top of the palace. "Chicken Lady – one confirmed hit and one probable," he bellowed. "Chicken thieves – Zip!"

Another round of barks and whoops went up from the group of young jarheads. "Make that 30 to nothing, Sir," laughed the lanky young marine. "The guys upstairs watch everything around here with night vision goggles, all night long. It's quite a show from up there."

"Thanks Corporal," said Trevanathan, uncertain if he was amused or horrified by what he had just seen. "What's your name?"

"Corporal Ahmed, Sir. 7th Recon."

"Thanks, Corporal Ahmed," replied Trevanathan, taking note of the last name. The Army and the Marine Corps had many troops of Arab descent – a situation of appreciable benefit for the military from those who retained any Arabic language or cultural knowledge.

"Corporal, don't we do anything to try to help her?" Smith asked in an incredulous tone of voice.

"Help her? Heck Sir, we'd have to help the Haji chicken thieves if we wanted to even up the odds," he laughed. "Plus we don't get involved in the inter-Haji fighting outside the camp at night. If we did, we'd probably end up shooting each other in the dark. Nah, she's fine, Sir. People learn to take care of themselves in this country…, or they don't last long."

After the Jaguar's initial concern for the lone woman's safety against the band of desperate poultry thieves abated, the Chicken Lady became the nightly entertainment for the team, who had no other diversions after sunset in their electricity-deprived barracks. Each night thereafter, like clockwork, the sun set, the wind gusted, the bats feasted, and the officers gathered on the side veranda to watch the light show. Every night the result was the same – the Chicken Lady prevailed.

"Why do they never fire into the camp?" inquired Doc Heller one night, as the row of chicken war aficionados relaxed with their feet up on the low veranda wall.

"A sentry told me," said Trevanathan. "All along the perimeter of the camp there are Marine snipers in gilly suits with night vision scopes waiting for any rounds to enter the perimeter. If they do, it's POW! 'Game Over.' As long as they just fire each other up outside the wire, we leave them alone. Kind of a gentleman's agreement."

"I don't know," said Doc, "sometimes I feel kinda' guilty sitting up here laughing and joking, while that woman is fighting off those thieves."

"Just think of it as a Haji reality show, Doc," said Trevanathan, laughing at his own joke. "Hell, this stuff is tame compared to some of the shows back in the USA."

The tactical significance of the surrounding countryside's darkness had not been recognized at first by the combat-inexperienced, part-time soldiers of the 538th. It was brought home to them in spades their first night in the palace, however. The first two serials of the 538th's convoy had arrived at Camp Babylon near dusk, two days before the Jaguars arrived. The lead element was settling into the palace as darkness fell, moving their equipment about, using flashlights to find their path through the clutter of cots and equipment that had yet to be stowed.

"Jeezus Christ! Who the Hell is making all that light in here?" roared a tall dark form standing in the wide entrance between the dining room and the ceremonial hall. The reservists stopped and stared at the large apparition, trying to discern its features without shining their lights upon it. "Who's in charge here?" demanded the gravelly voice of the shadow.

"That would be you, sir," whispered the brigade chaplain, Captain Clay, as he nudged the brigade adjutant, Lieutenant Colonel Stoat, who was at that moment the ranking officer present.

Snapping out of his hesitation, Stoat replied, "Aaah, aah, I am, sir," his thick, adenoid-laden voice breaking uncertainly through the silence.

"I'm not a 'sir'," the apparition spat. "I am Gunnery Sergeant Muldoon and this is my barracks! There will be no visible light in my barracks after sundown. Is that clear?!" The tone of Muldoon's baritone voice made it clear that his proclamation was a statement and not a question.

"Aaaahh, aah, I am Lieutenant Colonel Stoat, Sergeant, and...and these are officers' quarters," stammered the S1[40]. "And, aahh, I do not appreciate the tone you are using," he replied peevishly.

"I do apologize, SIR!" bellowed Muldoon, not moving from the doorway. "I had no idea that these were officers' quarters. I do apologize, SIR, and after a Haji sniper blows the top of your head off while you are flashing those lights around I will come and smartly salute your corpse. However, until that time," the Gunny growled, "I suggest you gentlemen maintain some light discipline so I do not have to clean your brains off of my nice clean marble floors."

No one responded. Everyone silently prayed that Stoat would keep his mouth shut so as to not further arouse the ire of this nocturnal martial beast that had descended upon them.

"Good night, gentleman!" bellowed Muldoon, as he turned and disappeared back into the dark interior of the palace.

"That was a warm welcome," laughed Captain Clay.

"Well, aaah, I did not find it amusing in the least," lamented Stoat. "He was, aaah, disrespectful and should be written up."

"He was also *right*, sir," countered the chaplain. "With the countryside so dark, our lights probably can be seen miles away through these windows," he indicated several large cathedral windows on the west side of the dining room that were missing glass. "That's just the way Marines say 'I care.'"

"Well, I plan to, aaah, talk to the commander in the morning about the attitude of these marines," whined Stoat, still smarting from the rebuke.

The chaplain, who knew Stoat's tendency to be thin-skinned from their time together at Fort Bragg, made one last effort to smooth matters over. "Maybe

---

[40] "S1" is the designation for the staff officer in units brigade and below, who is primarily responsible for personnel administrative matters and records keeping.

we should just try to fit in before we make waves, sir. We have to live with these guys a long time and getting in a pissing match at the start is maybe not a good idea."

"Well, aaaah, aaah, I'm primary staff and I will not be treated this way, Captain," concluded Stoat thickly, dropping petulantly into his cot.

Chapter 12
The POD

The executive officer, or "XO," for the brigade, Colonel Douglas Burr, was an Air Force ROTC graduate from Auburn University who worked as a mortgage banker in his hometown of Mobile, Alabama. Having had a short and relatively mediocre career as an Air Force officer, he had left active duty after four years and joined the Army National Guard. His efficiency reports from the Air Force had noted that while he was an extremely intelligent and capable officer, he was intensely disliked by his peers, who viewed him with distrust as a self-absorbed careerist. The reports also noted that he was not a team player, tending to put his own interests above the unit's when it was to his advantage.

Apparently the Army National Guard had not read the Air Force's evaluations, however, and Burr subsequently found an atmosphere where his career flourished. Under the Reserve system, where the prompt completion of status reports and fulfilling "block checking" training requirements were mistaken for military leadership, he had rapidly advanced through the ranks. When, due to a narrow promotion hierarchy, he could not find a way to advance beyond lieutenant colonel in the Alabama Guard, Burr had switched programs again, transferring to the US Army Reserve's Civil Affairs program. Civil Affairs was widely recognized throughout the Reserves as a place where an officer of even mediocre talents could advance to the rank of full colonel merely by hanging around long enough.

By way of example, the 538th mobilized for the Iraq invasion with 142 personnel, twelve of whom were full colonels and 23 of whom were lieutenant colonels (also known as "light colonels"). This top-heavy structure was due to the mission of a civil affairs brigade: to be able to administer an entire third-world country, if necessary. Accordingly, its ranks were filled with slots for doctors, lawyers, bankers and municipal engineers, who necessarily came with high rank by virtue of their extensive civilian expertise. Not one of them had heard a shot fired in anger in their cumulative 568 years of military experience, but they were, By God, ready to engage the enemy. Unfortunately, their civilian expertise did not always translate into military competence on the battlefield, and Burr was the epitome of this reality.

Burr's inability to lead or inspire soldiers was not a problem in the once-a-month training sessions at the Army Reserve center in Alabama. Burr, in fact, found the key to advancement was pointing out the deficiencies in his fellow officers' performance to his superiors; superiors who initially mistook his backstabbing traits as valuable insight into military affairs until they ultimately found themselves on the receiving end, as well. Dubbed the "Prince of Darkness" by those who knew him best, he was referred to by the shortened moniker, "the POD" within the 42d Civil Affairs Command.

Over time, though, it was the very traits that propelled Burr's career forward which caused General Merdier to jettison him to the 538th for the Iraq deployment. "That son-of-a bitch knows too much," said Merdier, aware of several deficiencies in the 42nd's property records that made Merdier vulnerable to an aggressive, careerist officer like Burr. "A year or two in the desert for Burr will give me the breathing room I need to correct those minor issues," he rationalized.

Upon learning of his peremptory reassignment, the POD knew that his temporary appointment as the number two officer in the 538th's chain of command was actually a unique opportunity for him. As BG Merdier's resources officer at the 42nd, he was basically immune from any real control by Colonel Hermann, the 538th commander, since Burr would ultimately return to being the higher headquarters' money man as soon as the war was over. While technically subject to Hermann's orders, Burr's power to control and oversee all funds for the 538th after the war gave him insulation in his current assignment. "If Hermann screws with me he'll never see another dime," the POD smirked to Colonel Rabbit, as they joined the 538th at Fort Bragg.

Colonel Hermann knew he was over a barrel as well. Although he despised Burr from prior disagreements the two had had over spending issues, Hermann understood that Burr had Merdier's ear and could do great harm to his own chances of promotion if they did not get along. Like many civil affairs brigade commanders, Hermann dreamed of being tapped for CACOM command and promotion to brigadier general. If he could bring the 538th through a major combat campaign without any embarrassing snafus on his watch, that possibility was virtually certain.

"Dick," said the POD, walking into the commander's small office at Camp Babylon without knocking. "We took some ground fire flying up from Kuwait last night. It was a close thing. I'm going to put in for an Air Combat Medal, OK?"

The POD's unquenchable thirst for awards and commendations he had not earned were already legendary throughout the unit by the time the 538th had been in Iraq for three months. No officer in US military history had so frequently claimed to have been under fire on so many missions, without suffering the slightest scratch.

"Are Army personnel even eligible for the Air Medal?" Hermann asked quizzically, looking up from his manning reports.

"Oh yes," said the POD with certainty. "I had Stoat research it last night after we got in. If Army troops are engaged in air combat they qualify. The way the pilot was jerking the helo around on his approach in, I'm quite convinced we were under fire."

Hermann noticed that the POD was sporting a new combat patch on the right shoulder of his uniform – a distinction that only soldiers who have completed a full combat tour may wear. The POD was wearing the distinctive eagle head patch of the 101st Airborne Division.

"Doug, were you in the 101st?" asked the brigade commander, eyeing the patch and trying not to sound accusatory.

"Well, I was last night," replied Burr, looking mildly annoyed. "It was a 101st Division Chinook helicopter that brought us up here from the finance conference in Kuwait. I was manifested on their roster, so I was technically attached to their unit at that time."

He paused as Hermann looked at him, speechless. *This man has no shame,* thought Hermann. *Kids spend a year in active combat for the privilege of wearing that combat patch and he slaps it on for taking a three hour bumpy helo ride.*

"Look, I'm pretty busy investigating the destruction of some government property. Can I just get a quick signature on this?" The POD slid the award recommendation across the brigade commander's desk.

"What investigation?" Hermann inquired slowly, as he had not received any reports of destroyed unit property.

"Well, some joker apparently took offense at my idea to conduct PT[41] formations at 0530 each morning, and pissed in my bunk. Ruined my sleeping bag and cot."

Hermann closed his eyes wearily. He had known the idea of PT formations was a bad one, as the troops were already exhausted from the heat and lack of sleep, but he had grudgingly acquiesced at Burr's insistence. Burr had posed the idea upon his return from a two week Iraq funding conference at the Washington, DC, Marriot. He felt that the troops looked tired and unfit upon his return. He insisted to the commander that, despite the average morning temperature of 105 degrees, more exercise was the solution. Burr, who had been living on room service, working out in the air conditioned hotel gym, and sleeping nine hours per night for the prior two weeks, was indeed in much better shape than those who had been living under oppressive field conditions.

"Doug, maybe we should back off on that idea. The troops are pretty ragged already, and Doc Heller thinks that if someone gets hurt due to the heat, there could be hell to pay."

"Dick, if we retreat now in the face of this attack on my authority, this unit will go to hell. We need to crack down and find this offender, not reward them by caving in."

Hermann looked down wearily at the award recommendation in front of him. It claimed that:

> On June 7, 2003, during a serious and determined attack by enemy forces upon a lightly armed CH-47 aircraft, COL Douglas Burr exhibited exceptional courage and presence of mind in maintaining order upon the aircraft, and preventing panic, resulting in the successful completion of the mission, with no Coalition losses.

Hermann sighed as he completed reading the military fairy tale before him and thought of the future, when he would need Burr's cooperation in obtaining training funds back in the States. He quickly dashed his signature across the recommendation block of the form. "Congratulations, Doug," he grimaced as he handed the form back.

---

[41] Physical Training

The POD took the form back, smiled smugly, and momentarily envisioned the unit ceremony back home where he would receive the award, his wife sitting proudly in the front row as BG Merdier pinned the decoration on his Class A uniform; Captain Hilton, admiring him expectantly. *Hah! Not even Merdier has an Air Medal*, the POD thought. *This will give me the inside track to getting a CACOM command when we get back.* Wrapped in his fantasy, he turned and strode from the commander's office without another word.

Chapter 13
The Court

The courthouse in Al Hillah had been spared much of the looting and arson that had been committed by the Iraqi people against government buildings following the fall of the regime. The orgy of self-inflicted violence had been the result of pent up frustration and hatred from Ba'athist abuse over many years. As the Iraqi military and secret police melted away in the face of the American advance, only the regime's buildings remained as targets for the collective release of anger. The courthouse had escaped serious damage, perhaps due to the local citizenry descending instead upon Saddam's compound at Babylon before the Marines arrived. Whatever the reason, the existence of the courthouse provided a starting point for the 538th to initiate the rule of law in a country that had been ruled by the whim of a tyrant and his two insane sons for over three decades.

As the Jaguar team drove into the center of the city, Trevanathan wondered what he would find. *Our orders are to assess the situation and do the best we can*, he pondered to himself. *That's some real clear guidance*, he thought cynically. *I don't even have a copy of the frickin' laws of this country and I'm supposed to tell these Iraqi judges what to do?*

Among the hurdles confronting the Coalition as it tried to restore order in Iraq was that most judges had simply abandoned their posts immediately before the invasion. Many had returned to their comfortable homes in Baghdad, Basra or Tikrit to wait out the war. Accordingly, even in cities such as Hillah where the courthouse had not suffered great damage, the immediate challenge was simply finding the judges and getting them to go back to their courts. Most of the Hillah judges had returned only when it became clear after two months of occupation that the Americans were not lining former regime officials up against a wall.

Trevanathan looked about the passing urban landscape. Hillah was a city of wide boulevards and relatively modern buildings, and home to perhaps 60,000. It had benefited over the years from being a retreat for Saddam, enjoying many modern amenities denied to other, more remote cities of comparable size, such as sanitation systems, clean water, well lit streets and modern schools. He noticed a group of young women walking down a sidewalk, wearing the traditional white blouses and dark skirts of high school students. They smiled at the convoy as it drove past. *We can make a real statement here*, Trevanathan thought, *if we do this right*.

Providing Saddam a refuge from the demands of terrorizing the country from Baghdad had not been without price, however. Saddam's two sons, Uday and Qusay, were infamous in the area for preying upon the local young women. A girl unlucky enough to attract their roving eyes, might be unceremoniously scooped up off the street by security forces and taken to the palace. After being ravished for two or three days to satisfy their perverse desires, she would be thrown back onto her family's doorstep, dishonored and a burden to her family who would not be able to find her a husband. In the interest of self-preservation, the citizens of Hillah had developed a network by which to quickly spread the warning whenever Saddam's sons showed up at the palace. Even so, not everyone was successful in avoiding their attentions.

One story told how a father was bold enough to complain to Saddam when his fourteen year old daughter was forcibly deflowered by Uday. As reward for his insolence, every woman in the his family – including his eight year old daughter – was raped in the father's presence. Whether true or not, the story was told with great conviction by the people of Hillah as a testament to the futility of speaking out against the excesses of the Hussein family. Reversing this mistrust of government and constructing a system where no man was above the law, was the Herculean challenge laid before Major Trevanathan and his team.

The Hillah courthouse was a cream colored, two-story structure surrounded by a low wall. A tall metal gate led into a narrow, rectangular courtyard in front of the entrance. As the two Jaguar Team HMMWVs approached the courthouse, Trevanathan saw a crowd of people milling around in front of the gate, waving papers. A green-shirted security guard inside the gate was waving his hands in response and shaking his head.

Trevanathan had brought Abu with him on this mission, not sure whether any of the Iraqi judges would speak English. "Cooper, stop across the street from the courthouse," he directed. Turning in his seat, he addressed Warden. "Sergeant Warden, take Abu and have the gate opened so we can park inside. I don't want to be sitting out here in the open."

"Roger, sahr," replied Warden seriously, tapping the side assist on his M16 to ensure the first round was well seated in its chamber.

The crowd ignored the HMMWVs behind them as the vehicles rumbled to a stop across from the courthouse. Warden quickly slid from his seat and checked his weapon again. "Watch that crowd," Trevanathan warned unnecessarily.

"Always, sahr. C'mon Abu, let's go say howdy to some of your cousins," Warden said, turning and walking toward the crowd, his rifle held across his chest, the barrel pointed down at a 45 degree angle.

"They are not my cousins," Abu whined to Warden's non-responsive back, as he scurried to catch up.

The two men pushed through the crowd up the 15 meter driveway to the gate. As Warden's presence was noticed by those in front of him, the crowd parted and became quiet, nervously eyeing the tall Texan with his flak jacket, helmet, and rifle.

"Do you speak English?" Warden asked the sweating, fat-faced security guard.

The man appeared relieved that the crowd had quieted. "Yes, yes. I spoke it very good," he replied eagerly, with a nervous smile on his round face.

"Great," replied Warden. "I need you to open this gate so me and my team can park in there. We're here to see the judges." Warden gestured toward the two HMMWVs behind him on the street.

"I cannot do that, colonel," said the guard, lowering his eyes and shifting his feet nervously. "The Chief Judge told me to keep this gate locked and the crowd outside."

"Listen, Muhammad: there's a new sheriff in town," said Warden impatiently. "Open the damn gate or we drive through it. Got it?"

The guard's eyes widened. "How do you know my name?" he gasped, wondering if this American had some secret knowledge of which he should fear.

"Lucky guess," responded Warden flatly. "Now we're pulling up here and I expect this gate to be open."

"Yes, colonel, it will be done," replied the guard, nodding in deference to the NCO.

Warden and Abu walked back through the silent crowd to the vehicles and resumed their seats within. "Any problems?" Trevanathan asked.

"No sahr," replied Warden. "The Haji guard thinks ahm a colonel, so it worked out just fine. Pull on up to the gate, Cooper, and he'll open her up for us."

The guard did as Warden had ordered, closing the gates behind the team as they pulled into the courtyard. Trevanathan quickly split up his team. "Ridlin, stay with the vehicles. Sergeant Leader, take Sergeant Mantis and Cooper and stroll through the building to make sure it's clear. Don't be too overt about it; smile and nod – you know the drill."

"Roger, sir," replied Leader. "Let's go," he said to his squad, and they quickly disappeared through the front door.

"Rick, would you keep an eye on the crowd with Ridlin?" Trevanathan inquired of Smith. "I want some adult supervision out here if that crowd gets unruly."

"You got it, sir," replied Smith.

Turning to Abu and Warden, Trevanathan said , "The three of us are going to find the Chief Judge and I'll brief him on our mission here. Abu, make sure that you translate everything, OK?"

"Yes, sir," said Abu. The Americans had already discovered that he had a bad habit of trying to sugarcoat whatever was said by the Iraqis. Despite his professed disdain for the Iraqi people, he had demonstrated a willingness to put everything in the best possible light, even if the resulting translation was less than accurate.

"Let's go."

Walking toward the front door and gesturing back toward the waiting crowd, Trevanathan asked Abu, "What are all of those people yelling about at the gate?"

"They are people who have legal petitions to file, sir," responded Abu. "They are asking to get access to file their cases, but the guard will not let them in."

"Hmm, OK."

Trevanathan entered the lobby of the courthouse, which was very cool compared to the late morning 120-degrees outside. Sergeant Leader met him, coming down a wide set of stairs on the right side of the lobby. "It's all clear upstairs, sir," Leader said. "The Chief Judge's office is at the end of the second floor hallway on the east side of the building."

"Thanks Sergeant Leader. Keep a position here with Cooper; send Sergeant Mantis outside to keep watch with Ridlin and Captain Smith," Trevanathan ordered, walking slowly up the stairs and down the narrow hallway, taking notice of the inactivity in the various offices he passed. Desks were piled high with papers, but no personnel were to be seen.

Abu pointed to a door with Arabic script on its frosted glass window. "This one, sir."

Trevanathan knocked on the door lightly, but there was no answer. Pushing the door open he saw a small, empty office, and another door. Stepping through the small room to the inner door, he reached for the handle.

"Be careful, sahr," Warden voiced softly over his shoulder. "I don't like it that no one is around." Trevanathan nodded, as he turned the handle to the next room.

Inside was a ten by seven meter room, lined with couches upon which sat perhaps a dozen middle-aged men in cheap suits, smoking and quietly talking. A cloud of blue smoke hung over the room. 1950s-style plywood tables sat at the end of each couch, covered with crowded ashtrays and cans of Pepsi.. As Trevanathan stepped into the room a metal ashtray clanged noisily as it fell to the tile floor and the men fell silent, looking nervously at the tall, armored figure stepping into their midst. "Salaam," said Trevanathan, forcing a smile. No one replied, as the men looked uncomfortably from one to another.

The Major turned to Abu and broke the awkward silence. "Abu, ask who is the Chief Judge."

Abu complied and flushed slightly at the response from one of the men. "They want to know if you are here to arrest them, sir."

Trevanathan almost laughed before realizing that they were dead serious. "No, tell them I am an Army lawyer and I was sent to meet with their Chief Judge."

Abu engaged in a round of discussion with several of the men, before again turning to Trevanathan. "Sir, I regret that they do not wish to identify the Chief Judge."

"Why not?" asked Trevanathan, wrinkling his brow.

"Sir, in Iraq an Army lawyer is the final person that an official would see before being taken before the court to confess and be executed. They are afraid you are here to take the Chief Judge to his firing squad."

Trevanathan looked at the anxious faces around him, their dark probing eyes betraying their fear. He considered how he must appear to them in his battle rattle, flak jacket, and weapon, with Warden's hulking presence behind him. *OK*, he thought, *we need to start over.*

"Warden, follow me." Stepping back out into the outer office Trevanathan removed his flak jacket and helmet, revealing his brown, matted hair. He then laid his rifle on top of the secretary's desk. "I think we may be scaring the crap out of them with all this gear," he said to Warden. "I want you to stay out here and watch my weapon. I'll go back in with Abu and try to break the ice."

"Sahr, I don't like it," warned Warden. A terrerist judge is still a terrerist. Don't trust 'em."

"I don't trust 'em either, but I have to look like I trust 'em or we're not gettin' anywhere. If there's any trouble, I'm confident you can pull me out of a group of middle-aged judges. I just wish someone had told me what the hell I'm supposed to tell them."

Warden just shook his head and looked unhappy.

Trevanathan stepped back into the room and smiled again at the group of men. An elaborate desk sat vacant at the near end of the room, and he walked behind it, admiring the leather chair. As the eyes of the men followed him, he sat down behind the desk.

Two men on a small couch quickly turned and looked at another sitting between them. *Well, now I know who the Chief Judge is*, Trevanathan smiled inwardly. He could also see the complexion of the small, gray-haired man color slightly in his displeasure at this infidel sitting at his desk.

Trevanathan had not planned a speech, nor had he been provided with any advice on what to say. "Do what is necessary," had been the only guidance when the General in charge of Civil Affairs had briefed them in Kuwait. *Well, I might as well sound important*, he thought to himself, *since I get to write the script.*

"Abu, translate for me."

"Good morning," he stated in a clear, deep voice to the anxious men staring at him. "I am Major Trevanathan of the United States Army. On behalf of President George Bush and the American people I bring you greetings." *I sound like I'm a Martian landing on earth*, he thought. "The regime of Saddam Hussein is gone and a new day has come to Iraq." Trevanathan paused and looked about the room, noticing that the men were now leaning forward and paying rapt attention to his every word.

"I am here to inform you that the laws of Iraq, as they were before the Americans arrived, shall remain in effect." The men in the room looked quickly at each other and began whispering among themselves.

"Those laws that supported the Ba'ath party and Saddam's security courts are hereby abolished." No one had told Trevanathan that this was so, but since no one had told him a damn thing he was going to do what made sense. He would apologize later if he was wrong. The men again buzzed among themselves, looking at Trevanathan and each other as they discussed each point as Abu translated.

"For now, each of you shall retain his current job and continue to administer the laws of Iraq," Trevanathan said. "The American General in Baghdad will decide later who will continue to be a judge permanently." Trevanathan knew that it was actually the Coalition Provisional Authority under Bremer[42] that would make the decision, but that was too complicated to explain at this moment.

"The court will reopen and begin to hear cases as soon as possible," he said. Again, Trevanathan was winging it, but he figured the country needed a legal system, and no one could really complain later that he had tried to jump start the process.

He paused to let his words sink in and to permit the judges to speak among themselves. Abu stepped next to Trevanathan and leaned down to whisper, "Sir, they are very afraid and confused. They are not sure what they are supposed to do."

"I just told them what to do, Abu."

The small, gray-haired man in the blue suit slowly stood and faced Trevanathan. As he began to speak, Abu translated. "I am Chief Judge Muhammad Al Elizar. In the name of Allah, the just and merciful, I bid you welcome."

"It is my honor to meet you," replied Trevanathan. Having accomplished his purpose of identifying the Chief Judge, Trevanathan rose from the desk chair and moved around to the front of the desk.

"While we wish to cooperate fully with the American authorities, we, of course, cannot begin to hear cases again until we have direction from the Minister of Justice in Baghdad."

"Sir, there is no Minister left in Baghdad to give you those directions," Trevanathan responded. "The Iraqi Government is gone. Your Minister of Justice is gone. The United States and the Coalition is now running this country. I am here to give you the authority to again hear cases."

A man who had been sitting next to the Chief Judge said something in a low voice, to which the Chief Judge nodded. "We believe that what you say is

---

[42] Ambassador Paul Bremer was appointed by President Bush as the civilian administrator for the US occupation government, known as the Coalition Provisional Authority (CPA).

true," said Judge Elizar. "We have heard it on our radios. But may I ask, who will tell us how to decide the cases?"

"I am telling *you* to begin hearing the cases again," replied the Major, slightly frustrated that he was forced to repeat everything three times and wondering if Abu was translating correctly. "I am the person to tell you to begin work again. There is no one else who will do so."

"Yes, I understand," said the Chief Judge. "But if there is no one in Baghdad, how will we know *how* to decide the cases? Will you be the one to tell us?"

A slightly sick feeling hit Trevanathan in the stomach. *Do they want to be told how to decide each case?* he wondered. *That's ridiculous.*

"No one will tell you *how* to decide each case," Trevanathan replied. "How to decide the case is for you alone to decide as the judge. You will hear the facts and decide under the law if a man is guilty or not guilty."

Judge Elizar turned and discussed this matter with the others. After what seemed like many minutes, he again turned to the Major. "We do not understand," he replied. "*Someone* must make the decision as to guilt or innocence. Who will this be?"

"It will be you, judge," Trevanathan said, slightly exasperated. "Each of you will decide your own cases. No one will tell you how to do it. You will apply the law and make your own decisions under the law from now on. That's what a judge does."

Judge Elizar turned back to his peers and an even longer discussion ensued, replete with raised voices, animated hand gestures, and the rolling of eyes. *These guys are nothing if not dramatic*, Trevanathan thought, watching one judge feign exhaustion and collapse at the response to a statement he had made to a third judge.

Judge Elizar turned back to Trevanathan. "We are not certain exactly how this will work," he said, "but if it is as you say, this is an amazing gift you bring to us. We have always taken direction from Baghdad on matters of such importance. You now tell us we may make our own decisions. How can this be?"

"Yes, you will judge. It is how things are done in America. I know you do not have juries here, but in America judges decide their own cases and no politician can make them change their rulings. If they try, the politician can even be put in jail."

"Truly a strange system," said the Chief Judge, "but we will do our best."

"Judge, I am here to be your contact with the US Army and Ambassador Bremer's people in Baghdad. Part of my job is to find out what you need to run this courthouse. I can't promise anything, but I will try to get you what you need."

"The first thing we need is money for the salaries," said Judge Elizar. "The workers have all gone home because there is no money to pay them. That is why we have sealed the gates to the courthouse."

"I will go to Baghdad Friday and find out about the money," said Trevanathan. "The other thing I need you to do is to make a list of supplies you need to run the courthouse. Paper, pencils, computers – whatever you had before to make this place run. I will come back for your list on Monday, OK?"

"Allah be praised," said the Chief Judge, stepping forward and grasping Trevanathan by both arms with a large smile on his face. "Thank you, Colonel, thank you."

"Ahh, I'm only a Major, sir," corrected Trevanathan as politely as he could.

"That is obviously a tremendous oversight by your Army," replied the judge, attempting to ingratiate himself to the officer. "A man of your talents and wisdom must surely be a Colonel soon."

The ice broken and the men reassured that Major Trevanathan was there to provide help and not make arrests, the rest of the meeting went smoothly. Each judge introduced himself and was very enthusiastic, with the exception of two men on a small couch in the corner. They shook hands with no particular warmth and appeared to be distant even from the other judges, who chatted very amicably among themselves.

"Abu, what's the deal with the two in the corner?" Trevanathan quietly asked his translator.

"They are not from here," replied Abu. "They are from Tikrit in the north, and were assigned here."

Tikrit? Trevanathan thought. *Saddam's hometown. Those two are probably spies on the rest of the judges,* he thought to himself. *I'll have to give Intel a rundown on them when we get back to camp.*

Leaving President Bush's greetings with the judges, Trevanathan excused himself from the gathering and returned to his team waiting downstairs.

"How'd it go, sir?" Leader asked as they assembled in the lobby.

"It's a start, but we'll have to see how it plays out. Let's go."

Chapter 14
The Leopard Man

The Jaguar team was returning from a legal training session with the Iraqi judges in Karbala, another provincial capital west of Hillah. Major Trevanathan's mission had been to teach the judges the new criminal procedural rules published by the Coalition Provisional Authority in Baghdad. The new rules required the appointment of a lawyer for an accused suspect and forbade the use of testimony obtained through torture.

"How'd it go, sir?" asked Warden as the two HMMWVs wound their way back toward Hillah.

"Great, great," replied Trevanathan wearily, as the merciless July sun beat down on his side of the HMMWV. "They'll warmly embrace the idea of a fair trial until about five minutes after we pull out of this country. Ya' know, one judge actually asked me what the police were supposed to do from now on to get evidence, if they could not beat a confession out of a suspect. He thought we were being unfair to the police." Trevanathan laughed bitterly.

Warden had noticed that Trevanathan was increasingly frustrated with the Iraqi judges. Over a period of several weeks, the judges had repeatedly demonstrated they cared more about their personal status and privileges than in improving their system. Attempts to get the Chief Judge in Hillah to put together an annual budget for courthouse operations had come back laden with requests for Range Rovers, televisions and satellite phones for the judges. Even after Major Trevanathan had rejected the first budget and directed that it be revised, "luxuries" such as legal books and paper had been conspicuously absent in the second draft, in favor of air conditioning units for each judge's office.

Warden noted that the Trevanathan's optimism for the mission had diminished somewhat after that. "Sahr, we're near the amusement park. Do ya' wanna stop in and see the lil' terrorist?" Warden knew that the occasional visits to the amusement park to see the boy had a positive effect on his Major's outlook.

"Sure, why not?" replied Trevanathan, perking up a bit. "We have a couple extra MREs and bottles of water in the back, don't we? We can leave 'em for him and his grandfather."

Cooper led the two vehicle convoy across the median of Highway 8, through the park's gateway, and down the now-familiar path to the utility shed where the boy and his grandfather lived. The visits had become part of the team's routine, and the boy seemed healthier on the calorie-rich diet of the team's spare MREs.

Today, however, young Saddam was not home. His grandfather had sent him off to the market to buy lamb, from which they would cook kabob for their evening meal. The old man sat alone in the shade outside the front door of the shed, smoking his acrid Iraqi cigarettes. The old man did not move as the desert camouflage painted HMMWVs rolled to their usual parking spot beneath the trees. He sat patiently and continued smoking, as the American troops dismounted and stretched from the long, hot ride from Karbala.

"Salaam Alekim," greeted Trevanathan as he walked up to the shed, touching the fingertips of his right hand to his heart.

"Alekim Salaam," replied the grandfather, returning the gesture and nodding his head in respect. The grandfather smiled and gestured for the officer to sit down on the ground next to him. As Trevanathan lowered himself to the ground in the cool shade, the old man offered him a bent and battered cigarette, which Trevanathan politely refused.

From several prior visits to the park over the past several weeks, Trevanathan had become friendly with the Iraqi. He learned that the old man had a strong grasp of English, as he had once been a veterinary school student in London. However, that academic career had come to a rapid close when the then much younger man had returned to Iraq to visit his young wife and infant child.

It was at the height of the Iran-Iraq war in the early eighties, when Iraq needed every man at the front to resist an Iranian offensive that threatened to wrest Basrah and the southern oil fields from Baghdad's control. The grandfather had been walking down the main street of Hillah to the market, when an Iraqi Army truck had pulled up beside him. Soldiers had descended upon him, insisting that he should be serving his country as a soldier. When he sought to explain that he was only a student visiting home, they had cuffed and beaten him, before forcibly loading him onto the truck and delivering him, along with eighteen other reluctant recruits, to the front lines after a miserable ten hour truck ride.

Battered and bruised, he had no training and no military equipment, but was nonetheless led through a series of winding paths into the trenches. There he was introduced to a large and sadistic sergeant named Hassan, who would own him and the other eighteen impressed recruits. Beaten again whenever he hesitated, the grandfather had quickly learned that weakness had no place at the front. Wearing only sandals and his dishdasha – a full length shirt-like garment, called a "man-dress" by US troops – he was assigned to the ranks of a badly-depleted mine-clearing unit.

Most of the men shanghaied with him had died within two weeks from undetected mines, Iranian snipers, or by the rampant disease in the filthy trenches. Bad food, dirty water, and unsanitary waste disposal quickly took their toll. Committed to seeing his family again, however, the grandfather had learned and adapted, picking up equipment and weapons from the dead, and learning survival tricks from Hassan.

Even that knowledge and equipment could not protect him, however, when the Iranians laid down a dense cloud of blister agent on the Iraqi trenches one morning, in retaliation for a mustard gas attack the Iraqis had launched days before to stop an Iranian offensive. The grandfather's unit had been caught in the middle of the attack, and he had suffered massive blisters and weeping sores over 90 percent of his body. Only his unrelenting will to see his wife and child again had kept him from dying at that moment. Medically evacuated in a donkey cart with the few other survivors of his unit, he had spent an agonizing year in a Basrah military hospital, slowly recovering as his body tried to grow new skin.

No longer fit for service, he was released from the Iraqi Army. He returned home to Hillah beneath a blanket in the back of a dump truck. His own family did not recognize him when he appeared in their doorway. He was nearly blind, and the skin of his body had yellowed, except where red, puckered lesions remained. The irregular, blotchy scars led to his being nicknamed the "Leopard Man" by the children of Hillah.

Unable to tolerate direct sunlight upon his tortured skin, and unable to find work, the Leopard Man's family had survived on the modest Army pension he received – the equivalent of $25 (US) per month. When his son, Ahmed, had reached the age to enter the university, he had passed the necessary exams to be accepted to medical school. Ahmed's lovely wife Fatime, had died in childbirth bringing forth young Saddam, shortly after Ahmed completed his studies. From that day forward, the grandfather acted as the primary caretaker for the boy in their modest three room home, adjacent to the local military base.

In March of 2003, the whoosh-roar of cruise missile engines launched from US Navy cruisers in the Arabian Gulf signaled the end of young Ahmed's medical career. When the Iraqi Army base next door was struck, Ahmed had responded to the screams of the wounded, many of them burned beyond recognition. His compassionate reaction coincided with the follow-on attack by US Marine F-18's that wiped the rest of the base, Ahmed, and their house, from the map.

Young Saddam had pulled his grandfather from the rubble of their home. The two of them lived on the streets of Hillah until the boy had come upon the empty utility shed two months before, during a trip to scavenge food.

Trevanathan had discussed the old man's story with him before and knew he must have conflicting emotions regarding the American presence. The Americans had taken his son from him, but were now providing assistance to his grandson that might mean the difference between life and death for the boy.

Warden walked up with an armful of MREs, as Trevanathan and the Leopard Man chatted. "Where do you want these, sir?" he asked the Major, ignoring the old man.

"Just set 'em here, Sergeant Warden. Thanks."

"Sergeant," the old man inquired, without preamble, "I sense you do not like our people. Is that true?"

Warden looked at Trevanathan, seeking a signal, but received nothing.

"Come sergeant, sit and talk to me," continued the grandfather without judgment. "I am interested in your views."

"Sahr, I don't have nuthin' to say," replied Warden as he turned away.

"Why did you come here, sergeant?" asked the old man as Warden began to step away, "You Americans go all over the world. You bring blue jeans and Britney Spears. You expect things to be like America and then are upset when they are not. Is that not true? Your Major is too polite to mention such things, but I sense your anger."

"I go where the Army tells me to, sahr. That's all there is to it," Warden said over his shoulder.

"Yes, I understand. I was a soldier too. But why the anger? Why do I see such hatred in your eyes?"

"Look sahr, we came to help you people," replied Warden turning back toward the old man in an uncharacteristic angry tone of voice. "We came to make your lives better. So maybe your grandson can grow up without fear. Now your people still try to kill us. I've been though this same bullshit in Somalia – you people bitin' the hand that feeds you."

"Is that really why you came, sergeant? So that there will be no fear?" The old man smiled, exposing brown, stained teeth. "There is no life in Iraq without fear. Fear is our natural state," he said in a whimsical manner. He paused as the NCO silently watched him.

"We fear our neighbors in Iran," the grandfather continued, drawing a crude map of Iraq in the sand with a stick. He stabbed at the rough location of Iran on the border. "In Iran, in Turkey, in Syria, in Saudi Arabia," he recited, as he sketched each country on his crude map, stabbing them in turn with his stick for emphasis. "We fear them all."

Warden looked again to Trevanathan for direction, but the Major continued to look at the map in the dirt.

"We fear the Government," the old man continued. "We fear each other. The Kurds fear the Turks. The Shiites fear the Sunnis. The Sunnis fear everyone as they have more to lose. We fear those who will hurt us and we fear those who say they will help – for no one helps without a price," he added.

"Do you fear the USA?" Warden asked.

"We do not fear America," the Leopard Man replied without hesitation. "We fear your weapons, but we do not fear your soldiers. You do not have the darkness and the strength of purpose needed to control Iraq – to control the *fear*. You have the weapons, but not the will. All the people know this."

The old man scratched out his map with the stick. "You do not have the heart of a conqueror," he continued evenly. "You destroy our army and then give candy to our children. You capture those who would kill you and then worry that you are too harsh to them. Your enemies here would cut your throat in your sleep, but you still want to be their friend. You want our gratitude. You seek our respect. Your newspapers cry out at mistreatment of men that would destroy your way of life. No," emphasized the Leopard Man gazing calmly at Warden, "there is no reason to fear you, because you will not stay. You will not be able to stay without becoming something you loath, and so you will leave and things will return to the way they were."

"Don't you people give a damn that we're trying to help you have a better life?" asked Warden sharply, irritated at the old man's fatalistic attitude.

"Let me tell you how Iraq views the man who comes to the door to bring help, sergeant," the old man smiled, his yellow eyes fixed upon the NCO's face. "Iraqis are the most charming people in the world – one at a time. We will invite you into our homes. We will feed you and entertain you, even if we ourselves must do without. It is a matter of honor. We will ask after your family and sincerely want to know all of the details about your children. Iraqis love children and love their families. We are a warm and friendly people – one at a time."

The Leopard Man now drew three stick figures in the dirt, scratching a circle about them. "Put two Iraqis in a room together and they will both seek to curry your friendship," he continued. "They will feed you and entertain you. They will give you the choicest cuts of the lamb. But they will quickly grow jealous of each other. Every favor that one does for you will be viewed jealously by the other. The first will accuse the second of seeking to embarrass him before the honored guest. The second will accuse the first of lying and seeking to alienate you from him by those lies. They will call each others' lineage, faith, and family history into question, forgetting their guest, and roll on the floor seeking to slit each others' throat."

Warden's posture relaxed slightly, listening carefully to the old man's words.

"Put three Iraqis in a room together with a guest," continued the old man, scratching a fourth figure within the circle in the soil. "Two of them will accuse the third of secretly trying to conspire with you, for your favor, to the detriment of the other two. The third will whisper in your ear that the first two are plotting against you and cannot be trusted. No rumor or falsehood is so extreme that it will not be repeated with the greatest sincerity and passion. The first two will declare the third a Zionist spy. The third will accuse the first two of being agents of Iran. The two will plot for the death of the third, and even while doing so, each of them will keep a wary eye on each other out of their mutual distrust. They will spend all of their time searching for treachery, conspiracy and deceit until the guest dies of starvation or throws up his hands and leaves in disgust."

Warden looked in wonder at the old man.

"You are not a guest, however," continued the grandfather in a friendly tone, looking up from his drawing with deep set eyes. "You are uninvited. You have invited yourselves into our homes, with your destruction and your promises of a better life. And yet, you believe you can bring this land together, where even an honored guest could not?" The old man tilted his head to one side and smiled. He gestured at the figures in the dirt. "These are the people upon whom you will spread your seeds of democracy, Sergeant. I believe your noble seeds may find the soil too hostile to grow." The old man laughed quietly, reached out with the stick, and scratched the figures out of existence.

"We need to give it a chance," said Trevanathan in a low voice. "That may be your past, but you can have a different future."

"Yes, by all means give it a chance," replied the old man. "But how many bodies will your country give to this chance, before there are no more chances left? Has anyone answered this question for you?"

Trevanathan was silent. This same question had haunted him. *Would all the suffering and death amount to anything when the Iraqis themselves didn't seem to be willing to change?*

"What about four Iraqis?" Warden asked, seeking to test the limits of the old man's analogy.

"Ahhh, four Iraqis," the Leopard Man smiled, revealing uneven, stained teeth behind dark gums. "With four Iraqis you have an army, and Kuwait should not sleep too well," he laughed, his yellow eyes flashing brightly.

On the return trip to Camp Babylon, Warden leaned forward from the back passenger seat to whisper in his Major's ear. "Sir, that's the most honest damned terrerist I've ever met."

Chapter 15
The Carpetbagger

Brigadier General Merdier's big moment arrived unexpectedly. Resigned to spending the war in Alabama, making the same nauseating, canned speech at Army Reserve Center Family Day functions week after week, he was caught off-guard when Major General Oldhaus called him in the middle of the night.

"Merdier?" came the forceful voice over the receiver.

"Mmphh, this is General Merdier," he replied, fumbling for the bedside lamp's switch.

"This is Major General Oldhaus. Pack your shit, and be at Pope Air Force Base tomorrow at 1800."

"Umm, umm, yes General… Can I ask what is going on?"

"Bob Smathers got himself whacked in Iraq and I need someone to take over command of the civil affairs effort there ASAP.

"General Smathers is dead, sir?"

"No. Worse. He's been relieved from command."

Merdier's head spun. "Relieved, sir?"

"What are you, a frickin' parrot, Merdier? Yes, *relieved*. He was in a briefing with the Undersecretary of the Army for Manpower Readiness, and the CG[43] in Iraq. He was asked his plan for follow-on troop deployments to continue reconstruction. Do you know what he responded? Do you?" Oldhaus' voice rose noticeably with the demand.

"No sir," replied Merdier groggily, wondering if this was some strange dream.

"He said, 'What plan?' Can you believe it? 'What plan?!' The CG fired him on the spot for incompetence."

---

[43] Commanding General

"That's pretty bad, sir. I agree. A real black eye for the civil affairs community. Umm, just for clarification sir, er, what *is* the plan?"

"There is no damn plan, you idiot! No one ever thought this goat-screw was going to drag on this long. But that's still no excuse for saying there's no plan, by God!"

"No sir. Definitely not, sir."

"We sent two thirds of our command over in the first wave. The rest of them are already in Afghanistan or the Balkans. There's no one left except the halt, lame and insane."

"Uh, so when I get there what shall I tell the CG when I arrive there, sir – ab..about replacements, I mean?" Merdier felt his pulse beginning to quicken, as he smelled another Oldhaus set-up designed to trash his career.

"I'm sure you'll think of something. It's a long flight." CLICK.

Brigadier General Merdier's C-130 transport flight from Kuwait landed at Saddam International Airport on the outskirts of Baghdad, launching a trail of flares on final approach which were intended to confuse the occasional surface-to-air rocket fired by locals who did not yet appreciate the benefits of being liberated. Typical of the irreverent humor of combat troops, some wag had altered the sign atop of the main terminal, thereby dubbing the airfield "ddam International Airport." "Lack of discipline," muttered Merdier, not amused by the defacing of public property.

Whisked by MP convoy to the new Coalition Headquarters at the former Republican Palace compound in the heart of the "Green Zone," Merdier quickly assumed charge of civil affairs reconstruction activities.

"We need to renovate this headquarters from the ground up," he exclaimed. "I can't possibly be expected to tolerate these conditions," he continued, adjusting the air conditioning unit that had been installed just prior to his arrival.

"General Maynard from the MP brigade has a tennis court behind her headquarters. I have an empty pool! What am I going to do with an empty pool, Shmedlap?" Merdier complained to his new aide. "I'll be a laughing stock. How will I show my face around the other Generals? By God, I bet the CG has done this on purpose to test me, to see if I will tolerate this abuse. Well, I'll show him a thing or two about the stuff I'm made of."

"Shmedlap!" he roared, ignoring the fact that Major Shmedlap was still standing only three feet away.

"Yes, sir?" replied Shmedlap, without enthusiasm as he continued to stare at his boots.

"Shmedlap, I want that engineering Major – Goldstein, Goldberg – some Jew name. Get his butt up here ASAP and put him on fixing this pool. I will not be made a laughing stock. The very honor of our branch is on the line here!" Merdier concluded, winded by his own outburst.

"Sir?" Major Shmedlap replied meekly, anticipating the negative reaction to his next comment, "Major Goldberg has been sent to Al Kut to restore the wastewater plant there. He'll be back in a week, though," he added hopefully.

"Wastewater?!" roared Merdier, his complexion flushing darkly. "This entire country is a goddamn waste. Get his butt back here, NOW. These people have been pissing in the streets for three thousand years. A few more days won't hurt them."

"Yessir," replied Shmedlap, backing quickly out of the office

The Green Zone was the pinnacle of Saddam's power and luxury. Sealed off from the general population, the area surrounding the Republican Palace had housed both Saddam's extended family and the families of his most loyal supporters. Shaded streets, lined by well-cared for trees and flowering shrubs, crossed the luxurious compound that measured two by five kilometers. Fountains and man-made ponds filled with flowers, aquatic plants, and exotic birds colored the landscape. Homes that would be considered mansions in America lined the cool streets, and were immediately turned into housing and headquarters buildings for the many Generals and civilian Coalition Provisional Authority (CPA) personnel responsible for getting Iraq back onto its feet.

There was no place like the Green Zone anywhere else in Iraq, and except for the occasional rocket or mortar round that dropped in unannounced, the duty there was better than on many military bases in the United States. Smartly dressed staff officers walked briskly through the air conditioned halls of the Republican Palace with self-important looks on their closely shaved faces. Pressed desert uniforms with razor sharp creases were reflected in the tall mirrors and chandeliers that lined each hallway. The looting that had reduced the grandeur of Saddam's rule to scrap in so much of Iraq had not touched the Green Zone, as the Coalition forces had seized the area before the looters could react. An AAFES[44] laundry and dry cleaning shop for the many staff officers had opened in the Green Zone, almost before the final echo of Saddam's statue being toppled a few blocks away had died out.

This country is not so bad, thought Merdier, as he settled into the high-backed leather chair behind the cherry wood desk that had been formerly occupied by a Republican Guard corps commander. *A little paint and some organization and we'll have this place running like a top*, he mused, as the drone of the AC unit lulled him off to sleep.

---

[44] Army and Air Force Exchange Service – the quasi-military entity that runs the PX, movie theaters, and other soldier support activities on US Army and Air Force bases around the world.

Chapter 16
The Sleeves

"Holy crap, look at this place," said Smith, looking at the line of crystal chandeliers that extended down the seemingly endless hallway of the Republican Palace. The Jaguars and Doc had just completed their first convoy to Baghdad in order to meet with the new Coalition Ministry of Justice officials, with whom they were to coordinate reconstruction of the provincial courts and medical facilities. With phone service between the far-flung provinces of Iraq not yet restored, and no radios of sufficient range available, in-person communication was the rule amongst the Coalition policy makers responsible for getting things done

"Feel that cold air. Look, I have goose bumps," Trevanathan added, holding up his bare arm to demonstrate his awe. Saddam's comfort had been ensured in his desert kingdom: his expansive Republican Palace was maintained at a temperate 72 degree Fahrenheit by massive air conditioning units. To the Jaguar team, grown accustomed to the summertime daytime highs in the mid-130 degree range, the palace felt like a meat locker.

"They have an espresso bar," Doc pointed to a busy little counter set off of the main lobby, where two Iraqi civilians were busy serving steaming cups of the bitter liquid to several smartly dressed army officers, waiting impatiently in line.

"Sir, they don't have weapons," whispered Warden, indicating the officers. "Where are their weapons?"

Trevanathan and Warden looked at their own small group, laden down with rifles, grenade launchers and pistols, a variety of combat knives hanging from their web belts. They had left their grenades in the HMMWV across the street.

"Ya' got me, Dorothy," replied Trevanathan with raised eyebrows. "We aren't in Iraq anymore."

"You men, there!" demanded a high-pitched, nasal voice from the intersecting hallway to their right. "What do you think you are doing?" Turning to the source of the terrier-like voice, Trevanathan was confronted with a rapidly approaching, crimson-faced Brigadier General Merdier. "That's the Civil

Affairs patch you're wearing on your shoulder, but you are out of uniform, mister," Merdier accused.

"Sir?" asked Trevanathan, bewildered.

"Who is the senior man here?" demanded Merdier, looking beyond Trevanathan at the salt-stained and frayed uniforms of the team. Several of their uniforms bore no rank, as they had been issued just before the unit had embarked on their flight to Kuwait.

"I am, sir," replied Trevanathan evenly. "Major William Trevanathan, 538th CA Brigade."

"Major, come with me," snapped Merdier, and he turned on his heel and strode quickly away.

"Rick, get the team something to drink," Trevanathan said to Smith over his shoulder, as he rushed to catch up with the rapidly moving General.

As he rounded a corner of the hallway to his left where Merdier had disappeared, Trevanathan found the General waiting for him, a scowl of displeasure on his face.

"Major, out of consideration for your rank, I did not wish to embarrass you in front of your men. But your uniform is intolerable."

"Sir, I apologize, but we only get to wash them once a week in a five-gallon bucket and they get pretty ripe."

"Not that, Major. It's the sleeves."

"The *sleeves*, sir?"

"The sleeves," repeated BG Merdier with a sadness of one mourning the loss of a close friend. "The sleeves are wrong."

"I'm sorry sir, I don't understand."

"Your sleeves are rolled up, Major. Don't you see what a problem that is? The uniform for all civil affairs personnel in theater is sleeves down, not sleeves up. I've made that quite clear in my daily briefings."

Trevanathan stood silent. He felt that somehow he must have misunderstood. He must have missed something. "You mean… the problem is that… I'm… wearing my sleeves rolled up, sir?" he inquired slowly, as he searched his mind for another possible meaning to the General's words.

"Of course, Major. How can I fight a war if half my people have their sleeves down and the other half have their sleeves up? There's no uniformity. No discipline. The enemy will be at our throats in a New York minute if they sense our discipline weakening." Merdier pounded his fist into his open palm for emphasis. "The difference between an Army and a rabble is discipline, Major. Discipline! Today it is sleeves and tomorrow we are all in a reeducation camp chanting out of a little red book. No, by God. Not while I'm in charge!"

Trevanathan's thoughts whirled and he felt light-headed. *People are dying out there, and we're discussing sleeves*, he thought to himself. *OK - focus*, he told himself — *focus*. "Uh, sir," Trevanathan started again slowly. "I'm with the 538th at Babylon. We don't get your briefings. We're assigned to the Marines and their uniform is sleeves rolled up. Colonel Hermann ordered us to follow the Marine uniform example, so we blend in."

"Hermann? *Hermann?*" demanded Merdier, his voice raising. He looked away from Trevanathan momentarily, his narrow eyes darting about, then lowered his voice and thought out loud. "Is he trying to undercut me? Is he trying to embarrass me to the Marines? Making me look silly for ordering sleeves down? Setting me up as the source of an inter-service conflict? That sneaky bastard Burr is probably behind this."

Recovering himself, Merdier again fixed Trevanathan with his narrow eyes. "OK, Major, here's the deal," he started, licking his lips nervously. "You're on my turf now. I want those sleeves down. I will not have Hermann mocking my authority, by sending sleeveless personnel into my area. You get them down and tell your men to get them down. But as soon as you leave this building, I want those sleeves back up again so no one can accuse me of undercutting the Marines. Do you understand me?" he spluttered, eying Trevanathan closely.

"Yes sir," said Trevanathan. "Sleeves down inside and then sleeves up once we leave."

Merdier nodded, his lips tight.

"Aaah, sir, point of clarification," Trevanathan continued, "Should we raise the sleeves right before we leave the headquarters or do we take off our blouses outside after we leave the building and raise them then?"

"Listen very, very closely, Major," replied Merdier, his voice hissing with displeasure. "I will not and cannot ever, *ever*, have sleeves up in my headquarters. Not now, and not just before you leave. It would generate chaos within my command. Anarchy! You will keep the sleeves down at *all* times that you are in the headquarters and immediately after crossing the threshold out of this building you will stop, remove your blouses, and re-roll your sleeves. Am I clear?"

"Yes, sir," said Trevanathan, revealing no sign that he thought Merdier was completely insane. "No sleeves down inside. Roll them outside. Got it, sir."

"Excellent Major," said Merdier, smiling through bared teeth. "I knew you would understand. Carry on." he ordered, and wheeled about to resume his rapid pace down the hallway, calling urgently after an NCO whose pant leg had come unbloused from his boot top.

Trevanathan walked slowly back into the lobby, feeling slightly distant from his surroundings, to find his team lounging against a wall, sipping strong cups of espresso, their rifles unslung and their offending sleeves still rolled up. "What did he want?" asked Smith nervously, with a look of concern.

"He was explaining the scope of his vision for reconstructing Iraq," replied Trevanathan. "Let's get to our meeting."

Chapter 17
The Clubhouse

The CPA Justice Ministry meeting had just convened as Trevanathan and Smith entered the ornate conference room. Two dozen US military officers and assorted civilian personnel sat around a long, dark wood table. Pitchers of ice water and glass tumblers were spaced along its length. At the near end, a silver-haired gentleman sat at the head of the table. Trevanathan recognized him from photographs as Judge Thaddeus Carpenter, the retired Third Circuit Court of Appeals Justice, who had been appointed Interim Minister of Justice within the US controlled bureaucracy responsible for administering Iraq.

Judge Carpenter was wearing khaki trousers and a peach colored polo shirt. He looked up and smiled as the two sweat-soaked officers entered the room. "Well, looks like we have some late arrivals," he beamed pleasantly. "Welcome gentlemen."

"Thanks sir." replied Trevanathan, "Sorry to interrupt – it was a bit of a haul up from Babylon."

"No problem at all," the judge replied warmly, "Have a seat." Judge Carpenter had a round, slightly reddish face. His balding, silver hair was accented by bright blue eyes that quickly assessed the two officers.

Trevanathan and Smith worked around the head of the table and squeezed down the other side to two empty, ornate, high-backed chairs made of some dark wood. As he awkwardly shuffled to his chair, attempting not to bump the other attendees with the plethora of field equipment strapped to his body, Trevanathan became aware that everyone was watching him. As he came abreast a large mirror on the far wall, he understood why. The vision of a gaunt, hollow-cheeked soldier standing across from him in a faded uniform obviously too big for him, caught him by surprise. He had not seen a full length reflection of himself in some time, and the reflection revealed that both he and his clothing were badly in need of a wash. Behind him, he could see the other officers sitting across from him in their fresh, new uniforms, closely trimmed haircuts, and clean hair.

"We present a pretty picture," he whispered to Smith, as they lowered themselves into the heavily padded chairs. Trevanathan's rifle clattered noisily on the cool marble floor as he unsuccessfully tried to lay it down softly.

"So, as I was saying," the judge continued pleasantly once Trevanathan and Smith were settled, "the Court of Cassation[45] will move to the former Republican Guards headquarters in the interim, until its damaged building can be repaired.

"Now let's go around the table and get an update," he continued. "Tom?"

A JAG Lieutenant Colonel wearing the unit patch of the Third Infantry Division spoke. "Sir, as you know, infrastructure damage caused by looting continues to limit our ability to get all of the courts in our area running, but I expect we will have 80% of them going within three months."

"Great, Tom, anything you need?"

"A one way ticket back to Texas?" the Lieutenant Colonel joked. Everyone laughed.

Trevanathan felt himself shiver involuntarily as the cool gusts of air poured out of vents placed high in the walls.

"Phil?" The judge asked of the next officer, a full Colonel wearing civil affairs brass and the 82nd Airborne Division combat patch. Trevanathan recognized the name on his DCU uniform as an attorney who was responsible for overseeing courthouse reconstruction across the entire country. *Wonder where he's been hiding?* Trevanathan pondered unkindly.

"Well, sir, we continue to have communications problems with some of our outlying legal teams," began the Colonel. "However, here in the capital things are coming together fairly well. All of the Iraqi judges and their personnel have been paid up current through the end of the month. We've been able to salvage many of the legal records that were damaged in the looting. We hope to have the legal gazette up and running by the end of next month, which will allow us to communicate new law changes clearly." He paused for dramatic effect. "If we could get some new coffee filters for my office, I'd even be a happy man," he joked, flashing a row of white teeth. Everyone in the room chuckled appreciatively, except Trevanathan and Smith. Still drained from

---

[45] The Iraqi Supreme Court

their convoy run through the desert and the encounter with Merdier, neither was in the mood for light banter.

"Do these guys realize this place is falling apart, outside Baghdad?" hissed Smith. Trevanathan shook his head slightly.

Judge Carpenter called on several other officers from units stationed in and around Baghdad. Each of them relayed all the positive things they were doing to restore legal operations in the capital. No one was present from any field unit in the provinces outside the capital – except Trevanathan and Smith.

"Well, now," said the judge, smiling as he turned his warm glow upon Trevanathan. "Major, what can you tell us about the situation in the *hinterlands*?" He chuckled at his own wit.

"Well, sir," began Trevanathan slowly, "it's a bit different away from Baghdad. We have no communications with the Ministry of Justice here or with our neighboring provinces. So we don't know what we are supposed to be doing and we can't coordinate with the other legal teams in the field. Right now we mostly just make it up as we go along..."

"Well, I'm sure you're doing a fine job," interrupted the Judge. "Anything else?" he asked in a tone, clearly indicating he had already heard enough.

"Ah, yes, sir," continued Trevanathan, not willing to be dismissed so easily. "What are the laws currently in place in this country? We don't have a copy of them, so we can't tell the judges what they're supposed to do. We've created some training materials on our own, but they are probably different than what you use up here. Can you give us a copy of the laws you want us to enforce, and which ones not to?"

Judge Carpenter glanced quickly over at the Colonel with the 82nd patch, but did not answer.

Trevanathan pushed forward. "The courts are closed in the South because there's no money to pay the court workers." Nodding toward the Colonel with the 82nd patch, Trevanathan continued, "Seems like you all have money here in the capital to pay your judges. How do we get some of that, sir?"

Carpenter shifted uncomfortably and again made eye contact with the Colonel, who quickly looked down at some suddenly very important papers lying on the table before him. "Well, Major, we're having trouble getting cooperation from the finance people…" His voice trailed off.

Trevanathan pressed on. "What are we supposed to be doing with the old judges that were loyal to Saddam? No one has given us any guidance. We've fired some of the bad ones in the South, but now we hear that you all here at CPA may reverse that. That'll be a problem if you undercut the field commander's decisions who are right there dealing with the issue. Also, many of the courthouses were burned in the provinces, so there are no cases being heard. That means the jails are overcrowded with criminals. If CNN or the Red Cross rolls up and sees these overflowing jails we're gonna' look pretty bad."

"Well that's quite a laundry list there, Major," said the Judge unsteadily, the warmth gone from his voice.

"Yessir," Trevanathan said briskly, ignoring the dirty looks he was drawing from the other staff officers. "We're hoping someone from CPA will come out to our area. I understand there's a proclamation you all issued that CPA is in charge of all legal functions in the country. Problem is there's no one from CPA doing any Justice work outside of the Green Zone, so I don't understand how that is supposed to work."

"Well, Major," interrupted a bald-headed man with wire rim glasses, in a white pressed shirt on the judge's left, "there is supposed to be a regional CPA legal liaison who will serve your area, that is coming out from the States. He was,… uh,… ah, supposed to be here this month, but now it looks more like September. The, um, various Departments are in a fight over who is to fund it – Justice, State, DOD. The old bureaucratic dance, you know," he ended with a half-hearted, nervous laugh.

"So, while they are fighting over the funding, who is in charge?" asked Trevanathan. "Who is supposed to tell us what the mission is?"

"Well, uh…, right now, no one, per se. I mean, we are overseeing things from Baghdad, but… uh, we don't have anyone we can spare to put out in your area."

"Sir, my *area* is the entire southern half of Iraq. There's not even one person from CPA that can be spared? Someone must have planned for this, didn't they? It seems kind of important that there's some coordination to run the legal system of half the country."

"Major," cut in the Judge, his eyes having turned to ice. "We are very aware of the struggles going on all over Iraq to restore the judicial system. We have studied it extensively." He coughed momentarily, and took a long drink of ice water before continuing. "I have a report right here from the Center for Strategic and International Studies assessing what challenges await us." He tapped his fingertips on the cover of a neatly bound report. "But we have a shortage of manpower and available funds. You'll just have to do the best you can until we can get someone down to you."

"Sir, I don't mean to press," countered Trevanathan, as he resolved to do just that, "but what good is some think tank report out of Washington? That sort of…," Trevanathan caught himself before the word *crap* came out of his mouth. "That sort of… *information* is great to kick around in air conditioned offices back in DC – but we're *here* now. We have the on-the-ground information of what needs to be done *now*. We can see it ourselves. Don't we need to be telling Washington what needs to be done, rather than the other way around?"

"Major," interrupted the civil affairs colonel, who had remained silent until now. "I appreciate your… enthusiasm," he added, softening his tone slightly, while fixing Trevanathan with a stern glare. "But those issues are being worked out above your *level*. What we need to know is, can you do the job?"

Trevanathan returned the Colonel's stare. *The old Army game*, he thought: *Raise an unpleasant reality to your superiors and if they have no good answer, they challenge your commitment.* "Yes, sir," said Trevanathan, refusing to waiver. "We can do the job, but I need guidance as to what the job *is*. Majors don't make national policy. What do you want us to do with the large number of prisoners that are about to overflow the jails in our area? With the courts not working, it's becoming a real issue having so many people packed to a cell. It's gonna' turn real ugly if there's a riot."

"Well, I believe that is an issue for the local commanders to determine," Judge Carpenter interjected curtly. "I appreciate your input, Major. I really do. You just need to realize that the challenge before us is great and requires further study and reflection." Shifting his view down the table, he continued,

"OK, I think we've spent enough time on this. Sam, what is your status out there at Abu Graib?"

"Can't complain sir,…" began the next officer, an MP colonel who had scooted his chair several inches away from Trevanathan during his status report. Trevanathan looked around the room as the assembly perked up again. *They're all smiling and nodding like those little bobble-headed dogs in cars. Christ, I can only imagine what bullshit is being transmitted back to Washington, if these people don't even know what is going on.*

Smith leaned over and whispered in his ear, "You tried…"

"Wonderful," Trevanathan whispered back sarcastically. "That doesn't mean much though, does it?"

Chapter 18
The Buddha

Returning from their futile Baghdad mission, the Jaguar team approached Camp Babylon and the usual gauntlet of local village urchins who hung about the main gate. As long as they did not get in the roadway and obstruct traffic, the Marine gate guards tolerated their presence. A makeshift market had even sprung up a hundred meters from the gate, where troops could buy Iraqi counterfeit Babylonian artifacts, Arab porno DVDs and grilled chicken.

"You know what these kids need? – a football field," said Captain Smith emphatically, looking at the several dozen pre-teen youths on either side of the roadway. The boys waved souvenir Saddam dollars and Pepsi cans at the passing soldiers, while the girls shyly clustered behind them. "We played football all the damn time when I was a kid, and it kept us out of trouble."

"Well, I don't know about football," replied Doc, who was riding in the back of Jaguar Two. "But I have seen a buncha' these kids kickin' 'round a soccer ball whenever we pass that little village back there."

"Shit, we could do it!" said Smith getting excited by his own idea. "There's that big old empty field across from the village where people just dump their trash. We could turn it into a sports field for 'em."

"Ya' know what you're going to have to do if ya' wanna' do that," said Doc.

"What?"

"See the Buddha."

"See the Buddha?" Smith repeated nervously. "Do you think so?"

"Nothing worthwhile happens around here without the Buddha's blessing. You want a football field, you need the Buddha's blessing," finished Doc.

"But…, I have nothing to offer," said Smith sheepishly.

"Hmmm, that is a problem. You don't want to appear presumptuous. A proper showing of respect is required," added Doc solemnly.

The Buddha lived in the cement walled utility building behind the 538th TOC, just in front of the latrines. The building was considered prime real estate, as it had a small square cement pad outside its metal double doors which was shaded in the late afternoon. Shade is a commodity whose value cannot be underestimated in a country where not a single cloud appears in the sky from April through October. The shady square was where the Buddha held court and dispensed his wisdom to those wise enough and patient enough to listen to his message.

"Richard, how are you?" the Buddha greeted Smith pleasantly, as the officer and Abu approached. Smith had brought Abu along for support, as he knew the Buddha had held long, philosophical discussions with the translator in the past. The Buddha's throne, a metal folding chair, was rocked back against the side of the utility shed from which the large, barrel-chested advisor looked serenely out on his world. "Salaam, Abu" said the Buddha, casting a warm smile upon the translator.

"Good afternoon, Lieutenant Colonel Magee," answered Abu.

"Please,…call me George," the Buddha responded. "I tire sometimes of the formality around here, don't you?"

The Buddha reached down to his side and opened the cover of a small Styrofoam cooler, "Would you like a drink, gentlemen?" he asked, producing a chilled, glass bottle of Snapple iced tea from the ice-filled cooler.

Smith had not seen a glass bottle since leaving Fort Bragg – instead living off of the hot, plastic-bottled water that lay in pallets about the camp. The chilled smoke of the ice wafted into the dry desert air, and Smith felt himself fixated upon the cold drink in spite of himself. "Sir, where did you get that?" he blurted out, before catching himself in the midst of the *faux pas*. But the Buddha did not appear offended.

"Oh, some friends of mine run a shuttle between Kuwait and Baghdad," replied the Buddha lightly. "On occasion, I am able to help them out and they express their thanks in different ways," he said holding the now dripping bottle up and turning it slowly in his hand as the cool droplets of water ran down his large, hairy forearm. "Have one," he said, lightly tossing the bottle to Smith. "Abu, may I interest you in a beverage?" asked the Buddha. "Sweet tea? Cola? Espresso?"

"You are very kind, Colonel Magee…"

"George," corrected the Buddha.

"Thank you, George," replied Abu. "Tea would be very nice if you have it." Abu looked about doubtfully at the three-meter square concrete pad, which seemed to be lacking a tea service or anything else; only a rather hairy, slightly overweight officer with brownish hair flecked with gray (too long by military standards), sitting on a metal folding chair.

The Buddha reached behind his reclining metal chair and rapped twice on the door of the utility shed. In an instant, a small Iraqi boy of approximately eight years of age appeared through the door, followed by a gust of cold air from within. "Muhammad, would you be so kind as to prepare some tea for my friend, Abu?"

"Yes, Meester George," responded the boy, quickly disappearing back through the metal doors.

The "Buddha," as he was known in the 538th, was a character of mythical dimensions. He had served in every major military deployment of the US Army over the preceding 18 years, including Grenada, Haiti, Bosnia, Kosovo, Gulf War I, and now Iraq. Officially, he was the Brigade S4, which meant he was responsible for all supplies and logistics for the unit. Keeping a unit supplied, fueled, fed, and maintained in the harsh desert conditions of an Iraqi summer was a Herculean job, and yet, no one could ever recall having seen the Buddha do any actual work.

While other staff officers fretted, fumed, gnashed their teeth, and burned the midnight oil to accomplish their important duties, Lieutenant Colonel Magee appeared to expend no effort whatsoever. And yet, the unit was always well-supplied, the vehicles were always fueled, the troops were always fed, and the equipment was well-maintained. When the commander needed to discuss a matter with his S4, he knew to send a runner either to the motor pool, where Magee slept, to the utility shed where he held court, or to the in-ground pool that the Navy Seabees had created out of Saddam's fish pond. Now, rather than stocked with fish, it could often be found stocked with US Marines and one middle-aged, Army Reserve lieutenant colonel, who had developed a deep, pre-cancerous glow that George Hamilton would have envied.

It was rumored that Magee had traveled extensively throughout Asia and the Middle East as a college student, from which he had gained an extensive knowledge of the region and its people. It was further legend that he had once met the Dali Lama in India, an encounter from which his nickname had originated. He had served in the liberation of Kuwait during the First Gulf War, which he referred to in a tongue in cheek fashion, as "the first great patriotic war." In Gulf War I he had been responsible for assisting in the restoration of the Kuwaiti civil government after the Iraqi Army had brutally raped and looted that country.

"Ah, sir," Smith began, "Major T suggested that you might be running low on suntan lotion and asked me to drop this off." He produced a large bottle of SPF 45 sun block from his DCU cargo pocket.

"That William – such a considerate person," said the Buddha warmly, opening the bottle and slathering a generous portion of the lotion onto his large hairy arms. "Ask him to stop by later if he has a chance. I have a new batch of Cubanos that a friend of mine dropped by, and he might enjoy one."

"Will do, sir," said Smith, shifting from one foot to the other. "Ahhh, sir, Major T also mentioned that you might be able to help us out with a little project down in the village."

"What's that, Richard?" said the Buddha leaning his chair forward, with a sincere look of interest on his face.

"Well, sir, as you know there are a lot of kids hanging around the camp, stealing stuff, getting into trouble and such, and well,… we thought if they had someplace to play away from the camp that it might not be such a problem."

"So, you want to build a playground, Richard?" asked the Buddha in a friendly manner.

"Actually, more like a soccer field, sir. We, um, have some soccer balls from the Red Cross and we thought if we put together a sports field where that dump now sits, opposite the village, that it might be good for the kids. And maybe the adults would see that we were here to help them, ya' know?"

"I see," said the Buddha. "Very commendable, Richard. Very commendable. I'd be pleased to help with this project. However, please keep one thing in mind," he said pleasantly.

"What's that, sir?" asked Smith eagerly, encouraged by the direction of the conversation.

"Never forget, Richard," the Buddha continued in his friendly conversational tone, "that no matter what you do for the Iraqis, and however great the sacrifice you make for their well-being, that they will slit your throat for the change in your pocket if it is to their advantage."

Smith was stunned. His mouth could not form words, as he looked with quick embarrassment at Abu. Abu stared at the ground, saying nothing.

"Am I wrong, Abu? Have I misstated the situation?" asked the Buddha with a calm smile, as he produced a massive cigar from his cargo pocket and wetted it between his lips.

Abu remained silent, his cheeks flushing slightly darker.

"You see Richard, this country has been 'liberated' many times," explained the Buddha, as he lit the massive stogie. "As the cradle of civilization and a major crossroads, it has been the target of every conquering army to come down the pike over the past thirty centuries. Greeks, Assyrians, Hittites, Mongols, Turks, British, and now the Americans. They all came here to conquer and rebuild in their own image. And in each instance the people of this land outlasted them. Whether they were called Sumerians, Babylonians, Bedouins or Iraqis at the time, the locals smiled and tolerated the invaders. They cooperated, survived, and adapted to each occupier – right until the moment where they turned on them and cut their throats. Cigar?" he offered Smith, pulling another from his cargo pocket.

"Uhm, no,... no thanks. But maybe it will be different his time..." Smith began, before his uncertain voice trailed off.

"I hope so too, Richard, but never lose sight of the reality. If you care too much in this land, you will go home in a bag or a strait jacket. I know. I was here in 1991 when we liberated the Kuwaitis from Saddam and then encouraged the Shiites in Southern Iraq to rise up against him."

The Buddha paused for a moment, as he gathered his thoughts.

"I sat on an observation post near Safwan," he remembered, as he looked off into the distance and his eyes became slightly unfocused. "We watched Saddam's troops butcher the Shiites just a few hundred meters away, because Saddam had figured out that the US would not intervene beyond the Kuwaiti border after the cease-fire was signed. The Iraqi special security forces mocked us and lined up men, women and children, and shot them down in plain sight of our lines. They would shoot one in the back of the head and then wave at us to come over. They laughed and jeered, and then they shot the next one. And we did nothing. It was our *policy* not to intervene."

"But we are here to help now…," objected Smith weakly.

"These are a people who remember for centuries," countered the Buddha politely. "They remember an insult or a slight against their family from generation to generation. You probably can't remember what you had for lunch two days ago, but these people will remember an insult that occurred to their great-grandfather by the great-grandfather of a neighboring tribe. And they will wait for the right moment to restore the honor of their family and to exact their revenge upon the descendants of that offender, if it takes two hundred years."

"The blood feud…," Abu murmured under his breath.

"Now we have humiliated these people twice," continued the Buddha, "both in the first great patriotic war and now in the second. We stood by while Saddam butchered their families after we encouraged them to rebel after the first war. Now we have killed their young men again, and we have bombed their homes again. Do you think against that background that a soccer field really matters to these people? Do you think that it will tip the scale even slightly in their minds as to our intentions?"

"I don't know, sir," said Smith, embarrassed that he had brought Abu to hear this. Even though Abu was Kuwaiti, Smith felt that as a Muslim he must take offense at the remarks. "But, I'm going to give it a try still, if you'll help."

"Of course, Richard," concluded the Buddha, as the young boy reappeared from within the shed with a silver tray holding three frosted glass tea cups. "For God and country. Just give me the grid coordinates where to be and I'll see what I can do."

Chapter 19
The Field

"Let's get moving, men," yelled Captain Smith into the enlisted area of their quarters. "We need to get working on this before it gets too hot."

"Roger, sir, be right there," said Staff Sergeant Leader. "Cooper!" he called across the room, as he fumbled with the button-up fly on his DCUs. "Time for your morning feeding. Get over here," he called in his thick Philly accent. Cooper just laughed and shook his head at Leader's off-color humor as he reached down to grab his M16 with one hand and an entrenching shovel with the other.

"All right, let's load 'em up," Warden barked through the main doorway. "This train is leaving."

Both the Jaguars and the medical team had donated their "day off," which came once every two weeks, to clearing the dump across the road from the village to create a soccer field. . Despite the worthy goal of having the local children use the sports field, rather than hanging around the dangerous road begging from convoys, Smith had been unable to convince the POD or the commander to designate it as an official Army project. "We build one soccer field and pretty soon everyone will want one," had been Burr's response, to which Colonel Hermann quietly demurred. Unable to get duty time for the mission, Smith had coordinated their off-time to make it happen.

In official Army parlance, the Jaguars were identified as CAT[46] B on the unit manning roster. Led by Major Trevanathan or "Major T," as he was now known to everyone, their primary mission focus was on government reconstruction. CAT A, known as the "Medical Team," was actually a hybrid team including medical, education, and "monuments," the latter discipline focused on preserving buildings and articles of historical importance wherever the Army might be operating. Tanks and old historical buildings generally do not play well together, so CAT A was in charge of coordinating unit actions, wherever possible, so that damage to old mosques, museums, and other historical sites would be minimized. Chaplain (Captain) Clay was dual-hatted as the 538th chaplain and the unit's monuments officer.

---

[46] Civil Affairs Team

As with the Jaguars, the Med team consisted of eight soldiers and two HMMWVs. Doc Heller was in charge of CAT A and was ranking officer aboard the HMMWV dubbed "Red Raider One." Red Raider One was driven by Private Tyler Jamie, a round faced young Texan with a future in NASCAR if his operation of Red Raider One was any indication.

Sitting behind Private Jamie, and manning the team's SAW was Sergeant Ramon Moncuso, a darkly handsome Latino of Mexican descent, who had earned the nickname "Monkeybusiness" due to his unquenchable thirst for female companionship and his impressive track record in obtaining it. Moncuso also had a gift with engines and mechanical parts that made him invaluable to the 538th in the harsh desert conditions that frequently brought the unit's vehicles to – literally – a grinding halt.

Chaplain Clay was the rear passenger side occupant. Clay, a likeable Methodist pastor, was on his first overseas deployment with the Army. He struggled daily with his role in keeping soldiers emotionally and spiritually fit enough so that they could continue a mission that might get them killed or result in the deaths of others.

"Red Raider Two" was the mutt of the unit: it was routinely pressed into service as the catch-all vehicle for carrying out a number of different missions. Corporal Tommy Sands was its driver and was renowned in the Texan faction of the 538th for never having been heard to utter more than two or three words a day. This was due, some hypothesized, to concern that with his slow Texas drawl he might run out of time to finish a full sentence before the sun went down. Sands was also the unofficial librarian of the unit, having the largest collection of comic books and pornography on the base.

The front passenger seat occupant of Red Raider Two was Captain Tammy Spandex, part of the Alabama contingent that BG Merdier had sent to "oversee" the 538th's mission. A modern dance teacher, the appropriately named Captain Spandex was the type of positive and cheerful person that everyone liked.

"I hate her," said Sergeant Floyd Saxe, the third member of Red Raider Two. "I knew she was bad news the second I laid eyes on her. Who brings a powder blue suitcase to a combat zone for God's sakes? It was absolutely frickin' embarrassing, standing there on the flight line at Pope Air Force Base, with her dragging that 'Barbie' case behind her. Those Air Force pukes were laughing their heads off at us." Saxe was the Public Affairs NCO for the Brigade, and it was his job to deal with the press, if any, and to get stories about the unit placed in newspapers back home to show the hometowns the good things their brave boys and girls were doing.

The last member of the Med team was First Lieutenant (1LT) Beth Gleason, a surgical nurse from Timonium, Maryland. A former enlisted Marine, Gleason was fully qualified as a combat medic, although her official duty title in the 538th was "Deputy Public Health officer."

On this day, however, both CAT A and CAT B had stepped outside respective areas of expertise to build a soccer field. Coordination with the village elders had been made by Smith and Abu the day before, so the locals would not be afraid of the sudden arrival of so many soldiers and equipment on their doorstep. The village of Al Salaam had benefited greatly from its close proximity to the Marine base, and the 538th had run several public health education programs in the village to emphasize disease prevention and nutrition. The Iraqi children reaped a continuous flow of candy that they wheedled from kind-hearted Marines and soldiers. Several of the village men had jobs on the base, working in the laundry or the mess hall, which brought hard dollars into the local economy, which were more stable than the wildly fluctuating Iraqi dinar.

Accordingly, the entire village of a hundred or so was waiting when the four HMMWVs rolled up to begin the project. Children smiled and waved at the reservists, chanting their usual greeting of "candy, meester; candy." The village elders came forth and solemnly shook hands with Trevanathan and Smith, thanking them and Allah for the generosity of the Americans. Women clustered together in the background, smiling with stained teeth and enjoying the festive atmosphere.

Following the perfunctory greetings, Trevanathan surveyed the site. The field lay along the opposite side of the two-lane road that ran past the village. Al Salaam was a collection of a couple of dozen brick buildings that sat between the road and the same Euphrates River canal that marked the western boundary of Camp Babylon. The village sat roughly two miles downstream from the camp, and on the same side. The distinguishing feature of the village, of which all of the villagers were extremely proud, was their modest two-story mosque. A leftover from the Middle Ages when Al Salaam had been much larger, the mosque was the religious and social center of the villagers' world. A light green, onion-style dome and a two-and-a-half story minaret towered proudly over the otherwise nondescript and hodge-podge collection of dirt colored buildings.

The area for the new soccer field was a flat, sun-baked patch of scrub and brambles, perhaps a mile square, bordered on its west side by a shallow irrigation ditch and the road. To the north, the field blended into low, rolling hills that faded into the distance. Two hundred meters south of the field, a large man-made hill rose steeply out of the plain. Legend was that Saddam had planned to construct a magnificent mosque on top that would have been visible from his palace.

A herd of goats picked amongst the trash that had accumulated on the near side of the site, which the villagers had been using as a dump for any items they could not easily pitch into the canal. The piles of accumulated trash suddenly looked larger to Trevanathan, now that the moment to remove them had arrived. "Rick, when was Lieutenant Colonel McGee going to be here?" he asked, scrupulously avoiding the use of the nickname "Buddha" due to the presence of civilians.

"0630, sir," Smith replied, looking about for any sign of additional help arriving.

"Well, it's 0650. I'm sure he'll be here, but maybe we should get started," said Trevanathan.

"Right. OK, Sergeant Warden, let's break out the tools and start cleaning up this area."

Although still early, the July morning temperature was already nearing 110 degrees. The 538th soldiers began to attack the widely spread trash pile with enthusiasm, stripping down to brown T-shirts to work. Their first objective was to centralize the trash, after which they would haul it away, clearing a space large enough for the new soccer field. As the sun rose higher, sweat quickly soaked their uniforms, but it felt good to be exerting effort on something tangible for a change.

The village elders had retreated back into the village after the obligatory pleasantries, as had the women. The children remained watching until it became clear that no more candy was coming their way, at which point they too wandered off. Several middle-aged men gathered beneath a gnarled tree that afforded them some shade, smoking cigarettes and critiquing the work being performed.

"They will never complete it," said one villager wearing a faded blue man-dress. "The Americans always try to do too much."

"Are they doing us a favor?" asked a second, who bore a long scar across his nose and right cheek. "We will have to walk further to dispose of our garbage. The dump was convenient."

"It will be good for the children," said a third who wore the traditional red and white checked khafir headdress. "But they are crazy to work during the day. It is too hot and they are not used to it."

"Their women work with them," spat a fourth man, a portly and sour-looking man missing the fingers of his left hand. "Look at them. It is a disgrace that this occurs on our soil. Look at that one," he gestured toward Captain Spandex, who was raking garbage into the growing pile. "Her breasts are there for the entire world to feast their eyes upon. Is this of benefit to our children?"

"It is of benefit to me," cackled a wizened older man who sat slightly apart from the others.

"Yes, you who already has four wives you do not care for. Very nice," retorted the man with the missing fingers with apparent disdain.

The old man shrugged and continued to watch Spandex work.

"Sahr, how 'bout I go give a shovel to them hajis sitting there in the shade and invite them to join the fun?" Warden asked the Major as he wiped sweat from his brow with a camouflage handkerchief.

"Give it time, Sergeant Warden," replied Trevanathan, pausing from his shoveling. "They probably aren't sure if we'd welcome their help. Let's just create a good example and they'll likely join in on their own."

"With all due respect, sahr, Ah've yet to see any haji in this country do much in the way of physical labor. Even the ones workin' on post mostly sit round in the shade waitin' for someone to tell 'em to move. Ah think they're just happy to see someone else bustin' their ass instead of them."

"Yeah, I know," replied Trevanathan, "but we gotta' remember that Iraq under Saddam was basically a socialist country. There was no reward for working harder. It's gonna' take a while for these folks to understand that they can build their own future."

"Well, Ah hope ya don't mind if Ah don't hold my breath, sahr," concluded Warden, returning to his work.

The low rumble of an approaching convoy came from the direction of the camp. *Must be a big one*, thought Trevanathan as he turned back to his work. *Maybe Bradleys?* he wondered, thinking of the large US armored personnel carriers used for scout work.

"Sir, sir – it's Lieutenant Colonel McGee," hollered Ridlin, pointing down the road at a long train of vehicles coming over a slight rise.

It was indeed the Buddha, standing upright in the open gunner's hatch of the lead HMMWV, a large cigar clenched between his teeth. He looked like a conquering general, leading a triumphal parade into his capital. In his DCUs and aviator glasses he made an impressive picture. What followed behind him was even more impressive, however: a platoon of Navy Seabees, with their two-and-a-half ton trucks, excavators, backhoes, bulldozers, graders, and a vehicle-mounted carpentry shop; a dozen heavy vehicles in all.

Smith stood in awe. He had hoped that maybe the Buddha would have been able to conjure up a few more strong backs and some tools for the project. Instead, McGee had brought a major portion of the construction resources available on Camp Babylon.

The convoy turned off onto a side-road over the irrigation ditch, and out onto the field. The HMMWV carrying the Buddha wheeled away from the others, and Navy engineers poured from their vehicles and began setting up for work. As blue-shirted sailors moved like relentless ants to assemble a small headquarters tent, a bulldozer bit into the soil.

The Buddha's HMMWV pulled up next to Trevanathan and Smith, and McGee dismounted before the speechless officers. "Good morning William, Richard," the senior officer greeted each in his calm, even voice. "I do apologize for being late. Our efforts required some further, …coordination to get the equipment off-post."

"Sir, this is amazing," gushed Smith, watching several sailors begin to survey the ground and lay boundaries for the field.

"I'm glad you're pleased, Richard. CPO[47] Baldwin and I came out last evening and looked at the area. With your permission, our plan is to put in the field running from east to west, one hundred meters long, with a modest set of bleachers running here along the road. We've brought in some extra dirt to level the field out. Is that acceptable?"

"Aaahh, yes, yessir," said Smith, still in shock at the scope of activity before him. "That would be great."

The Buddha spent the remainder of the day sitting on a soccer chair beneath a canopy erected for him along the roadway, smoking cigars and discussing Eastern philosophy with Abu, who had arrived with him. His right-hand assistant, Sergeant Major Wren, known as "Smadge" to her friends, coordinated activity with Smith and responded to questions from the Seabees.

Major Trevanathan approached the Buddha in his shrine, politely declined the offered cigar, and said, "Thanks anyway, sir, but this dust is playing hell with my breathing, and a smoke probably wouldn't help. I just wanted to thank you for making this happen. It means a lot to Rick."

"My pleasure, William. I know it means a lot to him, but that could be a problem in this country."

"What do you mean, sir?"

"Hopefully nothing, William. Would you care for a Snapple?"

Hours later, as the sun dipped toward the tops of the date palms in the west, the field had been magically transformed from a scrubby wasteland to a first class, hard-packed soccer field. Crisp, white chalk lines delineated the boundaries. Goals, constructed from four-inch surplus piping and Army camouflage netting stood solidly at each end. A small, four-tier set of stands, from which parents could watch their children, sat proudly beside the road.

---

[47] Chief Petty Officer, Navy equivalent to an Army Sergeant First Class.

The Seabees had even built a small scoreboard with the name "Salaam/Peace Field" lettered across the top. Once again, without apparent personal effort, the Buddha had accomplished the impossible.

"It's beautiful," Smith breathed, looking out over the field, as the last of the weary, but satisfied Jaguars loaded into their vehicles for the short trip back to camp. The smell of fresh turned earth, paint, and varnish filled the air. No sooner had the last Seabee vehicle left the field, than a parade of gleeful children broke from the village with a new soccer ball to inaugurate their gift.

Chapter 20
The Cloud

Morale rose perceptively within the unit during the last days of July. First, Colonel Hermann had cancelled the POD's morning physical training regimen, after a Marine Corps reservist had dropped dead during his own unit's training run in the oppressive summer heat. More significantly, though, the soccer field project had given unit members a sense of leaving a positive mark upon the country's restoration, albeit in a small way. Even those who had not been able to work on the project directly took pride in their unit's contribution. Most important, though, August would mark the sixth month since arriving in theater, and the rumor mill was ripe with stories that they would soon receive orders home.

But this morning, duty called again, with the Jaguars tasked to travel to the provincial capital of Al Kut, three hours to the east, so that Trevanathan could look into why the local judges were not yet hearing criminal cases. The reports from the Marine Governate Support Team (GST)[48] in Al Kut, indicated that the judges in Wasit Province claimed to be confused as to what law to apply, and so were not hearing cases. Trevanathan recognized the now familiar excuse used by many judges in other provinces under his supervision, who did not want to be perceived by the fledgling insurgent movement as cooperating with the Americans. He also knew that these judges did not want to give up their prestigious and relatively lucrative positions. After using reason failed to obtain the desired results, Trevanathan had quickly learned that threatening to fire the Chief Judge usually caused the local judiciary to suddenly remember the law. Trevanathan would use that effective message again today to the Chief Judge in Al Kut.

The team exited the main gate, with Jaguar One in the lead, as usual. Waves of heat were already shimmering across the blacktop despite the early hour. Winding around the familiar curves on the two lane road running from the camp to Highway 8, Trevanathan looked expectantly ahead to where the soccer field would soon appear. "Oh-my-God," he uttered flatly as the village

---

[48] GSTs were small groups of civil affairs personnel that worked to restore essential functions within the Iraqi governates. Ultimately, their goal was to supervise the return of these functions to responsible Iraqi control.

came into view. The soccer field was gone - completely obliterated. No remnant remained: the goals, stands and scoreboard were missing; the carefully graded playing surface was torn apart, pitted with ragged holes. A small heap of newly-discarded garbage was strewn across the traditional location next to the irrigation ditch.

"Stop," was all Trevanathan could say. Cooper complied and pulled off the left side of the road.

Jaguar Two pulled in behind, but Smith did not dismount. He sat, looking at the wreckage of his project through the windshield. He felt numb as he struggled to make sense of the scene before him.

Trevanathan dismounted and walked back to Smith's HMMWV, noting his friend's stare and clenching fists.

"I don't even know why the hell we're here anymore," said Smith, his shoulders slumped with despair.

"Men, could you give us a minute?" said Trevanathan to the remaining occupants of Jaguar Two, who nodded and quickly moved out of hearing range.

Trevanathan said nothing, deciding to let Smith get it off his chest.

Trevanathan looked toward the village, where several small changes were apparent. Pieces of Army camouflage netting hung from several of the windows facing the roadway. New sections of four-inch pipe had been laid from the northern base wall of the mosque, draining wastewater out onto the flat. Two women worked a fresh pile of dark soil into their meager garden on the left side of the village.

Smith's gaze followed Trevanathan's toward the village. "How the hell do you help a people who steal dirt?" he lamented.

Trevanathan remained silent.

"How do you help a people who will steal a chance for happiness from their own children so they can lay sewer pipe and patch windows?" he added, his sense of outrage growing. "I left my wife and kids to help these damn people! We kill ourselves, working our asses off, while they sit in the shade smoking and drinking Pepsi! We patrol their goddamn roads and get our legs blown off to make their country safer, and they don't give a rat's *ass!*" Smith's voice was raised and trembling with anger.

"This is a waste," he added, his voice softening and moisture welling up in his eyes. "The whole mission – a God-damned *waste*."

"It doesn't matter," said Trevanathan, looking calmly at the agitated Smith.

Shocked, Smith raised his head, looking through misty eyes to read Trevanathan's expression. His face displayed no emotion .

"What do ya' mean, it doesn't matter? It sure as hell matters to me!"

"The soccer field,…it really doesn't matter. The fact they tore it down. It doesn't matter."

"Jesus, what do you mean it doesn't matter?" asked Smith, his voice rising again. "Of course it matters. We killed ourselves to build that field. We gave up our free time. We worked in this God-awful heat, and they spit in our face. Don't tell me it doesn't matter," he emphasized by jabbing his finger in the general direction of the field. A tear ran down his right cheek, which he quickly brushed away with his dirty sleeve.

"Rick, it sounds harsh, but this mission is not about whether this two-donkey village has a soccer field or not. Whether they have a sports field or don't have a field isn't going to make a bit of difference in the future of this country. Whether we fix their schools or repair their hospitals. In the long run it doesn't matter."

"How can you say that? It's the reason we're here. If it doesn't matter, this is all a colossal waste of time."

"No, it's not," said Trevanathan evenly. "We've been told we're here to build schools and fix oil pipes and all that other crap. But it's not true. Just as they told us we were here to find chemical weapons that didn't exist. Just as the cynics say we're here to get the oil. It's all bullshit."

"What are we here for, then?" said Smith looking hard at Trevanathan.

"We're here to free these people," said Trevanathan. "We're here to try to free them from their lousy past and from themselves."

"Hmphh," snorted Smith.

"Rick, fifty years from now no one is going to remember the job you and I did here. They won't remember how many courthouses we rebuilt or how many miles of pipeline the Army repaired. They certainly won't remember this crummy little soccer field. Look, these people aren't gonna' change – not the adults anyway. These are the same people who applauded while Saddam raped Kuwait. These are the people who stayed silent when Saddam gassed women and babies in Kurdistan. These are the same stinkin' people who reported their neighbors to the secret police for real or imaginary offenses, before their neighbors could first drop a dime on them. Their lives revolve around fear and hate, and that's all they're ever gonna' know. Whether we build them a soccer field or get them clean water, they're not gonna' be grateful. They'll just say it was Allah's will and keep on plantin' their roadside bombs to kill the only people in the whole damn world who care whether they live or die."

"If you're trying to cheer me up, you're doing a shitty job. Why bother then?" asked Smith searchingly. "How do you stay so committed to trying to make a difference then?"

"The children," said Trevanathan. "The children can make the difference."

"How?" said Smith doubtfully. "They'll just grow up like their parents."

"They can't make a difference now," said Trevanathan. "Our current focus is all wrong. The President and all his cronies are trying to convince people that they can turn this place around in a few years. It's always next Spring or next Fall that things will be better. That's horseshit and they're either naive or just lying through their teeth. You don't take centuries of brutality and oppression and make it disappear overnight. All these people have known is hate and fear their entire lives."

"Yeah," said Smith without enthusiasm.

"But these street urchins who follow us around can make the difference. They haven't been poisoned yet. If we can show them there's a different way – that there's decency, commitment, and compassion in the world. Then, we will have made a difference here."

"That's a noble sentiment," said Smith. "But I don't see it."

"Rick, these kids are the same as kids anywhere in the world. They follow the lead of what they see. When I was stationed in Germany, families were cut in half by the Iron Curtain. I was stationed ten kilometers from the Wall dividing Germany when it came down. On our side the German people were smart, motivated, industrious. When we drove just ten klicks into East Germany the German people there were unmotivated, lazy, and selfish. They were a lot like the Iraqis. They wanted all the benefits of life in the West, without working for it. Same families, same gene pool. Completely different results."

"I suppose," said Smith slowly. "I saw that sort of thing in Croatia, too."

"Exactly. It's not the people. It's what they've been exposed to. 'The tree grows the way the twig is bent' sort of concept. You can't bend the tree once it's in middle age. That just causes it to snap. You've got to catch it while it's young. The difference we can make for Iraq is just by being here. By showing the kids the meaning of selfless service. By showing them the effort of trying to make their lives better – whether it results in a soccer field or not.

"Look, these kids are going to grow up. Had we not come, their view of the world would have continued to be the same as today's lazy, selfish adults, living in fear and hatred, trying to squeeze out some angle to outmaneuver their neighbors. We're trying to show them something different."

"We haven't shown 'em much yet, by the looks of things," Smith gestured toward the abused field.

"They don't understand it yet, but we're showing them a different way of life – an Army that comes to help, not to abuse them. We show them hard work and dedication. We show them that somebody cares. The importance of this won't sink in while they're kids, but when they get older and it is their turn to run this rathole, maybe they'll remember. They may remember that service and working for the betterment of their country is more important than lining their pockets with bribes. As far as I'm concerned, if I can keep even one kid from becoming another lazy, selfish, Haji SOB, then the mission is worth it. It's worth it because that kid becomes a seed who can carry the word to his children and his grandkids that there is a better way of life and that they can take responsibility for their actions instead of sitting around waiting for Allah to do it for them."

"Well, you have a lot more optimism than I do," said Smith, laughing bitterly. "I still think these people suck."

"Hah!" Trevanathan, laughed. "I think they suck too. I'm just willing to put the effort into making them suck less in the future. Now screw 'em. Let's do our mission"

Chapter 21
The Prison

Trevanathan walked into Judge Elizar's Hillah office, rendering the traditional greeting, "Salaam Alekim." The Chief Judge sprang from his seat and rounded the corner of his desk with his hands extended in greeting. "Hello, mister, hello," he replied with enthusiasm. The Iraqis called all US troops "mister," whether they were a colonel or a private. The judge took Trevanathan by the elbow and guided him to the sofa where he had sat during the previous visit.

"Your honor, I have both good news and bad news," began Trevanathan. "My most recent visit to Baghdad was successful and the officials at CPA indicated that they will provide whatever law books and research materials you need for the court."

"Ah, that is very good," replied the judge. "You are most generous," he smiled and nodded.

"I was also successful in obtaining the release of funds to pay every worker their back salary. However, there will not be a regular pay system in place until the Ministry of Finance approves a budget for the rest of the year. So, I cannot tell you when the next pay will come."

"Enshalla[49], it will come," said the judge.

"I would like to have the court employees gather in the main lobby tomorrow morning at 9, and we will distribute the money I have been given."

"You do not need to bother yourselves," replied the judge, a gleam coming into his eye. "Were you to leave the money with me, I can divide it among the workers."

Recognizing what a bad move this would be, Trevanathan responded politely, "You are very generous with your time. But my orders make it clear that I must be the one to distribute the money."

"As you wish," said the judge, slightly disappointed over the lost opportunity.

---

[49] Arabic for "If it is God's will."

"The other matter of importance is that I have been asked to check the conditions of the jail and determine whether there is sufficient space for the current prisoners," added Trevanathan.

"Aaah; there is much space," replied the judge. "Since we transferred the prisoners to the camp at Um Qasr, crowding is no longer a problem."

"That's good. Who can arrange for me to see the jail?"

"I will take you now if you wish," said the judge proudly. "It is only next door."

"Great," said Trevanathan, standing, "let's go, then."

The two men, followed by Warden and Abu, walked down the back stairway, out a rusted metal door and across the small alley behind the courthouse. Entering a small passageway leading to a side courtyard, Trevanathan saw a guard dressed in the green work shirt and pants of many Iraqi security personnel, sitting asleep on a chair before the door to the jail. A folded AK-47 rifle lay across his lap as he snored away, oblivious to the arrival of the guests.

The Chief Judge said something sharply in Arabic, which Abu translated to Trevanathan in a whisper, "He calls him the son of a dog." Walking past the still-sleeping guard and through the heavy metal door of the jail, the three men entered a large, poorly-lit room. A fat Iraqi guard with epaulets designating some level of authority sat across the room ten meters away, pushing a large baked chicken into his face. An SKS rifle lay propped against the wall next to him. He looked up at the group and quickly jumped to his feet, wiping chicken grease from his heavy mustache with the sleeve of his uniform.

The guard approached the Chief Judge without looking at the two Americans and began jabbering something in Arabic in an animated fashion, his arms and hands flying in the air in frustration and displeasure. Judge Elizar responded in an equally animated manner, pointing to the two Americans and slapping the back of his right hand into the palm of the other, as he spoke.

"Abu, what are they saying?" asked Trevanathan.

Abu related, "The corporal of the guard says that he was given no notice that there were to be visitors today. He says that it is not possible for the Chief Judge to come here today without first clearing the visit through the Chief of Police."

"Where's the Chief of Police?"

"That is what the Chief Judge is asking. The guard says that he is not here and will not be back until after the weekend. He says that it is impossible to visit now."

"Sir, if I may?" interrupted Warden. "I think I can work this out, one NCO to another."

"Go ahead," answered Trevanathan.

"Abu," began Warden, "Tell this terrerist shitbag that if he leaves my officer standing here for one more second that I am going to personally kick his ass all over this jail. I will hit him so hard I will kill his entire family."

Abu's eyes bulged. "Sergeant, I cannot say such a thing," he stammered.

"Oh, you can and you will. I'll be able to tell if you say it the way I did."

"Sir," Abu turned to Trevanathan in appeal. "I cannot speak to this man in this way."

"Sorry, Abu, this is NCO business. I can't interfere." Trevanathan replied, trying to suppress a smile at Warden's usual direct way of dealing with "local" issues.

With a look of despair on his face, Abu turned toward the guard and began speaking slowly in Arabic. The accuracy of Abu's translation was confirmed by the widening of the fat corporal's eyes. When Abu finished, the guard looked at Warden, took a step back, and replied, "Nahm (yes), Colonel," before stepping aside and waving them through with his arm.

"Very effective, *Colonel*," Trevanathan said to Warden with a grin, as he stepped past the shaken guard.

The jail was a simple arrangement. A glass-windowed control room sat just inside the door to the left of the vestibule they had entered. From the control room, a single corridor ran back into the cellblock. The walls were all painted a pale, institutional green: light green on the upper two thirds of the wall and dark green on the bottom. A single bulb hanging from a bare wire halfway down the corridor barely illuminated the dim, 20-meter passageway. Halfway down the hallway Trevanathan saw a large metal gate filling the right wall from floor to ceiling. It looked like a cell from an old western movie. On the left wall, opposite the gate, was a heavy, metal-banded door with a viewing slit. Warden followed closely behind Trevanathan, with Abu and the judge trailing in their wake. The guard remained at his post in the vestibule, smarting over the tongue lashing the "Colonel" had delivered.

As they proceeded down the hallway, the strong smell of institutional cleanser was slowly overpowered by the reek of human waste coming from the barred cell. Reaching the gate and looking into the dark interior, Trevanathan's saw nothing at first. The ten by fifteen meter chamber appeared empty – just a cold, dark room without lights, into which the shadows of the dangling bulb played. As his eyes adjusted to the dimness, though, Trevanathan saw two figures huddled against the back wall, their faces buried in folded arms atop their knees.

"Abu, come here," said Trevanathan, almost gagging when he forgot for a second to breathe only through his mouth. "Ask these men what they are in here for."

Abu called to the men. Two thin, middle-aged men rose slowly to their feet and approached the gate. The shorter of the two, barely Abu's height, appeared to be limping slightly. The two men said nothing, but approached cautiously as if stepping toward an unknown danger.

"Abu, tell them that I am here from the American Army and need to know what they are charged with," directed the Major.

Abu spoke to the men, and the one with the limp replied quietly in Arabic.

"He says that they were arrested for looting by an American patrol and brought here. He says it is a case of mistaken identity, as he was helping his cousin move his goods from his old house to a new house."

Trevanathan noticed a large weeping sore running down the front of the man's left shin. It seemed to pain him greatly when he placed any weight upon it. "Abu, call the corporal," Trevanathan directed. The corporal came waddling down the hallway when called, licking chicken grease from his pudgy fingers. He glanced at the prisoners without interest.

"Has this man had any medical treatment?" Trevanathan asked the corporal, pointing at the short prisoner. "That wound looks infected."

"No, Colonel," replied the guard through Abu. "We sent for a doctor when he was brought in three days ago, but the doctor refused to come. There is no money to pay him, so he will not come."

"How long will he remain here?" asked Trevanathan.

"Until the investigating magistrate completes his investigation, your excellency," the corporal replied. "It may be a week or even two. The judges have not been working either, due to the lack of money."

"That is a lie!" hissed the Chief Judge.

Trevanathan reached back into the fanny pack that dangled from the rear of his LBE.[50] Unzipping the pouch, he pulled out a tube of antibiotic ointment he carried for the minor cuts and scrapes that could otherwise turn nasty in the filthy Iraqi environment. He knelt near the bars and told Abu to have the man stick his wounded leg through the bars. Abu complied and as the man extended his leg, Trevanathan involuntarily pulled back with an oath.

"Jesus Christ," he exclaimed. "His feet and legs are covered with shit!" Looking behind the prisoners, Trevanathan could now see that streaks of fecal matter covered the floor and walls of the cell. "Don't these guys have a place to take a dump?" Trevanathan asked, turning angrily toward the guard.

Nervously, through Abu, the corporal replied, "General, they were given a pot in which to relieve themselves, but they broke it. There is no replacement. They must make due."

Trevanathan said to Warden. "This damn place makes a medieval French prison look like a palace."

"These people are animals, sahr. It's their way."

---

[50] Load Bearing Equipment – Army term for the belt and suspenders on which troops carry their equipment.

168

Trevanathan leaned closer to Warden and said, quietly, "Can that kind of talk, OK? I sense the judge understands more English than he is letting on."

"Sorry, sir."

Trevanathan turned back to the prisoners. "Abu, tell the one with the leg wound that I am leaving this medicine with him. There's no way I'm touching that. He should smear it on his leg four times each day and try to keep his leg out of the crap, OK?"

Abu translated and replied on behalf of the prisoner, "He said you are most merciful, sir."

"Wonderful," replied Trevanathan. "OK, now tell the judge I want these men brought before the magistrate tomorrow and either charged or released. No excuses."

Abu complied and the judge responded that he would make it happen. The judge then spoke to Abu in a low voice, away from the guard. Abu then sidled up next to Trevanathan and spoke softly in English. "Sir, the judge says that you are most compassionate to help this despised man. But he said you should know that your generosity will be wasted."

"Why?"

"The judge says that as soon as you leave, either the stronger prisoner will beat him to get the medicine or that the corporal will steal it to sell for himself. He says that the injured man will not keep it either way."

Trevanathan shook his head and sighed. "Allah the merciful and compassionate," he said in a low voice to himself.

"OK gents, here's the deal. Abu, you tell the corporal to keep the medicine. Tell him I am holding him personally responsible to see that the prisoner gets the medicine on his wound every four hours. Tell him that 'Colonel' Warden will be coming back tomorrow to check that it has happened. If it has not, or if the medicine is missing, he will answer to Colonel Warden."

As Abu translated, the corporal looked nervously from Trevanathan to Warden, both of whom glared menacingly.

"He says it will be done, *General* and that he thanks you for your mercy," replied Abu in translation.

"I bet," said Trevanathan. "OK, what chamber of horrors lies behind *Door Number Three*, here?" He gestured toward the large metal door with the sliding viewport.

"That is the women's section, sir," Abu translated.

"*Really?*" asked the Major, his curiosity piqued as he had not really thought of Muslim women being a "criminal" element. "Any prisoners?"

"Yes, sir, there are two," translated Abu from the guard.

"What are the charges?"

"Murder, sir," translated Abu. "A mother and daughter killed their nephew cousin."

"*Really?*" said Trevanathan, again surprised that such a thing would happen in a male dominated society. "Let's open it up."

The fat corporal looked through the sliding viewport, and then unlocked the heavy door with a large, iron key. The door swung into the corridor to reveal a much brighter room, cleaner than the barred cell, but again without furniture. The smaller room, perhaps 7 meters by 10 meters, was painted the same institutional green. Light streamed in through opaque transom-style windows on the far wall, set behind bars fifteen feet above the floor. On a small ceramic platform in the far left corner of the room was the opening of a "Turkish" style toilet – the standard throughout Iraq.

On the floor sat two figures, huddled together with their burkhas intertwined such that one could not see where one form began and the other finished. The women looked at the guard with disinterest as he opened the door, but their eyes widened in fear as the American soldiers strode into the room. Seeing their reaction, Trevanathan told Abu, "Let them know we are not here to hurt them. That this is a routine inspection." The look of fear and distrust did not dissipate as Abu relayed the message.

"Abu, ask them how they are being treated here." Abu complied and the older woman said a few words in Arabic, the younger woman remaining silent.

"The old woman says they have been treated well, sir." Trevanathan wondered if the answer was the truth or if asking the question without the guard present would reveal a different answer.

Not willing to take the guard at his word regarding their crime, Trevanathan asked, "Ask them what they are charged with." In response, the woman said a few words. Before Abu could translate she added several more, and finally she let loose with a flood of rapid speech that continued uninterrupted for the better part of two minutes, complete with animated hand motions and arm waving.

"The old woman says they are charged with the death of her nephew," Abu translated when she stopped. The "old woman," as Abu referred to her, was probably in her late thirties, but the Iraqi sun had a way of aging one's skin so that people looked decades beyond their true age.

"That was a whole lot of arm waving and speaking for that one sentence. Listen Abu, I need you to tell me *everything*. *Every* time. You are not to select what to translate and what to not translate, got it? We've talked about this before." Trevanathan glared at Abu, as the translator shifted uncomfortably from foot to foot.

"Yes, sir," Abu replied. "The old woman explained that her daughter was violated by Iraqi troops that had deserted from the army during the American advance. Many of them threw away their weapons and uniforms and tried to blend into the towns. This group of deserters attacked her daughter on the way home from school. They kept her for hours before they let her go."

"So the cousin was one of these rapists?" Trevanathan asked with disgust.

"Oh, no, sir," continued Abu. "In our culture if a woman permits herself to be defiled in this manner she brings shame upon the entire family. That stain can only be cleaned away by her marriage to the man with whom she had relations."

"Charming custom," Warden stated from behind Trevanathan, with obvious derision in his voice.

"So, what's the deal with the cousin?"

"The young woman had no brothers to perform the task, so her cousin was chosen by the elders of the tribe to remove the stain from the family honor. When he sought to perform his duty, the girl resisted and the old woman stabbed him from behind."

"I don't understand," said Trevanathan. "How was he to remove the stain?"

Abu looked at Trevanathan as if he were a simpleton for not recognizing the obvious. "It was his family duty as her closest male relative to put her to death, sir." Abu said it with an air that nothing could be more obvious under the circumstances.

"And so,...they are in here because they did not let her be killed?" Trevanathan asked, incredulous.

"No, sir," said Abu. "They are charged with murder for the death of the cousin."

"Sounds like self-defense," said Trevanathan. "Abu, ask the judge what the law says about such a situation in Iraq."

After several moments of conversation, Abu replied, "The judge says that such honor killings are not permitted under the laws of Iraq, but it is recognized that they occur. When one happens, it is usually left to the sheikh of the tribe to decide whether there was a basis for the action. If the man is brought before the court and is found guilty he will be jailed for six months – or maybe a year in a very bad case, if he is cruel."

"But what about the women? What if they are found responsible for killing the cousin in order to protect the girl?"

Abu translated for Judge Elizar again. "The judge says, sir, that he would have to consider the positions of all the parties and who the victim was. He would have to consider the motive of the cousin's actions. However, as the mother was not being attacked herself, she could be found guilty of murder. If that occurs, the daughter may be an accomplice and could face the same fate."

"What is the fate?"

"They would be executed under Iraqi law. But as the Americans have forbidden the death penalty in Iraq, they will remain in prison until that changes."

Trevanathan shook his head and looked momentarily into the dark brown eyes of the girl, before she quickly looked away. He could see pain and humiliation in that momentary glance. *What the hell are we doing here?* he asked himself, *if the end result of all the sacrifice and death is that this sort of abuse is going to continue?*

"OK, I've seen enough. Let's go," Trevanathan ordered briskly, turning and walking back into the corridor and back toward the control room.

"Sir, shouldn't we report this situation with these women to higher headquarters?" asked Warden, following in his path.

"I will," responded Trevanathan wearily, "and it won't do a damn bit of good. Those pukes in Baghdad don't know or want to know what's going on out here as long as it doesn't end up on CNN."

"Well, you're in charge of legal down here, sir, why not just order them released?"

"Not that easy. Merdier has put out orders that we are not to interfere and change the outcomes of cases. He doesn't want us to look like 'occupiers' over a puppet government. We're supposed to make sure Iraqi law is applied, even if we disagree with the outcome in a given case. All part of the plan to make the Hajis feel like they have a greater say in their own future now."

"So that girl gets gang-banged, beaten, and then executed," said Warden, letting loose a stream of brown tobacco juice onto the floor. "Nice."

"Welcome to the cradle of civilization," replied Trevanathan sarcastically. "Let's get out of here."

"Abu," Trevanathan continued. "Thank the judge for the tour and remind him we'll be back in the morning with the payroll."

"Salaam Alekim," replied the judge touching his hand to his heart.

"Yeah, peace to you, too, judge," said Trevanathan, turning and walking out the door.

Chapter 22
The Payday

Trevanathan spent a restless night bathed in sweat on his cot. Even the usual trick of pouring a half-liter bottle of water on the hot nylon sleeping surface before climbing beneath his mosquito netting hadn't helped. The cooling evaporation lasted about ten minutes before the surface was dry again, normally long enough to drift off into a semi-comfortable sleep. But that night sleep would not come. The eyes of the young woman who had been brutalized by her own soldiers and now shunned by her legal system haunted him. *I lectured Rick about hope for the future,* he thought to himself as he turned onto his back, *but that doesn't do a helluva lot for that girl, does it?*

In the early hours, shortly before dawn, sleep finally found him, as the temperature dipped to the daily low of 105 degrees. But the rocket motor roar of the UAV[51] launching from the short runway across the river soon nudged him from slumber as the sun climbed above the horizon. Following his usual morning routine, Trevanathan shook out his boots to ensure that no intruders had taken up residence in their cavernous depths during the night. After a quick visit to the piss tubes on the back of the hill, he found Smith readying his gear for the day's mission to pay the courthouse salaries.

"Rick, after you get breakfast, go pull the money from the unit safe and have it ready to go at 0830, OK?" requested Trevanathan.

"Will do. You look like hell. You gonna' go eat?"

"I'll just grab some Joe. If I eat another plate of T-ration eggs and sausages for breakfast I'll be searching for a rafter with a rope."

The two officers worked their way down the large hill and through the maze of tents between their quarters and the mess hall. The mess facility, which had originally been a reception hall for Saddam, had a large, covered veranda behind it which was an ideal place to eat before the heat of the day struck. The veranda ran along the width of the building, elevated two meters or so above the Euphrates River canal. Although the canal cooled the air slightly, it also

---

[51] Unmanned Aerial Vehicle – a small remotely controlled aircraft mounted with cameras for surveillance of the countryside.

brought swarms of flies to breakfast. The 538th troops had sufficiently acclimated to Iraq at this point that the presence of a dozen flies or so crawling over their food was no longer a deterrent to a robust appetite.

As Trevanathan and Smith sat down at one of the folding tables on the veranda, they noticed the flies were even lighter than usual – a pleasant development. It took only a moment to realize why, however: the corpse of a great bull had washed up on the sandbar immediately below the building. Every fly in the immediate area was fully occupied with this dormant feast. The water level of the canal was low this morning, leaving the beast stranded, one dead eye staring up at the two officers as they dined. "Mmmm," replied Trevanathan dryly, eyeing the corpse, "got an extra spoon?"

"Hell, we should put a dead cow down there every morning," Smith replied, as he dug into the prepackaged eggs and shriveled sausages. "This is the fewest number of flies I've ever seen out here."

"Well, if it's still here when we get back from the mission, we can have a barbecue," deadpanned Trevanathan.

"Mmmmm, love that Euphrates marinade," said Smith, shoving another forkful of greasy sausage into his mouth with one hand as he scattered a few flies from his eggs with the other.

"Morning, boys," said Doc, ambling out the rear exit of the mess hall with a tray of food in his hand. He glanced at the water buffalo and sat down next to Smith, without comment. "Did you hear that new Air Force weather officer got whacked yesterday?"

"The Air Force," chimed Smith through a half chewed mouthful, "a viable alternative to military service."

"No, we were down in Hillah, meeting with the Chief Judge," said Trevanathan. "What happened?"

"He went out on a convoy over to Al Kut to pick up some equipment. They stopped for a piss break and a Haji sniper shot him right between the shoulder blades."

"Flak jacket?" asked Smith, grimacing at the lukewarm coffee he was drinking.

"No plates," replied Doc. "He was wearing the vest, but they hadn't received their ceramic plates yet."

"Vest alone's not gonna' stop a 7.62 round," commented Trevanathan matter-of-factly, pouring his remaining coffee over the edge of the veranda onto the head of the staring buffalo. Several hundred flies whirled momentarily into the air in protest before settling back down on the bloated corpse.

"Anyway," continued Doc, "I saw Sergeant Warden on the way in here, and he said he'd have Jaguars One and Two ready out front in five minutes."

"OK," said Trevanathan standing, "Appreciate it, Doc. Have a great Army day."

"Is there any other kind?" asked Doc, as he too began to defend his plate against the assault of Iraqi flies.

Warden and the rest of the team were waiting for their officers in front of the mess hall. After giving the usual Rules of Engagement briefing, Trevanathan and the Jaguar team – carrying ten thousand US dollars in an Army laundry bag – began their trip to the courthouse.

Cooper led the way in Jaguar One down the familiar road out the main gate and onto the two-lane hardball road past Al Salaam and the growing trash dump on the former soccer field. They turned south onto Highway 8 toward the river canal and the two lane bridge that spanned the waterway.

"Sir, can I ask you somethin'?" queried Cooper, uncharacteristically initiating conversation as they approached the river bridge.

"Sure, Cooper, go ahead," replied Trevanathan, keeping an eye on the approaching bridge. Any roadway that forced his team through a choke point with no alternate routes of escape made him uncomfortable.

"Do you think that this is gonna' make a difference – you know, working with the judges?"

"Well, it depends on how you measure making a difference, Cooper. If you look at whether we can maybe make this paradise a little better place to live – yeah, we can make a difference. If you buy into all that bullshit from

Washington that this place is going to become a bastion of democracy, forget about it."

"Yessir, but now with Saddam Hussein gone they can be democratic if they want," suggested Cooper hopefully as they bounced across the narrow bridge over the canal.

"That's the point, Coop. Democracy isn't just appointing a legislature or setting up some elections. It requires the people in power to be willing to voluntarily surrender control of the government to their political enemies if the people say so. That's not gonna' happen over here. Never. About ten seconds after we leave, whoever is in power is going to declare a state of emergency because of security concerns, and these people will have a new, hopefully benevolent, dictator."

"Well, maybe they won't accept it, sir, ya' know, based on their experience with Saddam." Cooper turned left at the four-way intersection into downtown Hillah. As usual, one Iraqi traffic cop stood in the middle of the intersection directing traffic. Four full-time police lounged in the shade of a meter-high wall on the east side of the road, their assault rifles leaning against the wall.

Anyone opens up on those heroes from a passing vehicle, thought Trevanathan, looking at the careless police, *and they'll never get their hands on those weapons before they go to join Allah.*

"Sir?" continued Cooper. "What if the people just refuse to accept that?"

"Oh, uh, well, that's a possibility some day, Cooper. But these people we're dealin' with now – the ones who have spent their entire lives giving into fear and power under Saddam– they not only won't oppose a new strongman – they'll welcome it."

"I don't understand that, sir. They have freedom for the first time. You think they'll just give that up?"

"Cooper, this entire society is based upon a strong central figure calling the shots. A sheikh or Saddam,…whoever. There's a few I've seen in this country that would be willing to stand up for an abstract principle like democracy. But they'll be the first ones put against the wall when the others refuse to fight for it. The rest of the cattle will welcome the fact that they won't have to be responsible for their own affairs any more. It's a very comfortable thing to people in this part of the world to be told what to do. Democracy is hard. It requires respect for property rights, for the worth of the individual, the willingness to tolerate opposing viewpoints. These people want to deal with everything by killing their opponents. Democracy can't survive on that type of a foundation. Not yet, anyway."

"Yessir," said Cooper, pulling into the side street on which the courthouse sat two blocks ahead. *I'll never understand the Major,* Cooper thought to himself. *He can't stand these people and he's still willing to bust his ass to help them out at the same time.*

"Well, enough preaching," said Trevanathan, as they approached the courthouse. "Let's earn our pay."

A large group had already gathered outside the gates to the courthouse when the team arrived. As usual, Muhammad the guard let them into the courtyard parking area. For purpose of the payroll distribution, Trevanathan had decided to use the large downstairs lobby, which would hold the most people at one time. His plan was to have a line begin at a large table and extend out into the courtyard. Trevanathan had assigned Smith to make the payment to each worker, checking their identification against the roster provided to them by the Chief Judge.

The pay station was set up by 0855. Smith sat behind the table with the cash, and Warden and Leader provided security, standing on either side of him. Cooper was to ensure the line remained orderly and that no one cut in. Abu stood by behind Smith to provide necessary translation services. Everything seemed in order.

After double-checking that everyone knew their role, Trevanathan turned to tell Muhammad outside to admit the employees. Before he reached the door, however, Trevanathan noticed that the judges had already placed themselves at the head of the line, laughing among themselves in anticipation of receiving their salaries for the first time in over two months.

Trevanathan stopped and called Chief Judge Elizar over to his side. "Judge, it may set a better example if the judges do not go first in the line," he advised.

"Why?" asked Elizar, furrowing his brow in obvious confusion.

"It shows that you take care of your workers first, before yourself. It demonstrates leadership."

"I think it demonstrates foolishness," replied the judge, acting as if he had been insulted. "I am the Chief Judge. Why would I stand behind a mere file clerk? It is impossible."

"Judge, I'm not telling you what to do. In our Army the officers eat last, after the men. It shows that we are leaders and take care of our troops first, before ourselves. It builds loyalty and respect."

"They will respect me or they will have no job," declared the judge in an imperious voice.

"Have it your way," said Trevanathan with resignation, turning and walking out between the twin metal doors on the front of the building. He realized as he went that the judge had just openly demonstrated a perfect grasp of English for the first time. As Trevanathan stepped outside, he could see that nearly 200 people had gathered outside the metal gate – those in front wedged tightly against its bars. They reached their hands through the grate toward the building as if they could somehow slip through the narrow spaces if they tried hard enough.

Trevanathan began walking over toward Jaguar One to send a status report back to the brigade's operations center, when the cry of a woman mashed against the gate by the crowd caught his attention. Concerned for her well-being, Trevanathan called to Muhammad, "Muhammad, open it." Muhammad looked back momentarily from the jostling crowd toward Trevanathan with a questioning look on his face. "Open it," yelled Trevanathan again, making an "open" sign with his two hands.

Muhammad fished the iron key from his pocket and turned it in the lock. With the weight of the crowd against the bolt, it turned slowly but as it carried free, the two halves of the gate sprung inward, sending the guard backpedaling. The crowd surged forward, pushing those in front onto the ground as they lost their balance. Two persons whose arms were caught between the bars howled in pain as they were dragged forcibly aside by the springing gates. The crowd surged forward irresistibly, with those now on the ground disappearing beneath a tide of black burkhas and white man-dresses. Muhammad regained his own balance and dove out of the way just in time to avoid being trampled.

The surging crowd, eight persons wide, wedged into the courthouse doorway, built to accommodate two or three persons. The rest of the surge broke against the front wall of the building, spilling to either side. Trevanathan, now standing near the HMMWVs, watched Haji Darwinism, in embarrassingly graphic detail, as men shoved women to the side or onto the ground in their desperation to get to the money inside. Larger men punched and threw vicious elbows at smaller men who sought to enter the building before them. The air filled with oaths and the crying of the injured. Trevanathan saw one very large man, whom he recognized as a minor prosecutor, smash his fist into the face of a clerk who worked on the second floor. The smaller man fell to the ground and lay motionless as the crowd stepped upon him in its frenzy.

The scene at the door looked like a bad Three Stooges skit: despite the flurry of movement few were actually getting through. Trevanathan, afraid for the clerk who had disappeared beneath the uncaring feet of the crowd cried "Kuf, Kuf![52]" at the top of his lungs. No one paid attention, as they continued to elbow their way forward. Trevanathan stepped up to the flank of the crowd near where the clerk had disappeared and unsuccessfully tried to push his way into the flow. It was like a kid trying to leap aboard a moving express train. Despite his size and the added ballast of his flak jacket, Trevanathan simply bounced off the surging crowd.

Women were now beating upon the backs of other women in front of them, and slaps were rained down upon the younger women by the older ones near the rear of the pack.

Trevanathan knew he had lost complete control of the situation. His mind whirled on how to recover the operation before things got worse. For a moment, he considered firing a warning shot into the air, but that was strictly against ROE guidelines, and it might result in others in the crowd pulling weapons. Before he could act, the large prosecutor he had seen fight his way to the head of the line came flying out the courthouse doors over the heads of the crowd, landing in the middle of the mob and breaking its momentum. Several other bodies came flying or spinning out behind him, causing the crowd to stop and begin moving back.

Behind the ejected workers came Leader and Warden, two irresistible forces of nature side-by-side, grabbing those who fought to gain access to the

---

[52] Arabic for "Halt, halt."

interior and throwing them backwards with tremendous force into the crowd. Cooper and Ridlin followed behind them, quickly taking up flanking positions on either side of the NCOs, creating a semi-circle of four intimidating and very pissed-off soldiers. The door to the courthouse effectively blocked, the crowd paused, hampered by the many bodies that had been either trampled or flung back against their advance.

Trevanathan elbowed his way to the front of the crowd from the flank, being none-too-subtle in his approach. As he reached the door, Abu and the Chief Judge emerged behind the four soldiers.

Passing between his defensive linemen, Trevanathan turned, red-faced, upon the judge. "You tell these *people*," he spat, "that the salary distribution is cancelled. I have never seen such a display of selfishness in my life. There is enough money for everyone," he yelled, his voice rising, as he turned to face the crowd. "Everyone was going to be paid. What the hell is *wrong* with you people?"

The Chief Judge lowered his eyes and seemed to shrink before the outrage of the tall, lanky American. "We are a poor people," he said humbly. "You cannot understand the desperation of people who have nothing, until you have been one of us."

Turning back to face the judge, Trevanathan countered, "Judge – that's bullshit. Poverty is not an excuse for what I saw here today. I saw the strong taking advantage of the weak, when there was plenty for everyone. I saw officers of the court acting like street thugs to make sure they got their share first. It's the same old habit you people have, of the strong stomping the weak." Trevanathan regretted the indictment the moment it came out of his mouth. He believed the statement, but he gained nothing by insulting the judge. Not willing to back down, though, he ordered the judge, "Now you tell them payday is cancelled because of their conduct."

The judge stepped out in front of the four soldiers and spoke to the crowd in a slow, halting voice. The crowd reacted with a chorus of insults, shaking their fists in frustration. The judge took a step backward, looking concerned. Over his shoulder, Trevanathan saw the battered and now bloody face of the clerk who had fallen beneath the crowd's feet. His nose was smashed flat and both cheeks were streaked with blood. He looked through one eye, the other already swollen shut.

"C'mon Abu," Trevanathan commanded, moving out from behind his team to stand next to the judge. "Translate for me."

"Hear me, hear me," he yelled over the shouts of the crowd. Several stopped yelling and listened as Abu translated. "The money will not be given out today due to your bad conduct. Look at yourselves – look at the people you have hurt." Trevanathan pointed at an older woman who had dragged herself free of the crowd and sat upon the ground, rocking in pain as she held her injured arm. Several people shifted uncomfortably as she moaned in pain.

"I will be back in two days with the money," Trevanathan continued, raising his voice over the crowd. The crowd slowly quieted now and listened. "When I arrive there will be two lines – the women will be there" – he pointed along the right side of the wall outside the gate. "The men will be there." He pointed to the wall to the left side of the gate. "You will be let in one at a time." As Abu translated several of the men, including the large prosecutor, grumbled with discontent.

"If there is any pushing, any hitting, or any cutting in line, I will build a fire with your money and *burn* it right here." Trevanathan stamped his foot on the landing. "Do you understand?" he roared, his voice now rising again in anger. The crowd quieted completely in the face of his sustained outburst as they listened to Abu's equally animated – and nervous – translation.

Trevanathan spotted the tall prosecutor in the midst of the crowd, scowling at the ground and muttering. Trevanathan stepped down and waded into the crowd toward him, Abu following in his path. The crowd parted as Trevanathan approached. "And *you*," Trevanathan barked, pointing his finger into the man's chest, who towered over him. "You will be the last in the men's line and the last one paid." The man did not make eye contact with the angry American, but stood silently with downcast eyes like a scolded child.

Trevanathan turned and walked back through the crowd and into the courthouse lobby. As he passed Abu, the translator offered weakly, "I believe it will be better next time." But Trevanathan just glanced at him with an eyebrow raised in disagreement. He wondered, *How can this legal system succeed when the gatekeepers of the system use brute force to protect their own selfish interests?*

Once out of the line of sight from the crowd, Trevanathan leaned back against the cool interior wall. As he removed his helmet, he noticed that his hands were shaking, half from anger, and half from the adrenaline rush of his confrontation with the Iraqi workers. *Note to self,* he thought as he closed his eyes and drew a deep breath. *Hajis don't stand in lines.*

Chapter 23
The Convoy

The occupation of Iraq undertook a fundamental shift in August, 2003. As the defeated pro-Saddam forces reorganized from the overwhelming American battlefield victory in April, incidents of attacks on US facilities and convoys spiked sharply. While Pentagon spokespersons tried to characterize the attacks as a "few remaining disorganized elements of the former regime," there suddenly seemed to be a hell of a lot of "disorganized elements" to the troops on the ground.

While Administration "talking heads" continued to focus on the great military victory in their Sunday morning talk show appearances, Marine and Army base camps were once again receiving regular mortar fire and increased roadside bomb attacks upon their convoys. Troops in theater began referring to "the war" in the present tense again, a practice that had faded for a couple months after the fall of Baghdad.

Attacks occurring in a few troubled areas of the Sunni Triangle to the north that had previously seemed remote to the soldiers of the 538th, were now close to home. A two-vehicle convoy of lightly armed military intelligence personnel was hit by insurgents on MSR TAMPA, just eight klicks north of Hillah. Four of the eight members of the convoy were killed instantly by the detonation of a powerful IED that had been concealed in the body of a dead dog. The attack was well coordinated, with supporting small arms fire following the blast, wounding an additional three members of the convoy.

To the members of the 538th, who regularly traveled MSR TAMPA, a greater tone of seriousness began to accompany their convoy preparations. A second attack two days later, made the mood even more somber, when an unknown number of insurgents destroyed a CSH[53] supply convoy from a unit of the Michigan National Guard, twenty klicks south of Hillah.

The medical convoy had successfully driven through a smattering of harassing gunfire, stopping to assess any casualties at a roadside rest area two miles later. The insurgents had anticipated such a stop from observing prior

---

[53] Combat Support Hospital

US reactions to ambush, and slammed the door shut on the trap. They decimated the parked convoy with pre-targeted mortar fire and previously concealed IEDs that killed and wounded a dozen Guardsmen. The troops paid a bitter price for becoming predictable in their reactions to enemy contact.

Word of the attack hit particularly hard within the Marine contingent sharing the palace with the 538th, as Corporal Ahmed of the recon team was killed by one of the several hidden IEDs. Ahmed, who had survived many missions as a scout in front of the initial Marine thrust through Central Iraq, had died while a passenger in one of the trucks while en route for some R&R[54]. While a man is just as dead no matter how the blow is delivered, the fact that this likeable and highly skilled warrior had been struck down while being hauled like cargo in the back of a supply truck was particularly galling to the Marine warrior ethos.

As the ranking officer in the weekly convoy to coordinate reconstruction planning with CPA Justice officials in the Green Zone, Major Trevanathan was tapped as the convoy commander. In this role, he was responsible for all aspects of the movement to Baghdad and back. Today would be the team's first trip to Baghdad since MSR TAMPA had again turned into a shooting gallery, and tension was high. Jaguar One and Two would be accompanied by Doc Heller and his medical team in Red Raider One: the thinking was that the more rifles available, the better their chances in case trouble popped up. Red Raider was along purely to provide that additional firepower.

"OK, listen up for the ROE briefing," Trevanathan directed to the teams, as they gathered in a half-circle about him to hear their orders. Trevanathan pulled the current ROE briefing card from his pocket and read it aloud.

"Standing Rules of Engagement for Phase 3 combat operations remain in effect. If engaged by enemy fire you may engage at will. Do not wait on my order. If an individual points a weapon at you or other protected personnel or drives a vehicle at you or other protected personnel, you are authorized to employ deadly force. Use aimed fire on identified targets…." As he continued to brief the team, Trevanathan noticed that everyone was paying closer attention than usual to the rules on their ability to defend themselves.

---

[54] Rest and Relaxation – The R&R program in Iraq at the time was a three-day pass to Kuwait.

"Warning shots are not authorized," he continued. "The use of riot control agents or pepper spray are not authorized. The use of altered ammunition or "Dum Dum" bullets is not authorized. Any questions?"

As Trevanathan finished, Sergeant Mantis came jogging up, late due to having been delayed in drawing additional ammunition. "Sorry, sir," he breathed heavily.

"It's pretty simple, Mantis," interjected Staff Sergeant Leader. "If it screws with us, kill it."

"Something like that," smirked Trevanathan, amused at Leader's unvarnished summary of his briefing.

"What about frags[55], sir?" asked Mantis, who was hefting one of the orb shaped grenades in his meaty hand.

"We'll kill more of us than enemy if we use grenades from a moving vehicle. No frags. If we dismount – which is unlikely – only Sergeants Warden and Leader will use frags without my prior approval."

Mantis looked disappointed at the perceived lack of confidence in his abilities.

Mantis looks a little too anxious to use grenades, Trevanathan thought to himself. *I don't need any glory seekers on this mission.*

"We are in canvas covered HMMWVs with light weapons," the Major reminded his soldiers. "If we get engaged, our job is not to stand toe-to-toe and duke it out with the Hajis. We will put the pedal down and get the hell out of the area and call for support."

"You mean we're gonna' run?" asked Mantis with a mocking look of disbelief on his face.

"No, Mantis," interjected Leader before Trevanathan could respond. "We're gonna' build a bunker outta' your fat, dead ass and move into it for the duration."

---

[55] Army slang for *fragmentation grenades*.

"Knock it off," Trevanathan admonished, while silently appreciating Leader shutting down the mouthy young NCO. "This isn't the frickin' Sands of Iwo Jima, Mantis. Our mission is not to take ground and kill Hajis. Our job is to help rebuild this dump, if possible, and we won't do a good job of that with a bunch of dead and wounded personnel. So, yes, if we come under fire and we can leave, we will. The one thing that will not happen is that no one gets left behind. If we get whacked, Jaguar Two is the designated ambulance. Rick, your team will load any wounded in the bed of Jaguar Two while the remaining vehicles provide covering fire."

"Roger, sir," replied Smith in a professional, no-nonsense voice.

"If Jaguar Two gets whacked, then Red Raider One is the evac vehicle. Doc, you're our medic. Each team has one combat lifesaver's bag. OK, let's go. Keep your eyes open – 360 degrees. No sleeping."

"Sahr, may I say somethin'?" asked Sergeant First Class Warden.

"Sure, Sergeant Warden. Go ahead."

"Most of you know I was in Somalia, dealin' with those Hajis. I was there when they dragged that dead troop through the streets and danced 'round his body. You all saw it on TV. These are not people you wanna' get taken prisoner by, if it ever comes to that. They tried to keep a lid on it down there, but a whole convoy of Pakistani troops were butchered by the Somalis. That's their own Haji people. They cut the throats of the ones that surrendered and chopped the heads off the dead ones as a message. Point is, so long as you got ammo, keep firin'. There ain't no such thing as a Haji prison camp – especially with these terrorists we're fightin' now."

The team's usual light banter was missing as the convoy departed the camp on the two-lane road toward MSR TAMPA. This slice of Iraq along the canal was almost picturesque: tall date palms towered over the road, and exotic-looking green plants surrounded many of the small farm houses. Several children waved as the three vehicles drove past. As they left the hardball road and crossed the familiar short, two-track that intersected the MSR, however, both the terrain and the attitude abruptly changed. The terrain became open desert again, as the nurturing waters of the Euphrates were left behind. From the intersection with Tampa until they reached Baghdad one hundred kilometers to the north they would face open terrain and pounding desert heat.

The nature of the population changed also, for with every mile they traveled north, the relatively friendly Shiite population dwindled, and the number of Sunnis who had lost so much with the downfall of their champion, Saddam, increased.

Trevanathan looked about at the team. Each man was completely focused upon his designated security area outside of the vehicle. They had driven this route several times before, but today seemed like the first time again. The team knew that a popular location for ambush was any bridge over the MSR. The elevated concrete structures made these natural fortresses, from which grenades could be dropped upon vehicles passing below or a prone marksman could wreck havoc, without presenting much of a target. Accordingly, each of the thirteen bridge crossings between Hillah and Baghdad was a potential kill zone. "It's not in the ROE," Trevanathan had told his team before they departed, "but there's no legitimate reason for any Haji to be lurking on the far side of those overpasses unless he means us harm. If someone is sitting there, whack 'em."

The bridges were clear today, however, as the small convoy traveled north. The first sign of potential trouble was a small plume of black smoke far to the right of the highway, appearing to be significantly away from their path of travel. Something was always burning in Iraq, so Trevanathan did not give it much notice. However, the highway began to gradually turn in the direction of the plume, which grew in height and volume with each passing kilometer.

"All Jaguar elements," Trevanathan spoke into his handheld radio. "Be alert. Something is burning up ahead."

"Roger, One," came the response from each of the vehicles. The team had become increasingly frustrated with their highly temperamental SINCGARS radio systems over the past several weeks. On every mission at least one of the vehicles was unable to communicate due to radio problems. While the encryption capability afforded by the military radios was important when conveying sensitive information, their unreliability had become a pain in the neck when the team needed to relay routine information within a convoy, such as "Turn right" or "Stop". Accordingly, the team had purchased four Motorola handheld radios – "walkie-talkies," really – on the internet, which greatly improved their ability to communicate. The devices were officially prohibited by the Army because they could easily be intercepted, but as forbidden fruit, their popularity had naturally increased, resulting in many commanders and team leaders openly carrying the devices. In war, you go with what works or you don't last.

As they approached the source of the smoke, Trevanathan double-checked that his rifle was ready, tapping the "forward assist" button to ensure that the bolt firmly pressed up against the first 5.56mm round in the chamber. His thumb drifted down the left side of the rifle's metal housing and switched the safety switch from *safe* to *semi*-automatic. "Ease up on the speed, Cooper," he directed. "We don't want to run up on anything unpleasant too quickly."

Cooper nodded and slowed the HMMWV.

As the team came within half a kilometer of the billowing smoke ahead, five or six desert camouflage vehicles could be seen pulled off along the right side of the highway, with several similarly clad personnel moving about them.

"All Jaguar elements, it looks like we have friendlies up ahead. Stay sharp," Trevanathan spoke into his radio.

Twisting in his seat, Trevanathan made a 360 degree scan of the surrounding area as they neared the other vehicles. There were good fields of fire in all directions, except for the usual sand berms that the Iraqis had bulldozed into place before the war. These stood back roughly 200 meters from the highway, and the two-meter high hills always gave Trevanathan the feeling he was on the wrong side of a turkey shoot. *I can't understand why they don't get the engineers to bulldoze those*, he thought. *It would provide less cover for anyone wanting to lay an ambush.*

An Army soldier stepped into the highway a hundred yards ahead and signaled for them to stop. Trevanathan could now clearly see that there were six Army HMMWVs and a military ambulance on the side of the road, while a seventh, upside-down HMMWV thirty meters or so off to the right was burning fiercely. Its melting tires were throwing up the thick, black smoke they had first seen.

Trevanathan briefed the trail vehicles over his handheld. "Everyone stay alert: we're stopping. Remain in vehicles."

Jaguar One stopped fifty meters from the soldier in the road, and they waited as the figure briskly approached. Trevanathan watched him carefully, looking for any sign that might reveal he was anything other than what he appeared to be. HMMWVs and US uniforms had been stolen in Iraq, and nothing could be assumed.

"Afternoon, sir," said the young sergeant wearing the shoulder patch of the 800th Military Police Brigade. "Convoy got hit by an IED about twenty minutes ago. We're putting out the word to all convoys to keep their eyes open for a white Toyota pickup truck that was spotted fleeing from the area right after the blast."

"That describes about half the vehicles in Iraq," Trevanathan replied. Iraqis had a distinct preference for white Isuzu and Toyota pickup trucks.

"Roger that, sir. Unfortunately, that's all we have to go on now."

"What's the casualty count?" Trevanathan asked.

"Two KIA[56], two WIA[57]," answered the sergeant matter-of-factly. "Helo already took out the wounded. We're just cleaning up."

Trevanathan only nodded, taking in the carnage.

"The convoy commander in the death seat[58] – he caught the brunt of the blast," said the MP. "The bomb was alongside the road – probably concealed inside something, but hard to tell now. Driver lost control and flipped the vehicle, crushing the roof gunner between the roof and the road. Not a pretty sight," he stated. "You can proceed, sir, but keep your eyes open for Haji and be careful passing by the wreck as there's still a lot of busted equipment and metal on the road."

"Will do," said Trevanathan nodding to the young military policeman. "Cooper, let's roll. Keep it under five until we clear this area."

Jaguar One slowly rolled forward through the kill zone, crunching shattered glass and bits of debris beneath its massive tires. It was obvious where the bomb had been planted from the small crater, still smoldering along the right edge of the highway. Twisted water cans, MREs, and unidentifiable pieces of metal debris littered the roadway over a hundred meter section. As they

---

[56] Killed in Action.

[57] Wounded in Action.

[58] Front right seat, so named because it is the part of the vehicle that typically first encounters a buried mine, often resulting in the death of whoever is sitting there.

passed the first parked HMMWV, Trevanathan saw the ambulance crew walking along the road with large black trash bags. One female soldier, with strands of dirty blond hair sticking out of her helmet, bent and picked up a dirty, bloody lump of something and dropped it into the bag. She straightened and was looking about for more body parts before Trevanathan lost sight of her behind the next vehicle. Somehow it bothered him that her face was completely without emotion.

As they came abreast the burning vehicle, Trevanathan could feel the heat of it wash across his face. At that angle, the charred hull bore little resemblance to a HMMWV.

A rust-colored smear in the road immediately ahead of Jaguar One revealed where the doomed vehicle had initially flipped and crushed the roof gunner. *That has to be about the most dangerous job around*, thought Trevanathan. The 538th's HMMWVs had only canvas stretched across the roof support beams of their frames. However, many HMMWVs in combat units had an opening in the center of a hardened roof, through which a gunner on a SAW or a 50 caliber machine gun had a clear field of fire in almost every direction. The problem, of course, was that this also gave the enemy a clear shot back at the gunner, and if the vehicle flipped... well, it was hopefully over quickly.

Trevanathan was extremely alert as they cleared the last of the debris and began to slowly accelerate toward Baghdad. Haji often planted IEDs in series and would hit one convoy initially and then hit a second or even a third an hour or two later. IEDs were the poor man's weapon in Iraq, where the excess artillery shells that made the bombs were readily abundant and lightly guarded. The insurgents actually looted the shells from massive Iraqi ammunition dumps that US troops were supposedly guarding. However, the number of troops allocated to that mission was woefully inadequate.

His eyes searching for any irregularities in the road or the rail ahead, Trevanathan quickly noticed a container sitting out of place along the road next to a guardrail post twenty meters ahead.

"Stop! Stop now!" he barked at Cooper, who immediately locked the brakes on his vehicle. The screeching of tires behind him signaled that Jaguar Two had been surprised by their reaction, but had managed to avoid hitting them.

"Container by the side of the road," Trevanathan stated quickly into his SINCGARS handset, avoiding the Motorola for this sensitive information. "Dismount and give 360 security." Trevanathan stepped from the HMMWV, looking for any hiding place in the immediate area from which a bomb could be detonated. Looking behind, he could see the MPs and ambulance personnel they had passed now pointing in their direction. The rest of the Jaguar team quickly spilled from their vehicles, setting up a perimeter around the convoy. Ahead lay the misshapen, sand-colored container. *If that's some Haji's grocery bag, I'm gonna' be very embarrassed*, thought Trevanathan.

The Major walked cautiously toward the object, craning his head to see if any wires were visible from the container.

"You sure you wanna' be doin' that sahr?" called Warden over the hood of Jaguar One. "I don't recall you mentionin' bomb disposal as one of your hobbies." Trevanathan stopped, recognizing the wisdom of the NCO's caution. *If your wife could see you now, you would be in deep shit, boy,* he thought, as he squinted at the box. There appeared to be a pipe sticking out the rear of it, and the side facing the road was corrugated and somehow familiar.

As Trevanathan considered his next move, a gust of wind caused a flap of the box to wave. Trevanathan was shaken with the realization that the object was not a box at all; it was the bottom of a GI boot, blown out of shape by the force of the prior blast – its corrugated "alligator" sole facing toward him. He closed his eyes and tried to swallow, finding his mouth suddenly very dry. Covering his lips with his hand, he slowly moved closer.

"*Sahr...*" warned Warden, with a cautioning inflection of his voice.

"It's a boot," Trevanathan yelled over his shoulder. He stood and stared at it, unable to look away from the portion of fractured tibia and calf muscle that remained together within the top of the boot. The skin had been cleanly removed, making it look like a diagram from a biology textbook.

Jeezus, he thought, swallowing hard and trying to avert his eyes. *We must be at least two hundred, maybe two hundred and fifty meters from the detonation That was a helluva' blast.* Looking closer, he saw that on the side of the sole were written the words "NO IODINE," "A-NEG" and "GRAHAM."

Trevanathan reached back to his fanny pack and loosened the cover. As he did so, Smith came up beside him, peeking around his shoulder at the grisly remnant. "Whoa," was all he could utter.

Trevanathan pulled a small green roll from his fanny pack and untied it, then shook out his wet weather poncho. Stepping gingerly up to the boot, he kneeled and gently laid the poncho over it. Sliding his hands beneath it, he tucked the poncho underneath the boot. Fighting back the bile rising in his throat, he lifted the surprisingly heavy object into his arms. It was more cumbersome than he had expected and a trickle of blood leaked out of the poncho, running down his pants' leg as he stood up. *I don't want to touch the bone*, was the creeping thought that kept washing over him…*anything but the bone*.

"Bill…" Smith started, "you don't have to…"

"Yes, I do," replied Trevanathan. "This poor bastard bought it and I'm not leaving bits of him laying around for some frickin' Haji dog to feed on." Trevanathan's mind flashed back to their crossing at Safwan. "Not this time," he said aloud, then turned and began walking back toward the burning HMMWV. None of the men spoke as he passed.

Trevanathan walked slowly, feeling the grisly weight in his arms. It shifted once, causing the shaft of bone to momentarily rub against his hand through the light nylon fabric. A incontrollable shiver ran down his back and he fought the urge to retch.

The MP sergeant and the blonde medic met Trevanathan halfway to the ambulance, approaching without saying a word. They had guessed what he had found as he approached them with his burden and a stream of dark blood running from his left knee down onto his boot.

"Graham," Trevanathan stated dully, as they met him. "His boot."

"Yes, sir," said the female specialist. "I can take that from you, sir", she said kindly, gently holding out two hands covered with rubber surgical gloves.

Trevanathan slowly handed her the dripping package. "Not in the bag, OK?" he said, his voice cracking slightly. "I…I don't want it tossed in the trash bag."

"No problem, sir," she said sympathetically. "We'll take good care of him." The sergeant remained mute, looking down at Trevanathan's stained uniform.

"OK, then," Trevanathan said, his voice flat. He swallowed hard and moved to return to his convoy.

"Sir…," the medic called after him. "Your poncho…?"

Trevanathan turned and looked at the package lying in the young medic's arms, the trickle of blood now dripping onto her boots. "It's his now," he said tightly and turned away.

Chapter 24
The Unwelcome Guest

"All right, listen up," said Trevanathan as he walked into the ceremonial hall that doubled as the enlisted quarters in their hilltop palace. The enlisted members of the team broke away from their various tasks and gathered around their Major, waiting for his direction. "G2 says that they have intel that there's likely to be a mortar attack on this camp within the next 72 hours. It may or may not be coupled with some type of ground attack – infiltrators, or something like that."

"We're gonna' take some new precautions until this thing blows over. Everyone needs to be sleeping inside for the next three days. You guys who have a hooch set up out on the veranda need to pull inside the walls for a little bit. Everyone needs to be in full battle rattle anytime they go outside – even to the pisser. Flak jackets and helmets – so you don't go to your Maker with your drawers at half-mast." The team chuckled appreciatively at Trevanathan's imagery.

"Any questions?" Trevanathan asked. No one replied. "Oh yeah, one more thing. Anyone going out to the piss tube at night needs to take a buddy with him. Some Hajis have been probing the wire and if they make it inside, you don't want to get your throat cut while taking a leak. OK?"

Sanitation was a luxury that did not exist when an Army was on the move. However, the second it settled into a camp, good waste disposal became an absolute necessity to avoid sickness and disease. In most wars of the past, disease from poor camp sanitary facilities had killed more soldiers than the enemy. Without running water, slit trenches were dug behind the palace on the back slope leading down to the motor pool. The Navy Seabees had built multiple seat "outhouses," to centralize that particular activity and avoid disease. For convenience, the other invention of the desert Army was known as the "piss tube:" a six to eight-foot length of white PVC pipe that was driven three feet or more into the sand at a 45-degree angle. The result was an open air urinal that kept everything far underground that might otherwise attract animals or lead to the spread of sickness.

Despite the eventful convoy of the week before, the team had again settled into the monotony of garrison life at Camp Babylon. As such, it was a notable evening when Doc Heller received a large box in the mail from his wife. "Hey, it's my birthday," he said with surprise. "I had forgotten all about it."

"Open it Doc – see what you got," said Smith, hoping it would be cookies that might be shared. Doc pulled out his Leatherman tool and quickly cut through the packing tape. Opening the cardboard flaps he exclaimed, "Hey, it's a coffee press and coffee. Starbucks®."

"Oh, lordy-lord, I done died and gone to heaven," said Chaplain (Captain) Clay, effecting a fake, high-pitched accent.

"Don't walk toward the light, padre," cracked Trevanathan.

"Doc," said Smith, "Let's go set it up on the veranda. It's almost time for the Chicken Lady."

"Good idea," said Doc, "let me go grab my flak jacket and I'll meet you out there."

That evening's bull session on the veranda was one they would talk about for weeks thereafter. After they mastered how the French-style coffee press worked, which everyone jokingly renamed the 'freedom press,' they enjoyed large steaming canteen cups of strong, fresh coffee.

"Now, *that's* coffee," said Smith for the third or fourth time, deeply inhaling the aroma from his cup as he sagged happily into the canvas embrace of his soccer chair.

"I don't think I can ever drink that swill in the messhall again," said Doc.

"That crap in the messhall is an insult to good swill everywhere," joked Trevanathan, who had propped his stained desert boots up on the low, two foot high wall that ran around the edge of the veranda.

"Messhall coffee will eat through your cup if you leave it in there," added Clay.

"Well, one thing remains constant," said Trevanathan, standing up from his soccer chair and stretching, "this stuff runs through me pretty quick. I need to hit the latrine. Which one of you ladies wants to go with me?" he asked.

"I gotta go," said Clay. "I have a peanut sized bladder," he laughed in his usual jovial manner.

"Why is everything peanuts and cotton to you crackers down south?" Trevanathan asked, as they walked down the veranda's stairway to the dirt footpath that wound behind the palace to the piss tubes.

The well-worn trail surrounded the entire palace. It was a hundred meter walk from the upper veranda on the southwest corner of the palace where they were sitting, to the latrine area on the northwest corner. As they walked along the narrow path, with the Euphrates canal shimmering in the moonlight three hundred yards below them, Clay commented, "It's odd we haven't seen any fire tonight from the Chicken Lady yet. They usually make a run at her by now."

"Maybe they've given up," said Trevanathan. "Or maybe they're going into something more lucrative, like selling those cheesy Haji porno cassettes outside the main gate."

Trevanathan walked quickly the last few feet to the tubes, as the pressure of the coffee increased. "Aaah. That's more like it," he said, as he went about his business.

"A waste of darn fine coffee," teased Clay, sidling up to the empty tube to his right. "You should be ashamed…" He did not have a chance to finish his sentence, as a red streak tore across the face of the hill immediately in front of them. A dull report echoed across the canal in the general vicinity of the palm grove and the chicken farm.

A second streak flashed over their heads, as Trevanathan yelled, "Get down!" before diving into the dirt behind Clay's feet.

"Wha..?" asked Clay, looking about uncertainly. "Sniper!" barked Trevanathan, "Get down! Trevanathan reached up and hit the chaplain behind the knee, causing him to fall backwards in a heap on top of him.

Fifty meters below them, on the paved road that wound up the palace hill, the heavy bark of a 50 caliber machine gun roared to life, as one of the permanently positioned guard HMMWV teams flooded red tracers into the grove below. The high-pitched *crack!* of small arms fire came from several locations along the canal, as Marine snipers also zeroed in on their targets.

Trevanathan started to shake underneath Clay, his body quivering. "It's OK, Bill," the chaplain said soothingly, trying to shift his weight off of the prone officer beneath him. "It's gonna' be OK," he repeated. A squeak escaped from beneath him, worrying Clay's that Trevanathan was hysterical. "It'll be OK, Bill, don't worry," he said again.

Trevanathan raised his face up out of the sand where it had been driven when Clay landed on top of him. "Ohhh, I'm OK, Padre," he laughed. "I just started thinking about what kind of letter the Old Man would write home to my wife if I was shot while using a piss tube." Lowering his voice to that of a baritone FM radio announcer, Trevanathan intoned, "He bravely held his post, among other things, in the face of overwhelming odds," before resuming his laughter.

Clay was not certain whether to be relieved or concerned that the shaking he had felt beneath him was Trevanathan laughing at their ridiculous situation. "Well, I'm glad you're enjoying yourself," the pastor said dryly, as the last sounds of firing below them died away.

"All clear," a voice called up from the barely-visible HMMWV below them. "Anyone hit up there?"

"No hits," the chaplain called back down the hill. "We're OK."

"Did you get him?" Trevanathan called down

"Yeah, no problem," the voice answered. "Haji forgets we have night vision."

Trevanathan stood up and brushed himself off, quickly realizing that his pants were fairly well soaked through and coated with mud, a product of the Padre failing to turn off his plumbing as he fell to the ground.

"Very nice," he said ruefully. "Guess I better go change."

"Ya' did good, Bill," said Clay, wiping the dirt from his hands. "I appreciate you pulling me down. I didn't realize what was going on."

"No problem, Padre," said Trevanathan. "Can't let the Hajis make any new holes in my favorite chaplain. Just try not to piss on me next time, if it's not too much to ask."

Clay laughed, "Baptism by fire, my son…"

As Trevanathan walked back up the veranda stairs, Doc called to him, "Did you see all that fire over on the back of the hill? A guy said it was a sniper."

"Yeah, I had a front row seat," said Trevanathan, walking a little bowlegged as his wet pants began to chafe. "I think we know now why there was no Chicken Lady tonight. Haji was trying to set up a sniper attack and so they probably stopped anyone from going over to steal the chickens. We should remember that next time there's no light show."

Chapter 25
The Friend

With no light show that evening, the officers turned in early. His later than usual cup of coffee caused Trevanathan to toss and turn under his mosquito net, as the caffeine and the night's adrenaline made it hard for him to relax. Gradually, however, he drifted off into an uneasy sleep.

KAARUMPH...KARUMPH...KARUMPH! The noise from three explosions reverberated within the palace, and Trevanathan groggily felt the world turn upside-down. "Mortar attack!" yelled someone outside a nearby window.

"Incoming!" a more distant voice called. "Get away from the doors and windows!" another ordered.

Trevanathan rolled off his cot and hit the floor hard, bruising his arm. Even in his half-awake state he know that getting low to the ground was his best protection against a mortar attack. Mortar shells are shot from portable tubes in a high arc; upon impact they explode into a deadly cone of shrapnel, outward and upward from the point of detonation. The lower one is to the ground and the further away from that point, the better one's chances.

Shaking off the sleep, Trevanathan fished under his cot for his flak jacket and helmet. As his bunk was located near one of the windows, he did not stand nor kneel to put them on, as any shell landing nearby would blow shrapnel through the thin plywood sheet covering the lower half of the three-meter high frame. In the darkness, he could hear the slap of bare feet on the marble floor, as the other officers living in the converted dining room scurried toward better protection in the interior hallways. Pulling his helmet on, Trevanathan grabbed his 9mm pistol in one hand, and with his flak jacket in the other, ran to join his comrades. As he cleared the doorway he turned left, away from any opening that might expose him to a nearby hit. In the darkness were fifteen to twenty members of the unit. Some were in boxer shorts, some in less; but all were in flak jackets and carried weapons. A few wore helmets..

If this wasn't so serious, this would make a great picture, thought Trevanathan. *Jeesez; I've been here for six months with little trouble and now they try to grease me twice in one night.* Looking around, he could see that no one was taking control of the situation. *We need to get organized and figure out what is gonna' happen if someone starts firing into this building. At this point we're more likely to shoot each other than the enemy*, he thought.

The rumble of men in boots echoed down the marble staircase from the Marine quarters on the second floor, above. "Make way for the QRF[59]. Make way for the QRF," an assertive voice demanded. Seconds later the same voice roared, "Get your ass out of the way before I kick it between your shoulder blades!" as Gunnery Sergeant Muldoon and his men swarmed through the ceremonial hallway to take positions outside.

Inside the dark hallway, Trevanathan could hear Muldoon directing his team. "I want that SAW set up here on the veranda," he demanded. "Lopez, Contreras, get your butts down to that corner and make sure no one comes up that path. Corporal Penny, secure the left flank of the veranda with Bishop." Raising his voice, Muldoon yelled back into the interior of the building. "If you're not QRF, stay inside. If it's moving outside and it's not QRF it's gonna' die!" No one inside believed this was an idle statement. In the darkness, metal-jacketed rounds clattered on the floor as nervous fingers sought to load weapons and magazines.

"Ridlin, you point that weapon at me again and I'm breaking it over your head," said Mantis from down the dark hallway. "Sorry, Sergeant," came Ridlin's timid reply.

"Keep it down over there" said Trevanathan into the darkness. "Ridlin, maintain weapon discipline."

"Yessir," came the simultaneous replies from Mantis and Ridlin.

Trevanathan peered into the officer's quarters. It had been about five minutes since the explosions and there was no sign of a follow-on attack. "Well, this has been an exciting night," said a voice on his right, as Smith came sidling up next to him.

"All we need now is a plague of locusts and we can have our own book in the Bible," jested Trevanathan in a whispered voice.

---

[59] Quick Reaction Force – the team of soldiers detailed to be first responders to any attack.

A shadow caught his attention. "We got movement," he hissed quietly, his voice tense. Far across the rectangular officer's quarters, a dark figure moved stealthily into the room from the side entrance on the veranda. Silhouetted by the moonlight outside, Trevanathan could not make out any features.

"Get back against the wall," he whispered to Smith. *If anyone opens up in this place, trigger-happy idiots like Mantis will shoot us all by accident*, he thought. Trevanathan felt his sweaty grip on the pistol tighten, as the silhouette moved closer. The interloper moved steadily, looking side to side as if trying to detect movement. Hearing something, the intruder stopped abruptly in the middle of the room, tilting his head toward the hallway where Trevanathan was concealed. The Major slowly raised his 9mm pistol, centering its barrel upon the figure's chest.

I can't believe the QRF didn't see this guy, he thought. *If he has an automatic weapon I'm only going to get one shot before he hoses me down.* Trevanathan steadied his body and right hand against the frame of the doorway while his mind raced. *Do I call for him to halt, first? Or will that just give him a chance to nail me by giving my position away? What if he's just some knucklehead and not a Haji? But why is he sneaking around then?* Trevanathan could feel his heart pounding as he slipped his finger against the trigger.

As if he could hear the small movement, the figure spoke. "You gentlemen can come out," directed Gunny Muldoon. "False alarm."

Jeezus, thought Trevanathan, guiltily lowering his pistol sight from the middle of the Marine NCO's chest. He let out a breath that he felt like he had been holding since rolling from his cot. "Rick," he said to Smith, "Tell everyone to stand down and secure their weapons."

"Roger," said Smith, turning to walk back down the hallway.

"And Rick…," Trevanathan added, "make sure Ridlin unloads his weapon properly."

"Got it," said Smith.

"Gunny," asked Trevanathan as he stepped back into the room, "what happened? How was it a false alarm with all those explosions?"

"Well, sir," said the Marine, "turns out one of them helo jocks got a bit careless. A late patrol landed at the airfield about ten minutes ago. One of the pilots leaned on something unfortunate as he climbed out of his seat and sent three rockets streaking across the camp and into our backyard. They hit the dirt berm on the other side of the motor pool. No one hurt."

"Great," breathed Trevanathan wearily.

"You know the old saying, sir, 'Friendly Fire…isn't.'"

"Roger that, Gunny."

"G'Night, sir. Make sure your chicks secure all that ammo they were dropping around back there would ya,' sir?"

"Will do, Gunny. Good night."

Chapter 26
The Sheikh

Smith and Trevanathan sat in the rear seats of Gator One as it bumped along the dirt road ten kilometers south of Hillah. The sun hammered on the canvas roof, making the HMMWV an oven for the passengers inside. "So why is this Sheikh Ali so important anyway?" Smith asked Trevanathan.

"He was one of the first tribal leaders to turn on Saddam when the Marines entered this area," replied Trevanathan, glancing at the burned-out shell of an Army 5-ton truck that had been pushed to the side of the road. It had been stripped to its metal frame by the locals, who scavenged every destroyed Coalition vehicle down to the last piece of wiring. "He's friendly to the Coalition, and so we want to help him consolidate his position with the other tribes."

"It's not only that, counselor," said Colonel Rabbit, turning in the front right seat to address the officers behind him. "Sheikh Ali has land in the areas through which the oil pipelines run from central Iraq to the port at Um Qasr. By ensuring that he is on our side, we gain instant security along the pipeline from members of his tribe. They'll take it as a point of honor to protect the pipeline if we protect Sheikh Ali."

"Of course, it's not about the oil, right, sir?" joked Trevanathan wryly.

"Oh, no," said Smith with equal dryness, "That would be wrong."

Rabbit gave the two officers a blank look and turned back to searching for the turnoff into Sheikh Ali's compound. Trevanathan and Smith grinned at each other, amused that it was so easy to frustrate Rabbit's attempts to be insightful.

"Here it is, here it is." Rabbit pointed excitedly at a nondescript two-track dirt road leading back into the scrub, beside which a lone Iraqi wearing a stained, rust-colored man-dress stood, waving.

"Sir," Trevanathan said, leaning forward; "ol' Muhammad there has an AK-47 strapped across his back. Are you sure this is the turn?"

"I didn't think they were allowed to publicly carry weapons, anymore," commented Smith, shifting nervously in his seat. He and the other officers had been directed by Colonel Rabbit to leave their M16s at Camp Babylon as a sign of trust and respect for Sheikh Ali. Of course, each officer had shoved a 9mm pistol into the back of his pants underneath his BDU blouse, in a sincere sign of distrust of their host and Rabbit's judgment . Each one of them knew, however, that a pistol was about as useful as throwing rocks in a fight against an assault rifle.

"They're allowed to have weapons in their homes or in their tribal area," Rabbit said over his shoulder. "If we tried to disarm these tribes, we'd start another war, so it was easier to change the rules to keep everyone happy." He nodded at the Iraqi guard as the HMMWV turned.

As rough as the first road had been, the new track was worse, no better than a washboard that jarred the spines of the soldiers as the vehicle bounced unmercifully from ridge to ridge. Glancing back, Trevanathan saw that the three HMMWVs behind them, carrying the other Government Team members under Rabbit's direction, were completely lost from view behind the wake of dust behind them. *Sometimes it pays to be first*, he thought.

At the crest of a small rise, two boys of approximately 13-14 years of age stood guard beneath a gnarled old tree to the right of the road, folded AK-47s hanging from neck straps. They also waved to the soldiers as the HMMWVs passed. Trevanathan tried unsuccessfully to imagine his own teenage sons standing guard in the desert with automatic weapons.

Below, Sheikh Ali's compound sat in a small depression. Several small, white pickup trucks sat next to a long, rectangular tent that stretched into the middle of the compound. Blue smoke rose from a fire pit and hung lazily over the compound. "Looks like a West Texas barbecue," commented Smith happily, leaning forward to breath in the aromatic smell of meat cooking over an open fire.

As they stopped near the great tent, Trevanathan saw young men approaching from every corner of the camp, each bearing his own AK-47 slung casually across his chest or back. "This place is NRA heaven," Smith cracked, trying to reduce the tension of seeing heavily-armed Iraqi youths converge on their vehicles.

"I'm just glad they're smiling," said Trevanathan, noticing the relaxed gait and easy manner of the young men, who appeared to range in age from their early teens to their mid-twenties. "Hey sir, how do we surrender in Haji? Just curious, you know," Trevanathan quipped.

Rabbit ignored the banter behind him and quickly swung his feet out of the HMMWV, anxious to meet their host. The heel of his boot caught on the door lip, causing him to fall face-first into a field grade heap in the dirt.

"Nice entrance," Smith said quietly to Trevanathan. Trevanathan bit his lip to keep from laughing, and dismounted from the back seat to assist the colonel. A large man in a long white man-dress and a black and white checkered head scarf hurried from the side entrance of the tent, reaching Rabbit with speed surprising for a man of his size.

"Colonel, my Colonel," said the Iraqi in slightly-accented English, grabbing Rabbit's left arm and pulling him to his feet. "I apologize for the condition of my poor compound. Please forgive our rude welcome." He turned and called over a small wizened man standing near the door to the tent. He spoke sharply to the man in Arabic, and then struck the side of the smaller man's head that sent him reeling into the dirt several meters away.

Very nice, thought Trevanathan, observing the theater being played out before him. *Remove the embarrassment from the guest by placing the blame upon an underling. Very interesting how these Hajis operate*, he thought, while maintaining a pleasant smile. *Saving face and preserving honor is more important than the reality of the situation. I need to remember that in dealing with these people.*

"Come, and welcome to my humble tent," said the man, whom Trevanathan realized must be Sheikh Ali himself. He grasped Rabbit's hand warmly in both of his and shook it heartily, then released his grip and touched his right hand to his heart. "Salaam Alekim."

"Thanks, Sheikh," rasped Rabbit in his high-pitched Southern accent, missing the opportunity to return the culturally correct and expected response of "Alekim Salaam."

Rabbit wiped the caked dust off the right side of his face with his sleeve, then turned to introduce Smith and Trevanathan to Sheikh Ali. "Salaam Alekim," stated Trevanathan as he grasped the large man's hand and then touched his own heart. Smith followed suit, as the Sheikh inclined his head slightly, pleased that these American officers had learned the customs of his country.

"Please, please, come in out of the sun and refresh yourselves," said the Sheikh, opening a flap in the side of the tent and waving his hand. As they followed their host into the shade inside, Trevanathan felt that he had walked onto a movie set. Lining the walls of the tent were several dozen older men dressed in full length, white man-dresses and traditional head garb, sitting on rich rugs and sharing water pipes. The quality and cleanliness of their garments reflected that these were men of stature within the tribe. As the guests entered, these lesser sheikhs politely stood and waited expectantly.

"Permit me to introduce the elders of my tribe," said Sheikh Ali warmly. "As you see, the Mayor, the Chief of Police, and our Chief Judge are also in attendance," he said proudly, waving toward the head of the tent where the three officials stood on either side of a slightly raised platform.

Nice touch again, thought Trevanathan. *He shows the Haji officials how important he is by bringing the Americans to his tent. He shows us how important he is by having Haji big shots here. This guy is no dummy.*

Sheikh Ali led Colonel Rabbit to the place of honor on the platform, which bore expensive-looking rugs and embroidered pillows. Trevanathan and Smith followed as the remaining Government Team officers of the 538th belatedly entered the tent, blinking away the dust bath they had just endured behind Gator One. After urging Rabbit to seat himself, the Sheikh hurried back to greet each new arrival, drawing mixed success in his attempted exchange of traditional Iraqi greetings.

"Please, be seated, my friends," Sheikh Ali said to the assembled group. No sooner had the Americans and the other Iraqis done so, than servants appeared, bearing trays of Iraqi sweet tea. Iraqi tea is delicious, and one reason it is so acceptable to the American palate is that each four-ounce glass contains nearly an ounce of sugar. Because of the sweetness, the more one drinks, the thirstier one becomes. Still, it beats a mouthful of desert sand and the soldiers gratefully gulped down the hot liquid.

As they drank, Sheikh Ali began a long, rambling speech discussing the long and proud friendship between the United States and the Iraqi people – an observation that caused Smith's brow to crinkle in disbelief. "Steady," said

Trevanathan softly. He knew that after Smith spent six months in the desert in 1990 helping to run the Iraqi Army out of Kuwait, his fellow officer did not consider the Iraqis to be "longstanding" friends.

Once again the Sheikh shows us that saving face is more important in this culture than fact, observed Trevanathan.

During the next 30 minutes, Sheikh Ali spoke about the "criminal donkey" Saddam Hussein and the crimes the missing President had perpetrated upon the Iraqi people. He concluded his speech with a call for the Iraqi people to find new leadership with the strength and wisdom to lead them into a successful future with their American friends. "By which he means himself, of course," Trevanathan whispered to Smith, who nodded sagely as if agreeing with Sheikh Ali's last point.

Sheikh Ali sat down with a great grunt of satisfaction and signaled with his hands for Colonel Rabbit to say a few words. "Sweet Jesus, no," Trevanathan hissed to Smith, imagining himself and the others staked to an ant hill and smeared with honey as throngs of rifle-toting youths threw lots for their ears.

"Well, thanks a lot, Sheikh," said Rabbit as he stood, pleased as always to have a captive audience. "I shore do want to thank you and all the other sheikhs for your hospitality. You know a couple of years ago you boys were part of the axis of evil that the President said was a threat to civilization. Now we're sittin' here drinkin' tea together and getting along just fine…"

"Shoot him," said Smith through clenched teeth. "Shoot him now. I'll swear it was self-defense."

"…Anyway, it just goes to show what people can do together when they decide to cooperate. Thanks a lot." concluded Rabbit, smiling broadly at the silent tent.

"Or when three divisions of armor shove themselves up your backside," whispered Trevanathan to Smith.

"Thank you, thank you, Colonel," said Sheikh Ahmed, standing and embracing Rabbit warmly for all to see.

"The Sheikh has got to be thinking, 'How did we ever lose to these shmoes?'" Trevanathan commented quietly, causing Smith to choke a mouthful of tea down the wrong pipe, setting off a fit of coughing. "Damnit, Bill," sputtered Smith, recovering. "Don't do that!"

Sheikh Ali looked down the tent to ensure his coughing guest was OK, and then toward the tent flap where the servant he had cuffed earlier waited. The Sheikh clapped his hands sharply twice and the little man pulled back the cloth opening to allow a parade of male servants bearing large silver trays to enter the tent. The massive platters held mounds of rice upon which rested roasted goat and lamb. The smell of meat and spices filled the tent and Trevanathan's mouth watered. A thin, elderly man with skin baked red by years in the sun, placed one of the large silver platters at Trevanathan's feet. Upon the bed of rice lay the roasted torso of a young goat, split open like a baked fish, revealing the ribs and backbone. The old man, who Trevanathan thought looked like an Iraqi version of Gabby Hayes, knelt and motioned for the officer to pass him the small plate in front of him.

Trevanathan knew that the Iraqi custom was to eat with one's hands, or by scooping up rice and meat with soft flatbread, in one fluid motion. Fluid, that is, if one had years of practice since childhood – more often this was a mess for those unpracticed Westerners. Apparently there was no reliance on serving tools, either, as Trevanathan watched "Gabby" tear strips of goat meat off the carcass with his bare hands, adeptly flicking them onto his plate. He felt his initial enthusiasm for the meal begin to wane.

"Mmmmm," commented Smith in a low voice, "Can only imagine where those hands have been." His amusement at Trevanathan's discomfort was obvious.

Ignoring Smith, Trevanathan leaned forward and quietly asked his server, "Do you speak English?" The old man responded with a nod and a broad smile that revealed two teeth perfectly centered in an otherwise vacant set of gums – one on top and one on bottom.

Must save a fortune on toothpaste, thought Trevanathan as he had to force himself not to stare at the stained brown teeth clacking together happily in the middle of the man's mouth.

"You don't speak English, do you?" Trevanathan asked again pleasantly, eliciting the same happy, vacant response, who shoved the now-heaping plate toward the officer.

Beside the dentally-challenged man, a younger serving man with similar issues also pushed a plateful of hand-picked goat toward Smith.. "Oh, no, really," said Smith smiling his best fake smile. "I had a rather large brunch, really." The server jabbered something unintelligible in Arabic and motioned enthusiastically for Smith to try the delicacy before him.

"You know," commented Trevanathan, "My dad told me before I came over here that if you refuse to accept food from an Arab, it's taken as a huge insult against their honor, and they kill you."

"I could deal with that right now," said Smith staring dubiously at the gray, greasy meat on the plate before him.

"For God and country," said Trevanathan, grasping a handful of rice and goat from the plate and popping it in his mouth. He swallowed quickly and gave a wan smile to his server to show how truly delicious he found the slick flesh.

Smith followed suit and tried a mouthful, dropping half of it onto the rug. "Hey, it's not half bad," he said, pleasantly surprised that the first bite had somehow not managed to kill him. He scooped another handful into his mouth, managing to lose only a few grains of rice this time. Trevanathan watched him dubiously.

"Hey, what's that white stuff?" asked Smith, pointing at several glistening nodules inside the abdominal cavity of the animal. Taking Smith's motion as a request, the dentally-challenged server reached into the goat carcass and tore off a sizable piece of fat, before placing it onto Smith's dish. Trevanathan laughed at Smith's predicament, causing the eager-to-please server to deposit an even more impressive quantity of the gelatinous fat upon Trevanathan's plate.

"Not in a million years," said Smith under his breath, looking dubiously at the globules of pale flesh shining on his plate.

"Oh, yeah, Captain," nodded Trevanathan, "you asked for it, you got it."

Trevanathan scooped up a generous portion of rice with the pale fat from his plate in an attempt to mask the taste. His effort was wasted: the distinct, slimy texture of the jiggling fat overrode any attempt at camouflage as it traveled down his throat. Finishing a very hard swallow, Trevanathan smiled weakly at his server and said to Smith, "The good news...," he coughed and paused momentarily to fight his gag reflex. "The good news," he repeated with malice as Smith placed a pinch of the fat into his own mouth, "…is that it's half-cooked, as well." He watched the color drain from Smith's face as the raw goat fat slid down the back of his friend's throat.

"Keep it down, buddy," Trevanathan encouraged, as he saw Smith fighting the urge to forcefully return the offending substance to its point of origin. "This is why you make the big money."

Smith nodded, pinching his eyes together tightly as he fought off his body's objections with a shiver. As he recovered, he weakly gasped, "Just like mom used to make…" A peculiar greenish tinge accented his face.

The banquet continued for another two hours. Following the main course, servants brought trays of honey cakes and strong Arab coffee. Despite the fact that the cakes were truly delicious, the officers' enthusiasm for the meal had departed with the main course. Later that night, Smith lay on his cot in the palace at Camp Babylon and listened to the bats squeaking outside. He thought back to meals he had complained about back in the States, where the meat was just slightly too rare or well done. As his digestive track rumbled in protest, Smith swore to himself that he would never complain about some marginal variation in the preparation of food again. The thought of living in Iraq for the rest of his life, eating half-cooked goat, caused him to involuntarily shudder and groan, as sleep took him.

Chapter 27
The Unit of the Damned

"Hey Bill, me and some of the boys are trying to get a volleyball game goin' – are you interested?" asked Doc on one of the rare afternoons most of the camp had been granted "off," in this case for Labor Day.

"Thanks, Doc," said Trevanathan, reclining in his cot, "but I'm going to take advantage of the down time to write some cards home. You guys go ahead."

"OK, we're going to go challenge the chemical unit that's stationed on the other side of the airfield."

"Have fun," replied Trevanathan, settling back to his writing.

B Company of the 673d Chemical Brigade, Arkansas National Guard, had been attached to the Marine Expeditionary Force to provide additional decontamination capacity in the event the Marines came under chemical attack in their advance on Baghdad. As chemical warfare specialists, they were one of the most intensively trained and highly skilled units in the reserve system. Trained to respond to nuclear, biological or chemical attacks, they deployed to Iraq with high expectations of playing a pivotal role in the seizure of Saddam's stockpile of chemical weapons.

The chemical attacks did not come, however, and after the first few weeks of false alarms, a malaise had settled over the unit that seemingly had no mission. Its presence, initially so vital to the Coalition victory, gradually became an embarrassing reminder to Coalition officials that the claimed rationale for the invasion of Iraq had been a house of cards.

The command tent for B Company had originally been adjacent to the 1st MARDIV[60] tactical operations center so that precious seconds would be saved in case of a chemical attack. "I want that chemical commander so close I can feel his belt buckle," intoned the colorful MARDIV commander. As such an attack failed to develop, however, the unit was shifted to the edge of the cluster of command tents. Finally, as new coalition troops from Eastern Europe began to move into the increasingly crowded cluster wedged between

---

[60] 1st Marine Division

212

the palace and the mess hall, the B Company was "laterally reallocated" to the east edge of the camp, on the far side of the airfield. There, it was out of sight and mind of the busy combat commanders who were recasting Iraq's future and their own promotion potential.

As Doc and Sergeant Monkeybusiness walked up to the concertina wire that marked B Company's area, they noted that the makeshift guard shack at the entrance was empty. In fact, there was no apparent sign of life whatsoever among the cluster of GP-medium[61] tents behind the wire.

"Are you sure this is their area?" Doc asked his young NCO, as he looked about doubtfully. Two stray dogs lay flat in the shade of a nearby tent, tongues hanging out of their mouths as they endured the midday heat. "Yassir," said Monkeybusiness. "They are the only unit on this side of the airfield."

As the wind shifted from the north, the two soldiers heard the faint sound of music beyond tents to their left. "Well, sounds like someone's home," said Doc. "Let's check it out."

As the two soldiers made their way around the cluster of tents, they heard voices above the music. Rounding the corner of the last tent, they stopped in their tracks and stared at a group of civilians dressed in flowered shirts that would have made a Palm Beach retiree blush. The astonishing group lounged about a crude hot tub that had been set up under some camouflage netting. A pretty blond girl in a pink blouse sat on a stack of HMMWV tires, her hair tied back in a pony tail as she strummed an acoustic guitar. Another girl, wearing a bikini top and shorts, swayed to the music and sang a slightly familiar country-western tune. Three bushy haired young men, sporting multiple tattoos on their broad arms and shoulders, lolled about in the tub, which appeared to have been constructed from a giant field water bladder.

"Excuse me," stammered Doc. "I was looking for the chemical company." Monkeybusiness' attention eyes focused on the two sprightly young musicians and he flashed his most winning Latino smile at them.

---

[61] General Purpose, canvas tent; approximately 10 x 5 meters.

"You found us, sir," said one of the tub occupants, looking back over his shoulder. "I'm Sergeant Best, and this is the fighting 673d...," he chuckled, "or what's left of it."

"Aaahh, well, I'm Major Heller, from the 538th CA Brigade," said Doc slowly, still trying to reconcile the scene before him. "We, aahh,,... wanted to see if your unit was interested in some volleyball this afternoon."

"Man, that sounds great, sir, but we're a little shorthanded right now. Some of the boys are down at the Haji market outside the wire getting some fixin's for our, uh, trash can punch, and several others are over at the aid station trying to get profiles[62] for one thing or another."

"Is your commander around?" asked Doc.

"Ahh, yes sir, I believe he's in his tent. It's the first one on the right side when you come in the gate."

"Do you know there's no one at the gate?" asked Doc. "We just walked right in and no one stopped us or asked us our business here."

"Hmmm," said Best, trying to appear concerned. "I guess Private Weathers must have snuck off to the Haji market with his friends. I'll have to have a word with him when he gets back, sir."

"Ahh, sir," said Monkeybusiness eagerly, "would you mind if I stayed here a few minutes while you visit with their commander?" His eyes never left the now-smiling young women.

"Yeah, sure, Sergeant M," said Doc. "I'll come back for you in about fifteen minutes."

Doc walked back across the small compound, again encountering no one. A giggle and a high pitched whoop came from a tent to his left as he made his way to the commander's tent. A sign hanging from the flap of a GP-small[63] tent stated, "CPT Timothy Blaze, Commander."

---

[62] The written opinion of a medical doctor that exempts a soldier from duty based on illness or injury is called a "profile" in Army parlance.
[63] General Purpose, canvas tent; approximately 5 x 5 meters; commonly used for command posts or officer billeting.

One of the inconveniences of tents is there is no way to announce oneself, Lacking a doorbell or place to knock, one can only stand outside and yell, or perhaps shake a tent flap, hoping someone will notice. Or, one can simply enter the tent unannounced, which is what Doc did. Inside, the tent was dark: the small canvas window flaps had been tied down from the inside. The familiar, slightly moldy smell of military canvas, unwashed clothing and the unmistakable odor of cheap alcohol.

"Captain Blaze?" asked Doc, looking around as his eyes tried to adjust to the gloom. "Captain?" he said a little louder.

"MMpphh," came a muffled response from a pile of rumpled laundry atop cot against the left wall.

"Captain Blaze," Doc said a little louder, "I'm Major Heller."

At the mention of a higher rank, the man beneath the pile of laundry slowly swung upright and slurred, "OOhh, morning shir, do you have a mission for us?"

"Ahh, not exactly, Captain, I was hoping to get your unit to play ours in volleyball this afternoon, but your Sergeant Best said that the unit is shorthanded."

"Oh, we're shorthanded alright sir. Shorthanded…," he repeated again, his voice trailing off.

"Umm, do you mind if I open a tent flap or something?," asked Heller. The stale air inside the tent was quickly becoming overpowering.

"No, no, go right ahead, sir – make yourself at home."

Doc turned to the wall of the tent and rolled up the inner window flap. Light flooded into the room, causing Blaze to recoil. Doc examined the man before him, and saw a almost-wraithlike creature in a dirty brown t-shirt and boxer shorts, sporting a two-day beard and dark purple circles under each eye. Blaze had the look of a man who had been hit by a two-by-four between the eyes.

"Captain, are you alright?" asked Doc cautiously.

"Yeah, yeah, I'm fine, sir,…just waking up kinda' slow." Blaze rubbed the palms of his hands into bloodshot eyes.

In the light now flooding into the space, Doc saw that another, unoccupied cot sat against the opposite wall. This bunk was maintained in an immaculate military manner, with all of the owner's property stowed beneath, or hanging from a makeshift clothes line in the far corner.

"I'm sorry, sir," said Blaze again slowly, moving his neck around in a slow circle, as he rubbed the back of his neck, "Who are you again?"

"I'm Major Heller, 538th CA. Just came by for a social call." Doc's eyes dropped to the corner of Blaze's bunk, where a bottle of the local Haji whiskey commonly known as, "Five Dollar Rotgut" sat, three-quarters empty. Available at most Army refueling stations along the main supply route, Rotgut was usually hawked by small Iraqi boys who would chase alongside the convoys as they slowed to turn into the refueling point. Most US troops, even those desperate for a drink, knew better than to tap into Rotgut, which was rumored to be a combination of wood alcohol and rice wine.

"Captain, I'm a nurse by trade. So let's put rank away for a minute. What the hell is going on around here? There's no one guarding your compound. The people I could find were having a luau, and you're sitting in this stinkatorium three sheets to the wind."

Blaze looked blearily at the officer standing before him. "Sir, I'm not one to snivel, so I'd just as soon not talk about it, if you don't mind."

"Try me."

"Well, sir," Blaze paused momentarily to swallow deeply before continuing, "you asked, so I'm gonna' tell ya'. This here is one of the best chemical warfare companies in the Guard – not that you could tell by looking at us these days. The officers and NCOs of this unit spent years training for the day when some bad guy would let loose with a chemical attack and we'd get the call."

"Well that day has never come yet, thank God, so when Baghdad fell we were shifted over to the search for chemical weapons. It took a couple months to realize there weren't gonna' be any weapons found, but we were told to keep up the search anyways so that the President wouldn't be embarrassed. So, like good soldiers, we did. But pretty soon they even stopped sending us out on those missions, because it became a news event that we were still lookin' and coming up empty. So they parked us over here on the far side of this airfield with no mission and forgot 'bout us."

"So you cashed it in because you didn't have a mission, is that it?" Doc asked, trying to keep the edge out of his voice.

"Ohhh, that it was that simple sir. If that was the case I could just be called a bad commander and that would be a happy ending. But no…" The Captain closed his eyes and swayed on the edge of his cot for several minutes, as Doc waited.

"Well…?" asked Doc, unsure if Blaze was still awake.

Slowly opening his bleary eyes and focusing with some difficulty, Blaze continued. "Well.., after four months of nothin', they told us we were going home. Said to pack up and prepare to return home so we'd be available for 'next time,' whenever that may be. So we did. But nothin' happened. We sat and waited, and no orders came. Finally I sent a request for information up through my chain of command. It took a week, but then my brigade commander called and said no one is going home. Said the new General in Baghdad had come up with a 365 days boots on the ground policy, which meant no one leaves – whether they're needed or not – whether they have a mission or not. So we were told just to sit here and wait."

"And that's what broke your unit?"

"No, sir, not even that would have ripped the guts out of this unit. I mean, no one was happy with it, but these are experienced NCOs and officers, and we're used to getting screwed by Uncle Sam on a semi-regular basis. They had their pride to maintain and would not throw in the towel."

Captain Blaze looked slowly about as if trying to remember why he was sitting in this tent, before continuing. "No, the same military genius who came up with the 365 day policy also now realized he had a lot of unemployed troops sitting out in the desert and a shortage of military police to protect the highways and checkpoints. So, they called us up, told us we were now military police, not chemical warfare experts, and split us up to guard checkpoints. They gave us a three-day crash course on tactical MP security and put my boys out on the checkpoints along Highway 8." Blaze shook his head and rubbed the back of his neck gingerly as the memory still pained him.

"They took the best chemical warfare experts in the world and turned us into security guards," he stated bitterly.

"That sucks, Captain, but everyone over here is doing jobs that are new to them…" Doc began.

Continuing as if he had not heard, Blaze went on. "The first day on the job in Najaf, a Haji car bomber drove right through two of my young guys, who were uncertain how to react, and blew up another six of my guys in one blast. Wasn't hardly 'nuff of 'em left to even send home, but the Army put some scraps together in coffins and shipped 'em back to their proud hometowns.

"Well, that was enough for me and most of my boys. We didn't mind not bein' used and we didn't mind bein' misused, but when they started setting us up for failure by puttin' troops with no security or law enforcement experience in that position with bullshit training I had enough. I put in a formal protest and requested my unit be reassigned to 'more appropriate duties.'" A flicker of life crept into the Captain's eyes. "Know what happened?"

"Tell me," said Doc.

"Well, first of all, I was admonished for not being a team player and 'whining' about a tough mission. That's what they called it – 'whining.' The General said the most important thing to do was to get my boys right back out there – so they wouldn't lose their nerve. So that's what they did. Next night my boys were right back out there on the checkpoint, nervous as mother hens, waiting for their turn. I went out with 'em to try to keep up their spirits, ya' know?"

"Uh huh, so what happened?"

"Sure enough, another vehicle rolled up on one of our checkpoints and didn't immediately obey the signal to stop. Our guys were so jacked from the previous incident that they opened up on the car with a 50 cal. and turned the front seat occupants into a bloody pulp. Was like hittin' watermelons with a jackhammer." Blaze choked, his eyes filling with tears. "So…so we stopped that vehicle, by God."

Doc sat silently, watching the Captain closely.

"See sir, only problem was the occupants were just a family returning to their village. They didn't understand the hand signal to halt and one of our guys blew their brains all over the back seat. When we pulled their kids out of the car, they couldn't even talk. Two little girls, maybe 7 and 8, and a little boy, maybe 4 years old. The 'fifty' took the arm clean off one of the girls – she didn't even notice, she was in shock. The little boy had his parent's brains splattered all over his face and he just kept making this little animal whine. Not a scream and not a cry. Just kinda' like the high pitched sound an animal makes when it has its paw caught in a trap and can't understand why the pain won't stop."

Blaze paused and picked up the bottle of Haji whiskey. He looked at the label for a minute and then gulped a large mouthful before continuing.

"The kid just kept making that damn noise. I still hear it in my head. I hear it right now. He looked me in the eyes and just kept makin' that sound. I wanted to shake him to make him stop, but I just had to walk away. I hear it every night when I go to sleep and it's there when I wake up. Only the Rotgut makes it stop for awhile. It makes me so damn sick that I can forget about that sound for awhile."

"You need to get some help, Captain," suggested Doc. "There're people who can help with this sort of thing. Where's your XO?"

Blaze snorted, and motioned with his thumb at the empty bunk at the far end of the tent. "First Lieutenant Tripley, is my XO...was my XO," said Blaze. "They say that he ran about 50 yards with his clothes on fire after that car bomb went off before he collapsed. Then he just kind of twitched and rolled around in the dirt as they tried to put him out. He lived a few hours, but then that was it…." Blaze's voice trailed off.

"I haven't written home yet. I can't." he said, taking another long pull from the bottle. "Sir, we're the Arkansas Guard. Most of these boys come from the same twenty square miles 'round the Armory. I grew up with them and know their families… and I got 'em killed. How do I go home now? How do I tell my sister that her husband isn't coming home because he wasn't a good enough MP? That I let her husband die, because I couldn't get this unit home when it had no mission?"

"You know it's not your fault," said Doc. "Bad shit happens over here. Whether you're smart or whether you're unlucky. It just happens. Where's the First Sergeant?" asked Doc, hoping to find someone in authority who might take this situation in hand.

"Well, that's the good news in all of this," laughed Blaze bitterly. "They say that prosthetics have made a lot of progress since the First Gulf War and that he has a damn fine chance of walking again after his burns heal over....So we all have that to look forward to."

Doc stood there in silence, not knowing what he could say that wouldn't add to this man's pain.

"Sir, I'm feeling a mite poorly right now. You wouldn't be offended if I just laid down for a bit, would you?"

"No, no, you go ahead, Captain. I'll close this window flap for you."

"Thanksh, sir," slurred Blaze, as he rolled back onto his cot, his face to the wall and his back to Doc.

Doc slid out the flap of the tent into the blinding Iraqi sun. He stood there lost in thought, marveling at the beating this unit had taken – *and for what? They had lost their mission, their purpose, and most of their leadership. Not in any noble or meaningful battle or in accomplishing some vital military objective, but because someone had not had the balls or interest to send them home when they weren't needed any more.* "Set up for failure," Blaze had said. *There's a lot of that going on,* thought Doc sourly.

Christ, where are the bad guys like in those old John Wayne movies?, he wondered. *Over here all you see are dead soldiers and dead civilians. You never see the bad guys. There aren't any hills to take or enemy bunkers to knock out. There's just death, coiled up, waiting to lash out the second your guard is down for a second.*

Movement to his right caught Doc's attention, as Sergeant Monkeybusiness exited another of the small tents, adjusting his blouse and catching Doc's eye with a bright flash of his teeth. "Ready to go, sir?" he asked, as he walked up, beaming his winning smile. Doc looked over his NCO's shoulder as the guitar-strumming blonde left the same tent with a quick look around before darting back toward the hot tub.

"Well, I'm glad some things never change, Sergeant M," said Doc, with a tired shake of his head. "Let's get out of here and let these people rest in peace."

Chapter 28
The Long Haul

Colonel Hermann smoothed the pockets of his desert uniform as he waited for Brigadier General Merdier to meet with him. He stared out the window of the French doors into the lush rear garden, where a fountain shaped like a shellfish gurgled and splashed – a gross display of opulence in a water-deprived country like Iraq.

"I'm sure he'll be with you in just a moment, sir," said Sergeant Ben Flaherty, Merdier's driver and secretary. Flaherty was a bright young NCO from Jacksonville, Florida, who had received his sergeant's stripes at age 20. He had been halfway through his sophomore year at Auburn, maintaining a 4.0 grade average, when the call-up for Iraq came. Like so many other young reservists, he laid down his books, kissed his family goodbye, and went to fight and save people he had never seen before.

"Thanks, Sergeant Flaherty," said Colonel Hermann, noting Flaherty's neatly pressed uniform, a sharp contrast to his own rumpled DCUs, limp from the fourth day of wear since their bucket washing. Flaherty had always impressed him whenever he had visited Fort Rucker. Neither fawning nor aloof, he presented himself in a smart, professional manner. Eager to be of assistance when needed and smart enough to know when to duck out of the way, he was the epitome of the professional NCO. *A particularly valuable skill when working for Merdier*, thought Hermann.

The call to meet in Baghdad had come unexpectedly. Relayed from the Marine G3 Operations Center at Camp Babylon, the message had simply stated, "Report to BG Merdier at 1300Z tomorrow." Hermann thought that it must have something to do with their upcoming rotation home, as no other significant issues were looming. *Maybe this is his farewell speech*, thought Hermann, letting his mind wander. *Maybe he wants to congratulate me on a job well done. We have had some good feedback from the Marine Corps. He probably wants to pass on his best wishes to the men*, he thought. Hermann's congratulatory fantasy had occupied his mind over most of the sixty mile trip from Babylon.

"Flaherty!" roared a voice from behind the ornate parquet door leading into Merdier's office. "Yes sir," replied Flaherty, quickly scrambling to his feet and sticking his head inside the door.

"Send in Hermann," said Merdier briskly.

"Sir, the General will see you now," said Flaherty pleasantly, turning back to Hermann on the other side of the door. A little shiver ran down the Colonel's spine as he stepped quickly to the door, pulled it open, and entered the office in a purposeful fashion.

"Good morning, sir," said Hermann brightly, trying to balance being pleasant against looking overeager as he entered the office.

"Hmphh," said Merdier, continuing to review the papers on his desk. Hermann stopped before the General's desk at the position of attention and raised a crisp salute to the corner of his eye.

Merdier continued to read. Hermann stood before the desk, the salute still held in place, waiting to be put at ease.

Silence.

Merdier continued to read, taking no notice of the brigade commander postured formally before his desk.

"Aahh, you asked to see me, sir?" asked Hermann quietly, desperately hoping to ease the uncomfortable silence, as he continued to hold the now-awkward salute.

"Of course I *ordered* you here, Hermann," said Merdier, looking up with a sneer. "Would you be here otherwise?" He eyed Hermann narrowly, still not returning his salute.

Hermann had a reputation as a "comer" in the ranks of the Civil Affairs community. He had served in Haiti and Bosnia as a G5 – Civil Military Operations staff officer – before landing the brigade command. He had attended all of the appropriate military training schools and had been an honor graduate of his Civil Affairs Advanced Course. He was thought to be a likely candidate for a CACOM command in the near future, and was well-liked by his peers.

Merdier couldn't stand him. Looking the Colonel over carefully, the senior officer concluded that the brigade commander was too eager to please for his taste. *Would suck the brass off my belt buckle if it would buy him a star,* he thought, unkindly.

"Sit down, Hermann," said the General, with a wave of his hand toward one of the two high-backed wooden chairs across from his desk.

"Yessir." Hermann dropped his salute awkwardly and moved into the chair near the right-hand corner of the impressive desk.

"I hear good things about you, Hermann," said Merdier, trying to exude momentary warmth that was unnatural for him. "Your people are doing good work down there with the Marines."

"Thank you, sir, said Hermann with a smile. "That's very kind of you."

"Yes, yes," said Merdier quickly, wishing to cut off any ingratiating maneuvers by Hermann. "The MEF commander, Lieutenant General Cartwright, has informed me that you've become irreplaceable down there."

Not sensing the trap, Hermann gushed, "Well, we really enjoy supporting the Marines, sir. They're great war-fighters."

"Good, good," said Merdier, his voice taking on a smooth, hypnotic quality as his eyes danced with merriment before delivering the *coup de grace*. "That's good, because, …you see…you'll be here with them for awhile longer."

"Sir?" asked Hermann, his voice cracking slightly as he felt his stomach turn.

"Yes," said Merdier, bringing the axe down at full swing. "The CG is concerned about lack of continuity if we start rotating too many of our experienced units out of theater at this critical time." Merdier's eyes danced across Hermann's face, watching the color drain from his cheeks.

"But,…but, what about the 503rd, sir? They were to replace us," asked Hermann weakly, his head swimming as he tried to digest what Merdier was saying.

"Oooh, they're coming," said Merdier brightly. "They're certainly coming. It's just they're not coming for another three months." He could not longer conceal a smile at the power he felt watching Hermann squirm like bait on a hook.

"Uh sir, we're rotating out in three weeks. This is going to go down awfully hard with the troops," said Hermann, "I,...I...mean, of course, we are happy to do our part, sir. It's just this is kind of unexpected."

Merdier pursed his lips behind the fingertips he had raised together in a prayerful manner before his thin lips. "This is war, Hermann," he said, no trace of compassion in his tight voice. "Maybe we should ask Al Qaeda to schedule this fight around your other personal commitments?" One corner of his lip turned up in a mocking sneer.

"No, no – not at all, sir. It's just...what can I tell the men, sir? You know, to keep up morale?"

"Tell 'em what the CG told me, Hermann. There's not enough troops. We thought this thing would be over in a year and it's turned into a tar baby of Biblical proportions."

Hermann's head swam as he tried to recall any Biblical references to tar babies.

"We sent half our Army over here, Hermann, and these bastards still don't know that they're licked. We kicked their Haji butts from the Persian Gulf to the Turkish border and they barely put up a fight. Now that we've gone and tried to bring them a little of the benefits of Western-style living, they're throwing it back in our faces."

"Yessir," said Hermann weakly, his mind whirling over how to drop this bomb on his unit.

"Cradle of civilization?" mocked Merdier. "The people here don't live any better today than they did three thousand years ago. They still use donkeys for God's sake," he marveled, with a shake of his head. "Their problem is they don't know when they've lost, and they refuse to help themselves, so we need to stay and baby-sit them a bit longer. That requires bodies and Rummy doesn't have them right now."

"But, didn't anyone think of this, when the invasion was planned?" asked Hermann softly, mostly to himself.

"Look, Hermann," said Merdier flatly, "this is the deal and I need you to get behind it. You want that CACOM command don't you?" he asked sharply. Merdier saw that the mention of a higher command slot had recaptured Hermann's attention. "Sure, I know you do. You get behind this, support it, and sell it to your troops. Tell 'em it's necessary to protect their loved ones back home. They'll buy that. Team players get rewarded, and I need you on my team for this one. Can you do that for me?" Merdier asked with feigned sincerity, painting Hermann into a corner where only one answer was possible.

"Yessir," said Hermann, strength slowly returning to his voice. "But are we sure the situation will be any different in three months?"

"Oldhouse and CAPOC are cranking out a new raft of CA troops to ease the pain and get you out of here by year's end," answered Merdier. "They're recruiting like crazy back home. They just need a little more time."

A CACOM command, thought Hermann. *Well, this sucks, but what can I do but make the best of it? The men will understand.* He imagined his wife pinning General's stars on his shoulders at a Pentagon ceremony. Shaking his head to clear the vision, he said, "Sir, the 538th is ready to go the distance."

"Great, *great*. I knew I could count on you, Dick," said Merdier as he stood and moved around the corner of his desk, extending his hand with a cold smile. Hermann rose and shook the offered hand, looking warmly into the flat, reptilian eyes that gleamed back at him. "We won't let you down, sir."

"That's fine Dick, that's fine. Say, on your way out would you ask Sergeant Flaherty to come in?"

"Yessir, said Hermann easing toward the door while still facing the General.

"Oh, and Dick?"

"Yessir?"

"I don't want a raft of sniveling congressional inquiries coming out of this, do you understand? Ride herd on your people."

"Yessir," said Hermann, saluting crisply. With no indication from the General that his courtesy would be returned, he eased out of the room.

Flaherty entered the General's office seconds later, an expectant look on his tanned features. "Yessir? Can I get you anything?"

"Is Jessup here yet?" asked Merdier, referring to the 803d CA Brigade commander, who was the next one due to learn of his unit's extension.

"No, sir, but he should be here momentarily."

"Good, good," said Merdier. *It's time to rock his world as well*, he thought.

Chapter 29
The Honest Man

After Colonel Jessup numbly retreated from Brigadier General Merdier's office, Sergeant Flaherty slipped back in. "Sir, if I may, I couldn't help overhearing you mention that USACAPOC is training replacements. How long until the new troops are ready, sir?" he asked expectantly. He faintly hoped this news might mean he'd see his own young family sooner rather than later.

"Never," answered Merdier, as he filed papers into the three-drawer cabinet next to his desk.

"Sir?" asked Flaherty, a confused look on his face.

"There's no big recruitment campaign. Too expensive – can't afford the personnel. The word coming down from SECDEF is make due with what you have."

"Yes, sir," said Flaherty doubtfully, surprised that Merdier had blatantly lied to Hermann and Jessup. Flaherty had been with Merdier for nine months and knew that the General had a forceful personality that tolerated little dissent, but he had not seen this side of the man before, and it disturbed him.

"This war is a real opportunity, Sergeant Flaherty," said Merdier settling back into his large leather chair. "Those who realize it and seize the opportunity will be set for life." Flaherty stared without responding.

"Why," said Merdier, reclining in his chair and staring up at the large crystal chandelier that dominated the office, "I can see the Pentagon adding one or two more two-star slots within the Civil Affairs branch if this pace continues. There's no way that hack Oldhouse can keep a handle on things at Bragg and over here. They'll have to expand the command structure…and that means opportunity," he said with a wistful smile on his face, as he imagined receiving his second star.

"Yes, sir," said Flaherty, "but isn't there a chance we're gonna' lose an awful lot of people from the Reserves if this keeps up?"

The smile disappeared from Merdier's face as he rocked forward and fixed a stern look on Flaherty. "You think too small, Sergeant Flaherty," he chided. "You need to think of the big picture. A few weak sisters trying to cash out is no reason to miss this chance."

"Yessir, the big picture" repeated Flaherty, unconvinced.

"The system protects itself, Flaherty. No one is getting out," the General revealed, a gleam in his eye. "There is a stop-loss on now for all Civil Affairs troops in the Army. That means no one can leave. Period."

"Yes, sir," said Flaherty, trying to follow the General's logic. "But that can't stay on forever, and the longer it is on, the more people who will bail out when it is lifted."

"Nonsense," said Merdier. "Our troops understand that we are fighting against Islamic Fascism here. If we don't stop these bastards here, they'll be knocking down buildings back home again in a heartbeat. The men understand that by being here, they are protecting their families. They'll do what it takes."

"I think you're right, sir," said Flaherty, trying to not contradict the General. "But at a certain point it seems that people may start choosing to stay with their families when the deployments are becoming so long and so frequent. I mean, most of us didn't expect the Army to become our main job when we joined the Reserves, sir."

"Sergeant, let me let you in on a little secret," said Merdier, all residual warmth leaving his voice as he again leaned forward on his elbows. "America does not have enough full-time troops to fight these terrorist bastards and to protect our other interests in Europe, Korea, and in South America. Iran is next door and is the wild card in this region with their nuke program. That crazy bastard Kim Il is always about one dose of Prozac away from starting WWIII on the Korean Peninsula. We need a million troops to cover all those commitments and we have half that many. The Reserves are the plug to fill that hole. Anyone who is in Civil Affairs right now better strap in and get ready to spend the next six years out of ten overseas protecting the empire."

"Sir, this stuff is way above my level, I know. But why doesn't Secretary Rumsfeld and the President expand the number of active duty troops then?"

"Flaherty," sneered Merdier derisively. "You really are a boy scout. It's money, Sergeant – the budget. Presidents don't get reelected by jacking up taxes to pay for new troops. They get reelected by giving tax breaks. We add the four to six divisions this Army really needs and that's another ten billion dollars of tax debt per year. Not good politics."

"Well, what will they do when the stop-losses get lifted and Reservists start bailing out sir? Won't that have a bad impact on national security – unless they expand the active forces?"

"Not going to happen, Flaherty. Do the math. When you get home there is a 90-day "going home" stop-loss when you do not have to be at the unit. No one leaves then, get it? Then there's about three months of recovering at the unit, cleaning equipment and all that. Well, unless you're smart enough to jump ship during that small, three month window, we have you again."

"I don't understand sir," said Flaherty, confused by the General's explanation.

"Remember when we mobilized for this operation, Flaherty? There was also a no-transfer, no-resign policy 90 days before the deployment."

Flaherty looked at the General blankly.

Merdier continued. "It means, Sergeant, that if you don't get out within that small 90-day window when you first start drilling again, we can slap another stop-loss down and ship you out again nine months after the previous mission ended."

Flaherty felt his stomach sink as the reality of what he was hearing hit home.

You mean, sir, that the Army can send me to Iraq for two years, send me home and then mobilize me for two more years?"

Merdier grinned savagely and said nothing.

"And there's only 90 days in that four-year period when I can get out?"

"Well, technically those 90 days exist, Sergeant, but you know how slowly paperwork gets processed around the headquarters," Merdier replied gleefully. "Realistically, if you don't put in for a transfer the second the stop-loss is lifted we gotcha' for another two years."

"But sir, isn't there some two-year limit I heard about?"

"That's a fantasy, too, Flaherty. The two-year limit for deploying reservists is on each military operation, not on your total service. All we have to do is ship you back to Afghanistan instead of Iraq and we're covered – different operation, so no limit applies."

Flaherty stood before the General's desk, feeling a flush of anger touch his cheeks. "Sir, I don't think that's what anyone bargained for when they joined the Reserves. I know my family didn't. Active duty troops only have a three-year obligation. This is like bein' drafted for life."

"Watch yourself, Sergeant," said Merdier, a scowl crossing his face. "We are a nation at war. There's no room for freelancing and lack of resolve."

"Sir, I love the Army, and I love my country. I don't mean any disrespect. It just seems unfair that no one is bein' up front with the troops about what they are being asked…ordered to do."

"Soldiers need to obey orders, Flaherty. And they need to trust their leaders. There's no room for selfishness."

"What about the families, sir? They didn't enlist, but it hits them even harder."

"The families will understand Flaherty. In WWII our boys went away for years, and there wasn't all this sniveling and hand-wringing. Sacrifice is needed to maintain our freedom."

"Yessir," said Flaherty, with an obvious lack of enthusiasm. He thought of his wife and 16-month old daughter in their small ranch house.

"War is hard on everyone, Sergeant F. But the decisions need to be made by people who can see the big picture. The President not only has to win a war, but he has to keep the economy strong, the deficit under control, and taxes at a palatable level for the majority of families who do not have anyone in the service. We need to focus on our mission here and trust those bigger thoughts to others."

Flaherty stared down at his boots, lost in the moment. Merdier closely examined him, thinking, *I can't afford to have a malcontent stirring the others up around the headquarters. I've told him too much.* "Ben, I need to finish up this report. Could you send Major Shmedlap in here?"

"Yes sir," said Flaherty quietly, and turned and quickly walked from the office. His teeth clenched at the thought that his service and his family's sacrifice was just part of a big budgetary equation. *I'm not missing my daughter's childhood just so the Pentagon can stretch a nickel further*, he thought.

Moments later Major Shmedlap stuck his head in the General's door and inquired, "Yes, sir?"

"Close the door, Ken," ordered Merdier. Shmedlap pulled the door behind him and stood expectantly.

"Ken, I think Flaherty doesn't feel fully *challenged* in his current position. I'd like you to cut orders sending him out to Task Force Dragon."

"Fallujah, sir?" asked the Major, his eyebrows arched in curiosity.

"Yes, I think he needs more field time to season his outlook. Have him attached to that recon team that is trying to gather info on Zarkhawi, all right?"

"Yes, sir," said the Major, recognizing that Merdier had just ordered a transfer equivalent to being sent to the Russian front. "I'll take care of it right away."

Merdier slowly shifted his weight back into the great leather chair and exhaled a deep, cleansing breath. His eyes returned to the twinkling colors of the chandelier above as his promotion fantasy slowly formed again. "Yes," he said to himself drowsily, "the future is very bright indeed…"

Chapter 30
The Call

"Daddeee!" yelped Christa Smith into the phone with excitement. "I love you, Daddeee!"

"I love you too, sweetheart," said Rick Smith, sitting in the sweltering MWR[64] tent on Camp Babylon. Through satellite hook-up, the troops could now call home once per week using a phone card. *A benefit of the digital age*, thought Smith...*and a curse at moments like this.*

"Will you still be home for my birthday party, Daddee?" asked Christa in that flirtatious voice she had developed over the past year. Christa, Smith's oldest, was almost five years old now, resembling her mother more with each passing month. She was the apple of her father's eye, which she knew and used to fullest effect. Smith had been amazed at the changes that already were standing out in the weekly pictures his wife mailed him. *She's wearing her hair longer now*, he had thought after receiving the last envelope.

"Well, I thought so honey, but it seems that they need to keep us soldiers here a bit longer." He could feel the lead weight lying in the bottom of his stomach.

"Will you be home next week, Daddee?" Christa asked innocently into the phone, not yet having developed a real sense of time.

"Umm, probably not honey," said Smith, scrambling to find the words that could help her understand. "Remember how I said I had to go help protect some people from some bad guys?"

"Yes," came the soft and uncertain reply in his earpiece, quickly losing its former excitement.

"Well, ya' see, we haven't caught all the bad guys yet, so the Army needs me to stay a little longer, sweetheart."

"How long?" came the low voice again. "How long, Daddee?" she pleaded.

---

[64] Morale, Welfare and Recreation

"I don't know sweetheart. I really don't know. Maybe by Christmas time."

The line was silent.

"Honey, …honey, are you there?"

"I'm here." His daughter's voice was weak and quavering over the 8,000 miles that separated them.

"Honey, I'm really sorry. I thought I'd be home by your birthday…The Generals just changed their minds again."

"I don't love you anymore, Daddee," the child breathed into the mouthpiece.

Smith felt as if a knife had torn through his heart. He closed his eyes and grasped the phone receiver with white knuckles. "Ohh, don't say that, honey. You're just upset. I am, too. The fact that I'm away for awhile doesn't mean I don't love you." Smith lowered his voice so that the other troops sitting a few feet away, engaged in their own slender contact with the real world could not hear him.

"I want a new daddy," said Christa petulantly, her voice becoming sharper. "Caitlyn's daddy comes home every night and sings to her."

"Honey, I'll sing to you too. It will just take Daddy a little while to come home. It's not my choice to be here honey. I have to."

"Caitlyn's daddy doesn't have to. Brittany's daddy doesn't either," her voice cracked. "Only you. Only you!" she shrieked, then broke into deep sobs.

"Honey…," started Smith, then he heard the handset on the other side of the world bounce on the kitchen floor. He sat there for a minute or two, pressing his own handset hard against his ear, willing the child to return and pick up the phone. He imagined the scene back home: Christa had most likely run crying into her room, where his wife would have followed; she probably didn't realize the phone was still off the hook. Finally, he replaced his handset on its cradle and numbly lowered his head onto the small plywood counter if the cubicle in which he was sitting. An overwhelming wave of despair washed over him: he no longer cared, nor was aware, that someone might see him in such a vulnerable state.

It's too much, he thought, slightly rocking his head from side to side as a low moan escaped his lips. *It's too much to ask of someone. To tell them that they're going home. To get the hopes of their family set on that homecoming, and to then rip it out of their hands at the last moment.*

How can a four year old girl understand it? he wondered, bitterly. *I can't even understand it. Christ, it's not like Pearl Harbor just got hit or the Germans rolled out of the Ardennes. We've been at war since 9/11, and they've been planning this mission since 2002. How can they not have planned for replacements?* A fresh wave of despair rolled over him.

It's not the being here, he reasoned to himself. *I was prepared for that…and a lot worse. It's the continuous mind-game of "You're going home, You're not going home; the tour has been shortened, the tour has been extended." Stop-loss policies that hold you like a slave; the tease that maybe you'll see your family soon – only to have it torn from your grasp because some asshole in the Pentagon couldn't plan more than six months out.*

This is it, he thought angrily, his teeth grinding in frustration. *I am never putting myself in the position again where someone else can tear the heart out of my little girl. If I die doing my mission, that's one thing. But I am not going to lose my family or break that little girl's heart because some politician or frickin' General sitting in Washington didn't think ahead or didn't want to spend the money to have enough troops available.*

"Sir…?"

As soon as I get back I'm getting out, thought Smith decisively. *I have to do what's right by my family. They've changed all the rules on us.*

"Sir,… are you OK?"

Startled, Smith looked up to see a solemn young Marine standing next to him, a look of concern on his face.

"Hrmmp," Smith cleared his throat and quickly wiped his eyes with the back of his hand. "Um,…yeah,…I'm fine," he said, haltingly. "Um,...sorry, son. I just learned my, uh,…Grandma died," he lied. "We were, ah, close."

"I'm sorry about that, Sir," said the Marine. "That's a shame,…But she's in paradise now, at least," he said earnestly in a Midwestern twang.

"Thanks, son," said Smith, appreciating the young warrior's effort. "But where does that leave us, then?"

Chapter 31
The Break

Smith sat in the plywood latrine constructed by the Seabees, and reflected on his situation, as several flies buzzed about his ears. *I am sitting in a makeshift outhouse, in Iraq, crapping into a tin bucket,* he mused, *and this is the high point of my day.* He quietly laughed to himself, remembering the sage observation of Sergeant First Class Warden back at Fort Bragg: "Ya'll haven't lived 'til you've spent time in a 130-degree port-a-shitter."

Still, I have it better than a lot of guys over here, he considered. *Hell, I remember when we had to use trench toilets at Whitehorse. You'd just squat down next to a line of strangers occupied in the same pursuit and give the old heave-ho. Seems like a million years ago, now.* His thoughts shifted to his coworkers at the processing plant in Lubbock. *Aahh, if they could see me now. When people are having their heads blown off around you, taking a public dump really isn't high on the list of things to worry about. I wonder if they'd be able to even begin to understand? Over here, it's just the law of diminishing expectations.*

Trevanathan had come up with "the law of diminishing expectations" while they were still in Kuwait, living in the tent city at Camp Commando before the outbreak of hostilities. "The Army has a way of lowering your expectations so that you come to expect the worst as being normal," he told his team as they sat huddled in a bunker during a chemical attack drill. "If you came directly here from your nice cozy home in Maryland or Pennsylvania, you'd say this place really sucked and question how people could stand to live like this. But the Army takes care of us and makes us appreciate the luxury of our current situation." He had laughed at the absurdity of his own words.

"Luxury? What luxury do we have here?" Smith had asked him at the time.

"Well, think about it," explained Trevanathan. "When we got mobilized we first went from our homes to the Reserve Center, where we got used to living in hotel rooms and eating restaurant food. Then we went to Fort Bragg and got used to group living in an open-bay barracks, eating Army mess hall food, and using a shared bathroom. Then they shipped us to the processing center at Camp Arifjan here in Kuwait, where we lived in a warehouse with 500 other troops, ate contractor mass prepared meals, and used those nasty toilet trailers. Now we live in a tent in the desert, eat T-ration spaghetti for breakfast, lunch and dinner, and use porta- johns that are rumored to have been the source of the Black Death in medieval Europe."

"So, what's your point?" Smith had asked, feeling that he had missed something.

"Let me ask you this: what would you do if instead of spaghetti tonight, you could have a meal back in the mess hall at Fort Bragg?"

"Oh, man," Smith had replied, "hot coffee, that crumb cake – and fresh fruit! I'd give a month's pay."

"*Exactly*," said Trevanathan. "That's the law of diminishing expectations. That institutional food at Bragg is something you wouldn't even touch if you were home, but now that you're here, it seems like the most wonderful thing in the world that the Army ever did for you. Your expectations for anything good are so low after a few weeks in this dump that anything else, no matter how shitty it really is, seems wonderful." Trevanathan had beamed at the simplicity of his philosophy.

"I guess I know what you mean," Smith had acknowledged. "When I was in Hungary for the Bosnia mission, I lived in a ten by twelve room with three other guys in an old Soviet barracks. A buddy of mine found an old abandoned building near the airfield that we took over and divided into 'rooms' using blankets and bunks. Man, I thought having a twelve by twelve space all to myself was living like a king."

Lost in his recollections, Smith was startled by the sound of the bucket beneath him – actually half of a 55-gallon oil drum – scraping across the concrete. One of the ,base Hajis whose job was to burn the waste in the buckets had opened the small hinged door on the back wall beneath the platform on which Smith unceremoniously sat.

"Hey, I'm working in here!" Smith yelled over his shoulder to the unseen collector.

"Sir, sir; is that you?" came an out-of-breath voice from in front of Smith's stall.

"Jeesez Christ," lamented Smith, "is it asking too much for five minutes to do my business in here? What am I, a tour bus stop?"

"Sorry, sir," came the voice, now identifiable as Ridlin. "Major Trevanathan ordered me to find you right away. Said it's an emergency. He needs you at the operations center five minutes ago."

"Wonderful," said Smith, giving up and tugging his pants up around his waist. "I'll fill out a scheduling form from now on so my bodily functions don't conflict with the crap collector and Major T's emergencies." Buttoning his fly, he buckled on the pistol belt that had been carefully placed on the plywood seat farthest from the hole. As Smith reflexively glanced back through the hole where he had been sitting, he was surprised to see the smiling face of the crap master staring up at him with a toothless grin. The interloper happily rambled off some phrase in Arabic, gave a quick wave of his hand, and slid an empty bucket back into position through the small opening and dropped the door.

"You have to respect a man who loves his work," mumbled Smith dryly, as he turned and lifted his 25-pound flak jacket from the one dry corner of the otherwise wet floor. Unfortunately, this motion dislodged his helmet from its carefully balanced position on a small piece of dry wood: it fell and rolled across the urine-soaked plywood at his feet. The dry cloth camouflage cover soaked up the stinking liquid.

"Beautiful," grumbled Smith, as he picked up his helmet and examined the large urine stain. "That's just great." He pushed open the door to find Ridlin still waiting outside. The young soldier glanced at Smith's helmet and grinned. "Looks like you dropped your helmet, sir," he said.

"Mmpph," replied Smith sourly, turning and moving into a quick walk toward the Brigade TOC. Thirty seconds later, he entered the single-story building, noticing the cooling effect of its thick concrete walls. Trevanathan sat at the Government Team's computer, a serious look on his face.

"What's up?" Smith asked, fearing the answer.

"I've got some bad news, Rick," replied Trevanathan flatly. "The convoy from the 814th CA Battalion that was due in today for leave was delayed and won't make its flight in time."

"That sucks," said Smith, "But what does that have to do with us?"

"What it has to do with us," said Trevanathan, "is that today's slots are now up for grabs. *You*, my friend, are going home for two weeks." His face broke into the grin he had been trying so desperately to hide.

"Home?" whispered Smith, his heart seeming to flip over in his chest.

Trevanathan kept grinning, but nodded.

"You bastard," Smith laughed, "I thought that something bad had happened!"

"Well, it did," cracked Trevanathan, pausing for dramatic effect, "for the 814th. You, on the other hand, have exactly 30 minutes to grab your shit and get back to the muster point behind this building. Warden is going too."

"Oh, man, my wife is gonna' have a cow when she sees me."

"Very attractive metaphor," said Trevanathan. "Now you've got 29 minutes. Time, tide and leave wait for no man, Captain, as the 814th is discovering. I suggest you move it."

"That's an order I can happily obey," replied Smith, moving toward the door. "Hold on," he paused, his forehead wrinkling, "with both of us gone, how will you run missions?"

"CAT Team A is going to float us Monkeybusiness and Jamie," said Trevanathan. "We'll be OK. 28 minutes."

"OK, OK, I'm moving!" said Smith as he bolted out the TOC door.

"And wash that helmet cover before you come back!" Trevanathan gleefully called after his disappearing friend.

Chapter 32
The Box

Smith's trip to the airfield near Al Kut was made in the open cargo bed of an Army 5-ton dump truck. Each soldier going on leave was required to carry a weapon in case of a problem en route, but due to the presence of two escort vehicles mounting heavy machine guns, the unit had sent them forth with the more portable 9 mm pistols, rather than M16 rifles.

"Ah feel nekkid without mah rifle," complained Warden, exaggerating his southern drawl as he climbed down from the truck at the end of the three-hour, sun baked haul.

"Yeah, it's strange," acknowledged Smith, wiping away the sweat trickling down his cheek. "I keep looking around like I've forgotten something – I'm so used to having it with me."

The Air Force C-130 that would fly them to Kuwait was already idling on the runway as the last passenger jumped down from the rear of the truck. A bright eyed, lanky Air Force officer carrying a clipboard walked up to the gaggle of soldiers and marines that had just arrived. "Gentlemen, I am First Lieutenant McGovern of the 1st Theater Air Wing Command," he said. "I will be your escort to the aircraft. Please remove your headgear, grab your bags, and follow me out onto the flight line." He turned and walked purposefully toward the aircraft. Behind him, a wobbly line of troops struggling with their over-packed duffel bags followed. At the base of the loading ramp, the line paused as the Lieutenant handed over control of the passengers to the aircraft's crew chief.

"All right, listen up!" yelled the chief, trying to make himself heard over the engine noise. "This is a full flight, so I need you to all squeeze into every available seat along both sides of the aircraft! Stow your gear in the middle of the floor behind those caskets and take a seat! Move now!"

Smith felt his stomach flip. *Caskets? What is this, some sort of Air Force joke? A way to mess with the ground pounders?*

Unfortunately, it was no joke. The troops climbed up the ramp in two lines, one on either side of the cargo bay which was already occupied by six metal caskets: they looked like large silver wall lockers lying on their backs.

"Ah'm having words with mah travel agent, that's for shore," said Warden, stepping around the end of the first casket on the left as he walked toward the front of the aircraft.

"I thought we never put passengers on flights carrying dead?" Smith asked of no one in particular, as he followed Warden, sobered by the grim reminder of the cost of this operation.

"It's up to the pilot," Warden said over his shoulder. "Usually they won't, but they must be hurtin' for aircraft. Either this or they leave a buncha' troops sittin' in the desert. Can't blame 'em, Ah guess." He reached the furthest-forward seat still open and dropped his duffel bag onto the deck beside the first casket.

"Hey, sir," said Warden, "here's a guy named Ben Flaherty." He pointed at the handwritten nametag behind a small plexiglass window on the casket's cover. "Isn't that the name of General Merdier's driver?"

"Umm, …I know Merdier has a Sergeant Flaherty working for him, but I don't know his first name," said Smith, settling into the nylon seat next to Warden along the bulkhead. "He's in the Green Zone in Baghdad, though," he added, somberly eyeing the caskets with growing discomfort. "Unless he got backed over by a USO truck or choked on a shrimp cocktail, I doubt that's him."

Warden called to the crew chief as the Air Force NCO passed them on his way toward the cockpit. "Hey, Chief: do ya' know where these unlucky guys are from?"

"Fallujah," the crew chief responded without looking.

"Must be a different guy," said Warden with a shrug, as the roar of the engines revving for take-off drowned out further conversation.

Chapter 33
The REMFs[65]

"All right, pay attention," said the muscular master sergeant in starched DCUs. He had met the plane at Ali Al-Salem Airfield in Kuwait and introduced himself to the arriving passengers as the Army Liaison for the leave detachment. "We're dropping you here at Camp Doha for a couple of hours to take care of any personal needs before you go home. There's a barber shop, mess hall, PX for souvenirs, a food court, and a laundry. You may want to square yourselves away before you get home with your loved ones. From the smell on this bus I also recommend that some of you use the shower trailers that are along the back wall of the camp, behind the PX."

Smith looked at Warden quizzically. "What smell?" he asked out of the side of his mouth.

"Dunno', sir, guess these REMFs are a bit sensitive," he replied, loud enough to make sure the master sergeant heard him.

"Do you have a comment, Sergeant?" asked the Liaison in a condescending tone, as if catching a child speaking out of turn in school

"Ahh, yes, Master Sergn't," countered Warden evenly, "I was asking the Cap'n here if we were supposed to tip you, or if this was your full time job?"

The Liaison flushed but did not reply, glaring back at Warden with flashing eyes. Warden noted that the other NCO wore the Third Army "Circle A" patch on his left shoulder, but no combat patch on his right. *Probably spends four hours a day in an air conditioned gym making himself beautiful,* Warden evaluated, observing the master sergeant's broad chest and thick neck.

"Any other questions?" the Liaison asked the rest of the bus. The only response was the sniggering from a couple of enlisted men in the back row.

"OK, meet back here at 1700. Do not be late or we will leave without you." Shoving a lever at the front of the bus, the burly NCO opened the doors and stepped down to the parking lot pavement, below.

---

[65] Ask any soldier. They'll tell you.

"Nice move," said Smith to Warden sarcastically, as they stood up to edge into the narrow aisle where other soldiers were already shuffling off the bus. Warden shrugged and moved forward with half steps toward the exit. Upon stepping down onto the asphalt, he felt a large hand on his arm that spun him nose to nose with the massive master sergeant he had just heckled.

"You're real funny, cracker," hissed the Liaison. "Just remember, you're not in Iraq anymore. That hoorah front line bullshit don't cut it back here. You best remember you're in the Army again."

Warden gazed coolly at the large NCO. Without any emotion he replied, "You have three seconds to take your hands off me. Then I'm going to hurt you."

The Liaison's eyes widened slightly, but he did not remove his hand.

"One," began Warden, counting slowly and evenly; "Two,…"

Smith jumped down from the bottom step of the bus, intentionally wedging his smaller frame between the two men as if he had tripped. His "fall" broke the grip of the larger NCO. "Whoa, excuse me," he said, feigning a recovery. "Thanks a lot for the ride, Master Sergeant," he said to the towering Liaison. "C'mon, Sergeant Warden," he added, taking Warden by the elbow. "Let's get some chow."

The two NCOs separated slowly, like two dogs not wanting to back off from a scrap. "Roger, sir," said Warden, stepping around Smith while maintaining eye contact with his larger counterpart.

"1700, sir," said the master sergeant, averting his eyes from Warden. "We'll meet right back here."

"Got it, see you then," replied Smith continuing to move away with Warden in tow. The two turned and walked across the large parking lot in the general direction of the mess hall.

"Sergeant Warden, let's try to play nice with these REMFs, so we can get out of here, OK? I'd like to spend my leave in Texas, not in the detention cell at the MP station."

"Roger, sir," said Warden, staring ahead, disappointed that Smith had stepped into the matter. He was even more disturbed by his own reaction to the entire situation. *I need to decompress,* he thought; *that guy was a self important asshole, but I don't normally look for a fight. I badly wanted to have a piece of him, though: that's not good.*

The sign outside the Camp Doha mess facility boasted, "The best Army dining facility in theater." Like almost every other building in the complex, it had been converted from a warehouse that formerly serviced the Doha port, west of Kuwait City. "Well that's not much of a distinction," snorted Smith, thinking of the quality of the food he'd had so far during the deployment. The two Civil Affairs operators pushed open the gray double doors. As they entered, a wave of cold Arctic air washed over them, sending an involuntary shiver down Smith's spine.

"What the hell is that?" asked Smith, looking about in bewilderment as another icy blast touched him.

"Ah believe it's air conditioning, sahr. Ah heard about it once." Warden stopped to enjoy the cold air.

"Amazing," said Smith as two young soldiers in clean, pressed uniforms slid by, with an "Excuse me, sir."

Before another set of double doors twenty feet inside the first, a specialist and a young sergeant sporting fresh haircuts and uniforms with razor-edged creases checked identification cards and greeted each diner with a "Hello, sir" or "Good afternoon, sergeant," as each approached. Fishing his identification card out of the ID badge holder, Smith stepped up to the sergeant, whose nametag read "Thompson."

"Good afternoon, sir," said the sergeant, "I'm afraid you gentlemen can't come in here with weapons."

"Wha..?" gaped Smith in disbelief.

"No, sir," said Sergeant Thompson: "Post Commander's policy." He looked disapprovingly at the pistols in their stained holsters.

"Does the post commander know there's a war on?" asked Smith, laughing in mock disbelief.

"I wouldn't know, sir," replied Thompson without smiling. "I just know that firearms are not authorized in the dining facility."

"Waddya' do with your weapons while *ya'll* eat?" asked Warden over Smith's shoulder.

"Oh, we don't have weapons issued to us, Sergeant," interjected the specialist. "If we need them for some reason, we can go check one out of the arms room. I haven't held a weapon in nine months," he concluded brightly.

"Amazing," said Warden, shaking his head. He had not been out of arm's length reach of a weapon in seven months.

"Well, where's the arms room, so we can go check them in?" asked Smith.

"I'm afraid the arms room is closed on Wednesday afternoons for sergeant's time," replied Thompson. "You won't be able to get in there until 1800."

"Sergeant," said Smith slowly, his voice beginning to tremble slightly. "We just traveled twelve hours from Iraq. We're tired and hungry, and we need to eat. Now what can we do to fix this situation?"

"I'm afraid I don't know, sir" replied the sergeant with a look of feigned sympathy. "It's the post commander's orders. I can't let you in."

"Screw this, sir." said Warden, "let's go grab something at that food court by the PX."

"No weapons in the food court," replied Thompson in a helpful tone. "Nor in the PX."

"I'm not going anywhere. I'm going to get something to eat," said Smith loudly, drawing quick looks from two privates who flashed their IDs as they walked quickly past the two greeters. "Who the hell ever heard of not feeding soldiers in a goddamn war zone because they're carrying weapons?" he ranted, his voice gathering in volume. "I've been carrying a frickin' weapon for seven months and have *yet* managed not to blow someone away while I'm eating. Maybe my good luck can somehow continue, do ya' think, Sergeant Thompson?" Smith was now yelling, attracting looks from within the dining room whenever the inner doors opened. Inside, table upon table of weaponless, neatly clad soldiers were trying to enjoy their evening meal, despite the disturbance being caused by two shabbily-dressed individuals at the door.

"Sahr,…uh, sahr," said Warden, gently laying a hand on Smith's arm. "Sahr, Ah got a buddy we can leave our weapons with."

"Uhh, yessir," added a visibly shaken Sergeant Thompson quickly. "Maybe you could leave your weapons with the sergeant's friend. That would work."

"Leave my weapon, so I can eat: *that's* just beautiful," said Smith to himself, his voice still angry, but at a reduced volume. "Hope no one tells the Japs about this place or we're screwed," he fumed. "Your post commander really knows how to look after the troops, Sergeant," he bristled as he turned to leave.

"C'mon, sir," said Warden, coaxing Smith toward the door.

"*Whatever*," said Smith, storming out.

Outside, Warden led his officer behind the concrete blast barrier 10 meters away from the mess hall's doors.

"Sir," said Warden, removing the pistol from his holster, "just stick it in the back of your pants." He lifted the hem of the DCU blouse at the top of his thighs and snugged his pistol under his belt. When he dropped his shirt back in place, the bulge was hardly noticeable.

"Hmmph," said Smith, following his NCO's lead. "Hiding my weapon so the Goddamn Army will feed me. Simply amazing."

"OK, let's go, sir" said Warden, stepping back around the blast wall. In a moment, they were both again walking through the gray double doors.

"Good afternoon, Sergeant," said the specialist, brightly.

"Good afternoon, Sir," said Sergeant Thompson happily, eying the empty holsters at each ragged soldier's hip. "Enjoy your meal," he added helpfully, before fixing his plastic smile on the next group entering the building.

Smith and Warden nodded to the two mess hall guardians, and then, as two smugglers in the night, they walked into the dining room.

Chapter 34
The Reserve Center

"I'm not healthy enough to deploy," complained Captain Mesquite. Mesquite was one of the "victims" of the epidemic of *sleep apnea* that had torn through the 538th the previous fall, when the possibility of mobilization had originally been raised. "I can't rest at night. My doctor says I wake up 20-30 times a night without even realizing it. I'm bushed."

Smith, who was awaiting transport back to Baltimore Washington International Airport, looked slowly up from his magazine. He had just completed his leave, including a trip to Disneyworld with his family, and had reported back to the 538th Reserve Center to begin his return trip to Iraq.

"So, essentially you're stating that you're not healthy enough to die in the war?" Smith asked in a bored tone, eyeing Mesquite with undisguised disgust.

"That's right," said Mesquite briskly, failing to pick up on the derisive tone in Smith's voice. "War is a very serious business, and it's no place for sick people," he added.

"*Really?*" said Smith unenthusiastically, trying to return to his magazine.

"Look, I can't help it if I have a medical condition right? I mean, if I'm not fit for duty, it would put others at risk for me to deploy, right?"

Smith gave up and laid down the magazine, sensing that Mesquite was going to keep yakking, despite his best attempts to ignore him. "Don't you feel bad about drawing Reserve pay all these years and then bailing out on the unit when it really needs you?" he asked pointedly.

"Not at all," Mesquite bristled slightly. "I'm very engaged here at the Reserve Center. I'm liaison to the spouses' association. I do the unit newsletter, and I speak to community groups about the brave sacrifice our men and women make overseas. It's very stirring, actually. Hardly a dry eye in the house when I'm done."

"Sounds very moving; how *do* you do it?" asked Smith, his voice dripping with sarcasm.

"I wish I was as fortunate as you guys – getting all the glory...," he said enviously, taking a large bite out of a cream-filled Bismarck, "...but hmmmff, mmmff, hrmmmmm...," he added, aggressively chewing the mass. Swallowing hard, he concluded, "...and I count myself among them."

"Your parents must be very proud," said Smith.

"Oh, they are," said Mesquite, wiping a dab of cream from his chin. "By the time I finish this tour I'll have added the National Defense Service Medal, the War on Terrorism Campaign Ribbon, and maybe even a Meritorious Service Medal, if General Merdier likes the family newsletter. Plus, if you guys win any unit citations, we here in the rear get those, too," he smiled. "With those types of credentials, I'll have an outstanding chance for making Major at the next promotion board."

Smith resisted the growing impulse to rub Mesquite's face in the Bismarck as one would do to train a puppy after an accident. *This has been a great break*, thought Smith, *but these urges to seriously go upside some asshole's head are a bit disturbing. I didn't used to feel this way.*

"Sir?" asked a young private, sticking his head in the door of the administrative section where Smith was waiting. "Sir, the van is ready to go."

"Thanks, private," said Smith, quickly standing to end to the conversation with Mesquite.

"Well, good luck. Rick," said Mesquite, taking a long pull on a latte. "Make us proud."

Smith looked at the other officer. A large glob of the thick, white filling was now sliding unnoticed down the front of Mesquite's green BDUs.

"That shouldn't be too hard," Smith replied, as he walked out the door.

Chapter 35
The Homecoming

After an 18-hour flight from the United States to Kuwait, an hour-and-a-half C-130 hop to the airbase in Al Kut, and a 45-minute ride in a Marine helicopter to Camp Babylon, Captain Smith and Sergeant First Class Warden were back in the box.[66]

At the small airfield that serviced the camp, Doc was waiting for them with Sergeant Monkeybusiness. They had brought a HMMWV with which to carry the returning soldiers and their bags back to the palace. "Welcome back," Doc cheerfully greeted them, extending a hand to each as they hauled their loads up to the vehicle

"Thanks for nothing," laughed Smith good-naturedly, returning the strong handshake. "I expected you guys to win this damn war while I was away. What were you doing while we were away?"

"So, Manuel," said Warden to Monkeybusiness, "How's your girlfriend? The hot little number from the Chem unit?"

"Oh, that was two Chiquitas ago," replied Monkeybusiness, flashing a mischievous smile. "I'm seeing this specialist in the aviation unit now. Man, she wears nothing under that flight suit. RRrRrrrrr," he trilled with his tongue. "I think this one is the real deal, Sergn't. True love."

"I'm sure your wife will be relieved to hear you're finally settling down," Warden teased, slapping him on the back.

"My wife is a good woman," said Monkeybusiness, soberly. "She understands that a man has needs."

"Yeah, that's what she told me while I was sleeping over at your house last week," Warden jibed, as he climbed into the back right seat of the vehicle. Monkeybusiness grinned at the joke as he climbed into the other rear seat.

Doc climbed into the driver's seat and turned the engine over. The Marines were always scandalized that Army officers drove themselves, as the Marine

---

[66] The Box – military slang for the combat area of operations.

tradition was that an officer always had an enlisted driver. Doc released the hand brake as Smith settled into the last seat for the drive back up the steep hill to their quarters in the palace.

"So, Rick, how was it to be home?" Doc asked, genuinely interested to hear any news from the States. The longer the 538th was in country, the more it seemed to those who had not yet taken leave that *home* was a fading illusion.

"Ya' know," said Smith. "I'm not sure what 'home' even means anymore."

"Really?" said Doc surprised. "What could be bad about two weeks out of this cesspool?"

"No, no, it was really awesome to be home and see the kids and Susan, …man, they've grown a ton in the little time I've been here. But it was like a giant hourglass was hanging over the entire thing, ya' know. Every day I woke up, and it was like, 'twelve more days at home, 11 more days….' It kind of hung over everything unsaid, and made everything a little artificial. I almost felt like a guest in my own house with everyone being so nice to me. I almost wish that she would've yelled at me to take out the trash – would have seemed more real."

"Must have been a nice feeling to walk though the door of your own house though, huh?" Doc asked, focusing on the road, as he steered the truck onto the long spiral up the hill on which the palace stood.

"Yeah, I made love to my wife on the kitchen floor…and then I took off my rucksack," cracked Smith

"Sahr, you need some new jokes," Warden piped up from the rear seat. "We used to use that one in boot camp."

"How'd people react to you?" asked Doc. A fear seldom expressed out loud among the troops in Iraq was that they'd be received home as their Viet Nam counterparts had been – reviled due to the growing split in the country over the invasion.

"It was absolutely amazing," said Smith. "I ended up being the senior officer on the flight home and the stewardess came up and gave me a kiss in front of all the troops, saying she couldn't resist a war hero."

"Damn," exclaimed Monkeybusiness from the back seat. "I gotta' get me some of that leave."

"When we got into Baltimore, it was 0600, and we were all bagged from the flight," continued Smith. "Each guy grabbed his shit from the baggage carousel and was on his own to make his connecting flight. I grabbed mine, and when I went out the doors of the international terminal there was a crowd of people there applauding me. A guy from the VFW came up and shook my hand. He said that people gather there every morning to greet the troops coming home on leave to show their appreciation. They're not even catching flights. They just come out and cheer each soldier who comes off that plane." He cleared his throat, "Hrrmmph," before continuing. "Man, I still get choked up every time I tell that part."

"That's awesome," said Doc, also moved by the story. "Now for the really important question," he asked, as the vehicle circled up and around the hill, "What did you have to drink?"

"The first thing I had was a margarita about the size of a coconut in the airport bar," Smith laughed. "Best drink I've ever had." He paused, before continuing, "That was another thing," he recalled. "When I went to pay the bartender, this guy walked up out of nowhere and slapped a ten on the bar. He just said "It's on me," and walked away. Never even gave me his name. I was so shocked I forgot to even say thanks."

"Hell, I may never take this uniform off when I get home, at that rate," laughed Doc.

"Believe me," said Smith, "I got out of it as soon as I could. I couldn't believe all the clothes I had at home. I couldn't even decide what to wear. Here I have two ratty uniforms, and there I have about twenty different shirts, and pants, and suits. It's ridiculous. You don't realize how little you really need to get along until you come to a garden spot like this," he mused.

"Then it's too late," laughed Doc.

"My house too," Smith continued, caught up in his own observations. "Before, I was thinking that maybe we would get a new place when I got back from here, because the house seemed a little small. Now I look at the place and think about all the wasted space. Man, we could put a whole platoon of guys in my house, and they'd still have more room than we do here."

"Different perspective now, I guess," observed Doc, pulling the vehicle to a stop in front of the side entrance to the palace. "Welcome to the Hotel California," he joked: "you can check out any time you want, but you can never leave."

"Thanks for the lift, Doc," said Smith.

"Yeah, thanks Sahr," added Warden, climbing out of the vehicle. Smith paused and lingered behind, as Warden shouldered his duffel bag and walked up the dirt path to the veranda.

"You know something,' Doc?"

"What's that?"

"It was great to see my wife and kids. But I never really felt like I was at home, ya' know? Like how home is supposed to feel? Relaxed and natural – like you belong there? That was gone."

"Yeah?" asked Doc, leaning on the steering wheel and looking at Smith closely.

"I just felt guilty as hell." Smith looked away down the hill over the camp. "I felt more like I was coming home when I got on the plane to come back here. Almost relieved, ya' know?"

"Why?" asked Doc, wrinkling his forehead.

"I...I was afraid. I was afraid that while I was away one of you guys was gonna' buy it. And I wouldn't be here to stop it. I couldn't live with that possibility."

"You're mental, Rick. If I ever get out of here, I'm not ever looking back," said Doc.

"I thought the same thing," said Smith, looking Doc square in the face. "I swear every night when I go to sleep here that I can't wait to get out of here and forget all you ugly bastards." He laughed bitterly. "Then when you get home – after a few days – it's different – not the way it used to be. You wanta' be back here. Doesn't make any damn sense."

"Well, you got your wish. You're here, and 'T' has a mission going out tomorrow. Are you ready to get back in the saddle?"

"Wouldn't miss it for the world," Smith replied, as he hefted his 60-pound duffel bag onto his shoulder and walked slowly around the front of the HMMWV. The sun beating down on the grayish-white sand between the pavement and the palace creating a blinding reflection that caused his eyes to water. A hot breeze blew around the cap of the hill, carrying the familiar, sour smell of rancid latrines. The endless *chug, chug, chug* of a generator pounded away at the base of the wall below the veranda, adding strong diesel fumes to the mix.

"Home," breathed Smith under his breath, as he trudged up the slope to the veranda.

Chapter 36
The Chance

Major Trevanathan sat on the rusty folding chair outside the Buddha's hooch, squinting into the sun in the direction of the combat support hospital. "So, why are they suddenly willing to help the kid?" asked Sergeant Major Wren, the NCOIC of the logistics section, as she leaned back against the wall in her metal folding chair.

Sergeant Major Deborah Wren was a twenty-eight year veteran of the Army and Reserve system and served as the Buddha's right hand. When something needed to be done, or an "impossible to locate" part needed to be found, Wren made it happen. Barely five feet tall, with a sun-baked complexion, she was referred to as "Smadge" by her friends, and as "Yoda" by some of the other wags in the unit, due to her diminutive size.

"Doc apparently went to school with this guy at Texas Tech," said Trevanathan. "They had been staying in touch on the 'net, because he knew he was getting deployed, and by dumb luck they posted him here. So Doc asked him if he'd take a look at the kid's neck and he agreed. It's not authorized to treat the Hajis at the CSH unless it's a matter of life and death – which we caused – so they took the med team and this guy down to the amusement park to have a look at him."

"Here they come," said Wren, seeing Doc's slightly bowlegged form walking around a sandbagged bunker on the path to the CSH. Following Doc was a short, solid figure partially hidden from view by the man in front.

"Hey! Doc!" yelled the anxious Trevanathan as the pair approached. "What's the deal?"

"Mornin', T," replied Doc. "This is Doctor Fred Miller, a buddy of mine and a fellow Red Raider. He used to date my sister – no accounting for taste."

"Don't be jealous," quipped the stocky man with the five-o'clock shadow. "You wouldn't put out and she would." He laughed as Doc rolled his eyes in mock irritation.

"Fred demonstrated a complete lack of judgment in joining the Navy Medical Corps, believing it would keep him safely in the US or on a nice safe ship," Doc told Trevanathan and Wren. "He failed to read the recruiting brochure where it said the Marines draw their medical care from the Navy."

"Doh!" camped Miller, effecting a halfway-decent Homer Simpson impression.

"Nice to meet you, sir" said Trevanathan, standing and extending his hand.

"Fred Miller. Good to see ya," Doc's buddy replied, returning the firm handshake.

"I used to be Bill Trevanathan," the Major replied in a friendly fashion. "Now I'm just 'T'," he added with an awkward smile, as his voice trailed off.

Miller nodded, understanding, and said nothing.

"So, what's up with the boy?" asked Trevanathan quickly, anxious to get beyond the social pleasantries.

"Well, it's a good news - bad news situation," said Miller, suddenly very serious and professional. He met Trevanathan's inquiring stare directly. "The growth appears to be a type of benign tumor that sometimes affects children in his age range. The good news is they are usually very operable and there is a good chance of a complete recovery when the patient receives prompt medical treatment."

"And the bad?" asked Trevanathan, warily.

Miller shook his head. "The bad news is that it's a complex surgery that requires advanced diagnostic testing, sophisticated monitoring, and a recovery period that is not available in the bare bones setup of a field CSH. I'm a big fan of the 'Ask forgiveness, not permission' school of thought, and the fact that we're not allowed to treat the locals wouldn't stop me. But this boy needs the type of care that is available only in Germany, England or the States. Due to lack of treatment, the tumor has reached a size and advanced stage where it will soon start impinging his trachea."

"Which means what?"

"Well at first it will just be discomfort when swallowing," said Miller. "But left unchecked it will eventually grow to the point where he will not be able to swallow at all, and it could impair respiratory function."

"So it just keeps growing until…?" Trevanathan's voice trailed off.

"Until he can no longer eat or breathe, and then that's it. Or until the growth impairs blood flow to the brain – another possibility – which could trigger a stroke."

"Pheww.," Trevanathan breathed out heavily, feeling a bit overwhelmed. "So, did you tell Bo?"

"Bo?" asked Miller, uncertainly.

"Bill here couldn't get used to calling the boy 'Saddam,' so he renamed him after his favorite Yankee football coach," Doc provided. "The boy calls him 'Keptin,' for 'captain,' 'cause he can't pronounce 'major' very well." Turning to Trevanathan, Doc said, "We told him that the lump was a sickness that happens to a lot of people, and we were going to look into how to help him. No promises."

"So, what are the options, Captai…. I'm sorry, I should know Navy ranks, but I don't," stammered Trevanathan.

"He's the equivalent of a light colonel, T – a Commander," added Doc helpfully.

"Call me Fred," Miller said again. "I don't follow that rank crap much, except when I'm around the jarheads. I'm an emergency room doc back in Abilene."

"Is there anything we can do for him here, Fred?" asked Trevanathan, searchingly.

"If we tried to operate here, we'd probably kill him. Simple operation with the right equipment, but we're only set up for bare bones trauma surgery here."

"What about a medical evacuation back to Germany?" suggested Doc.

Miller shook his head again. "It's a tough sell," he said. "The rule is that no Iraqis are to leave country without express permission from CPA.[67] They're worried about the floodgates opening and a brain drain starting if we let people start to get out."

"Who has the call on that?" asked Trevanathan.

"Ministry of Justice in Baghdad controls medical exit visas," replied Miller.

"My boys!" Trevanathan exclaimed, lighting up at that news. "Well, looks like we'll be going to visit our friends at MOJ[68] on Friday," he said happily to Doc.

"Well, if you have some pull there, that might help," said Miller. "The word we get down through medical channels is that unless someone is a direct relative of a major sheikh or an important politician, don't even ask."

"Thanks, Fred," said Trevanathan. "I'll be sure to put on the charm," he said with a laugh.

---

[67] Coalition Provisional Authority – the occupational civilian government established by the US Government to administer Iraq after the fall of Saddam Hussein.
[68] Ministry of Justice

Chapter 37
The Other Half

The weekly visit to the Coalition Headquarters in Saddam's Republican Palace in Baghdad was always an irritating reminder to Trevanathan that the rest of the world did not live in a bug-infested, looted building with no lights or running water.

This week, however, he looked at the neat uniforms of the staff wonks with a little less derision. He did not bristle when the gate guards made him call into the massive building from the gate for an escort, like he was a peddler. Nor did he feel his usual resentment when the familiar blast of cold air from the palace's extensive air conditioning system washed over him. This visit, his entire focus was upon finding out how to arrange Bo's medical evacuation, and hopefully accomplish something of worth in this land that sucked hope from one's soul.

Walking down the marble hallway to the Ministry of Justice office he let his mind ponder a future that Bo might have if he just got out of this hellhole. *No more drinking and using water from the same canal that was used as a latrine by the villagers; the chance for an education in a real school; a life with dreams and a future, instead of one filled with fear and intimidation.*

"Hmmph," snorted Trevanathan, shaking out of his reverie as he reached the massive wooden doors of the Justice Ministry. *You're getting to be an idealist*, he chided himself.

The Ministry office occupied a Spartan area of perhaps 10 by 30 meters, cluttered with cheap metal desks, filing cabinets and makeshift cubicle walls. In contrast to the opulence of the palace, the furnishings seemed dismal and out of place. Hidden by a makeshift wall of metal filing cabinets in the far corner was the desk of Brian Shelty, the Ministry's operations officer and the only person in CPA who seemed to appreciate the funding needs of the provincial courthouses. While Trevanathan had been frequently frustrated by the lack of support coming out of CPA, he knew that Shelty was working hard to change that, regularly working 18 to 20-hour days, trying to keep his nose above the flood of demands for his time.

As he made his way toward Shelty's desk through the maze of furniture, Trevanathan thought, *this guy is trying to do a job that they would have 25 staff attorneys working on. back in the States. Hell, any US Attorney's office in a medium sized city in the USA would have several dozen assistant attorneys on staff. Here they have one guy trying to coordinate rebuilding the legal affairs of an entire war-torn country.* Trevanathan did not count the titular head of the office, Judge Carpenter, as a working asset: that man's greatest function was shaking hands with Haji officials and parroting that "President Bush was counting on them."

As he rounded the filing cabinet that sat next to Shelty's desk, Trevanathan began, "Hey Bria…," but stopped short. Sitting in Shelty's chair was a young woman furiously clacking away on the keyboard in front of her. Her back was toward Trevanathan, giving him a moment to try to process a picture that included a slender figure in a tight-fitting white sweater, a blonde pony tail held in place with a pink scrunchie, and the smell of potpourri and shampoo. The twitching of the pony tail as the woman pounded away merely contributed to Trevanathan's confusion. *Wha..?*

The woman ceased her assault upon the keyboard and turned around in her chair. At the sight of her visitor, a small sound somewhere between a squeak and a choke escaped from her mouth as her eyes locked upon Trevanathan's rifle and attached grenade launcher, which the officer held at a 45-degree angle across his sweat- stained flak jacket.

Recovering from his surprise – and her reaction – Trevanathan said, "Excuse me, I'm looking for Brian Shelty."

"Do,… d…do you carry that thing everywhere?" she asked, with a mixture of alarm and surprise, her eyes still locked on the weapon.

"Yeah, it comes in handy when twenty million Hajis want you dead," replied Trevanathan without amusement. "Where's Brian?"

"Mr. Shelty is gone," she replied officiously, regaining some composure.

"When will he be back?"

"I'm sorry, but he won't," she said, managing to finally make eye contact with Trevanathan's weathered face. "He's rotated back to the States. I'm his replacement, Bethany Dillmonger."

"Whaaat? Did he get sick or something?" Trevanathan furrowed his brow.

"Oh, no," she laughed. It was a clear, pure laugh, "He was due to rotate. Actually, he was overdue to rotate by more than three months. His boss in the States finally forced him to leave. We had such a nice party for him."

"He was only here six months. How could he be *due* to rotate after only three months?" Trevanathan asked with annoyance.

"Oh, that's the normal tour for our Iraqi Task Force," Bethany gushed, completely recovered from her initial surprise. "DOJ[69] wants to make sure anyone who wants the chance can come over here, so we've split the tours up into three month sections so everyone can do it."

"There are… that many people lined up who want to come here?" asked Trevanathan in disbelief.

"Oh, heavens yes," Bethany responded, her pony tail bobbing in affirmation. "This is an absolute plum assignment for anyone who wants to go anywhere in DOJ. You put a tour like this on your resume, and you can pretty much name your next assignment. I'm hoping for appellate litigation in San Francisco. It's so beautiful there." She sighed.

"Wow, that's great," replied Trevanathan half-heartedly, resisting the temptation to grab the pony tail to stop its hypnotic bobbing. "Umm, look, Barbie…," he continued.

"Bethany…," she corrected him, and laughed, flashing a set of perfect, white teeth at the dusty soldier. "You can't imagine how many people make that mistake."

"I can't imagine," repeated Trevanathan flatly, his imagination picturing how she would look in a plastic, aquamarine-colored convertible.

"Uh, Bethany, I had a number of open items with Brian. Did he go over the status of the court personnel funding requests in Al Hillah with you before he left?"

"Ohh, I know he said something about money for a courthouse in one of those Arab-sounding towns, but I haven't had a chance to look at the file yet. I've

---

[69] US Department of Justice

been trying all day to get the customs people to release my personal shipment from the airport. Can you believe I've been here three days and only have two sets of clothes to wear? It's embarrassing. Everything else is being held hostage in my trunk at that dreadful airport. I'm writing a memo to Ambassador Bremer right now about it." Her bright blue eyes flashed with the passion of the righteous, the pony tail bouncing in agreement.

"Wow, that is pretty bad," said Trevanathan, almost choking on his words. "I know some of the MPs over at the airport. Maybe I could look into that for you?" he inquired, setting her up for the kill.

"Oh, I would sooo appreciate that," she quickly replied.

Sounds like southern California, thought Trevanathan. "No, problem," he said, "we'll hit the airport on the way out of town and check that out for you."

"You are a sweetheart," Bethany gushed.

"No problem at all. Say, umm, the other thing that Brian was working on with me was getting this Haji kid med-evac'd out of the country," lied Trevanathan. "Has a big growth on his neck, and he needs surgery right away."

"Gross," said Bethany wrinkling up her button nose.

"Yeah, well, it is kinda' unsightly, but he's a good kid, and we want to help him out. Sort of a good humanitarian project sort of thing – maybe good for some positive press, ya know?"

"Sure, I'd be happy to help out." She began pulling open a drawer of her rickety metal desk. "Is he already on the list?"

"List?" Trevanathan asked, raising his eyebrows in uncertainty.

"Uh-huh," she said brightly. "The MEAL ticket we call it – Minors Evacuation Alternates List. Ummm, what's his name?"

"I don't think he's on there yet," said Trevanathan, with a sinking feeling. "His name is Saddam Al-Hassani."

"Hmmm..," Bethany pursed her lips as she ran a well-manicured finger down what appeared to be an extensive list of names. "Nope, don't see it," she said brightly. "Lots of Saddams though," she tittered.

"Can we get him on the list?"

"Sure, sure," she said brightly. "I have a slot in July 2005 that just opened up. How's that?"

"2005?" Trevanathan choked. "This kid is gonna be dead in six months if we don't get him out."

"I'm afraid that's the best I can do," she said with a sympathetic pout. "Unless he's someone important, you know? Like the son of an official? Medical Command only allocates one evac slot per month for Iraqi minors for medical care. We usually try to choose a high profile case – get some good PR, you know? Son of a Minister or some kid who loses his arms to a terrorist bomb," she beamed.

"What if you're not high profile enough?" asked Trevanathan, irritated now at the bureaucracy barriers that were between Bo and the medical attention he needed. "What if you're just going to die an anonymous and painful death from a disease we could treat in an hour back in the States?"

"Umm…," Bethany hesitated as she pursed her lips again. She furrowed her brow in thought for a moment, and then said, "They didn't cover that in orientation. Can I get back to you on that?"

"Yeah, well let's get him on the list in the meantime," said Trevanathan. "Maybe we'll get lucky and some of the important ones will die in the meantime."

"We can always hope," she said cheerfully, spinning her chair back around to enter Saddam's name in a spreadsheet on her computer screen. "Oh, and please don't forget to check on my trunk, dear," she smiled over her shoulder.

Trevanathan smiled weakly. "Of course."

Ten minutes later Trevanathan met his team at the espresso stand in the headquarters lobby, where he found them sprawled across several salmon-colored love seats. They were drinking small cups of bitter Turkish coffee while waiting. General staff officers who called the edifice "home" took wide detours around the unsightly and aromatic group.

"So, how did it go?" Smith asked Trevanathan with a hopeful look.

"Two year wait on a MEDEVAC."

"Two years," said Doc somberly to no one in particular. "He doesn't have that much time. It's going to start blocking his breathing if it grows any more."

"Well, that's not the only good news," said Trevanathan bitterly. "Shelty is gone and some ticket-punching Suzie Cream Cheese is coordinating CPA legal reconstruction for Iraq. They're all on 90-day tours from here on out."

"Ninety *days*?" asked Smith, incredulous. "Hell, that's plenty of time to master a foreign culture, learn their customs, problems, biases, needs, and effect meaningful change. No problem!"

"Sir, we got a serious problem," deadpanned Sergeant Leader. "There's been a terrible mistake. I've been here longer than ninety days, and my replacement hasn't shown up yet; I need to go tell General Sanchez right away." Leader stood up and feigned looking seriously about the heavily gilded foyer for the V Corps Commanding General. "General,... General Sanchez," Leader started calling in a whining overloud voice. "There's been a terrible mistake. Someone forgot to send me home...Ohh. General..."

"OK, knock it off," Trevanathan ordered, the lopsided grin on his face revealing that he agreed with Leader more than he could let on. "You never know when the old man or some other 'star' is gonna' walk through here. Let's grab our shit and get on the road before it gets dark."

"Rajah, sir," Leader cracked, as he stooped to retrieve the light machinegun that was his charge for the day. As the rest of team also collected its gear, Smith sidled up to Trevanathan and asked in a low voice. "Well, now what are you gonna do?"

"Not sure. I'm going to talk to Fred Miller again and see if there's a way to get the kid into Kuwait. We're runnin' outta' options."

Chapter 38
The Long Sleep

The morning after the trip to Baghdad , Doc sat on the lower veranda of the Palace, his feet up on the low concrete wall. Saturdays were his self-declared "off duty" time, when he rose a little later, had a couple strong cups of the coffee his father had sent, and then washed his DCUs by hand in a 5-gallon bucket of water. *Quality time.*

In the 538th, the owner of a plastic bucket was a man of status. A man with a bucket could wash clothes at a time of his convenience at least once a week. Drying was not problem: a piece of laundry was ready to go within 30 minutes of hanging in the dry Iraqi air. A clothesline of 550 cord had been strung between two corner posts of the veranda for the soldiers' use. When the line was full, draping items over the concrete rail worked almost as well.

Taking a couple of hours off, as well, Trevanathan found Doc in his usual spot, staring off into space. Beside his chair, the little camp stove hissed merrily away, heating the water in the metal canteen cup balanced on top.

"Morning, Doc," said Trevanathan, cheerfully. "Coffee time, huh?"

Doc continued staring out over the date palms, not responding to the obvious statement.

"Maybe we'll get some good news today about gettin' the kid to Kuwait," continued Trevanathan, happily. "Waddya think? Sure could use some."

Again, Doc didn't make any effort to reply.

Trevanathan paused, puzzled by Doc's uncharacteristic silence. "Hey Doc, you OK? Not very talkative this morning," he inquired.

"He's dead."

Trevanathan froze, a spear of ice ripping through his stomach at the unexpected declaration. He tried to form words, but found his mouth would not cooperate.

"He died in his sleep," continued Doc in a flat monotone voice. "His heart just gave out."

"Wh… Wha?," Trevanathan finally choked out, his mind racing to think what Bo had looked like when he had last seen him. *Had he looked worse? Had he given any sign?*

Doc looked slowly up at where Trevanathan stood beside him, for the first time. "Fred Miller," he said. "Found him in his cot this morning."

"Wh…what?" stammered Trevanathan, completely confused as he desperately tried to piece together what he was hearing. "Fred found him dead?"

"Fred Miller is dead," said Doc slowly and evenly. "They found Fred dead in his tent this morning," he explained, looking at Trevanathan quizzically, not understanding why what he was saying was not getting through.

Trevanathan felt an enormous surge of relief, followed by an immediate wave of guilt that someone other than Bo was dead. "But we just saw him yesterday," he said, his cheeks burning with embarrassment at the confusing emotions that were coursing through him. "What happened? Was he sick?"

"Sometimes people just die," said Doc, his gaze now focused on a hole in the top of his boot.

"I don't get it, Doc. He was fine yesterday. How can he be dead in his sleep?"

"Sometimes people just die," repeated Doc, his voice rising slightly.

"People don't *just die*," countered Trevanathan, bothered by Doc's pronouncement. "They die of something…*don't they*?"

"Heh," snorted Doc sourly. "You've got to be kidding, Bill. Look at the way we live. It's 135 during the day and 105 at night. We work 18-hour days under constant stress. We eat badly, crap our guts out half the time from bacteria, and are always a hair's breadth away from dehydration. Once a week or so somebody tries to kill us just to spice things up. If you're an 18-year old Marine your body can put up with that abuse. With a middle aged guy like Fred Miller, sometimes the body just can't take it and checks out. Everyone has different limits, and he reached his."

"That's scary," said Trevanathan, sitting down on the wall. He felt his knees tremble as the initial rush of adrenaline left his system. "You go through the entire combat part of this thing – survive SCUDS, mines, snipers, and then die in your frickin' sleep? What the hell...," he trailed off.

Doc lowered his feet from the low wall without replying and slowly bent to prepare his coffee in the now-steaming cup. The two men were quiet for a moment before Trevanathan quietly spoke.

"You know, Doc, sometimes I get the feeling that it doesn't matter what you do over here as to whether you live or die. It's almost random, ya' know? Guys who are really field smart get blown away by IEDs. Knuckleheads like Stoat survive no matter how stupid they are. Do ya' know he left his loaded 9mm in the shitter the other day? A Haji toilet cleaner found it and gave it to Monkeybusiness to find the owner. If that Haji had stolen it, or given it to a Marine, Stoat's career would be over."

"Couldn't happen to a nicer guy," snorted Doc, taking a trial sip of his coffee. "Wanna' cup?"

"Nah. Thanks, but my guts have been in an uproar for a couple days. Smells good, though."

"You feel that way," started Doc, "because you're trying to make sense out of what happens over here."

"Hmmph," snorted Trevanathan. He looked down over the tops of the endless rows of palm trees that stretched toward the western horizon.

"People who have never been to war think that it's a bunch of bad guys on one side of a field and the good guys on the other side, and they shoot at each other. That's a Hollywood war," Doc said, bitterly.

"Mmmm, hm," murmured Trevanathan.

"Folks back home have no idea that a huge percentage of deaths over here have nothing to do with fighting the enemy. Remember that kid who fell off of the roof last week?"

"Yeah, he splatted right outside our living area. Bloodstain's still there. What a waste." Trevanathan shook his head.

"Exactly. There's no *reason* to it. He probably trained for two years to be a high-speed Marine and fight the enemy. Now he's dead because his boot got tangled in some camo netting on the roof. Remember Tyson? The guy had 13 years in and had been on deployments in Grenada, Haiti, and Kosovo."

"Yeah, I know," said Trevanathan, remembering the personable officer from their subordinate battalion.

"Guy has a one-year old daughter at home and walks into a port-a-shitter and blows his brains out."

"I don't know why they didn't get him out of here," wondered Trevanathan. "Everyone could see he was depressed."

"Yeah, well, did you know he was taking Methaquin, because his stomach couldn't handle doxycycline? A guy with three combat deployments just suddenly decides to shoot himself? I don't think so. The Army knows that frickin' malaria drug is whacking people out, but they just keep handing it out like candy."

"I'd rather have the malaria," said Trevanathan.

"My point is that there's no way to rationalize who lives or dies in this thing. People get backed over by trucks. They die in their sleep. They fall off roofs. None of it is glorious or makes for a good movie, but you're still just as dead in the end, and that's hard to accept."

"So how do you deal with it?" asked Trevanathan.

"Just do the best you can, Bill. Do exactly what you do every day. Take care of your team the best way you know how. Protect them from shitheads like Burr who would spend them in the quest for some piece of ribbon…or chocolate milk." The memory brought a sad smile to Doc's face.

"Great." Trevanathan gave his friend a sardonic look. "Don't ever let anyone accuse you of being a therapist, Doc. You suck."

"My pleasure," said Doc, taking a long pull on his cooling coffee and returning to the contemplation of the hole in his boot. "The service for Fred is tomorrow at 1000 hours in the mess hall," he added.

"I'll be there," said Trevanathan.

Chapter 39
The Double Dip

On Thanksgiving morning, Major Trevanathan walked down the two-lane road that bisected Camp Babylon. Word had spread the moment the POD had appeared in his new Goretex, desert camouflage jacket that Supply had received new wet weather gear. Trevanathan hoped that something in his size was left, as his six-foot-three frame didn't fit into the normal "medium" sizes that Army clothing seemed to come in. With the rainy season settling over Iraq, daily temperatures had dropped into the 70s, and the veteran troops, acclimated to the 135-degree summers, shivered miserably. The first downpour had covered the parched Iraqi desert two nights before, leaving a thick slurry of mud throughout the camp.

Earlier in the week there had been a ripple of excitement throughout the camp when the first clouds in over six months appeared. The idea that anything other than the merciless sun could occupy the sky was inconceivable to the baked troops. Grown men stood outside and stared in awe at the miracle of water hanging in the sky. Beside the promise of rain – and shade – the arrival of clouds lifted moods within the 538th for another reason: it confirmed that time was actually passing, and the end of their tour – already extended – was near. The 538th would rotate back to Fort Bragg, North Carolina in mid-December, with the excellent likelihood that they would be spending Christmas at home. Spirits throughout the unit were high.

Trevanathan approached the supply shed with anticipation: a Goretex jacket would help keep him somewhat dry and comfortable for their few remaining weeks. *It might even make a nice souvenir of this goat screw*, he thought. For the fourth time since leaving the palace, he checked his pant's cargo pocket for the Cuban cigar he had bummed from Smith, who had received a box from a friend stationed in Kuwait. Trevanathan knew the Buddha's weakness for good cigars and hoped that his offering would please the Grantor of All Clothing and Equipment Prayers.

Outside the supply room door Smadge was sitting on a metal folding chair she had propped back against the wall on two legs, enjoying the cool morning. She looked up as Trevanathan came near. "Mornin' sir," she smiled at the tall officer. The level of familiarity between the two over the past six months had reached the point that neither expected the NCO to stand when the officer approached.

"Morning, Smadge. Is *he* in?"

"Yessir," she replied. "He's doing an inventory on a load of winter boots that just came in."

"Hah!" blurted the Major. "He should be packin' 'em up, not unpacking at this point. Twenty days and a wakeup." Trevanathan beamed happily.

The smile faded from the Sergeant Major's face. "Ah, sir, you... ah, may, uh,...want to talk to him about that."

Trevanathan felt a cold shock down his spine. "Waddya' mean, Smadge?" He looked warily at her face, which bore no expression he could read.

"Sir, I'm not sayin' nuthin'. I don't know nuthin'. I just think you better talk to him." She looked away from the Major, unable to maintain eye contact.

Trevanathan experienced an uncomfortable *deja vu* feeling. Afraid of what awaited on the other side of the heavy metal door, he felt the strength draining from his legs. *God, not again...*, he thought.

Gritting his teeth, he heaved the door handle and stepped inside.. As his eyes adjusted to the gloom, he saw two soldiers lifting pairs of heavy winter Army boots onto a wooden shelf that ran along the right hand wall. The Buddha reclined in a red leather easy chair, a clipboard in his large hands. He turned to see who had entered his sanctum and smiled when he saw Trevanathan, waving the visitor to his side.

"Good morning, William," he warmly greeted Trevanathan. "What a pleasure to see you. How is everything in JAG-land?"

"Morning, sir," replied Trevanathan unevenly. "It was pretty good until a moment ago. Is something up? Smadge hinted that you had some news."

"She did, did she? Hmm, I'll have to take a donut out of her paycheck." He chuckled. "Well, it's all coming out at staff call this afternoon, so I suppose there's no harm in giving you a preview."

"Yes?" Trevanathan encouraged, as the Buddha paused and pursed his lips.

"Well it seems that our leaders in Washington have suddenly realized that there will be a partial turnover of sovereignty to the Iraqis after the first of the year."

"They've known that since June," said Trevanathan, sensing the very bad direction this was going.

"Yes, well they've also come to the recent understanding that there is an insurgency going on over here. I'm sure you've read about it. It's in all the papers."

"So I've heard," said Trevanathan flatly, slightly impatient to cut to the chase but knowing there was no rushing the Buddha.

"Well, it seems that some bright young minds in Washington have figured out that changing a Government in the middle of a war could lead to some hijinks by our insurgent friends, and they feel that more troops on the ground would make that process smoother."

"More troops," said Trevanathan closing his eyes, feeling slightly lightheaded.

"Actually more of the *same* troops," added the Buddha. "A new stop-loss/stop-movement order came down last night. All rotations out of theater are frozen for at least three months. We're here until March."

Trevanathan felt that he had been clubbed between the eyes. Disbelief washed over him as he thought, *Jeezez, I feel like a frickin' mouse being toyed with by a cat. There's no way out of this nightmare.*

Trevanathan steadied himself, aware that the two enlisted men in the room were listening to every word, and he could not allow himself to show any emotion in their presence. He knew if he displayed any lack of resolve that every person in the unit, including his own team, would hear about it before lunch.

"Could we give the men a break?" he asked the G4, nodding toward the two soldiers who had nearly filled the wall with boots.

"Certainly, William. Thomas, Manuel? Take off for fifteen or so, would you? Thanks a lot."

As the two men filed out the door, the Buddha opened a scuffed red cooler on the other side of his chair and removed a dented metal thermos. Retrieving a plastic cup from a nearby table, he removed the cap of the thermos and poured something into the cup before handing it to the shaken officer. The strong smell of alcohol wafted up to Trevanathan's nostrils – a smell he had not enjoyed since Fort Bragg nearly eight months earlier.

"Here's to General Order #1[70]," joked the Buddha, half filling his own coffee mug from the thermos.

Trevanathan sipped cautiously at the cup, and felt the liquid burn down his throat. "What is it?" He croaked.

"That, my boy, is 25-year old Scotch," the Buddha replied, raising his coffee mug to his nose to take an appreciative sniff. "My brother mailed it to me."

"Aren't you worried about customs?" Trevanathan asked.

"The customs officer received the other bottle as a token of my appreciation," the Buddha said with a slight smile.

"Sir,…why?" Trevanathan choked the words out, as he sat down heavily onto a folding chair.

"William, that is the kind of question that can cause you to go mad in this war," the Buddha began slowly. "In a war, things just are. If you spend time trying to rationalize every bad thing that happens, you will go insane."

"But it doesn't make any sense…," Trevanathan began in protest.

"Remember that young Marine who drowned in the canal last week?" the Buddha interjected.

"Yeah, he fell in and couldn't get out of his flak jacket," Trevanathan recalled.

"Did that make any sense? That young Marine had survived eight months of combat and died because he tripped." The Buddha paused to take a deep swallow from his cup before continuing. "A local boy got run over outside the

---

[70] General Order #1 proscribes what constitutes illegal contraband in the theater, including alcohol.

main gate yesterday chasing after a candy bar someone in a convoy threw to him." The Buddha looked levelly at the Major. "None of it makes sense – and if you try to make sense of it you are going to lose your edge."

"My edge," Trevanathan repeated without enthusiasm.

"You know what I mean, William. You are a different person now than when you came over here. You have become a creature that knows how to survive in an environment that is designed to kill you. You know what to look for. You keep your team alive by not thinking 'Why?,' but by reacting with instinct. That's your edge. Once you start asking 'why,' you have had it, because while you're thinking that way, someone is going to put an RPG into you or your team, and it's *game over*."

"Yeah, well that's great sir, and I understand what you mean about those other things, but I have to make a call home that's gonna' tear the guts out of my family. The kids have been telling everyone I'm going to be home by Christmas, and now I get to break their hearts – again. I need to know why, damn it."

The Buddha sighed and stared into his cup as if it were a crystal ball. "Do you want the short or the long version?" he asked quietly.

"Oh, by all means the long version. I have three more months to kill."

"I have a friend in G3 Plans at the Pentagon who told me this was coming over a month ago," began the Buddha. "That's why we have winter clothing and wet weather gear arriving now," he gestured at the wall filled with boots. "The bottom line is we have no replacements."

"No replacements? How the hell is that possible, sir? The wonks back in the States have had nine months to plan our rotation out of here," Trevanathan demanded.

"Oh, they've been planning all right. But the planning came a bit late. You and I know that there was no plan on how to reconstruct this country when the fighting stopped. The Generals assumed it would take six months to take Baghdad and so they assumed they had plenty of time to figure that piece of the puzzle out."

"Yeah, and they were wrong. That's old news, though," said Trevanathan.

The Buddha adjusted his position in the chair, turning slightly to face Trevanathan squarely. "Well, what is news is that the Pentagon has decided it's not going to provide new active duty troops. They are going to turn this theater over to the Reserves."

"What do you mean?"

"Look, William. Since the huge drawdown of troops after the Soviet Union fell apart, there has been this fiction –a lie if you will – that our country can fight two major regional wars at the same time. Everyone bought into the lie – the "peace dividend" – because it allowed various Presidents and Congressmen to spend money on domestic issues and grant tax cuts at the same time, and that allowed Mr. and Mrs. America to buy their big houses and SUVs without concern for national security."

"I still don't understand how that impacts us."

"The point is that the forces we have right now are not capable of protecting all of the interests and commitments we have across the globe. If North Korea made a move southward, or if Iran came across that eastern border into Iraq, we would have to roll out the nukes to stop them. The Pentagon knows this. So they have two choices. One, is they can roll back the tax cuts and rebuild the military to the point where it really can fight two regional wars, or…" The Buddha paused.

"Or what?"

"Or,…they can use up the manpower they have in the Reserves and Guard," the Buddha finished.

"But that doesn't make sense," countered Trevanathan. "The Reserves train to support the active duty force, not replace it. We don't have the firepower or equipment to do it."

"William, how much firepower do you need to fight Hajis waging a guerrilla war based on recycled artillery shells detonated with garage door openers? It is just as easy to put a reservist at a checkpoint to get blown up as it is to deploy much more expensive active duty troops."

"You've lost me there. Why are the active troops any more expensive than we are? We all draw the same paycheck."

"You're looking at the short term. Think big. Over 40 percent of the Pentagon budget is personnel costs. You're right – when they deploy us to a garden spot like this, we get paid the same as active duty personnel – sometimes even more. *But,*" the Buddha emphasized, leaning forward and looking Trevanathan full in the face, "when we are done, we are done and we go back to our private homes and our private jobs and our private healthcare, and are off of Uncle Sugar's nickel. With active duty troops, when they are done over here, they go back to Government housing, they keep drawing Army paychecks, their wives go to the post medical clinic, and their kids are in Government schools. The overhead is enormous from a business perspective. And that doesn't even factor in the pension issue. Active duty troops can retire as early as age 38 with twenty years' service. That leaves DOD paying them a pension for 40 years, maybe more. Reservists can't draw a pension until age 60; some of 'em don't even make it that far."

"Wait… if you're telling me that we're being extended because we're cheaper, sir, I don't believe it."

"You don't have to believe it, William, but it's the reality. Do the math. My friend in G3 Plans told me that after Afghanistan the Pentagon bean counters studied how to fight future wars on the cheap that do not require so many active duty troops. Rummy fell in love with the idea of a handful of relatively cheap Special Forces guys on horseback, backed up by high-tech weapons, knocking off the Taliban. That's the model for the future. Few troops, lots of tech, and if you need bodies, call up the Reserves – they're cheaper by the dozen."

"So we get another three months – and maybe someone in my team dies – not due to operational necessity, but so the Pentagon can use us as a cheap labor force?" Trevanathan stared down at his boots and shook his head. "That's beautiful."

"William, war has always been about economics. Colonies, trade routes, raw materials – it has always been about money. There's nothing new about that. The only difference about this war is that it's being designed around personnel costs, and the cost of this one is being outsourced to the Reserves."

"I know I'm a mere Major, sir, and better minds than mine have supposedly worked all this out, but what happens when these 'cheap' reservists have to go up against a real army like China's or North Korea's, and not a bunch of third-world rag pickers like here?"

"Why, I imagine the same thing will happen that occurred at the start of every major US war, William. We'll get our asses handed to us, just like at the start of WWII and Korea and even back to the Civil War. All of the politicians who are responsible for our current state of disrepair will be back in corporate America by then, and a lot of young men will die needlessly in the name of tax breaks. We'll just have to hope that the enemy in the next major conflict makes the same mistake as our prior enemies did to give us time to rebuild what we are giving up now."

"Hmmph," snorted Trevanathan, rising from his chair. "Well, thanks for the gouge, sir. Oh, yeah, I brought you a Cubano that was lookin' for an owner," he said, pulling the large cigar out of his pocket and handing it over to the Buddha.

"Why, thank you, William," said the Buddha, running the cigar under his nose appreciatively. "And before you go, make sure to grab a pair of boots and one of those nice Goretex jackets."

Chapter 40
The Tourist

"Why are we stuck with the VIP detail again?" asked Smith.

"This Assistant Attorney General of something or other is on a fact-finding mission about war crimes. Since we're the legal team, we get to escort him," said Trevanathan as he replaced the rifle bolt he had just cleaned into his weapon. "Hand me some of that graphite spray, wouldja'?"

Smith handed the aerosol can to his OIC and watched him put a light shot onto the bolt. "This stuff is a helluva improvement over oil," commented Trevanathan as he worked the charging handle of the weapon back and forth to his satisfaction. "Doesn't gum up so easily with the dust."

Undeterred, Smith said in an irritated voice, "He should be here by now." He was not happy about having to baby sit anyone, VIP or not.

"Relax, we got all the time in the world," said Trevanathan, as he began to disassemble his 9mm pistol on the hood of one of the three Jeep Cherokee SUVs they had drawn for the day's mission. As if on cue, the faint but steady *thumpa-thumpa* of helicopter blades could be heard. "Sergeant Warden, wake the men up so we're ready to roll as soon as His Nibs gets here," ordered the Major.

"Roger, Sir," said Warden, and began to move among the team resting in the shade of the vehicles. The soldiers had acquired the skill of being able to sleep anywhere at any time when given the opportunity. "Alriiigght, ladies; time to earn your pay. Get up, Ridlin," Warden ordered, delivering a kick to the bottom of the boot of the snoring private.

To the north, a heavy Marine CH-53 cargo helicopter could be seen in the distance, escorted by two Marine Cobras. All three were painted the same bluish gray that made them so hard to spot at a distance.

"He must be someone important," commented Smith. "That's a lot of firepower."

His hands moving quickly, Trevanathan reassembled his pistol in anticipation of the large dust cloud that would kick up when the helicopters swooped in to the landing pad. "All right, smile, everyone," he joked.

The entire team was now watching the approaching aircraft. Trevanathan smiled to himself;; *troops love helicopters*, he thought. The pilot of the big transport was obviously someone with some expertise, he noted, watching the helicopter come in low over the date palms to avoid taking any ground fire; the Cobras on either side flew a little higher, taking advantage of better visibility afforded by altitude. As the field opened up, the two escorts broke left and right to work the perimeter as the CH-53 quickly dropped onto the pad, having presented only the briefest of targets to any insurgent who might be lurking around the camp. Above, the Cobras buzzed like a pair of angry hornets, looking for threats to their charge.

After the inevitable storm of dirt had washed over and past them, Trevanathan motioned to his team to remain with the vehicles while he went to find their guest, tucking his chin against his chest as he walked under the spinning blades. He passed a number of soldiers and Marines as he approached the ramp at the rear of the heavy aircraft, but did not see any civilians. *No sign of our boy*, Trevanathan wondered, looking around to see if he might have missed him. Not seeing anyone that could be his VIP, Trevanathan approached the flight-suit clad Marine crew chief stacking boxes of medical supplies on the end of the ramp and yelled up, "I'm looking for a civilian coming down from Baghdad! Supposed to be on this flight! Do you know if he made it?"

The Marine swiveled his helmet-covered head toward the officer, looking like a huge bug behind his smoked face shield. "There's one guy still in there, Sir! Doesn't look too good, though!" he yelled back.

"Thanks!" yelled Trevanathan, climbing up into the vibrating machine. Inside, the sharp smell of hydraulic fluid and the musty smell of sweat filled his nostrils. Near the forward bulkhead, a sole remaining passenger was doubled over in one of the nylon seats on the left side of the aircraft.

"Ohhhh, God." The figure moaned and convulsed before blowing a projectile stream of vomit onto the deck of the helo. "Ohh, God, I wanna' die," the figure gasped between dry heaves.

Trevanathan rolled his eyes, and began breathing through his mouth to minimize the stench spreading inside the helicopter. *The crew's gonna' be pissed*, he thought, and then leaned down to address the sick man. "Are you Mr. Patterson, sir?"

The figure raised its head and nodded with blank eyes, before turning back and adding to the already voluminous contribution at his feet.

"Let's get you off here and get some air, sir." Trevanathan reached down and pulled up on the man's arm. With his other hand, he popped the buckle on the man's seat belt. Marines didn't normally bother themselves with safety harnesses inside aircraft, but the crews were always a little more careful about their "guests." Trevanathan began to slowly lift the man to his feet.

"I need to sit awhile," the VIP protested weakly.

"You need to get off this barf bucket for some fresh air, sir. The smell in here would knock a buzzard off a shit wagon." Trevanathan urged the man quickly down the ramp and into the glare of the late morning sun. They passed the crew chief just as the smell of vomit did. The Marine stopped what he was doing, looked into the helicopter at the mess on the deck, and then at the backs of the Army officer and the stumbling passenger. "Hey!" he yelled. Trevanathan glanced back with an apologetic look to the crew chief and shrugged his shoulders. *Yep, they're pissed.*

"Need to sit…," the man began again as his escort guided him toward the waiting vehicles.

"Sir, you can sit over there," Trevanathan insisted, gesturing toward his team. "This helo is leaving in five mikes[71] and you don't wanna' be near it when it lifts off."

As they approached the team, strength began to return to Patterson's legs. "Well that was a helluva' first impression, I'm sure," he muttered, trying to force a laugh. "I never was much of a flyer."

"No problem, sir. I'm Major Bill Trevanathan, and this is my Number Two, Captain Rick Smith. You'll get to meet the rest of the team as we go along.

---

[71] military slang for minutes

We do need to get moving, however, if you want to visit the site today," Trevanathan observed, looking doubtfully at Patterson's greenish pallor.

"Good to meet ya', sir," said Smith, extending his hand.

"Please, call me 'Chip,'" replied Patterson, trying to be magnanimous.

"OK, Chip, welcome to Camp Babylon," said Trevanathan. "Here's the drill today: our mission is to get you to the site and back in one piece. We have a grid for the site and will be traveling to the objective in these civilian Cherokees to try to minimize attention. It's only about twenty klicks from here up Highway 8. We have ten members of the Government team and our translator, Abu."

"Great, well, I'm feeling much better, so I'm ready when you are."

Trevanathan paused to examine the slightly dumpy bureaucrat before him. He had been in Iraq for so long that he had almost forgotten how overweight everyone was back in the States. Almost everyone in Iraq had a lean, wolfish look about them after a month or two. At least, everyone outside the Green Zone, did. The constant fluid loss also seemed to take body fat right off a person, leaving them looking slightly gaunt. Next to the poor quality of one's uniform, another sure sign of an Iraq veteran was his sunken eyes and cheeks.

Trevanathan resumed his briefing. "OK, a couple ground rules before we go out. We don't expect any trouble, but that's usually when it happens. If we take any fire while en route I need you to get on the floor of the vehicle and stay there, understand?"

"I'm not afraid, Major. You don't have to worry about me," Patterson said with a just a hint of defensiveness.

"Well, that's good to hear, sir, 'cause I'm scared shitless every time I go out. My job is to get you out and back in one piece. So if we take fire, do me a favor and get on the floor of the vehicle. An AK round will go clean through one of these babies, so sitting up is gonna' do nothin' but get your guts splattered all over my nice clean upholstery."

Patterson began to open his mouth again, but Trevanathan turned away, cutting him off. He wasn't interested in objections from some non-tactical VIP from Baghdad.

"Sergeant Leader, come here, please," Trevanathan said to the large NCO leaning against the side of the second vehicle.

"Yessir?"

"Pete, this is Mr. Patterson: he's yours. If any shit goes down, I want you to get him out of the AO[72]".

"Got it, sir." Leader turned to Patterson, "Good to meet ya,' sir," said the muscular NCO, dwarfing the civilian's soft hand in his own calloused paw as they shook hands.

"Is all this really necessary, Major?" asked Patterson in a slightly exasperated voice. "They told me in Baghdad that there was no reason for concern – that this is a relatively quiet area of Iraq."

Trevanathan looked out the corner of his eye at Smith, who had suddenly found the toe of his boot extremely interesting. "Well sir, maybe you should talk to Lieutenant Commander Slattery about that."

"Fine," said Patterson in a clipped bureaucratic tone. "Where is he?"

"Over in the morgue, *Chip*. He was a brand spankin' new NIS[73] officer who went into quiet old Hillah a couple days ago without an escort, because this is such a *nice quiet area*. A Haji walked up behind him while he was at a stop sign and blew his brains out – shot him in the back of the head. He was in country two days."

Trevanathan watched the color drain from Patterson's face, and pressed his advantage. "Lesson One, Chip: those starched monkeys in the Green Zone don't know shit about what is going on down here. Not one of them has been out here, and they are fighting the war from leather chairs in air-conditioned offices. That's just fine, but don't rely on them for advice on how to survive out here in the sand."

"OK, I get your point," admitted a chastened Patterson. "What else do I need to know?"

---

[72] Area of Operations
[73] Naval Investigative Service

"Just stick with Sergeant Leader: he's your lifeline. If he says move, then move. If he says run, run fast."

Patterson nodded somberly.

Trevanathan decided that he'd gotten through to their visitor and that a little reassurance was in order. "Look, nothing is going to happen. But it's by being ready that we ensure that will be the case. The second you let your guard down around here, the Hajis can smell it and you're toast."

"Hajis?" asked Patterson.

"Umm, a term of affection for the local populace," said Trevanathan quickly, realizing that a civilian from Washington would probably not be understanding of the derogatory reference. "All right, let's mount up," he ordered his team. "Standard rules of engagement. Chip, I'd like you to sit between Staff Sergeant Leader and Sergeant First Class Warden, here, if you don't mind."

The team moved to depart through the eastern camp entrance on a route that led them past the reconstructed Ishtar Gate, the historic entrance into the ancient capital of the Babylonian empire. Just beyond, they passed a dirt track leading off toward an onion domed building.

"Tower of Babel," Trevanathan stated simply, pointing down the road.

"Wha...? What do you mean?" asked Patterson. "*The* Tower of Babel...like from the Bible?"

"Yeah," said Trevanathan unenthusiastically. "Just the foundations are there now, but you can see the outline from at the palace. Hajis built a mosque next to it."

"That's really something," commented Patterson. "I thought that was an old wives' tale... like the Loch Ness monster."

"Nah, outside of Israel, Iraq has the most known Biblical sites in the world. The ruins back there are Nebuchadnezzar's palace. It's where Daniel was tossed into the lion's den. The throne room is where Alexander the Great died, after conquering the known world. We stopped at Ur on the way up from

Nasiriyah and saw the birthplace of Abraham. It's all here – it's just these people are too busy killin' each other to know what they have."

"Amazing," sighed Patterson.

Trevanathan continued. "If they ever do stop killin' each other for a minute and think about it, they could turn this place into a tourist haven worth billions. But….," he let his voice trail off.

As the three vehicles eased up to the guard post at the outer gate, a young Marine Lance Corporal stepped out of the sandbagged bunker to check the vehicle dispatches. "Morning, Sir," he addressed Major Trevanathan, identifying him as the ranking officer in the lead vehicle. "Where are you heading?"

"Gravesite near Abu Shalil. Site inspection," answered Trevanathan.

"Roger, Sir. Have a safe one." He motioned, and another sentry stepped forward from the shadow of a large evergreen tree on the opposite side of the road to pull back the concertina wire barrier across the pavement.

Trevanathan picked up his Motorola radio and depressed the SEND button. "All Jaguar elements, this is Jaguar Red. Lock and load." They had changed their call signs for this mission to correspond to the civilian vehicles: "Jaguar Red" for Trevanathan's Jeep, "Jaguar Blue" for Smith's, and "Jaguar White" for the third, commanded by Doc Heller.

Patterson started slightly as the soldiers in his vehicle slapped magazines into their rifles and chambered rounds with silent efficiency. He noted that the big sergeant beside him had tapped his magazine on his helmet before inserting it into his weapon. *Must be for luck*, he thought, incorrectly. He also noticed that the tall Major in the front seat had also loaded a pistol. *Is all this really necessary?* he wondered.

Moving forward past the two Marines, the team maneuvered their vehicles through a maze of concrete barriers that required them to slowly zig and zag – a defensive measure that made sure that no one could ram through the gate at high speed.

In the rear seat next to Patterson, Leader squirmed uncomfortably. "Sir, this isn't any damn good," he said in a frustrated voice. "With these windows up we have no fields of fire and I have to keep my weapon between my knees. If some Haji lights us up, by the time I lower this window and shoulder my weapon, we're screwed."

"Hmm, I see what you mean," said Trevanathan, glancing at the semiautomatic rifle that sat uselessly between his own knees, the weapon's butt on the floor and barrel pointed at the roof. Within the tighter confines of the civilian SUV, it was too long to lay across his lap with the door and window closed. The HMMWVs they customarily used had no doors, providing no impedance to their weapons. The Cherokee was built for comfort and hauling passengers, not as a fighting platform.

"OK, so much for a low profile." Keying his handset, Trevanathan said, "All Jaguar elements, this is Jaguar Red. Lower your windows and maintain weapons ready status."

Breathing a sigh of relief, Leader quickly lowered the pane beside his head and extended the barrel of his rifle out the side where it might be able to influence future events.

The three-vehicle convoy followed the route to the intersection with Highway 8.

"Speed is our friend today, Cooper," Trevanathan told his driver as they approached the first bridge crossing. "The faster we go, the harder we are to hit. So keep it up above 65. Anyone runs in front of you, that's their bad luck, OK?" Cooper nodded his understanding, not taking his eyes of the road. Beside him, Trevanathan reflected for a moment how orders that could result in someone's death came easier to him these days. He did not allow himself to consider this for long, however, refocusing on his search for potential threats in the passing terrain.

As they slowed to allow the vehicles behind them to negotiate the turn onto the highway, the usual parade of orange and white Iraqi taxis zipped around them. The early days of the occupation, when military vehicles were the only traffic on the roads, were gone. Now, rusty and dented Iraqi cars of Soviet and French make fought for space with HMMWVs, Army fuel tankers, and the plethora of oversized SUVs that someone at CPA thought would blend into traffic. It was a ludicrous mistake. Such expensive, modern vehicles were easily recognized as US vehicles: few Iraqis drove vehicles less than ten years old if they had a vehicle at all.

A white Fiat chugged past the convoy in the left lane of the divided highway. A small wooden coffin balanced on the small car's roof, secured by ropes looped seemingly haphazardly about the box and through the open windows.

"My God, what is that?" asked Patterson, pointing.

"Hajis don't have hearses," answered Leader, paying close attention to the passing vehicle. "When Gran'ma kicks off, they slap her in a homemade box and take her off to the bone yard themselves. For awhile there, Haji had figured out we didn't want to disturb their dead, so he started smuggling weapons in the coffins. Now the MPs do random stops and checks. Mmmhmm, there's some nice duty," he laughed, "crack open a box with an old dead Haji in it that's been baking at 135 degrees for a day or so."

"Broasted Haji. MMmm, now that's good eatin,'" laughed Warden, from directly behind Trevanathan.

Trevanathan chuckled at the gallows humor in the back seat. It had become a natural part of the banter on their missions: the Jaguars, like police or firefighters who frequently encountered disturbing situations, had adopted the defense mechanism of joking about the horrific as if it were inconsequential.

Caught between the two NCOs, "horrific" was just the word that Patterson was thinking, appalled that these were the supposed "best and brightest" that the military had to offer. *These men have no heart*, he thought. *How the hell are we going to win over the Iraqis with a bunch of callous idiots who laugh at a dead body being carried on the top of a car in an old box?*

Trevanathan could see Patterson's discomfort in the small mirror hanging on the sun visor, but had no patience to explain their mindset to a rookie.

Static crackled from the handheld radio tied to Trevanathan's vest with 550 cord. "Jaguar Red, this is Jaguar White. We have company."

"Go ahead, White," Trevanathan responded.

Doc's voice crackled over the handheld. "White Isuzu pickup truck with three Muhammads sitting about two feet off our rear bumper. When we slow, they won't pass. They're just sitting there, probing us."

Trevanathan thought for a second, considering their options with their VIP aboard. The main mission was to protect him. *Then again, if the Hajis are trying to distract us or test our reaction by tailgating they're putting everyone at risk.* There was no doubt in his mind that they knew US personnel were aboard the three SUVs. He made his decision.

"Cooper, on my order, I want you to cut into the left lane, brake hard, and when the Hajis pass us on the right, come up behind them." Trevanathan spoke into his radio: "Jaguar Blue this is Jaguar Red. Jaguar Red is falling back on the left. Take the lead." Without waiting for a response, Trevanathan turned to Cooper. "Now!" he barked.

Cooper swerved into the left lane and simultaneously braked, decelerating the large vehicle. Jaguar Blue and White flew past on the right side with the white Iraqi truck close behind.

"Go, go, go!" Trevanathan urged Cooper. "Leader, Warden, I want weapons on that vehicle!"

Cooper floored the gas pedal, rapidly accelerating the large SUV as he cut back into the right lane. Leader and Warden each leaned out their respective windows, completely filling the openings with their large frames.

To the driver of the white pickup truck, the image suddenly filling his rear view mirror seemed like a great bird of prey swooping down, semi-automatic weapons bristling from its wings. The game of cat and mouse he and his brothers had found so amusing moments before just as abruptly lost its appeal, and in his panic, he cut his wheels too hard to the right. The vehicle veered off the highway onto a broad swath of sand and scrub brush at high speed. The sand grabbed the wheels of the truck, tearing control from the driver's grasp, and spun the vehicle two complete turns before it lurched to a stop.

Hoots of pleasure came from Warden and Leader in the back seat. Trevanathan looked in his side mirror and saw one of the occupants of the offending truck tumble out onto his hands and knees. Satisfied that they no longer posed a threat, Trevanathan turned back to his driver. "Good driving, Cooper," he said, "No red shirt for you today."

"Thanks for the assist, Jaguar Red," came Doc's voice over the radio.

"Roger, Jaguar White, Red out." Trevanathan turned in his seat to check on his passenger. The seat between Leader and Warden was empty. Leader pointed toward the floor, where Trevanathan saw that Patterson had dutifully gone for cover during the maneuver, and was now wedged tightly in the limited space between the front and back seats.

"Everything's OK, Mr. Patterson," Trevanathan said. "You can get up now. Good job on getting low when things got interesting."

With a helping hand from Leader, Patterson slowly pulled himself to his knees and paused a moment to take a deep breath before shifting his weight back up onto the seat. He was once again drained of color, but otherwise looked none the worse for wear. "Is,… is it always like this around here?" he asked in a slightly shaky voice, looking back and forth between Trevanathan, Warden and Leader for an answer.

"No, no," said Warden soberly. "This is the Haji weekend so things are kind of quiet. Stick around until Saturday, and we'll show you some real exciting drivin'." Warden winked at Trevanathan.

The remainder of the drive was uneventful. After the adrenaline left Patterson's system he still felt a little shaky, but was alert enough to notice the many monuments and shrines to Saddam alongside the road that had been defaced. He also noticed several formerly-walled compounds, almost completely leveled, which looked like they may have been military in nature.

Trevanathan checked his GPS[74] as they approached a small cluster of buildings by the side of the road. He had purchased the device off the internet when the bulky and complex military "pluggers"[75] they had been issued turned out to be too user unfriendly. It had taken three weeks for the device to reach him, but it was worth its weight in gold in the trackless wastelands that were much of southern Iraq.

"I think this is it, Cooper," he said. "Yeah, I remember that orange body shop." As they pulled off the highway into the hard-packed dirt parking lot,

---

[74] Global positioning system
[75] A military GPS system issued to troops that weighed several pounds and was the size of a large desktop radio.

Trevanathan pointed. "Pull around the back on that side road. Remember? There will be a two track leading up onto the levee."

"Yessir," said Cooper, who knew he would never forget the first disturbing trip the team had made to this site.

The road ended at the double path that climbed approximately five meters up onto the narrow levee, the tracks all that remained to show that heavy machinery had once been there. At the base of the levee, Trevanathan directed Warden to dismount and check for tripwires or evidence of mines planted since their last visit. Following behind the NCO's cautious pace, the three SUVs growled up the path in low gear.

On top of the levee, the passengers found themselves elevated above the surrounding countryside. The earthwork, only slightly wider than the vehicles, meandered across a large, grass covered plain as far as the eye could see. The smell of swampy soil and putrid water filled their nostrils as they proceeded.

"Stay alert, Jaguars," Trevanathan reminded his team over the radio, not liking how tall the swamp grass had grown since their last visit. *Must be nearly two meters high: plenty of cover for Haji to hide in with an RPG, waiting for some knuckleheads like us to come along,* he worried.

"So, this leads to the gravesite?" Patterson asked from the backseat, having recovered from his earlier shakiness.

"This is the gravesite," Trevanathan responded without emotion. "Cooper, stop at the next point that widens a bit. Yeah, up there on the left," Trevanathan pointed to a broad spot in the track across the top of the levee.

"I don't see it," said Patterson, impatiently. "Is it in all that grass?"

"You're on top of it," Trevanathan replied without looking back. He spoke into his radio again: "All Jaguar elements, dismount and establish security."

The convoy stopped and the team spilled from the doors without a word, each soldier glancing left and right to make sure that as a team they had eyes and weapons in every direction. Some chose a modicum of cover behind the SUVs, leaning their elbows on the hoods to stabilize their rifles. Others simply knelt as they scanned the countryside. Patterson began to climb out behind Leader. "Why don't you just sit tight, Mr. Patterson, until we make sure the area is clear," the NCO suggested with a calm, firm authority that Patterson recognized was not a suggestion at all.

After several minutes patient surveillance of the immediate area, Trevanathan waved and nodded to Leader that it was OK for Patterson to come out.

"Now wher…," Patterson started to ask as he climbed down between Leader and the SUV. His question was interrupted by a crunching sound beneath his feet. Patterson looked down and stopped. "Oh my God!" he exclaimed as half of a small ribcage popped up from the soil beneath his boot, forced up by his weight upon the still connected vertebrae. The chalk-colored bones wrapped themselves around the side of his boot.

Patterson jumped back reflexively. As he did, several other more ribs popped out of the soil. "Oh shit," he involuntarily squeaked, feeling that he had somehow wandered into a Kafka-esque nightmare.

Trevanathan looked sadly at Patterson, remembering that his first reaction to this place had not been dissimilar. He could still recall the sick feeling when he had kicked a hip ball joint up out of the dirt, and how it had tumbled along the dirt track and down the side of the levee to disappear into the weeds at the bottom. He had felt like a child who had broken an expensive vase in a shop. He had fought his urge to chase the errant joint and retrieve it, as if putting it back would somehow make things better. Even in his horror, he knew how ridiculous it would make him appear before the troops, and yet the urge had remained. The memory haunted him still. Today, he stood silently and felt the great weight of tangible evil as he looked about. *The waste… the waste…*

"Mr. Patterson...Chip," Trevanathan called. "Come over here, and I'll give you a brief rundown of what you are seeing." Patterson walked to Trevanathan's side, carefully examining each patch of ground before taking each step.

"This site is known as Hotel 17, a mass grave of Shiites who were executed by Saddam's security forces sometime right after the First Gulf War. As you may recall, after we retook Kuwait in 1991 we encouraged the Iraqis to rise up against Saddam. The Shiites here in the South did indeed revolt and when we did not assist them, Saddam let loose what was left of his military and secret police upon them. This site was discovered about six weeks ago and so has not been secured for any forensic work yet."

"So how do we know who these people are or why they died, then?" asked Patterson.

"After the locals figured out we weren't here to harm them, they led some of our Special Forces guys here. They told them that from 1991 to 1993 hundreds of thousands of people and their families who were believed to be involved in the revolt were collected by the regime. They were brought to sixty or so sites like this across southern Iraq. Army trucks, buses – anything that could move was used. The locals saw the trucks come through the town full of passengers and then go back out empty. This levee did not exist here before 1991. The Ba'athists put down a layer of bodies, covered them with ashes and dirt. and then laid another load of bodies on top. Eventually the compacted bodies became the road on which more victims were transported for execution."

"How were they killed?"

"Shot. Not very efficient with that many people, but the Hajis aren't as efficient as the Nazis were. Same end game, though."

"Why were they killing children, too?" asked Patterson, pointing to a child's book bag, laying near the edge of the road. Its fading rainbow pattern still showed, despite years of being exposed to the elements.

"Two reasons, mostly. First, it is a very effective deterrent against anyone in the future to consider opposing Saddam when they know that if they are caught, it's a death sentence for their entire family – children included."

"And?" asked Patterson as Trevanathan paused.

"Arabs believe in the concept of the blood feud. If you do a wrong to my family and my grandchildren take revenge upon your grandchildren two generations from now, they are acting hastily," said Trevanathan. "By wiping out the entire families and tribes of those who opposed him, Saddam was buying an insurance policy that neither the children of the victims, nor their children's children, would come back on him or his heirs in the future."

"Incredible," said Patterson. "How are we supposed to show these people how to form a government when we are centuries apart in the way we think about things?"

"Don't know," replied Trevanathan. "Wish someone had thought of that before we became the landlord."

Trevanathan's gaze found what looked like a piece of a dirty pink rubber band sticking out of the ground. Momentarily forgetting his training, he reached down and pulled on it, dislodging a small sandal from beneath the ash. He knelt and cupped the small item in his hand. Months of fatigue caught up with him, and he felt his defenses drop as he thought of the terror and bewilderment the young girl –of what? maybe six or seven year's old? – must have experienced as she was led to her death, clinging to her mother's skirts. He imagined some fat-bellied Iraqi soldier sneering at her fear, anxious to finish the job so he could return to the barracks and get out of the sun. *What kind of person puts a pistol to the back of a little girl's head and pulls the trigger?* he wondered, lost in the thought for a moment..

With effort, he shook the vision from his head. *Oh, no you don't,* he chastised himself silently, standing up quickly and dropping the sandal back into the dust. *I don't have the time or luxury for getting all emotional. Do that, and someone doesn't go home to their family.*

Not noticing Trevanathan's lapse, Patterson spoke to no one in particular, "Jesus, you read about stuff like this in the newspaper or see the numbers in some government report, and it's like it isn't real. It's just numbers. But he really slaughtered these people. Kids, women, old people – by the thousands. It's right here." He took a deep breath and looked down the length of the levee that stretched as far as he could see. He struggled to maintain his composure for a minute and then gave up, turning to heave the remaining contents of his stomach onto the powdery surface.

Trevanathan stood silently beside the VIP, allowing the man a moment to compose himself. "This is what it's about, Chip. It's not about frickin' Exxon and the oil, and it's not about turning these power hungry Iraqi bastards into Thomas Jefferson. That ain't gonna' happen. For me, it is and always will be about that sandal laying there and that kid's book bag over there. I see that shit when I go to sleep at night and know for the first time in my life that there is a real thing called evil in the world. Putting a stop to kids and women dyin' is what makes this worth leaving my wife and kids; to cobble this worthless country back together."

"They don't pay you guys enough," said Patterson, holding his arms across his chest and feeling cold, despite the warm sun beating down on them. He felt light-headed.

"They don't make enough money to put up with this, ever," said Trevanathan. "It's our duty. That's enough. We can look at more if you want, but this just goes on like this for the next kilometer or so."

"No, I've seen enough for a lifetime. I'm ready to go."

Trevanathan turned to his team. With a few hand signals relayed among his team, they fell back back into the SUVs. Eyes and weapons directed outward, they turned the vehicles around and left the killing fields.

Chapter 41
The Order

"All right, that's all I have," said Colonel Hermann to the assembled staff officers. He could sense the depressed mood of the group since the second tour extension had been announced and wanted to keep the meeting moving. Trevanathan and Smith sat in their usual chairs along the back wall during the daily briefing. "Let's go around the room. S-1?"

The bookish Lieutenant Colonel Stoat, who made it a point of honor to never travel outside the wire and the protective Marines guarding Camp Babylon, responded. "Thir," he began in his adenoid-laden voice, "We have 142 present for duty. Three are on the R&R program in CONUS[76]. One pax[77] is down with Saddam's revenge and on two days bed rest. That's all, thir."

"Thank you," said Hermann. "Eth-2, err, S-2?"

Major Robert (Bob) McHenry, a tall sandy haired officer with a heavy coating of freckles, stood up. "Sir, this morning's low was 62 degrees. The afternoon high is expected to be an unseasonably high 82." As usual, McHenry's weather report was greeted with a wave of good-natured hisses and boos from the other staff officers.. McHenry was one of the few brigade officers who had actually served on a combatant command staff while in Korea, and was one of the bright stars in the brigade. He ran his shop professionally and efficiently, showing favoritism to no one and requiring his staff to conform to active duty military standards. He was despised by the majority of the senior staff, who found him insufficiently deferential to their rank and status. The POD especially hated him for having turned down a citation for valor during the initial move to Babylon, when McHenry's convoy had come under fire. After that incident, in which he had provided covering fire on a sniper so the rest of the convoy could escape, McHenry had declined the proposed Bronze Star for valor, saying, "I didn't do anything except my job. Give the medal to someone who deserves it."

---

[76] CONUS – Continental United States

[77] Pax – technically, *passenger*, but commonly used when referring to "personnel."

"How selfish can a person be?" the POD had demanded of Colonel Hermann. "Those awards reflect on this entire unit. He owes it to the rest of the unit to accept it. Besides, it sets the bar higher for the rest of us if he turns it down."

Today, McHenry provided his situation briefing with the same calm that he had demonstrated under fire. "There is increased insurgent activity near Fallujah, west of Baghdad, and as far south as Farisiya at the north tip of our area of operations. JTF7 G-2[78] reports increasing incidents of arms and foreign personnel being smuggled through the western desert from Syria."

"Any sign of increased enemy activity in our area yet?" asked Hermann.

"No sir, but Farisiya is only fifty klicks north, so the Marines are preparing for the possibility. There have been a couple rumors of planned mortar attacks on this post, but nothing concrete. Subject to your questions, Sir, that's all I have."

"Great. Thanks Bob. No questions. S-3?"

Colonel Scarrey, the operations officer, gulped nervously as he addressed Hermann, his fish-like eyes darting around the room. "Uh, sir, we have a new tasker from General Merdier. Colonel Burr spoke to him a half-hour ago by satellite phone. I'll let him cover it."

All eyes turned to the POD, who rose from his seat behind the commander.

"General Merdier recognizes that this is a battle for the hearts and minds of the Iraqi people. We have to show them that our arrival here has made life better for them than they had under Saddam. If we can't do that – and quickly – malcontents like Al Sadr and the Sunnis up north may gain the momentum and blow these scattered attacks we've been seeing into a full-fledged civil war." The POD paused to let the drama of this message take effect. Confident that he had everyone's attention, he continued. "Under Saddam, only a privileged few were permitted to enjoy the benefits of this society. If you were a loyal Ba'ath party member you got certain privileges. Otherwise you got squat. Our new assignment is to ensure that the people at all levels enjoy the good things this society has to offer."

---

[78] Joint Task Force 7 was the corps level combat command responsible for all military operations within Iraq. G-2 is the intelligence section at the division or corps level.

"An AK-47 in every pot," Smith whispered in Trevanathan's ear. Trevanathan smirked.

"Those of you who have been south of town," continued the POD "have seen the abandoned amusement park, that was only for Ba'ath party members. General Merdier has ordered us to help restore that facility to working order, so that everyone in Hillah can enjoy it. I'm personally very excited about this mission and think it can be a real feather in the cap of this brigade."

"He's jokin', right?" whispered Smith.

Hermann cleared his throat. "Doug, is General Merdier going to dedicate any other personnel or assets to this mission?"

"Sir, the actual work will be performed by the combat engineers. We are to help facilitate cooperation between the community and the Marines and to work with PSYOPS[79] to promote this effort."

"Sir," Trevanathan spoke, directing his question toward Colonel Hermann, "Most of these people do not have clean drinking water, jobs, or even feel safe in their own homes. How is opening a carnival going to help them? Or help us win their hearts and minds? I mean, I like a good time as much as the next guy, but if my family's broke or in danger a carnival is not high on my list."

"Major," interrupted the POD sharply. "Our job is not to question orders. Our job is to carry them out. A lot of people with more experience and more brass on their shoulders than you worked through the pros and cons of this. Our role is to implement it. Not question it."

"Yessir," said Trevanathan not flinching from the POD's angry stare. He knew Burr's tactic of "winning through intimidation," and had grown tired of it over the many months in Iraq. "It's just that we have about half the court employees about to walk off the job down because CPA still can't get the payroll down here regularly. If the courthouse stops working, the jails are gonna' overflow. The hospital still has a shortage of IV needles, and only half our area has regular electrical service. Seems like we're diluting our effort for a feel-good moment when there's a lot of 'must haves' still on the plate."

---

[79] Psychological Operations

"I'm well aware of our other mission priorities, Major," hissed the POD. "You just need to learn to be able to handle more than one thing at a time."

"Sir, I don't think we're handling anything particularly well at the moment. We kick out a lot of self-serving reports that make ourselves look good, but what real difference have we made?"

"Gentlemen," interrupted Hermann, sensing the ugly turn the conversation was taking in his headquarters. "I understand everyone's concerns. I'll discuss this with General Merdier when I go to Baghdad next week for the commander's conference. In the meantime we have a tasker from the General, and we need to move forward on it."

The POD continued to glare at Trevanathan. Smith feigned interest in his boots and whispered, "Shut up," to his friend.

"Sir, I don't mean to beat a dead horse," Trevanathan ignored Burr's glare and faced Hermann, "but you also need to know that that park is currently home for about twenty refugees who are living in the outbuildings on the property. What about them?"

"How long have they been there?" asked Hermann, who had not been briefed on that information before..

"As far as I know, since the start of hostilities, sir" replied Trevanathan. "We've made contact with a couple of them who lost their homes in the fighting. They have nowhere else to go."

"Well, since you have a relationship established, of sorts," leered the POD, his eyes aglow, "you can go over there and tell them to get out. That property is now a project of the US Department of Defense, and we can't have a bunch of foreigners hanging around."

"I think the XO is right, Bill," said Hermann. "Those people are going to have to relocate. We can't renovate the property and maintain security with locals squatting in the buildings. Besides, you know that they'll steal any improvements we put into the place unless we secure the property."

Trevanathan could only nod, recognizing that the old man had a valid point about the thievery. The experience of the soccer field was still a source of pain and embarrassment.

Hermann continued, trying to be sympathetic. "Why don't you and the Jaguars run over there tomorrow and give them a warning order that they're going to have to move soon. That will give them time to start looking. We can even distribute some MREs to soften the situation."

After the meeting, Smith and Trevanathan discussed the situation during the long, steep walk up the hill to their quarters in the palace. "Not one of your smarter moments, Bill," Smith chided him. "You can't expect to take the POD on like that in front of the entire staff and win. He eats Majors for breakfast."

"I know," said Trevanathan glumly, stirring up the fine Iraqi dust as he trudged up the long incline. "I just keep fantasizing that some day the old man is gonna' grow a pair and do the right thing, instead of the right thing to get his star."

"Don't hold your breath," Smith said, pausing to catch his own before continuing. "So, now what?"

"So tomorrow we go over and demonstrate the benevolence of the American people by throwing those homeless people out into the street."

"What about the kid?"

"Don't know yet. We're going to do something, though. He's been through enough"

Chapter 42
The Storm

Trevanathan stewed as Jaguar One entered the familiar grounds of the amusement park. *Here's a 'CNN moment,'* he thought: *"I'm sorry Mr. Refugee, the United States needs to kick your ass out of your little hovel so we can have a carnival. I'm sure you'll understand."*

The two HMMWVs followed the path toward the trees near the Leopard Man's utility shed. *I guess I just tell him quickly and not beat around the bush*, thought Trevanathan. As they approached their usual parking area near the carousel, Trevanathan could see the Leopard Man sitting in the shaded spot outside his door. The old man slowly raised his hand in greeting.

Man, this isn't what I signed up for, Trevanathan mused. The team quietly dismounted, without its customary banter. Nobody had much enthusiasm for the day's mission.

Gathering himself for the unpleasant task, Trevanathan stood beside his HMMWV for a moment, thinking back two years earlier, when he had interviewed with Colonel Hermann for the JAG slot at the 538th. "We go to Honduras, dig a few wells, take some photos of our contribution and come home," Hermann had said during his recruitment pitch. "Once you've earned your spurs, you may even get a chance at one of the MEDCAP missions in the Caribbean."

"MEDCAP, Sir?"

"Yeah, we take one of the medical teams down to some island, give out a few inoculations, drink a boatload of rum, declare victory and come home. Good duty if you can get it," the commander smiled

"What about deploying sir? Any chance we go to Afghanistan?" Trevanathan had done his share of mindless Reserve duty in other units, and was looking for a more meaningful contribution in view of 9/11.

"Well, of course, we're ready to go if called," Hermann had told him, shifting uncomfortably in his chair. "But right now we're the hearts and minds guys for the sweetest real estate in the world. Stick with us and you'll be lying on warm sand...."

CRUMP! Trevanathan found himself lying on warm sand as the first mortar round struck the carousel. Two of the colorful wooden horses were turned into splinters, adding to the deadly shrapnel of the round itself.

CRUMP! The earth heaved again as a second round disintegrated a lemonade stand 25 meters away, showering the now prone team with dirt and twisted metal.

"Take cover!" yelled Trevanathan as he rolled into a shallow drainage ditch next to the cart path.

Whump. Something hit Trevanathan in the back, driving his face into the dirt and splitting his lips over his teeth: Cooper had dove into the same ditch on top of him. "Sorry, sir," he said.

"Cooper, unless you're gonna' buy me dinner first, GET OFF ME!," Trevanathan sputtered, blood running down his chin. Cooper pushed himself off the officer and scrambled a few feet down the ditch, where he buried his head under his arms.

"Sir! They've got us zeroed in!" yelled Warden flopping into the ditch nose-to-nose with Trevanathan.

"I'm right here, Sergeant Warden; stop yelling at me. Where's it coming..." Trevanathan's inquiry was interrupted by the third round blasting one of the twisted cypress trees into a spray of deadly wooden shards.

Trevanathan fumbled in his pants cargo pocket for his satellite phone. All convoy commanders carried one for just such emergencies as this. Relieved to see that the phone had survived his dive into the ditch and was showing a satellite signal, he hit the speed dial button for the 538th TOC at Camp Babylon. The phone rang three times – and eternity to Trevanathan – before someone answered.

"538th Tactical Operations – this is...Specialist Sands,... Can ah help you sahr or ma'am?"

"Bravo 1-6, Bravo 1-6, this is Jaguar One! We are taking mortar fire!" Trevanathan said quickly into the microphone, spitting dirt and blood as he spoke.

"Uh,...sahr,...this is Specialist Sands," replied the slow Southern drawl. "Did you...uh....say that you're on fire...uh...sir?"

"Oh God, it's *Sands*," said Trevanathan to Warden. The NCO shook his head in dismay: Sands spoke slower and more deliberately than anyone he had ever met.

Crump. The fourth round landed harmlessly 75 meters to their southwest.

"No! *Listen*, Sands," Trevanathan spoke into the receiver. "We're at the amusement park. We are taking mortar fire...*mortar* fire!" he yelled, his frustration causing his voice to rise.

"Umm...OK, Jaguar One...Gimme a minute..."

The phone was silent. Trevanathan felt his heart hammering against the inside of his flak jacket as he waited another eternity for Sands to come back on line.

"Uhh,...Jaguar One...," Sands began, "Colonel Burr...uh,... says you should probably get out of there."

KARUMPH! With a mind-jarring explosion, Trevanathan's HMMWV erupted skyward, performed a mid-air summersault, and landed upside down in a burning heap of scrap metal ten meters from the ditch where its former occupants lay. The heat from the burning vehicle washed over the men in the ditch.

"Hey, that's *great*," the officer spat. "Warden, the POD thinks we should leave. Waddya' think?"

"I could be convinced," muttered Warden, trying to work himself even lower in the shallow ditch.

"Hey 1-6, maybe I'll knit a HMMWV to leave in since mine is frickin' BLOWN UP!" Trevanathan roared into the phone. Recovering his composure, he lowered his voice, "But in the meantime, we need the QRF here ASAP."

"Ahhh,... let me check on that, Jaguar One."

"Sure, sure, I got the rest of my life. *Take your time!*"

CRUMP! *A sixth round impacted twenty meters north.*

"Sahr, we need to get out of here," advised Warden. "They have us zeroed in. We're in more danger sitting here than running for it." His head jerked up at a new sound adding itself to the cacophony.

Crack!.

"We're takin' small arms fire, sir!" Cooper said.

Crack!

"That's an improvement," said Warden; "at least the frickin' Hajis can't shoot."

"I don't think so – I think that's the ammo cookin' off in the HMMWV," Trevanathan replied. The smell of burning plastic and diesel fuel choked the air.

"Too far away, sahr," Warden corrected.

"Cooper, slide backward down the ditch and try to get as far from the fire as you can in case any thing else explodes.," ordered Trevanathan. "I'll follow you. But keep your head down."

"Uhm, Jaguar One, this is…uh… Bravo 1-6," came the thin voice over the satellite phone. "The QRF is at…uh… an Organizational Day event. Ah'm sending a runner over there. Umm…what's your situation?"

"Unbelievable," muttered Trevanathan. He imagined a somber officer in Class A uniform knocking on the door of his home in rural Pennsylvania. "I'm sorry Mrs. Trevanathan, but your husband was killed due to a unit picnic."

"Sir, sir; it's stopped," said Warden. Other than the roar of the burning HMMWV there was no sound of either mortar or small arms fire.

"Everyone stay down!" Trevanathan yelled over the edge of the ditch to the rest of the team. "They may be trying to suck us into the open again." He cautiously peered out. The park was a junkyard of debris and flaming equipment. The carousel's roof was gone, and pieces of the brightly painted horses were scattered about. Several trees were now just smoldering stumps. Molten asphalt steamed at the bottom of a small crater in the cart path.

Trevanathan slowly raised to his knees, ready to drop again at the first sound of incoming fire.

"Rick, are your people OK?" Trevanathan called, seeing Smith peeking over the edge of a concrete fountain twenty meters away.

"Yeah, we're in one piece!"

"Stay down, until I'm sure this is over!" Trevanathan ordered.

"Sir, we got company," Cooper warned, pointing beyond the burning HMMWV.

Trevanathan squinted in the direction Cooper indicated, but smoke blocked his vision from this angle. Looking quickly about for cover, Trevanathan spotted a large piece of drain pipe ripped from somewhere during the attack and quickly knelt behind it, peering through the smoke and raising his rifle barrel in the direction Cooper had pointed. *Shit, I'll never hit anything like this,* he thought as his hands shook, causing the barrel to quiver as if he had a fish on a line. *Deep breaths, deep breaths*, he calmed himself, and his shaking abated somewhat.

Through the smoke, the indistinct outline of a man slowly approached. *He has a weapon*, Trevanathan recognized, seeing a rifle barrel silhouetted across the figure. He bent his head to the sights on his M16 and took aim on the target as it cleared the smoke 20 meters away.

The man stopped and looked calmly at Trevanathan before speaking. "My mama's gonna' be real disappointed if you pull that trigger, bud," came the slow drawl. "I'd feel a might better if you would point that bad boy in a less interestin' direction."

Trevanathan looked up from his sights. The picture before him was so out of place that he wondered if his brain had been scrambled by the blasts. Although the stranger wore no military uniform, he was just as certainly not Iraqi, nor even Arab. He wore a Harley Davidson T shirt declaring "Highway to Hell" beneath a nondescript black jacket, and dark green dungaree coveralls with large cargo pockets. Knee protectors were strapped around each leg, and on his head was a small, black hockey-like helmet. The man's weapon was a heavy caliber German model with a telescopic sight. It had a collapsible stock and dangled from a guitar strap that said "ZZ TOP" in faded red letters.

"Looks lahk you boys had a bit of excitement," he laughed, running a large rough hand over a dirty red beard. Trevanathan thought he looked like one of the steam grate dwellers he had seen in DC before the war. "Well, them boys won't be botherin' you anymore," he chuckled.

Trevanathan was trying to stammer something intelligent as he stood up, but the words would not come. His ears rang from the concussion of the mortar rounds. Walking slowly up him, the stranger said, "Hey sahr, you might want to sit down for a few. Ya' look a might pekid, if you don't mind me sayin so."

"Wh…who are you?" Trevanathan stuttered, noticing pain in his mouth for the first time.

"They call me Red Dog, sahr. Ah've been huntin' them Hajis with the mortar tube for a couple weeks now. Sneaky little bastards. They drop five or six quick rounds from the back of a truck, jump in and speed away before we can bring counter-battery down on 'em. They had a spotter on you up in that mosque," he pointed, directing Trevanathan's attention to the three-story minaret half a klick east of the park. "Ah took care of him."

A small radio buzzed on the stranger's chest. Pressing a clip under his throat, he said "Yeah?" Trevanathan noticed a wire running up from his collar to an earpiece stuck in his right ear. "Got it. Good job. Head for the barn." He looked back at the Major. "Mah partner took care of the boys with the tube. They had unloaded it this tahm to get a more stable shot at ya'al, so he was able to get up on 'em."

"Well, thanks for your help. We're lucky you were in the neighborhood," said Trevanathan.

"Nuthin' lucky 'bout it, sahr. We figgered thay'd be takin' a shot at you soon, seein' how you always come here and set up in the same place. Kind of like an invitation for Haji to whack ya', if ya' know what I mean. So me an' my partner 'Bear' decided to stake the place out for a few days, and it paid off."

Trevanathan was stunned. "You mean… you knew we were going to get hit?" he slowly asked as his head began to clear a bit.

"Pretty much everyone in town knew it, sahr, the way you boys been comin' out here all the time, giving out food, bein' nice guys. You get predictable and you're toast, sahr. You boys are 'bout as predictable as they come concernin' this park."

"*Who* are you anyway?" Trevanathan demanded, feeling his temper grow.

"Sahr, you know better than to ask that," chuckled Red Dog, flashing a white smile through his dusty red beard. "I don't exist."

"Why the hell didn't you warn us?" Trevanathan flashed backed angrily. "We could've been killed!"

"I warn you, and I don't get Haji, sahr. Mah job is to get Haji – not babysit you fine gentlemen. No hard feelings sahr, but y'all were the best bait in town."

"Are you Delta?" Trevanathan probed, looking at the high powered sniper rifle. Red Dog beamed and laughed, shaking his head. "Now sahr, you know Delta don't really exist. Just think of me as a good samaritan."

"*T!*" Doc called from near the shed. "T, get over here!" His urgency was unmistakable. Trevanathan abandoned his conversation and ran toward the voice.

"Shit!" exclaimed Doc, bending down next to the still-seated Leopard Man. The old man had been hit by a spear of wood blown off the carousel by the first mortar round. The shard, almost eighteen inches long and two inches thick had pierced his throat, tearing away half of his neck, and pinning his body to the wall of the shed in a ghastly fashion.

"Aaacch," Trevanathan exclaimed, as he saw the old man from behind Doc's back. Doc glanced up at Trevanathan and gave a definitive shake of his head. Trevanathan stared. *How come there's not more blood?* he wondered. The vertebrae at the back of the old man's neck was visible through a mass of purplish twisted tissue, transfixing the Major.

"Hey sir…," called Mantis, quickly walking up from wherever he had taken cover. He glanced down the old man and froze in mid-sentence, all color draining from his face. The ragged shreds of flesh dangling from the darkening wound were not something he had ever seen. Mantis felt his stomach flip twice, and he swallowed. He opened his mouth to get air, but it was no use: he quickly spun on his heel and turned his head and vomited into the dirt. "Ohh, shhiit," he barked, as his body convulsed again, gagging up the morning's breakfast. Slowly, almost as if in slow motion, he dropped to his knees and bent forward as if praying, resting on his helmet top in the dirt.

"Nice,"said Leader as he walked up to Trevanathan, looking with derision at Mantis, prostrate. "Hey, anybody got a fork?" he asked, looking around in wide-eyed mock wonder, as if he expected one to be produced.

Mantis choked again, his stomach spasming painfully.

"Not now, Pete," said Trevanathan quietly.

"Roger, Sir," said Leader obediently. "Captain Smith asked me to let you know the QRF is arriving."

"OK, thanks. Look, we can't leave the old man out here like this. Ask Captain Smith to radio back to the TOC to find out what the procedure is to deal with a dead Haji."

"What about the boy?" asked Doc.

"Crap!" said Trevanathan, "Where is he?" He looked around quickly for Bo. "Where was he when the first round hit?"

"Dunno," said Doc. "Didn't see him."

"OOoohhh," moaned Mantis, his body rocking back and forth on his knees.

"Pete, get him cleaned up and on his feet," said Trevanathan, looking at Mantis. "We don't want to embarrass ourselves in front of the Marines."

"Roger, Sir," said Leader, stepping over to lift Mantis by a beefy arm. "Come on, hero," he said as he slowly lifted Mantis onto his shaky legs. "You stay in that position too much longer, and I might not be able to restrain myself," he cracked, shooting a parting grin at the Major.

"Well, I'm glad someone still has a sense of humor," said Doc somberly, as he draped a camouflage neckerchief over the old man's face and neck

"Yeah, well, I'll check inside," said Trevanathan as he pulled back the dirty piece of cloth that served as the shed's door. Stepping inside, he had to wait a moment for his eyes to adjust to the dimness of the 3 meter by 4 meter dirt-floored room. Against the left wall, he could make out a pile of blankets that was apparently the sleeping area. An empty fuse box was mounted on the wall above. In the center of the room were two small rugs rolled up next to two bowls stacked inside each other. A pile of loose boards, a broken shovel and a tire occupied the far right hand corner.

Movement under the blankets caught Trevanathan's attention. In the darkness, he could just make out a small, dirty foot extended out from beneath. "Saddam," he said softly, surprised at the sound of his own voice in the stillness of the room. "Saddam, are you OK?" he asked, his voice lifting slightly in inquiry.

A blue eye peaked out from a corner of the pile, "Keptin," Bo said softly, "You OK?"

"Yeah, yeah; I'm fine, kid," said Trevanathan. "How are *you* is the question?"

"I am fine, Keptin. I am not hurt."

"Good. That's good," he repeated to fill the awkward silence. "Look Sadd…" Trevanathan started feeling his own stomach flipping with the unpleasantness of his next task.

"Do not call me Saddam, please," stated the boy slowly, raising himself to a half-seated position in the tangle of bedding. "It is an evil name. All of the death – my grandfather – it is all due to that name…"

Trevanathan was struck silent.

"My name is Bo, now. It is the name you gave me. It is a name that means good things, doesn't it?" he asked hopefully, his eyes meeting Trevanathan's in a serious and questioning stare.

"Yeah, it means good things," said Trevanathan softly. "Uh, Bo, you know your grandfather… he ah, didn't make it, you know?" he stammered, trying to find a way to soften the news that the child's last family in the world had just been torn from him.

"Yes, I know Keptin," said Bo somberly. "I was sitting inside the door when the bomb went off. He did not suffer…," the boy trailed off, tears blinking in his eyes.

The soldier knelt silently before the boy. The boy looked back. Eyes locked.

"I will go to America with you," Bo said matter-of-factly.

Trevanathan felt as if he had been punched. The kid had lost everything in his universe. Was he supposed to deliver the last kick in the ass to him by saying that wasn't going to happen? "Ahhh, Sadd…errr… Bo, that may not be too easy," he stuttered, trying to find a way to sidestep a more complete explanation.

"It does not matter, Keptin," said Bo with great certainty. "You will find a way."

"Ahh, sure Bo, sure," said Trevanathan, looking about the room again, trying to avoid contact with the piercing eyes of the boy. "Look, you can't stay here alone. That gang of kids you fought with will have you for lunch. Pack your shit…errr, things together and we'll figure out where you can stay after we get back to camp."

"I am going to the American camp?" asked Bo, his eyes lighting up in excitement.

"Just for a few hours," said Trevanathan. "Until we figure out what to do with you."

"I am going to the American camp," said Bo briskly, rising quickly and grabbing one of the two blankets. He then stepped swiftly over to the smallest of the two rugs and tucked it under his small arm. Last, he picked up his bowl. "I am ready to go to the American camp," he said again for emphasis, staring up at the soldier who loomed over him.

"OK, but it's just for a few hours. OK? Don't get too used to the idea."

"We will go now," said Bo decisively. "I will go to the American camp, and then I will go to America with you." He stepped past Trevanathan, through the blanket door, and out into the light of day.

Chapter 43
The Red Dog

Outside the shed, the team waited for Trevanathan and the boy. While the QRF secured the area, Red Dog sat down with the NCOs and broke out some jerky to share.

"No, thanks," said Mantis, still a little green around the gills. "Man, that was nasty," he commented, wiping his mouth with his camouflage neckerchief.

"You boys need to keep your officers sharp," Red Dog said to the three sergeants. "You need to make sure you're not predictable."

"Major T is pretty good," Warden said in Trevanathan's defense. "He *thinks*, ya' know? He just has kinda' a blind spot about this Haji kid, though."

"Well, that's good he's a thinker, but blind spots are what get ya' killed over here," replied Red Dog.

The group chewed the jerky for awhile without speaking.

"Let me ask you this," said Red Dog, gnawing off another large piece of the dried meat. "What's the one thing this party has in common to every big war we've been in?

"We've won," said Mantis quickly.

"Hah," laughed Red Dog. "Who's settin' in Saigon right now, bud?" Mantis shut up.

"There's some good lessons ya' can draw from history if ya' pay attention," said Red Dog. "Comes in handy in my line of work. No, the thing they all have in common is we get our butts handed to us at the beginning of every major war, but somehow we end up stronger in the end. Ya' ever wonder why that happens?"

"Waddya mean?" asked Mantis.

"The British kicked us from one end of the colonies to the other 'til Washington figgered the way to win was to outlast 'em. The Union lost the

Civil War for 2½ years before finding a fighting general who would attack instead of just talk about attackin'. In WWI, we didn't even have an army at the start of it. In WWII, the Japs and Germans beat on us for the first two years. We even almost lost Korea 'til we figured out how to fight that one."

"So?" asked Mantis. "The point is we're a good fourth quarter team?"

"Nah," replied Red Dog patiently, as he slowly chewed. "The point is that wars are won by fighting men, not by politicians. We lost those early battles because our peacetime generals sucked and the politicians tried to micro-manage things. A peacetime army doesn't produce great warfighters: it produces great administrators. Paper pushers. Guys who move up through the ranks because they avoid controversy – they play it safe, say what the politicians want to hear, and move up. But when the crap hits the fan and some ass-kickin' is needed, they're worthless."

Red Dog paused to spit a piece of gristle onto the ground before resuming. "Eventually, when enough boys get killed because of unimaginative tactics, the politicians and paper pushers start to hide out, and eventually a real fighting general stands up. Only time the politicians didn't get out of the way was Viet Nam – and look what happened there."

"Yeah," said Warden, thoughtfully. "Eisenhower was only a colonel at the start of WWII and he ended up runnin' the show."

"There's lot of that," agreed Red Dog. "US Grant was a sales clerk when the Civil War broke out, and only became a great general by taking risks and killing the enemy. McClellan was a political general who got more troops killed by his inaction than Grant ever did by attacking. Hell, look at Patton: he was considered a nut and an outcast – until he started killing Germans. Same with Halsey in the Pacific. The thing that saved us in each of those instances was that the politician-type generals got canned when they couldn't produce, and the fighting generals rose to leadership."

"What about this war, though?" asked Mantis. "We kicked ass from Day One."

"This war ain't over, bud. We kicked the crap out of a disorganized third-world army that had no will to fight. We took 21st century technology and bulldozed a 1970s-Soviet-supplied army and then congratulated ourselves on our fighting spirit. You see all those dead tanks between here and Baghdad?

Every one of them was hit from behind, running from the fight. Hell, even McClellan could have won here," Red Dog laughed.

"Them bubbas we greased in March and April had no will to fight and die for Saddam Hussein," he continued. "But the boys we're fightin' now ain't runnin'. They're hittin' and scootin'. They move fast, hit hard, and move on to the next soft target. They know they don't have to beat us. They just have to outlast us – just like George Washington. These people think in terms of centuries. We think in terms of weeks and months. No, they don't have to beat us: they just have to be more patient. And time is on their side. It's a different kind of war. We have to win, and they just have to wait us out."

"But with our weapons and technology, don't you think we'll get the upper hand eventually?" asked Mantis, disturbed by the thought that victory was not as inevitable as he had assumed.

"The problem with this war is we won so fast that we became overconfident," replied Red Dog. "Our troops went through the Iraqi Army like crap through a goose, and we declared victory. We didn't know the real fight was just beginning. We have the world's best military, and now we're cooped up in a bunch of base camps by a bunch of uneducated guerillas. We have total command of the air, but we don't use that advantage because it puts too much wear and tear on the 'copters and the fixed-wings. When's the last time you even saw an A-10 over here? When's the last time you saw a helo doing recon along the highway to prevent IEDs? It's not happenin'. Too expensive to keep runnin' all that high-tech searchin' for a threat that might not be there.

"We're huddled up in these camps telling people we control the country, and Haji is runnin' around out there in the open. We're so worried about casualties that we've taken our victory and gone on the defensive. We can't travel in small groups. We can't travel at night. We can't go into certain parts of Baghdad. Tell me who's winning again?"

Warden and Leader sat quietly, contemplating the words and becoming uncomfortable with the idea that this unkempt prophet from the desert might have a point - no army ever won a war by sitting on the defensive.

"We didn't beat the Iraqi army because our generals are so great," Red Dog continued. "Our problem is we won so fast against poor opposition that now we're saddled with a buncha' cautious old men leading us, who are using the same tired tactics that got the British thrown out of every country in their empire, lost the French Viet Nam, and are sending home a few dozen body bags a month to Bugtussle, USA, for no apparent gain. Hell, they've even started doing the 'body count' thing again that was so meaningless in Viet Nam, because they have no other way to show any progress."

"Well, I think we'll eventually wear them down with our better weapons," argued Mantis defensively.

"Oh yeah?" retorted Red Dog. "And how do we use those superior weapons? Haji hits fast and light and we take weeks to plan massive offensives to crush small pockets of resistance, so that everyone from Muhammad the shit sucker to my Aunt Tilly knows when and where we are going to attack. Hell, we even tell CNN where we'll attack ahead of time so they can capture our 'victory' on film. You think the head bad guys stick around for that attack? Hell no! They leave behind their cannon fodder and scoot off to the next quiet spot to plan their next attack, while Hopalong Haji and the Dumbshit Brothers go to Allah covering their rear. We then congratulate the generals for spending a couple hundred million dollars' worth of ordnance to grease a few dozen bad guys, hand out another round of medals, and once again declare victory. It's pathetic."

"So how would you do it?" Mantis challenged. He did not like the fact that this freelancer was chipping away at ideas he firmly believed in.

"You want to beat Haji? You need to fight like Haji," said Red Dog, his eyes flashing. "Next mosque we find stuffed with ammo, take the Mullah in charge out right then and shoot him in the street. Hang his body from a bridge and let the crows pick at it awhile. I guarandamntee you that no other Haji mullahs are gonna' store weapons after that." He licked his lips quickly. "We take sniper fire from a minaret? Drop a 2,000-pound bomb on it. There won't be any more damn snipers in minarets. You want to beat the devil, you better fight like the devil. Or be prepared to crawl home with your tail between your legs."

Warden nodded; he had thought much the same thing after his tour in Somalia.

"But…," Red Dog said, slowly standing up and wiping his hands on his pants. "That would be wrong. We would offend the UN. The stinky-cheesechompin' surrender monkeys in Paris would be outraged. No, we want to wear the white hat and be liked by everyone; so, it's better to send Mrs. Jones her little Johnny home in a baggie, than to be accused of being tough on these poor, misunderstood people."

"Well, looks like your boss is ready to go," said Red Dog, gesturing toward Trevanathan and Bo as they exited the shed. "You gentlemen have a nice day."

"Where ya' going now, Red?" asked Warden.

"Well, I think I might mosey over to that mosque and explain to the man in charge that he had a bad man on his roof. I'll bet he didn't even know that," he smiled wryly, biting off another piece of jerky. "You be careful, sir," he said to Trevanathan, with a nod. Slinging the sniper rifle across his back, Red Dog strode away through the wreckage of the park.

Chapter 44
The Tenant

The Jaguars had sequestered Bo out of sight on Camp Babylon for a week before the command group learned of his presence. During that time, the boy had kept a low profile in the palace, doing laundry – at $1 per bucket – and consuming more than his share of surplus candy. Even the Marines turned a blind eye to his existence as the story of his situation got around.

The team had set up a small hooch for Bo, next to Trevanathan's cot, and Doc was keeping an eye on the boy's health: he was not happy that the mass on child's neck seemed to be still growing. Bo seemed to be happy and healthy otherwise, but Trevanathan noticed that he became very fatigued toward the end of the day. The team's officers spent hours discussing ideas late into the night as they sat on the terrace., without finding a long-term solution.

It was Trevanathan's bad luck that when word got to the TOC, Colonel Hermann was in Baghdad attending a commanders' conference: he was summoned by the XO, Colonel Burr, who delivered both barrels.

"Are you under the misapprehension, Major, that we're running a day care on this post?" sneered the POD, sitting behind Hermann's desk.

"No, sir," replied Trevanathan, standing at the position of parade rest. He knew that this would be a one-sided conversation.

"Could it be that you were confused as to the fact that Iraqi nationals are not to be within the wire without authorization?" In his anger, the POD was practically spitting.

"No, sir."

"Well then, you are telling me that you intentionally violated post security procedures. Is that correct?"

"Yes, sir."

"Not that I really care, Major, but humor me," the POD probed with an insincere smile. "Why?"

Trevanathan thought through a variety of possible responses before responding, but knew that any rationale, humanitarian or otherwise, would fall upon deaf ears.

"No excuse sir. I screwed up."

"Hmm," murmured the POD, surprised that the JAG officer was not weaseling and squirming on the hook in his own defense. He was slightly disappointed that Trevanathan was not providing more sport.

"Well, this will be reflected on your evaluation report, Major," stated the POD coolly. "Now get out of here, and get rid of the kid."

"Yessir," said Trevanathan, snapping to attention and saluting before exiting the small office.

At the top of the steep dusty path up to the palace, Smith and Doc were waiting for him. "Well?" Doc probed.

"He said get rid of the kid."

"That's all?" asked Smith. He had been worried that Burr might try to institute formal charges against his friend.

"Oh, well, he's going to hose me on my OER[80]," chuckled Trevanathan. "I was worried he was gonna' send me to Iraq or something serious like that."

"Well, I have some good news," said Doc.

"What, another extension?" replied Trevanathan sarcastically.

"No, Abu was poking around down in the village and found a widow who said she is willing to take the boy. She's the sister of the Chicken Lady. Name is Fatine."

"Can we trust her?" asked Trevanathan, who had come to question the sincerity of any purported acts of kindness in this country.

"Abu sniffed around, and she seems legit. She gave tours of the ruins and the museum before the war. Lost her husband in the First Gulf War."

---

[80] Officer Evaluation Report

"Does she know he's sick?"

"Yeah, but she didn't seem to care. I think it would be a good idea to leave some money with her to help out, though. She didn't ask for any, mind you. Probably would help. She gets money from her sister, too."

"OK, let me meet her, and then we'll make the move."

Trevanathan had been satisfied that Fatine was sincere in her desire to help Bo, although she still insisted upon calling the boy "Saddam."

"Bo?" she had asked, incredulously. "What is a 'Bo?' There is no such name in Islam." The boy had not been happy with the move, but after Doc explained that staying on the base would get the "Keptin" into trouble, he had accepted it graciously.

For the first few weeks, Bo had appeared to thrive on the steady diet of chicken that Fatine put on the table, but his condition gradually began to decline. He became less active, and swallowing was more of an effort. Doc obtained some medicine from the CSH that reduced the discomfort somewhat, but he could do nothing to stop the slow and constant growth of the tumor.

Christmas in Iraq was just another work day for the troops on Camp Babylon, who tried to stay busy and avoid thoughts of home. Boxes of food and chocolate which would not have survived the summer temperatures, now poured into the camp from the States. Trevanathan and the Jaguars made a visit to the village on Christmas morning to present Bo with a wrist slingshot they had ordered from the internet, along with a stocking full of candy. "Just great," said Warden as he watched the boy dispatch a lizard with his gift: "Now we're arming the terrorists." But he was smiling.

Meanwhile, Trevanathan unsuccessfully exhausted avenues to find the boy a way out of the country. During his frequent missions throughout Southern Iraq, he sought out anyone who might have contacts or influence to help the boy. In every instance, he found sympathy but no answers. The few international aid groups that remained in the country claimed that it was a government matter. Behind the walls of the Green Zone, CPA hid behind its waiting list. The Kuwaitis were apologetic, but said that such a thing was not possible when Iraq had yet to account for so many missing Kuwaiti children from the First Gulf War. Trevanathan even lowered himself to seeking help from the French, who had maintained strong business interests in Iraq over the years despite the UN embargo. *"Ce'st impossible"* had been the predictable response by the French military liaison in Baghdad.

Chapter 45
The Goodbye

Trevanathan saw Bo sitting by the edge of the canal just outside the village, a long stick in his hand. As he approached, he saw that the boy was poking at a green water snake that coiled angrily about the offending instrument in protest. The rest of the Jaguar team remained with their vehicles, parked in the shadow of the village mosque nearby.

The village had at one time been a center for traders plying their bronze goods up and down the length of Mesopotamia. During the age of Nebuchadnezzar and the Diaspora, Jewish slaves had occupied much of this area, raising their children in exile in the shadow of the great capital city of Babylon. During the failed attempt by Britain to colonize Iraq in the early twentieth century, the village had been an important communications station between Baghdad and the desert tribes who defeated the British advance. At all the varied times and passages of history in the region, one organized faith or another had been the glue holding the village together.

To the Jaguars, who represented the latest conquering army to slash its way across the wastes of Iraq, the mosque was a good place to park their HMMWVs out of the late afternoon sun while their Major bade farewell to the boy he had vainly hoped to save. Easter was approaching, and while no one was getting his hopes up too high this time, thoughts were once again slipping homeward. Behind their machineguns, Ridlin and Cooper kept watch while the rest of the team relaxed in their vehicles.

"Hey, Bo, what's up?" asked Trevanathan with false cheerfulness. From behind he could see that the growth on the boy's neck was beginning to affect the angle at which the child could hold his head.

"Keptin!" Bo responded cheerfully, keeping one eye on the coiled serpent weighing down his stick. "Give me five," he said sticking out his one free palm in the direction of the soldier.

Trevanathan tapped the boy's hand and then squatted beside him, observing the angry snake. "I hate snakes," said Trevanathan. "Don't know why. They never bothered me when I was your age, but now – oooohhh!" Trevanathan feigned a shiver for emphasis.

"The snake does not bother me," said Bo. "It is a creature like all others. No better, no worse."

"Maybe," replied Trevanathan. "Say, uh, look Bo, I've got some news. It, uh, seems that the President is going to finally send us,…uhm,… home to America. We got our orders."

"That is very good for you, Keptin," Bo said, seriously. "You will be able to see your sons. They will be very proud of you."

"Yeah, well, uh,… We, uhm, leave in two weeks, and another group of soldiers will take our place."

"I must remain here?" Bo asked, dropping the stick into the canal and turning to face Trevanathan for the first time.

"Um, I think so, Bo. Your name is still on the list in Baghdad to go someday, but it will still be awhile yet."

"It does not matter," said Bo, matter-of-factly, returning his gaze to the canal where the snake was now skimming quickly away across the surface.

"Why do you say that?" asked Trevanathan.

"I will die soon," said Bo.

Trevanathan felt a cold shock to hear the boy say such words so calmly. "Don't say that," he replied quickly. "You aren't going to die."

"Keptin, friends do not tell each other false things. It is already hard to breathe, and 'it' is bigger. I cannot run anymore, because there is no air. I will die, I think."

Trevanathan said nothing. *What the hell does one say to a kid who is so accepting of his own mortality?* he asked himself.

"I am not afraid to die, Keptin," Bo continued. "I have seen many die since last winter. My father. My grandfather. It does not look difficult. They lie down and do not get up again. That is all."

"Bo…," Trevanathan started with a faltering voice. "You can't give up hope."

"I am not very old, Keptin, but I have learned some matters. I know it is sometimes harder to live than to die. When the boys beat me because they thought I am marked by evil. When the women stare and whisper – afraid that I will pass my sickness to their children – I think it would be easier to lie down and not get up again at those times."

Trevanathan was silent, unable to think of anything that would not sound silly and common in comparison to the wisdom of this eight-year old child. Moments passed as the pair stared at the swift current of the canal washing by.

"Bo, I have left some money with Fatine to take care of you. You don't have to worry ever again about not having a place to stay." Trevanathan thought his words sounded hollow, but he was fighting to keep a brave front for the boy. *Too much emotion would be even worse*, he thought.

"Do not be sad for me when you are gone," Bo said to the stream, without looking up. "You have done much for me. I will never forget you." Saddam reached up and placed his hand into Trevanathan's. Trevanathan squatted down silently beside him, looking across the canal into the date palms on the far bank. They sat that way - side by side, quiet - as the western sky turned orange and then purple. A single star appeared, low and red above the palms, as the first foray of bats darted back and forth across the water, snatching insects for their evening meal.

"What are they doing?" asked Mantis, standing next to Jaguar Two. He was increasingly uncomfortable with his officer sitting along the canal as the sun set, holding the boy's hand. *It's not the right image to send to these Hajis*, he thought.

"They're saying goodbye, asshole," said Leader. "The kid is dead when we leave here, and it's eatin' the boss alive."

"He doesn't talk about it," countered Mantis; he had grown immune to the barbs thrown at him by the tall NCO.

"That's how you know it's killin' him," Warden said from the front passenger seat of Jaguar One, his legs hanging out the doorway. "That's his way; Now just shut up."

The team remained waiting, giving their officer time to finish his personal mission. Shortly, Warden saw Trevanathan slowly rise. In the failing light, the boy remained on the bank, staring out across the canal. The officer reached down and touched the boy on the shoulder, then walked back toward his soldiers.

"It's done," Trevanathan said flatly to Warden as he approached Jaguar One. "Let's go."

Chapter 46
The Relief

Against all reasonable expectations – and fears – to the contrary, replacements for the veterans of the 538th arrived in March of 2004. The 803rd Civil Affairs Brigade from Milwaukee, Wisconsin, would be stationed in An Najaf, an hour south of Camp Babylon and more central to Southern Iraq. A side effect of this stationing plan was that the departure of the 538th would significantly decrease the daily civil affairs presence in Al Hillah. The fact that the 803rd was also deploying with 2/3 the number that the 538th had on the ground had raised some eyebrows among the latter.

The 803rd spent its first week deployed in Kuwait, absorbing the latest memos and after action reports of the 538th before moving north into Iraq. The respective command groups had directed team-to-team transition operations, and so it was a few days later that the legal teams of the two brigades were to meet face-to-face for the first time at the courthouse in Al Hillah. Trevanathan wanted to personally introduce the replacements to the judges, and the 803rd's people had responded to the idea with enthusiasm: the message from the new OIC was that his team was looking forward to meeting its predecessors and was ready "to continue making a positive difference in guiding Iraq along the path toward democracy." Accordingly, when the Jaguar team walked into the Al Hillah courthouse that morning, a snapshot would have shown an army existing in two different worlds.

The hollow-eyed, wolfish appearance of the 538th team caught the 803rd soldiers off guard. These did not look like the cocky, victorious US troops he had expected, but more like scarecrows in ragged uniforms, attempting some ridiculous masquerade. Salt stains covered the backs and legs of their faded, frayed DCUs. Pocket covers flapped open where buttons had long ago liberated themselves from their hold. Small tears, frayed collars, and stained helmet covers completed the picture. Hardened eyes darted about the lobby looking for anything out of place. At first glance, the new OIC assumed these were some other troops, until he spotted the name "Trevanathan" marked on one's ammo pouch. Realizing this was the man whose reports he had been reading for the past several weeks, the 803rd officer rushed forward with a smile.

"Hi, I'm George Busch, your replacement," said the short, slightly overweight and prematurely balding JAG Major, extending his hand toward Trevanathan.

"Well, George," said Trevanathan with a tired grin, "I want you to know I think your war sucks." He took the other's hand, idly noting the sharp appearance of the brand new desert uniform worn by his replacement.

Busch looked uncertain for a moment and then laughed. "Oh yeah," he chuckled, "The name – I get a lot of that."

"Sergeant Warden," said Trevanathan over his shoulder, "do a loop upstairs and make sure everything's secure."

"Roger, sir," said Warden tapping Jamie on the shoulder before climbing the lobby stairs in tandem, M16s lowered, but ready. Jamie was with the team today, as Mantis was down with a nasty case of *Saddam's Revenge*.

"Oh, everything's fine" said Busch. "We were just up there talking to some of the prosecutors. Seem like a nice group of fellas. Offered us a Pepsi," he beamed.

"Uh- huh," replied Trevanathan, quietly evaluating the newbie.

"I gotta' say I'm really looking forward to this mission," said Busch. "Everyone's been real friendly. I think we can do a lot of great things with the locals if we work together."

"Uh-huh," said Trevanathan.

"Oh, here's my deputy, First Lieutenant Maraguez," said Busch, as a young, portly female officer waddled into the lobby carrying an M16 slung over her shoulder. The weapon was nearly as tall as she was.

"Jeez," whispered Leader into Cooper's ear. "Her ass is almost as big as Mantis'." Cooper grinned, and struggled not to laugh out loud. A quick look from Trevanathan told the two of them to knock it off.

"How ya' doin', El-Tee?" said Trevanathan, turning around to shake hands with Maraguez.

"Ooohh, sir, it's so good to meet you. I've heard so much about the great work you've done over here. We've been reading all of your SITREPs[81] , getting ready to come up here. I think I've read just about every book on Iraq I could get my hands on, too. It is such a thrill to finally be here and meet you...."

Trevanathan stared at Maraguez and could see her lips moving, but all that reached his brain was a high-pitched babble. *She's wearing make-up*, he realized. The light blue eyeliner and rose blush on her cheeks stood out in stark contrast to her desert tan and brown uniform, from which the clean smell of soap and perfume wafted, offending his nostrils. *The second those canal mosquitoes get a whiff of that, they're going to set the table for the whole family*, he mused. *She has earrings, too. Some Haji will cut her frickin' ears off to get those diamond studs.*

"...so I hope you'll tell us all about it," she ended in an excited, panting voice as Trevanathan tried to refocus on what she was saying.

"All clear, sahr," said Warden, as he and Jamie rumbled back down the stairs. "The Haji judges are all gathered in the Chief Judge's office as usual, smoking up a storm."

"El-Tee," said Warden to Maraguez, as he passed behind her; "your weapon is off 'SAFE.'" Maraguez flushed and looked at Busch.

"Ah, well," stammered Busch, "I had, uh, briefed everyone last night to ah, keep their weapons ready in case anything surprised us when we came up from our camp."

"No disrespect, Sahr," said Warden, "but the surprise you're gonna' receive is when your lieutenant puts a round in your back when she drops that rifle. It's practically dragging on the ground now the way she has it slung."

"Well, Sergeant, I think we know what we're doing," said Busch, coloring slightly. "I've been in the Army for 13 years, and where I come from NCOs do not correct officers in public," he ended defensively.

"OK, Sahr," said Warden nonchalantly. "Just tryin' to help."

---

[81] Situation Reports – military slang for status reports

Trevanathan made eye contact with Warden, "Get the team ready to roll. I'll be about 15 minutes."

"Roger, Sahr," said Warden. He, Jamie, Cooper, and Leader quickly went out the door.

Busch looked uncomfortable as Trevanathan turned to him without saying a word. "Sorry to correct your NCO there, Major Trevethanon," said Busch, butchering Trevanathan's name. "But he came on a little strong."

"Heh," said Trevanathan ruefully, as he took a step closer toward Busch and put his arm tightly around the shorter man's shoulders. Busch recoiled slightly as the sour smell of Trevanathan's uniform hit his nostrils.

"You said you wanted to learn about Iraq, George, so I'm gonna' tell you. Miss Perfume over here too," he said gesturing at the horrified, plump face of Maraguez.

"One: there ain't no Hajis in this country who are 'a nice bunch of fellas.' They all want something and you're just the way to get it. If they can get it by smiling, they'll do that – but if they need to cut your throat, well, they'll do that, too."

Busch tried to gently pull back from Trevanathan's embrace, but Trevanathan held him firmly, shoulder to shoulder.

"Two: the next time you come into any Haji building without properly clearing it, you're probably gonna' die, sure and simple. Probably a third of those nice fellas upstairs are selling information to the insurgents as a life insurance policy so they don't get whacked for playin' nice with us. You trust them, and you and your people are goin' home in bags."

Busch looked desperately at Maraguez, seeking help to escape the hold of this foul-smelling desert creature.

"Finally, Mr. President," said Trevanathan flatly, turning and placing his nose inches from Busch' now sweating face. "Your '13 years' in the peacetime Army don't mean shit. Anyone who has spent two months in this hell-hole knows more about soldierin', dyin', and survivin' than all of you gung-ho, gonna'-save-the-world newbies wrapped together. So the next time a combat-experienced NCO tries to save your life, put away your ego and listen to him."

Busch tried to open his mouth, but nothing came out but a nervous squeak.

"Salaam Alekim," said Trevanathan, releasing his grip and walking toward the stairs. "Let's go meet the judges."

Behind him, Busch stood stunned as Trevanathan disappeared up the stairs. Beside him, Maraguez puffed indignantly, "Well, sir; that was the rudest officer I have ever met. You should report him." Busch didn't reply. The flat, hollow stare of his predecessor remained in Busch's memory. He had heard through the JAG grapevine that Trevanathan was an outgoing and gregarious officer: this man withdrawn and confrontational. *I wonder what he's seen,* thought Busch.

"Sir?" asked Maraguez.

"Put your weapon on safe, Lieutenant," ordered Busch, "and go wash off that perfume."

Chapter 47
The Final Day

"Do you really think we're going home this time, sir?" asked Cooper, as Trevanathan climbed into Jaguar One outside the courthouse.

"I sure hope so, Coop, because I think I just pissed off the new neighbors," Trevanathan laughed. "Let's move out."

Jaguars One (replaced) and Two started off on the familiar route back to Camp Babylon for the last time. At 0300 the next morning, trucks would arrive at Camp Babylon to take them to Baghdad Airport and from there to Kuwait and then home.

Trevanathan had longed for this day, every day, for the past twelve months. He had expected to be excited, but now that it was here he only felt numb. The world outside Iraq didn't seem to exist any more. Family had been reduced to anxious and supportive voices coming out of a phone receiver in the Morale Tent; his law firm job was a hundred years ago, and the thought of wearing a tie and sitting behind a desk all day seemed ridiculous. His early enthusiasm for going home had become quiet, gnawing concern for how he would fit in there. There had been a period of readjustment after his Bosnia tour, too, but this was different. He had not just regained an "active duty" mentality on this deployment – he had become something different.

As Jaguar One led the usual winding route back to Camp Babylon, each mile brought back memories of the past year. The courthouse, now operating again, lay behind them. The jail, too, where they had first seen the Iraqi concept of rehabilitation in action. The narrow bridge over the canal where they had expected to get hit so many times. *You can't count on anything in this country,* thought Trevanathan, as they safely cleared the short span for the last time. *The locals don't even have the common courtesy to ambush you where they should.*

He thought back to his conversation with the Buddha about whether this had all been worth it – whether they had really made a difference at all, other than just repairing a few crummy buildings and handing out some trinkets to the natives.

"Sahr, the village is just ahead," yelled Warden from the rear seat, where he was manning the SAW behind Cooper. "Ya' wanna stop in and see the lil' terrerist one last time?"

Trevanathan thought about the last goodbye he had made with Bo and the look on the child's face as he had walked away. "No, I don't think I could take it again," he replied. "That tumor is a death sentence, and I let the kid down. Can't face him again."

The 122 millimeter artillery shell had been carefully secured behind the guard rail that morning by a team of six Syrians and Saudis who had infiltrated south from Fallujah over the past several day to destroy the appearance of stability in the South. The shell had been looted from a vast and lightly guarded ammunition dump southwest of Baghdad. The insurgents had laughed that the Americans took such good care to secure ordnance that they could then easily steal and turn into roadside bombs. They had developed tactics that served them well. The six had traveled across the country under the guise of refugees returning to Iraq from exile in Jordan. Provided with false papers showing temporary legal residence in Jordan, they were able to move through US checkpoints under the fiction of returning to homes they had fled under Saddam's brutal rule. They had identified the village of Al Salaam as a good point from which to launch their first attack in this area, as the Americans often slowed down through the narrow stretch of road due to the many animals and children present. Hitting the enemy this close to the vaunted Marine Corps headquarters would also send a strong message that no place was safe.

On this day, however, the children and the animals had been herded away from the road. Gathering the village elders at dawn, the insurgents had been very clear that any warning to the Americans would result in the immediate execution of them and their families. The children had been hustled away to the mosque under the ruse of receiving school supplies from the Americans. There they were held by two of the insurgents, along with the village's women.

Jaguar One rounded the curve at the base of the hill atop which Saddam Hussein had intended to build his mosque, and slowed as the village came into sight. *The road is strangely empty*, thought Trevanathan. "You can speed up Cooper," he said to his driver, "no one out today."

As Cooper pressed on the accelerator, the thumb of the Saudi team leader depressed the doorbell button linked to the detonator by two hundred meters of copper wire. The shell strapped to the back side of the rail detonated just as Jaguar One passed, missing a clean hit due to Cooper's last-second acceleration. The blast simultaneously demolished and lifted the rear half of the truck into the air, spinning the vehicle clockwise and throwing its passengers forward against their seatbelts. Abu, in Warden's usual seat behind Trevanathan, received the brunt of the blast, the unarmored side panel of his flak jacket pierced by dozens of jagged metal fragments. His jaw was ripped from his face by a particularly large piece of shrapnel and smashed into Warden's helmet, spraying the NCO with blood, bone splinters, and teeth. The only blessing, if any, was that the force was so sudden and overwhelming that Abu never felt the pain of his death as the searing hot metal punctured his body.

Though stunned, Warden and Cooper were spared the brunt of the blast by being on the opposite side of the HMMWV from the explosive. Warden in particular was saved by Abu's body absorbing much of the shock. Trevanathan was knocked unconscious and suffered multiple shrapnel wounds to his upper right arm. Had it not been for his too-small flak jacket, his injuries would not have been severe: instead, a thin steel sliver entered his lower back just below the edge of his body armor, tearing through his right kidney and large intestine before blowing a baseball-sized hole in his abdomen as it exited the other side of the officer's body.

The HMMWV slammed down with a screech onto its shredded tires, facing the way from which it had come - spilling fuel and engine fluids into a pool beneath itself.

Jaguar Two skidded to a halt 50 meters behind the stricken vehicle as automatic weapons fire reached out from the village. Smith gazed at the scene of horror in disbelief. *Not now,* he thought, *not now!* Rounds rang off the bumper of Jaguar Two as he ordered, "Take cover! We're not leaving them!" He fumbled with his seatbelt release, freeing himself quickly enough to roll out the right side of the vehicle onto the hard pavement. The rest of Jaguar

Two's team also dove out the right side, scrambling for cover behind the ample body and thick tires of their vehicle.

"Can anyone tell where they're firing from?" Smith demanded, his voice cracking slightly.

"Sir, all the fire is coming from the village," said Sergeant Leader as he reached up to pull the SAW out of the passenger compartment. He quickly checked that the mechanism had not jammed, and crawled to the rear of the truck. Partially shielded by the left rear tire he sent a short burst of fire into the village.

"What are you firing at?" yelled Smith, peaking up over the HMMWV's hood before ducking down again.

"Anything that moves, sir" said Leader between bursts.

"How can you tell who's a bad guy?" asked Ridlin uncertainly from where he had taken cover behind the right front tire.

"If it's a Haji, and its movin' out there, it's a bad guy," replied Leader calmly, squeezing off another burst at movement in a window. *Bup, Bup, Bup*, came the throaty reply of the AK-47 moments later, confirming that Leader had indeed smelled out an enemy position.

"Ridlin! Jamie! I need you to find out if anyone is still alive from Jaguar One," ordered Smith. "I can't see with all the smoke."

"OK, sir," answered both troops simultaneously.

"Wait until Sergeant Leader opens up with the SAW and then run like hell, got it? Use that ditch for cover," Smith directed, pointing to the depression along the road that prevented the heavy winter downpours from flooding the village.

"OK, sir," repeated Jamie. Ridlin nodded.

"Now!" yelled Smith, as he popped the barrel of his M16 over the hood of Jaguar Two and began squeezing off bursts of covering fire. Leader began traversing the buildings with the SAW, his rounds kicking up dust from the walls wherever they hit. Ridlin and Jamie broke from cover: Jamie into the ditch as ordered, while Ridlin – within his own little world as usual – ran straight down the open road toward the smoking hulk of Jaguar One. Behind him, Smith could only gape, expecting the young troop to be hit at any second.

As Ridlin approached the twisted remnant of Jaguar One, he could see Trevanathan still strapped into the front seat. The Major weakly raised a bloody hand, waving him off. To the right, he saw another hand waving to him from behind the rail above the drainage ditch. "Get in here, you idiot!" Warden yelled.

A burst of fire from the village chewed into the pavement in front of Ridlin, and he veered from his original path into the ditch. He flopped into the bottom beside Warden just as another set of rounds bit at his heels.

"What the hell were you doing?" Warden demanded.

"Tryin' to see if you were alive, Serg'nt. Captain Smith sent me."

"Well, don't bother," said Warden. "Abu is dead and I'm pretty sure Major T bought it, too. They caught the brunt of it."

"Major's alive Serg'nt," said Ridlin quickly. "He just waved me off."

Cold, gnawing guilt bit Warden's stomach. *Damn it, I left him out there*, he thought. Depressing the SEND button on his handheld radio, Warden called to Smith. "Jaguar Two, Jaguar Two: need MEDEVAC ASAP. We have one KIA and one critical WIA from blast."

"Bravo 1-6, this is Jaguar Two; over," Smith spoke into the handset of his SINCGARS radio. The cord was just long enough to let him crawl halfway into the front seat of the vehicle and hide behind the dashboard as he radioed for help.

"Bravo 1-6, this is Jaguar Two; over," he repeated, as sweat trickled into the corners of his mouth.

"Ah, hi sir. This is Bravo 1-6, what can I do for you?" came the bored voice of Lieutenant Hilton. "No one is really around. They're all off packing; over," she said petulantly.

"This is Jaguar Two, base; we have been hit by an IED. One dead and one badly wounded. We are taking small arms fire. Prepare for a nine line MEDEVAC request; over."

"Sir, are you joking? I don't think this is very funny," Hilton said in the same bored tone.

"Bravo 1-6, this is no Goddamn joke!, Damnit, prepare to copy!"

Back at the 538th TOC at Camp Babylon, Hilton could now hear small arms fire over the radio, deep AK-47 shots merging with the high pitched chatter of the SAW. "Oh my God," she cried, scrambling to find a pen as her voice shook with the realization that this was not a practical joke.

"Line One:" started Smith, "Whiskey Kilo, seven niner five, four seven three; break.

"Line Two: Jaguar Two; break,

"Line Three: one patient, Alpha; over!"

"Ahh, sir, I can't find my sample medical EVAC card here," interrupted Hilton, fumbling amongst the pile of papers on the staff duty officer's desk. "Can you tell me what Alpha means in Line 3?"

Smith fought back an urge to scream as several rounds bit into HMMWV hood above him.

"Listen, El-Tee: Line three, we have one urgent case! Break!

"Line Four: none; break!

"Line Five: Lima, one; over!"

"Sir, tell me that in English can you?" Hilton begged. "I don't have a card, remember?"

Smith barked into the microphone, "We have one litter patient. One frickin' litter patient! That is, if he's still alive when you finally get your shit together!"

"I'm sorry, sir" said Hilton, beginning to sniffle into the handset. "I've never done this before," she choked.

"Listen up, El-Tee: we're in a bad way out here. I need you to focus and get this right, OK? Line Six: multiple shrapnel wounds and probable burns; break!"

"Oh God," sobbed Hilton, tears streaming down her face and staining the pad on which she was scribbling.

"Line Seven:" continued Smith, as Leader slapped another magazine into the SAW, "Charlie – smoke; break!

"Line 8: US military; break!

"Line 9: open scrub. Hot LZ under small arms fire; over!"

"Got it, sir," sniffled Hilton into her handset. "What do you want me to do with this?"

"You're the Staff Duty Officer, Hilton! Contact the Division G3 operations section, let them know our situation, and send a MEDEVAC; over!"

"Ah, yes sir, but no one ever showed me how to do that. I'm just kind of minding the radio while Colonel Burr is packing."

Smith buried his face in the passenger's seat, not believing what he was hearing. *We're going to die here*, he thought, *so everyone else can make sure they've packed to go home.* "El-Tee," he snapped into the radio, "I want you to take that message you just wrote down and run – *frickin' run* – to the 1st Division TOC and ask for the Staff Duty Officer. He'll know what to do; over."

"OK, sir," came Hilton's shaky reply.

"Jaguar Two; out," spat Smith, dropping the handset and sliding back out of the passenger compartment to the covering safety of the truck's massive body.

"We're hosed," he replied to Leader's inquisitive look.

"Serg'nt, we gotta' get him out of there, before the Hajis light him up or the HMMWV catches fire," Cooper said, nodding his head toward the smoking hulk of Jaguar One. The incoming fire had momentarily abated, permitting Warden to briefly survey the scene.

Warden could see the silhouette of Trevanathan's helmeted head hanging down on his chest, but the smoke from the wreckage and the steam from the pierced radiator obscured any detail. He peered past the edge of the smoldering hulk toward the village, looking for movement. A momentary flash of white between the outer buildings and the small mosque caught his eye.

"Movement!" he roared, pointing his gloved hand toward the street corner where the flash had come from. Jamie, who had assumed operation of Jaguar One's SAW from Warden, rapidly swiveled the barrel toward the target area, letting loose a stream of 5.56 mm rounds that flew too high, splattering against the small minaret behind the intended target. A short figure in a white, ankle-length man dress stepped out into the open from behind the building in front of the mosque, and turned to face the Americans. He stood still, making no attempt to conceal himself. Jamie quickly lowered his barrel and slowly squeezed the trigger.

"CEASE FIRE! CEASE FIRE!" screamed Warden. An ounce of pressure before the trigger mechanism released the firing pin, Jamie released the trigger and breathed heavily. The small figure in white continued to stare back at them impassively, motionless: it was Bo.

"It's the lil' terrerist," said Warden to himself. "Cease fire!" he yelled again toward Ridlin to ensure that no mistake was made.

"What the hell's the kid doing?" he called to Jamie, who was five meters to his left and had a clearer view past the destroyed vehicle.

"Nuthin, serg'nt, he's just standin there," replied Jamie. "Wait," he corrected, "he's moving. He's moving toward us."

"Damnit!" exclaimed Warden.

"Serg'nt," said Jamie, "he's leading something – it's a frickin' donkey." Warden, frustrated by his blocked vantage point, half-scooted, half-crawled down the ditch toward Jamie to get a better vantage point. Just as Jamie said, Bo was walking slowly toward them out of the village, calmly leading a donkey with a rope halter.

"Go back!" Warden yelled, partially exposing himself above the top of the ditch to wave the child away. "Get back!"

Bo did not acknowledge the order and continued to walk slowly and purposefully toward them, the donkey trailing sadly behind.

Warden heard the snap of rounds passing inches over his head before the *BUP, BUP, BUP,* of an AK called from inside a small, mud brick outbuilding on the left flank of the village. He dropped flat into the ditch as Jamie shifted his body weight to bring the new threat under fire, letting loose a three-second burst around and through a window. Supporting fire joined in from Jaguar Two.

Warden lifted his face out of the dirt, spitting sand out of his mouth. "Ridlin!" he barked, "Crawl down the ditch that way," he pointed behind the young soldier, "and get an angle on that kid. Tell me what you see. They have me zeroed in, here!"

Ridlin cradled his rifle the way he had been taught in basic training and crawled down the ditch on his elbows and knees. The ditch curved slightly toward the village in this direction as it followed the slight bend in the road. When he reached a point approximately 30 meters from Warden, he looked back at the sergeant, who signaled for him to take a look. Ridlin slowly raised himself onto his knees and peeked quickly over the lip of the ditch before dropping back down. Bo had walked two thirds of the distance to the destroyed Jaguar One: he was still making no effort to conceal himself or to hurry.

"Sergn't!" Ridlin yelled to Warden. "He's still coming – and the donkey's dragging something!"

Warden's heart pounded. *The Hajis are using him to drag an IED to us, because they don't think we'll shoot the kid.* His mind whirled as he tried to decide what to do. He knew the Major was attached to the kid, but he couldn't put the team at risk. He knew that once the boy reached them that an explosive could easily be remotely detonated from the village using a cell phone or a garage door opener.

"Jamie, the kid is draggin' somethin' behind that donkey," Warden repeated. "They're using him to get at us." Jamie's eyes widened as Warden's words sank in. "We can't let that happen," Warden said flatly. Jamie did not respond.

"On *three* I need you to put as much covering fire as you can onto the village. I've got to drop that donkey or we're dead."

"Sergn't" said Jamie, "You're gonna' haveta' shoot right through the kid to get it."

Warden hesitated, knowing that the Private was right. The odds were high he would hit the boy before the donkey. "Just do what I said, Jamie," he said tersely.

Warden moved onto his knees, crouching as he prepared to spring up and shoot. He glanced quickly at Jamie, who had done the same thing, holding the SAW along his side as he prepared to lift its barrel above the edge of the ditch.

"Get ready," Warden ordered: "One,…Two….,THREE!" he barked, and Jamie popped the barrel above the lip of the ditch and released a stream of automatic fire. Simultaneously, Warden popped up, weapon at his shoulder, ready to fire, and saw…nothing.

Warden glanced quickly about, knowing that the boy could not have simply evaporated. Then he saw the forehead and ears of the donkey on the far side of the HMMWV.

"Get down!" he yelled to Jamie. Both soldiers dropped below the lip of the ditch.

"Where's the kid?" asked Jamie.

"I think he's on the far side of the HMMWV," said Warden. He looked down the ditch toward Ridlin and signaled for him to take another look. Ridlin quickly peered over the edge and dropped back down. He had seen the back of the boy's head moving on the far side of the vehicle and a set of donkey ears, but nothing more.

"He's doing something behind the HMMWV," Ridlin called to Warden. "But I can't get a clear view."

Warden sat with his back against the sloping wall of the ditch closest to the village. *What is the kid up to?* he thought. *Looting? That would be pretty stupid in the middle of a firefight.* But he had seen just such things in Nasiriyah, where the Hajis had not been deterred from public thievery either by the regular fall of harassing Iraqi mortar rounds or the immediate presence of US troops.

"Jamie," he said, "Ah don't know what he's up to. But if he moves toward us I'm gonna' have to drop him. God knows what those bastards in the village have strapped on him or behind that donkey."

"Sergn't, Bo wouldn't do that," said Jamie.

"He might not know any better," replied Warden tersely. "He may not even know it's us. I'm not shipping you home in a bag if you're wrong."

Warden rolled slowly onto his knees again, feeling the stiffness of kneeling in the ditch for so long catching up to him. As he looked up toward the top of the ditch his stomach flipped. Bo stood there, looking somberly down at him.

"Keptin is hurt," the boy said, breathing heavily. "Hep him."

Behind Bo stood the gray, nervous donkey, trailing a makeshift litter upon which the torn body of Major William Trevanathan lay.

"Christ!" yelled, Warden. "Jamie! Covering fire!" he cried as he sprang up to grab the boy. Jamie launched himself up and steadied the machinegun's bipod on the edge of the ditch as rounds kicked up the dirt in front of him. An angry *BUP, BUP, BUP,* screamed from the minaret.

Behind Jaguar Two, Leader saw the gunman lean forward too far in the open window of the tower to get a better shot at the kid and the wounded soldier. As the gunman's AK-47 opened up, Leader squeezed off a burst with the SAW that stitched the Syrian across the breadth of his torso: the man fell back into the minaret.

Jamie maintained a steady volume of fire into the village as Warden dragged Trevanathan off the litter and into the bottom of the ditch. The officer was pale and had a gaping hole in his abdomen. Pieces of intestine poked out from beneath the edge of his flak jacket. The wounds to his right arm looked nasty, but were not life threatening.

"Kid, you got a brass pair," Warden said to Bo as he tore open the first aid pouch on Trevanathan's web gear to remove the field dressing inside. He felt around the officer's back searching for any other exit or entry wounds."Shit!" he exclaimed, finding the small hole in the Major's lower right back. "Cooper, give me your hand," Warden barked. He stripped off his own field dressing and placed it in Cooper's hand. He positioned it over the exit wound and directed, "Keep firm pressure on that hole, while I roll him on his side."

"OK," gulped Cooper, turning a little green.

Warden rolled Trevanathan onto his left side and applied the second bandage to the entry wound, using the long wrappings attached to the dressing to secure it in place before rolling him onto his back again. Cooper kept pressure on the front. "Good thing his lanky ass doesn't weigh very much," puffed Warden, winded by his efforts.

"Will the Keptin be OK?" wheezed the boy, tugging at Warden's sleeve.

"I don't know, kid," said Warden. "It's all in your Allah's hands, now."

"Then he will be OK," said Bo certainty in his voice.

Warden looked into the boy's eyes, seeing the quiet resolve of faith there. "OK, kid; OK," he said softly. "Stay down, alright?" He called out to the soldier on his left, "Jamie, you seein' anything?" Warden asked.

"Nuthin' serg'nt. Maybe they're pullin out?"

"Maybe," said Warden. "I'd expect the cavalry to be comin' soon – this close to the camp."

Warden turned back to address the kid again, but saw that the Iraqi boy was scuttling down the ditch toward Ridlin. "Kid,…Sadd…Bo…get your ass back here!" he yelled. "This ain't over yet!"

"I must go back," replied Bo. "I must help Fatine!"

"Bullshit!…I mean, no! You can't do anything! Get back here!"

Bo ignored Warden, however, crawling past Ridlin and disappearing around the turn in the ditch where it bent under the road toward the village.

"Stubborn li'l bastard," said Warden with a touch of admiration in his voice. He turned back toward his casualty to see how he was faring. Trevanathan looked very pale and still. He thought he heard a faint, rhythmic sound in the distance.

Whup, whup, whup whup whup…

"Do you see it?" Warden called to Ridlin.

"No."

Whup Whup Whup Whup…

"No, but I hear it."

The steady pulse of the rotors cutting through the thin desert air came closer…

Chapter 48
Taps

Trevanathan stared up into the evening sky. Since early in the deployment it had bothered him that some of the familiar constellations he knew at home were not present in the Iraqi heavens. Orion, which stood out so clearly, high in the Central Pennsylvania sky, was nowhere to be seen. He had often pointed out the belt of Orion to his son Alex on warm summer nights, when they played basketball in the yard until it was too dark to see the hoop. *I don't know why it bothers me so much to not see it*, he thought now. *Just makes it seem that much farther from home, I guess.*

The pretty young medical specialist who had cared for him in the critical surgery ward leaned over his stretcher, smiling. "Well, this is it for you, sir," she said warmly. "We need the beds for the really sick patients."

"Don't make me laugh, Ski," he said to Specialist Karpinski, "Makes my stitches hurt."

"You take care of yourself, sir," she replied. "This is Sergeant Bradley, who will be your flight nurse to Germany. She'll take good care of you."

"Thanks, Ski; I 'preciate it. You better get out of here before Haji drops a mortar on you."

Baghdad Airport had been one of the major objectives in the fight for Iraq in April, 2003. Now it bore little resemblance to the smoking battlefield it had been back then. Surrounded by hundreds of shipping containers and tents, it had become the major military resupply point in Iraq. The one consistent feature from the previous year, however, was the terminal sign which still read "..ddam International Airport." It earned its name, for despite the high security the airport was still the frequent target of mortar attacks launched from the nearby urban areas.

"Evening, Sir," said Air Force Staff Sergeant Bradley, a no-nonsense-looking female NCO, wearing the blue flight suit favored by air crews.

"Evening, Sergeant Bradley."

"Sir, we have you bound for Landstuhl Army Hospital in Germany. This C-141 is an air ambulance that will fly us there. It is a seven-hour flight. Any questions, sir?"

"Umm, no, Sergeant. But do you know if anyone from my unit has been by?"

"Sorry, sir. I don't know. These two fine airmen will load you now, if that's OK."

"Sure, let's go," said Trevanathan. *Well, I'm finally getting out of here,* he thought, *although not the way I intended.* Two young Air Force enlisted men took opposite ends of Trevanathan's stretcher and carefully carried him up the rear ramp into the waiting aircraft. The interior of the plane was truly impressive, with a full array of medical monitoring equipment mounted on the bulkheads. A double-row of stretcher racks ran up the center of the hold. The men gently carried Trevanathan up the left aisle and snapped his stretcher into the bottom slot.

"Thanks guys," said Trevanathan.

"No problem, sir. Have a good flight," replied the taller of the two before they departed.

Trevanathan stared at the roof of the plane through the empty rack slots above him, wondering how long he might be at Landstuhl before he got back to the States. The doctors had told him that his greatest threat at this point was infection, as a substantial amount of foreign matter had gotten into his abdominal cavity during the firefight at the village. The surgeons had basically pulled out his intestines, cut out two meters of damage, cleaned up the rest and stuffed it back in. At least, that's how the Army trauma surgeon with the lousy bedside manner had explained it.

A warm breeze blew up the ramp of the aircraft, carrying with it the evening smells of Iraq. *Eau de Baghdad. A subtle combination of diesel fuel and crap,* Trevanathan recognized.

The shudder of one of the engines on the left wing kicking to life momentarily caught his attention. *Man, I'm really leaving,* he thought, experiencing a pang of guilt: the rest of the 538th was not due to leave for another four days. *I wanted to go home with the team,* he thought, wondering what they were doing. He had seen Smith and Warden for just a few moments a couple days after his surgery. Warden said that the Colonel Hermann had submitted him for a Bronze Star for Valor to go with his Purple Heart. That news had made Trevanathan smirk, until his stitches reminded him that extracurricular humor was currently off limits. He marveled at an awards system that memorialized his being unlucky enough to get his guts blown across southern Iraq – as well as getting his translator killed – as making him somehow more *valorous. They should give a medal to the guys who are smart enough not to get wounded*, he thought.

The 538th was temporarily camped in an assembly area just off the airport, cleaning their vehicles and shipping equipment in advance of their own flight home. Their mission was over and now it was just a matter of waiting for an aircraft to be detailed to take them back to Fort Bragg. *And then home...*, Trevanathan thought. *I'm not even sure I remember how to be a civilian lawyer any more. I've been doing a lot more soldierin' and a lot less lawyerin' than I would have ever imagined.*

A large figure loomed over his stretcher. *One of the airmen is back*, thought Trevanathan absently.

"Jeesez Christ, Sahr," said Warden in his lazy Texas drawl. "Beggin' your pardon, but the taxpayers ain't exactly getting their money's worth with you layin' around all the time."

"Warden, what the hell are you doing here?" Trevanathan asked weakly, smiling affectionately at his team NCOIC. "Trying to stow away?"

"No, sahr," said Warden, effecting a mock look of hurt. "With all you officers layin' 'round all day, us NCOs hafta' keep this Army running."

"Si, that's right," said Sergeant Monkeybusiness from the opposite aisle.

"Aaahh, me no work. Me lay in bad all day looong," said another familiar, yet invisible sing-song voice beyond Monkeybusiness. "Let NCO do all the work. He no need medal. He no need Bronze Star. You kick him in ass. He happy."

"Stop, stop," Trevanathan begged, laughing at Leader's banter. "You clowns are going to kill me," he said holding his abdominal stitches with his good left arm.

"What is going on here?" boomed the humorless voice of Sergeant Bradley. "What are you men doing on my plane?" she demanded.

"It's uh, my team, Sergeant Bradley," said Trevanathan weakly, still holding his stitches. "I guess they came to kiss me goodbye."

"Now hold on, Sahr," interjected Warden, "as much as we deeply love and admire you, we are here on official US Army business." He reached into the pocket of his DCU and removed a piece of paper, which he handed to Sergeant Bradley with a flourish. She examined the document, her brow wrinkling, as she absorbed its contents. "OK, OK," she snapped. "Put it down here next to the Major," she directed. "Then get off my plane. We are wheels up in ten Mikes." She turned and stalked away, checking on the other rows of stretchers forward.

"Charming thang," said Warden looking after her.

"Oh, I don' know, Sergn't," said Monkeybusiness from the other aisle as he and Leader struggled with their load, "she seemed nice to me."

"Monkeybusiness, if I ever see you near my sister I'm gonna kill you," said Leader. "No, make that my grandmother too."

"Anyway, sahr," said Warden, "we need to get going, but we wanted to say 'adios,' and we'll see you back in the States."

"Thanks, Sergeant Warden," Trevanathan said quietly, painfully raising his left forearm to shake hands with the towering NCO.

"Keptin."

Trevanathan froze.

"Keptin."

Trevanathan closed his eyes as an electric charge seemed to run down his spine.

"Keptin, we go to 'Merica now?" asked Bo's soft voice.

Trevanathan strained to turn his head to the left, the smallest movement taking all of his strength. The boy lay on a stretcher that Monkeybusiness and Leader were sliding into place in the adjacent rack. One large blue eye peeked out of a dressing that covered most of the boy's head.

"Bo," Trevanathan half-whispered, half croaked, as tears filled his eyes.

"Keptin, why you cry?" chided the boy. "We go to 'Merica, just like you said." He smiled.

"Just like I said," Trevanathan repeated, softly. With effort, he rolled his head back toward Warden, whose red rimmed eyes also fought back the moisture gathering there.

"How?" Trevanathan asked, his soft voice now unsteady. "How?"

Warden did a quick wipe across his left eye with the back of his hand. "Well, sahr, after the firefight at Al Salaam, the lil' terrorist here was touch and go for a few days. We pulled him outta' some rubble near the mosque after you were evacuated and got him to the CSH. Couple broken bones and a skull fracture. Was in a coma for a day an'a half, and the docs weren't sure what was gonna' happen. He woke up, though, and came off better'n most of the folks in the village."

"But the list...?"

"Well, the story got round how he pulled you outta' that HMMWV under fire and he's become a bit of a celebrity. Me and Monkeybusiness took the opportunity to go discuss the situation with Ms. Creamcheese up at CPA, and it turns out there's some exception to allow lil' terrorists who save careless officers to jump to the head of the line. Leastways that's how Monkeybusiness explained it to me after he had a private chat with her."

"Or two," beamed Monkeybusiness over Warden's shoulder.

"So the kid is a hero now and some politician back in Texas thought he should be taken care of – back in the States. That's what happened. Just dumb luck, I guess," Warden finished.

Trevanathan smiled wearily. "Thanks."

"Oh, it was my great pleasure, sir," said Monkeybusiness, flashing his trademark grin. "Adios, muchacho," he said to Bo, leaning over Trevanathan to squeeze the boy's exposed big toe before turning and walking down the ramp.

"Take care, sir. Stay outta' trouble, kid…and keep the Major outta' trouble too," added Leader, before following Monkeybusiness out of the airplane.

"You're becoming a softie in your old age, Sergeant Warden," Trevanathan quietly teased his NCOIC, after the other two had departed.

"Not a damn bit, Sahr," said Warden briskly, looking offended at the mere suggestion. "I just figger' this country can do with one less terrerist, so gettin' this one outta' here is a good idea."

Trevanathan looked silently at Warden, who seemed embarrassed at the suggestion that he might care what happened to the kid. "Roger that," he said, "see you at home station."

Warden nodded, turned, and walked down the ramp of the C-141. Halfway down, he paused and looked back toward the officer and the boy. The two lay side by side – a striking contrast between the small brown frame of the boy and the lanky, pale officer. Both had suffered in the war and in the unquiet peace that had followed the Coalition's "victory." Each had given so much to change the lives of others and the jury was still out as to whether it would make any difference or not.

But for now, the future of Iraq lay in two cots, side by side, recovering from wounds that are so often borne in the violent struggle for the dignity of men. Warden watched for a moment as the stick-like arm of the boy reached out from under his blanket and grasped the large hand of his 'Keptin' beside him. Trevanathan squeezed the small hand and closed his eyes.

Warden brought himself slowly to the position of attention and raised the tips of his right fingers to his right eyebrow in a salute to the two veterans. Then he turned and was gone.

CPSIA information can be obtained
at www.ICGtesting.com
Printed in the USA
BVHW041420131222
654128BV00004B/41